The House of
Six Doors

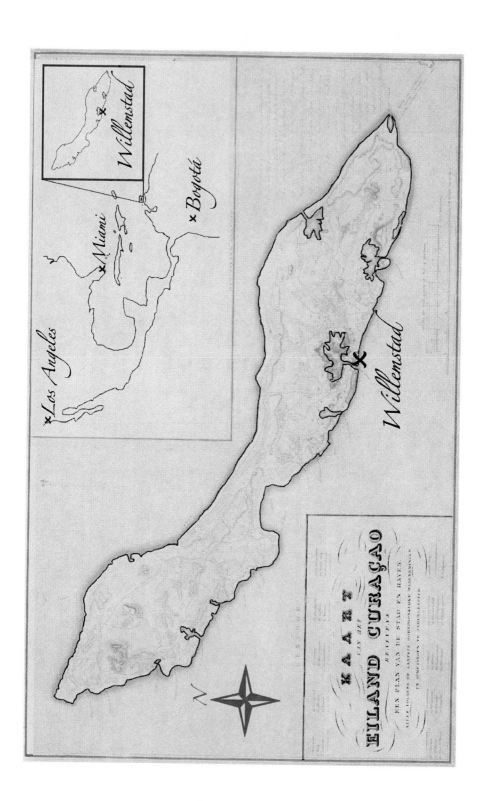

Los Angeles

Miami

Bogotá

Willemstad

Willemstad

KAART
VAN HET
EILAND CURAÇAO
BEVATTENDE
EEN PLAN VAN DE STAD EN HAVEN

The House of
Six Doors

— a novel —

Patricia Selbert

Publishing by the Seas
Santa Barbara, California

Publishing by the Seas

Publishing by the Seas, Inc., 1187 Coast Village Rd. Suite 1-530, Santa Barbara, CA 93108

This is a work of fiction. Names, characters, places, and incidents either are the product of the author's imagination or are used fictitiously, and any resemblance to actual persons, living or dead, or business establishments, events, or locales is entirely coincidental.

The House of Six Doors

www.publishingbytheseas.com

www.thehouseofsixdoors.com

Cataloging-in-Publication Data is on file with the Library of Congress.

ISBN: 978-0-578-06440-6

Book art, photography, and design by Isaac Hernández/IsaacArt.com

To my husband,
Jim,
and my two sons,
Stefan and Spencer,
the loves of my life.

— Part I —

MAMA'S HANDS FLUTTERED LIKE FLAGS in the island's trade winds, as they always did when she was nervous. She smiled at the Miami International Airport customs officer, who asked her again whether she had anything to declare.

"No. No, we don't," Mama answered. "Hendrika, doesn't he look just like Johan? Is he not handsome with that dark, curly hair and those nice brown eyes?" Although she directed her words toward my eighteen-year-old sister, I knew they were meant for the customs officer. I thought she was right; he was handsome, but he didn't look anything like my brother Johan, who had straight, light-brown hair and hazel eyes.

"Please proceed to the inspection area," the customs officer said, his frown deepening.

"But we have nothing to declare. We should move on so you can attend to these other people," Mama said, pointing to the line behind us.

I turned around. The lady after us pulled her young daughter closer to her as if she did not want to be near us; the man next to them tapped his passport against his leg and clenched his jaw. I glanced at Hendrika, but her eyes were darting from the officer to Mama and back again. Mama hung her purse on her arm and started to walk away, but the officer intercepted her. "*Wat doet die man toch vervelend,*" Mama muttered in Dutch to Hendrika, telling her how annoying the officer was.

"Right this way, ma'am," the officer said firmly as he guided her toward the baggage inspection area.

We followed Mama. At the inspection area, another officer ordered, "Please open your suitcases."

"But we have nothing to declare," protested Mama, her index finger moving from side to side, emphasizing her words.

"Then you won't mind opening your suitcases, will you?" said a young, bald officer standing next to him.

"*Ay nò*, why are you wasting your time opening our bags?" Mama complained. "You should be looking for drug dealers, not nice families like us."

Reluctantly, Mama opened the suitcase in front of her. My eyes met Hendrika's. She shrugged her shoulders. Hendrika and I watched in silence while Mama stood gazing down at the officer inspecting the suitcase, arms crossed. He felt around inside the case. He pulled out a small bag, opened it, smelled its contents, and nodded to the second officer who took the walkie-talkie from his belt and asked for backup. "Ma'am, do you understand it's illegal to bring plants into the country?" Mama's eyes opened wide in surprise.

"Ma'am, would you like a Spanish translator?"

Mama stretched up to her full height of five foot eight. "I am not Hispanic. I'm from Curaçao—that is a Dutch island. I not only speak English; I also speak Dutch, Spanish, and Papiamentu." Two more officers came up behind us, and we were surrounded.

"*Dios mío*. What is going on? What are you doing? This is not right. We are not criminals," Mama complained.

"Please follow these agents," the first officer ordered. "We need to determine what you're trying to bring into the United States."

I squeezed myself in between Hendrika and Mama.

"But officer, but officer …" Mama stuttered.

I wasn't sure whether she was outraged, panicked, or both. I grabbed Hendrika's hand and held on tight; she was five years older than me. The officers separated us and took each one of us by the arm. They escorted us down a long hallway with white walls and brown doors. They walked fast, and I had difficulty keeping up.

Mama was not even trying to keep up; she refused to be hurried. All I wanted to do was get back on the plane that had brought us here and return to Curaçao.

"Do you think they are drugs?" Mama said to the man escorting her. "They are not drugs, they are all natural herbs. They do only good."

The officer kept walking and looked straight ahead, stone-faced.

"Those herbs have healing powers! They work for all kinds of problems. I could help you." She tapped him on the shoulder and her pace picked up. "Are you having money problems, love problems? That is what these herbs are for. These herbs are to help, not to harm."

The officers looked at each other and rolled their eyes. They led us through one of the brown doors into a cramped, stark room.

"You people from the islands are all the same, always trying to sneak things by us," one of them grumbled. "Please sit down and wait here!" he ordered, shaking his head in an expression of disgust.

As the officers left, the last one locked the door behind him, leaving us huddled together. There were four white plastic chairs lined up against one wall and in a corner behind a paper-thin partition stood a battered wooden table with two more plastic chairs on either side. We went over to the row of chairs and sat down. I squirmed around in my seat trying to adjust the bra Mama had bought for my thirteenth birthday. Wearing a bra was new to me and it felt uncomfortable.

My heart pounded. My stomach was turning as if I were seasick. I focused on Hendrika to make the feeling go away. She sat in her chair, clutching her camera on her lap. She wanted to be a professional photographer and hoped America was the place where her dream would come true. She had long skinny limbs, red hair, and her body was covered with freckles. When she stayed out in the sun too long, her skin matched her hair and we called her Lobster.

"Hendrika, I'm scared," I whispered, not wanting Mama to hear me. "There's no one here to help us. I miss Oma. I want to go home." I clasped my hands together, trying to hold onto something.

Hendrika gave me a half smile but didn't answer. She started humming "*La Vida Sigue Igual*," a Spanish song with a refrain that meant life goes on. She always sang when she was worried or sad.

The clock on the wall ticked, turning the minutes of waiting into an hour. I thought about our flight from Curaçao. We had been full of anticipation. Mama promised that here in America we would live in a house with a lawn and I could go to high school and later on to university. I dreamed of becoming a reporter and working at a newspaper like the one my grandfather had owned in Curaçao.

As I stared at the squares of the linoleum floor, I thought I could hear the voice of Oma, my grandmother, something that often happened when I felt scared or confused. "Don't worry, *mi dushi*, worrying doesn't do you any good. Take a deep breath and feel the earth under your feet, look around and see where you are, become very quiet and listen to your heartbeat. Remember, there is only one pursuit—finding your essence in an ever-changing world." I didn't always understand everything Oma told me; I just knew that I felt better when I was with her.

On the other hand, with Mama I always felt worried. She was perpetually pursuing prosperity. In her eyes, prosperity brought security. She was relentless in her search. She had traveled to many places trying to find it and America was where she was going now. Oma once told me that Mama was different after she came back from the war in Europe. Oma said that was when Mama's obsession with money started. I leaned over to pick up the small red-and-white plastic purse Oma had given me before we left, and I set it on my lap just the way Oma did with her purse, but minutes later the purse was in the crook of my arm as if it were a teddy bear.

"Serena, stop playing with that purse," Mama snapped.

Now I understood that she had been hoping they wouldn't find her hidden treasure of herbs and incenses: verbena, aloe vera, valerian root, yerba buena, myrrh, patchouli, and sandalwood. Oma had taught Mama about the healing properties of plants, and although Mama thought those healing properties were trivial compared to the power of the pharmaceuticals she had learned to use in the Netherlands, nothing she had experienced there could replace for her the mystical aspect of working with the herbs.

Mama turned to Hendrika. "What bad luck they found them." Hendrika nodded in agreement. Mama had calmed down, but I knew she was still upset, by the way she examined the ceiling while the left foot of her crossed legs rhythmically kicked in the air.

After another half hour, two of the officers returned. They spoke quickly, and I couldn't understand everything they said. I hated the sound of English. To me, it sounded like cats fighting. I preferred the music of more familiar languages. I liked the sound of Dutch, which was spoken from the back of the throat and sounded strong; Papiamentu, the local language of Curaçao, which was playfully repetitious; and I loved the soothing and lyrical sound of Spanish.

An officer asked Mama to step behind the partition. I could hear the conversation between them.

"If you put the belladonna with some of the oregano and a sprinkle of verbena in a jar, let it sit in the sun for two full days and then bathe with it for two nights, it will change your whole outlook on life. Luck will follow you everywhere."

I had seen my grandmother use belladonna to reduce fever, verbena to relieve cough and sore throat, and oregano to calm an upset stomach. When Oma used these herbs, miraculous cures often happened. Mama had been educated as a nurse in the Netherlands and trained to use conventional medicine, but she was superstitious about herbs because Oma had saved her life with them. Using herbs made Mama feel as if she could fix anything. But they didn't always work. It worried me, when she was so sure of herself. I held my breath again, thinking it might help me hear better.

"No offense, ma'am, but I think you might be needing that good-luck bath more than me. We'll be testing the substances you brought in. You will have to wait here."

"Go ahead and test. You'll see it's all natural, all from the earth to help you."

I could imagine her hands, again waving in the air. I was used to Mama's finagling, but in this case her negotiations frightened me.

"Even if they aren't drugs, what you tried to do is illegal. You cannot bring live plants into this country."

"But I can help you if you let me keep my herbs," Mama pleaded.

The officer ignored her offer and told her to sit back down in a chair on the other side of the partition. Then he called me. It was easy for him to see that I didn't speak much English and he dismissed me. The officer called Hendrika in. I stared at Mama sitting in her chair. Her sturdy build, dark hair, khaki-brown skin, and erect posture had always reminded me of an Arawak Indian warrior, but now the sight of her slouched in her chair worried me. Hendrika came back from behind the partition and sat down.

"What if they don't let me keep them?" Mama fretted. "Oh, I hope they don't take them away. I'm not sure we can find all these things here, and even if we can, we don't know what they are called, or if they are of good quality. I hope this is not a sign of bad luck. I should have sprinkled the suitcases with lemongrass, caraway, and lavender to prevent losses." Her head hung down and she stared at the floor.

Two more hours passed before one of the officers came back. It was the young, bald officer from the inspection area. "You are released, but all of the agricultural products have been confiscated," he declared.

Hendrika immediately stood up and moved toward the door, and I followed her, but Mama turned toward the officer. "If you let me keep my herbs, I'll make a special ancient Arawak Indian potion to make you grow hair." Mama leaned toward the officer. "You would look so handsome if you had hair on your head." For a second he looked intrigued. "There are no bald Arawak Indians, you know," Mama said flirtatiously.

"Now that's enough. I could arrest you for the attempted bribery of a federal officer and I could have you sent back to wherever you came from."

"*Ay, Dios mío,*" Mama exclaimed as she stepped back in surprise. She stood paralyzed for a moment. "No, no, officer—there is no need for that." She quickly turned around and walked to the door where we were waiting. Together we retrieved our bags. "They just do not understand," Mama muttered under her breath as we headed for the exit. A blast of hot, humid air enveloped us as we stepped through the door and onto the sidewalk.

"Welcome to the United States," a luggage porter called out, and we embarked on our new life.

ॐॐॐॐॐॐॐॐ

I HUNG MY HEAD OUT of the window of the taxi that took us to a nearby motel. I was astonished at how organized everything seemed. The wide streets were smoothly paved, and the traffic lights even had signals for pedestrians. Palm trees in Curaçao grew wherever they wanted; here they seemed to grow in rows.

At the motel the lady behind the front desk wore attractive pink lipstick and matching nail polish, but her permed and bleached hair reminded me of straw.

"What can I do for you?" she said, chewing gum while she spoke. I recognized her accent from *The Andy Griffith Show* reruns I had watched on television in Curaçao on the national television station. There was a fan on the end of the counter, blowing straight at her. "Would you like a room or a studio with a kitchenette?"

"We would like a studio for a week, please," Mama answered, her body rigid. She held on tightly to her purse as if she wasn't going to let anyone take anything else away from her.

"Gerald, is studio seven done up?" the lady shouted, leaning back through the office doorway. "Gerald? Can you hear me?" She turned back to us and handed Mama a registration card and a pen.

"Where is the nearest grocery store?" Mama asked.

"About two miles away," the lady answered, pointing her thumb over her right shoulder. "You'll have to take a taxi."

"Is it always this humid here?" Mama asked, fanning herself with the card. We were all sweating.

"Last winter we had freezing temperatures and this summer we're having a heat wave," the lady said. "Nineteen seventy-two is proving to be quite a year."

Curaçao was hot, but the constant trade winds made the heat tolerable. I had never felt humidity like this before; I felt sticky all over.

I wiped my forehead, glanced around the tiny office and noticed it connected to the living room of the manager's apartment. The living room was immaculate, and I wondered if anybody actually used it. The sofa and chairs didn't appear as if they had ever been sat in. On the coffee table stood a vase full of plastic flowers, a clean ashtray, two crystal statues, and a square box, all perfectly arranged. On the wall hung seascapes that matched the color scheme of the room: everything was baby blue and cream—even the plastic flowers.

I had never seen a room like this: perfectly matched and completely unused. The walls of the rooms in Curaçao were painted in bright colors: red, green, turquoise, pink—anything but white. Furniture was used and the rooms were lived in: an open book here, a cup of tea there, a pair of shoes under the sofa, pillows stacked just right to throw yourself onto, and, most of all, people enjoying the space. Perfect was pretty, but it didn't make me feel welcome.

"Of course studio seven is ready," a man's voice responded from somewhere beyond the living room. "We haven't rented that studio in weeks."

"Okay. These ladies will take it."

Hendrika and I carried the bags as Mama led the way to studio seven. She wrestled with the door. A kick from her left foot released it, and a whiff of stale air greeted us. In the corner two twin beds at right angles to each other doubled as a couch. In the opposite corner was a square wooden table with three chairs. Behind the table was a Formica-topped counter with a compact, built-in refrigerator; a sink; and a hot plate on top. Mama pulled back the rust-colored curtains and opened the windows; then she walked to the door and swung it back and forth, trying to get some fresh air into the room. "Come, help me make this place cozy," she encouraged us. We placed our suitcases on the beds and Mama opened them. She handed us piles of clothes that Hendrika and I put in the closet.

"I have nothing to clear the vibrations in this room," she lamented, glancing around. "Let's put the chairs and table outside; it is cooler there and it will be fun to watch the big American cars drive by." Sitting on the porch and watching cars go by was something we often did on hot afternoons in Curaçao. Hendrika and Mama carried the table and the chairs outside.

"What are you doing with my furniture?" I heard the lady from the front desk shouting. I peeked out of the door to see what was happening. Mama and Hendrika were sitting in the chairs they had just put out.

"You can't do that!" she exclaimed, breathless from running.

"Do what?" Mama asked, confused.

"You can't put the furniture outside."

"It's too hot inside, so we thought we would sit outside. What is wrong with that?" Mama asked.

"This is not patio furniture and this is not a patio. Please put it back immediately." She spat out each syllable of "patio" and "immediately," to make sure we understood.

"But it is so hot and the air conditioning is not so good."

"Please put the furniture back or I'll have to call my husband." Her finger pointed toward the door of the studio. Hendrika and Mama got up and brought the furniture back in.

"I do not understand," Mama muttered. "Why can we not put the furniture outside?" She closed the front door and stood in front of the air conditioner, staring through the glass of the window as if it were a crystal ball.

I switched on the television and clicked the dial through the channels, amazed that there were six stations; in Curaçao there was only one and it broadcast only from five o'clock to ten o'clock each night. I wanted to see *The Brady Bunch*. I fantasized about having a house in a neighborhood with lots of kids my age. I thought that American families were large and everyone lived in a new house with fancy appliances and a lawn. But *The Brady Bunch* wasn't on and I settled for channel three, which was showing *Green Acres*.

Mama returned to rearranging the furniture inside the studio, when she remembered what the lady at the front desk had said about the grocery store.

"*Ay nò*. There is no good public transportation here," Mama sighed. "We cannot afford to take taxis everywhere. I did not plan for this. If I do not find a job right away, we are going to run out of money."

Mama's comment surprised me. She had promised things would be better here, but so far everything had been worse. I felt as if we were playing the game Sorry. In Dutch it was called Don't Irritate Yourself. Mama called that game Stupid, and every time we asked her to play she'd refuse, saying life was frustrating enough.

Mama had a nursing license and was confident she could easily get a job. Three years earlier, she had answered an ad in our local newspaper offering any Dutch registered nurse legal residence in the United States to help meet the nursing shortage caused by the Vietnam War. She had left the four of us with Oma in Curaçao and worked in California for almost a year.

"It is time to buy food," Mama announced. "I will call a taxi."

When the taxi pulled up, Mama told the driver we had just arrived in America and asked him to take us to the nearest supermarket.

"Welcome to *los Estados Unidos*," he said with a smile. The driver was Cuban and his radio was tuned to a Spanish-language station. Hendrika was excited to hear Spanish. She asked him the frequency and wrote the number down. Mama kept glancing at the taxi meter.

The taxi dropped us off at the Publix supermarket. We'd never seen anything so opulent. The market was inside a large, air-conditioned building with aisles eight feet wide and shelves packed with more kinds of food than I had ever imagined existed. The floors were so shiny they reflected the overhead lights.

When we arrived at the produce section of the market I just stared, but Hendrika was taking pictures of the emerald-green broccoli and asparagus, varieties of exotic mushrooms, fresh Brussels sprouts, plump strawberries, golden pears, and dewy peaches. Hendrika and I had never seen any of these before.

"Look, Hendrika, raspberries and blueberries. Do you remember reading about them in our Dutch schoolbooks? Now we get to taste them," I said, pointing at the display.

"*Eh-eh*, we are in a land of real fruits and vegetables," Hendrika said, smiling. Mama followed us around the store, beaming. We walked around the display tables, each mounded chest-high with a pyramid of gleaming, fresh produce.

We walked up and down the aisles, amazed at the fantastic variety of American cereals, snacks, drinks, toothpastes, shampoos, soaps, and cleaning products. "American grocery stores are much better than even the grocery stores in Holland," Mama said.

I had never seen a grocery store in Holland, but there was one Dutch grocery in Curaçao. It was called Zuikertuintje, or Sugar Garden. We could only afford to shop there once a month while Mama was married to Papa because it was very expensive. The store was in a blood-red *landhuis,* an old plantation house, in the rich Dutch residential neighborhood of the island. All of the items sold there were imported directly from Holland. Zuikertuintje did not sell Dutch fruits and vegetables because they could not survive the long boat trip or the heat of the Caribbean.

In Curaçao, we usually shopped at Shon Bila's store. She was a seventy-year-old black spinster and her store was simply a room in her house with a door onto the street. The doorway had a glass counter built into it. Little shops like hers were found in each neighborhood. We'd stand outside and request the products off the shelves: Spam, corned beef, canned hot dogs, canned sardines, canned tuna. The vegetables were canned string beans, canned corn, canned carrots, and canned peas. The fruits were canned fruit cocktail, canned pears, canned peaches, and canned tangerine slices. There was also canned margarine, canned powdered milk, canned evaporated milk, Ovaltine, Tang, instant coffee, and bagged tea. Four burlap bags sat on the floor: one filled with rice, one with black beans, one with cornmeal, and one with black-eyed peas. A wheel of old Dutch cheese sat in the corner, oozing fat in the heat; a salami hung above it. Once a week Shon Bila sold fresh eggs.

Shon Bila's counter held my favorite items: minicans of condensed milk, shredded coconut candy, chunky coconut candy, peanut butter candy, milk candy, guava candy, and Chiclets gum. It was not unusual to see a cockroach scurrying across the floor as our groceries were placed on top of the counter. Mama hated cockroaches. Every time she saw one she said, "Only backward countries have cockroaches. Holland does not have cockroaches." I hated cockroaches too, especially when I had to stomp on them and hear them crush under my shoe.

In Curaçao, we purchased fresh produce at the floating market, where boats came in from Venezuela every other day and tied up along the waterfront in town. They sold cucumbers, tomatoes, herbs, cabbages, yucca, paprika, and lemons. They sold fruit—bananas; coconuts; mangoes; *mispels*, which tasted like a very sweet kiwi; and *kenepas*, an orange lychee fruit. Mama always said these fruits were worthless, since they perished within forty-eight hours in the island heat. She told us they had proper fruit in Holland, not common tropical fruits like mangoes, which caused mouth rashes and diarrhea if you ate too many.

We bought vegetables from Shon Cheche, a thin, tall black woman. She was a *Shon di Kunuku*, a Lady of the Countryside. These women were farmers' or fishermen's wives, and they walked for miles, balancing large wooden trays, filled with produce or fish, on their heads. These trays were so heavy the women needed two people to help lift them off their heads and onto the ground to display their goods. If we wanted goat or chicken we would order it from Shon Cheche, and she would bring it the next day.

Now, in America, we were silly with excitement by the time we got to the meat, poultry, and fish sections.

"They must have a lot of people who shop here. Are they going to sell all this today?" I asked Mama. I had never seen so many pieces of meat. An image of Shon Cheche frantically killing chickens and goats popped into my head. The vision horrified me.

"No, that would be impossible," Mama told us.

"This looks nothing like Shon Lita's tray of fresh fish," Hendrika remarked. Shon Lita, another *Shon di Kunuku*, the wife of a fisherman, came by our house every day with fresh fish. I could identify each kind of fish on her tray, but in these displays every fish was filleted and unrecognizable. We filled our Publix grocery cart full of all the good things America had to offer and took another taxi back to our studio.

Hendrika cleaned and cut the strawberries, peaches, and pears into quarter pieces and arranged them on a paper plate. Mama stood in front of the hot plate simmering the chicken, onions, tomatoes, paprika, and garlic, to which she added lemon, nutmeg, and a dash of coconut milk. The familiar smells made our modest studio feel a bit more like home. Hendrika and I sat down at the square table and ate the fruit while we watched Mama cook. After she finished, she joined us at the table to savor our first home-cooked meal in America.

Mama raised her glass of water high in the air and proposed a toast.

"To getting a new job tomorrow, and to our new lives, which will be overflowing with American comforts and pleasures." Her face was radiant, as if she had already gotten a job and our lives had already been transformed. I loved seeing her this way.

Hendrika and I clicked our glasses against hers. I felt better. Mama had instilled a confidence in me that made all my doubts disappear.

ৡ৶ৡ৶ৡ৶ৡ৶ৡ৶ৡ৶

HENDRIKA AND I HAD AGREED to take turns sleeping in the second bed, and the next morning, I woke up stiff from sleeping on the floor. The unfamiliar smell of the sheets puzzled me. I looked around the studio and remembered we were in America. A wave of excitement came over me. Today Mama was going to get a job and soon we would live like the Brady Bunch. Hendrika was already dressed and on her way out to get the *Miami Herald*. Mama was making coffee and toast at the counter. She had finished making the beds, their avocado-green bedspreads pulled tight and tucked in hospital-style. I turned on the television. A man stood in a big parking lot full of cars, prices painted on their windshields. He was on roller skates and so was a chimpanzee standing next to him. "Look at this, Mama," I called out. Mama came over to see. The man was singing.

If you need to buy a car, deal with Dan,
If you're going oh so far, deal with Dan,
If your wheels are roller skates,
And you don't have cash to waste,
Deal with Dan, deal with Dan, deal with Dan.

"What is he singing, Mama?" I asked. Mama explained that he was selling cars. I tried to mouth the words along with Dan, thinking it might help me sound American. After Hendrika returned with the paper, we all sat around the table while Mama circled all the classified ads for registered nursing jobs. Mama had university degrees from the Netherlands in nursing and midwifery. Hendrika searched on the map for the location of the hospitals. We were ready to find Mama a job.

Around eleven o'clock in the morning, we called a taxi. I was proud of the way Mama looked: she wore a white suit she had made herself and a red shirt that made her appear very professional. At the first hospital, a modern brick building five stories tall, she was asked to fill out an application by the interviewer, who was an overweight woman with curly blond hair, a kind smile, and gaps between her teeth. After Mama handed back her completed application, the interviewer looked it over, "May I see your license and your green card, please?" the interviewer asked. Mama took her license and green card out of her purse and handed them to her.

"This is a California nursing license," said the interviewer, surprised. "This is not valid in the state of Florida."

"What do you mean?" Mama gasped in shock. "I got this license in California just three years ago. I worked there. Of course it is a valid license!"

"You don't understand," said the interviewer. "Each state has its own licensing laws. Your nursing license is only good in California. You have to pass the Florida State Nursing Boards to get a license in Florida."

Mama was outraged. I could feel my heart speed up.

"*Ay nò.* That's not possible!" she said. "This is one country. I've never heard of anything like this! How could this be? You must be wrong. Let me talk to your supervisor." Mama's shock had changed to determination, as it did when things did not turn out the way she expected. We had often gotten in trouble when Mama had assumed things instead of investigating them. But this time it felt as if we were being treated unfairly, and her outrage seemed justified to me. All we wanted was for Mama to get a job.

"These are state laws, ma'am," said woman. "They are on the books and we can't change them. My supervisor isn't going to tell you anything different. I suggest you call the Florida State Board Licensing Office. You can ask them any questions. By the way, your California license expired in 1971, almost a year ago."

She handed Mama her license, which was now worthless, her green card, and her application, turned back to her desk, and started typing as if we weren't there. I began to see a pattern in the way people treated us. The customs officer, the lady at the motel, and now this woman, they all treated us as if we were stupid.

"How is it possible? How can one country be run with a different license for each state? A diploma is a diploma. I've worked all over the world and no other country does this. I've worked in the Netherlands; I've worked in Colombia; I've worked in Venezuela." Hendrika moved over to Mama and gently put her hand on her shoulder. Mama shrugged it off. "I've worked in Curaçao, Aruba, and Bonaire. The Dutch diploma is recognized all over the world. Even here in America they recognize the Dutch diploma, but what is this licensing business? A diploma should be enough. I passed their test in California—that should be enough! *Ay nò*, this cannot be right. I cannot believe a country can be run like this. It does not make sense."

Hendrika touched Mama's shoulder again. "You're right, Mama. Let's just go," she said in Dutch. "It's ridiculous to have to get a license in each state."

I felt embarrassed and sorry for Mama as she stormed out of the hospital, striding quickly along the pavement, muttering in disbelief about the licensing system while Hendrika and I struggled to keep up with her. When Mama was like this we knew not to interrupt her, yet at the same time we knew she needed our attention to feel reassured that we were on her side.

Back at the motel, I escaped to the tiny bathroom, where I stood, listening. I didn't understand why Mama took such risks. I often wondered how I could be her daughter. I was nothing like her—I didn't even look like her. I looked more like my father, who had white skin, freckles, and light-brown hair. I tried to be quiet, agreeable, methodical, and cautious. Mama was dominant, loud, and daring. I loved her and wanted to be proud of her, but often I found myself being embarrassed by her and that made me ashamed.

I could see Mama and Hendrika reflected in the bathroom mirror. Mama was talking to Hendrika as she carefully folded her red shirt and hung up her white suit. She seemed to be going through a mental tug-of-war, trying to explain and understand what had just happened. Hendrika lay on the bed, agreeing with every point Mama made. We knew not to ask her what she would do next. Asking could be interpreted as a lack of faith in Mama, which could result in another lecture about how capable she was and how blind we were for not seeing things her way.

Not much was said in our family over the next couple of days; the television did most of the talking. Mama was in an unpredictable and frightening state of mind. Hendrika and I speculated about whether her silence was meant to show us she would not tolerate any lack of confidence in her, or whether this was the beginning of another period of darkness. She had never hurt us physically, although she had often told us we were ungrateful beings who just didn't understand her, but in this state, which Oma called *e la pèrdè strea di nort*—she has lost the North Star—Mama could harm herself.

Sitting in the corner of the studio, I remembered how dreadful that could be.

ᒿᑊᒿᑊᒿᑊᒿᑊᒿᑊᒿᑊᒿᑊ

WE MOVED FROM CURAÇAO TO Colombia when I was six. Only my father, Jan Brink, stayed behind. Mama and Papa had decided that their children should go to university in Bogotá, Colombia, because it was much cheaper than Europe or the US. Mama thought it was best to make the move while my fifteen-year-old brother, Johan, and my sisters, Hendrika and Willia, who were then twelve and seventeen, were still in high school and young enough to learn a new language. After almost a year Mama discovered she couldn't live on the money Papa sent her each month. She asked him for more, and when he said he did not have any, she returned to Curaçao to check on him and took me along. The day we arrived we went to Oma's house and stayed in her guest cottage next door. Mama was mad at Papa and did not want to stay with him. That afternoon he came over to see us. They had an argument.

"How could you leave me stranded with four children?" Mama screamed. I could see the veins in her neck swell and her face turn a bright red. "What kind of irresponsible father and husband are you? We agreed that I would move with the children to Colombia so that your salary could support four children all the way through university. There are bills to pay; people are knocking at my door wanting their money. You know how embarrassing that is? *Hè!* And here you are, living the good life. So irresponsible." She waved her hands as if she were slapping the air. My father pointed his finger at her and shook his head. The corners of his lips turned down.

"I did not leave you stranded. I send you my entire paycheck every month. I even got an extra job to pay for my own expenses here. You're the one who wants to live like Queen Juliana. It's never enough for you! You always want more, more, more!"

I felt awful for Papa. I had heard them argue like this many times before. Papa always tried to calm Mama down. Sometimes, Mama

ᬵ *19* ᬵ

threatened to kill herself. Then Papa would give in and do everything he could to make sure she did not. I hid in the corner of the room behind the bed, quietly crying, wishing they would stop fighting.

"I want a divorce!" Mama yelled. "I don't need you. You always leave me stranded. You've been nothing but a disappointment." I wondered what Mama meant. Papa had always lived with us. He helped her around the house. He even cooked sometimes while Mama was out delivering babies. Colombia had been the first time we hadn't lived with Papa.

"That's it. You're right. We should get a divorce." Papa said, his body rigid. "I've been trying all these years for the children's sake, but I can't live up to your expectations. I can't do it anymore." Silently, he shook his head from side to side and then he walked out the door.

Shocked, I stopped crying. I wanted to run after him and yell, "Wait for me!" But then what would happen to Mama? I could hardly breathe.

Mama looked stunned. She lowered herself into a chair and stared into the distance. I had never heard Papa like this before. I prayed that he would come back and give her more money, although I was afraid he wouldn't. I thought about how much I had missed Papa's good-night kisses every evening in Colombia, the way he tucked me in and urged me to close my eyes before the sandman came, the smell of rum on his breath.

Later that evening, we lay in bed looking, out the window. Mama gave me tiny sips of her wine as we ate small cubes of Gouda cheese on top of saltine crackers.

"Serena, we'll be much better off without him. We'll live here in Oma's cottage, and I'll make him give me the money to bring your brother and sisters home. I'll take care of all of you."

It was one of the moments I felt closest to her. I was filling the space that was empty in her heart, and I was doing a great job. I felt important. Maybe things would be all right after all. I liked the attention and I was going to do everything possible to help her get over her sadness.

Papa did not come back. In a desperate attempt to make him return to her, she ordered all of us to stop speaking to him. But Johan and Willia would not do that. Mama was crushed. Arrangements were made for Willia, Johan, and Hendrika to return to Curaçao in a few weeks.

A few days after Mama and Papa's argument, I came home from school to find an ambulance in front of the cottage. I felt my stomach tighten. My grandmother intercepted me and pulled me into her house.

"Where's Mama?" I asked.

"She's not feeling well," my grandmother said. "Come with me."

I followed her into the kitchen. Oma filled a glass with water and added a few drops of tincture of valerian root. Its purpose, I knew, was to relieve shock and anxiety. Valerian water was only used if someone had died or if a serious accident had happened. She handed me the glass; I drank the mixture.

"Mama has tried to kill her body again," Oma said in Papiamentu, putting her arms around me. "*E la pèrdè strea di nort.* She will have to go to the hospital. There they will pump the poison from her stomach." It was the fourth time she had tried to kill herself. My grandmother took the empty glass and set it on the counter.

"Come on, *mi dushi*, let's lie down and rest our bodies," she said, and she steered me into her bedroom. I lay in Oma's arms as the valerian-root drink relaxed me. I needed something familiar. I looked up at her and asked, "Oma, will you tell me the story about how you and Opa met again?" She smiled, stroked my hair, and began.

"You know, *dushi*, I was raised by my grandmother, who was your great-great grandmother. She taught me how to read and write, how to sew, and how to use herbs. She used to say, 'Elena, when I am gone you must leave Aruba and take the boat to Curaçao, that's where your destiny awaits you.' When she passed away, she left me an envelope with enough money for the journey.

"The trip took the entire day. In the golden light of the late afternoon, as the boat neared the harbor entrance, I could see two menacing stone forts rising out of the ocean, one on either side of the long, narrow entrance channel. The waves beat against the massive stone walls, which were studded with several large cannons. For a moment, I doubted my grandmother's advice. Then, I could not believe what I saw. An orange-yellow palace stood next to the fort on the right side of the channel. That was where the governor lived. Next to the palace was a canary-yellow building that housed the printing press where your grandfather worked, but I did not know that then.

"Next to the printing press stood the blood-red post office. Then came Penha, the jeweler's, in hot pink; La Bonanza, the fabric shop, in sky blue, where I found a job two weeks later; Bata, the shoe shop, in bright green; and finally, La Ganga, the hardware store, in turquoise. All the rooflines of the buildings were decorated with plaster, like icing on a wedding cake. Some roof trims had stair-step patterns, others had undulating lines with spiral endings, and still others had combinations of both. It was like looking into the window of a pastry shop and admiring all the different creations.

"The two sides of the harbor were equally colorful, although the buildings were fancier on the governor's palace side. That side also had big *flamboyan* trees with bright-orange flowers that were in full bloom.

"As our boat reached halfway down the narrow channel, the pontoon bridge connecting the two sides of the harbor swung open like magic. There were no cars in those days—only donkey carts and pedestrians. I stood on the deck, taking in all the beauty. The wind blew my hair back and I remember feeling as if I had flown right into the gates of heaven. I put my hand over my pounding heart, and whispered to myself, 'Curaçao, my new home.' *Curaçao* comes from the word for *heart* in Portuguese, and I knew my grandmother had been right.

"I was working at the tailor's shop one spring day when Diego Ferreira-García, your grandfather, came in. He stood perfectly straight, claiming every bit of his five-foot-four-inch height. He had an air of self-importance. I had to look down in order to see his face.

"'I want you to make a dress for my mother,' he said, not looking at me. 'Show me your best fabrics.' He ran his eye over the rainbow of colored bolts of cloth on the shelves. I took down the expensive brocade, the thick red velvet, and the raw silk. I put them on the counter and he looked down to examine them. I noticed that his eyes were level with my breasts. He rubbed each fabric between his fingers and asked, 'Which one do you like?'

"'The silk,' I answered. He glanced up, and as his eyes met mine, his expression softened. He stared at me, spellbound, as if I were the Virgin Mary herself. My heart was pounding. I had never felt so beautiful before. At that moment, I knew this was the man I would share my life with.

"Your grandfather was born and raised in Curaçao. As the only son in his family, he had to support his mother and two sisters because his father had gone insane and had become a vagrant. His father wandered the streets of Curaçao, searching, as if he had lost something that he could never find.

"Your grandfather got a job setting type at the island's newspaper. Opa was an eager and fast learner. The owner had no children and groomed Opa to run the paper. At the age of twenty-one, he was given the position of assistant publisher. In celebration he had decided to buy his mother a tailor-made dress."

My grandmother paused to see if I had fallen asleep. My eyes felt heavy and the warm breeze made it difficult to stay awake, but I was still listening.

"*Dushi*, you are never alone in this world, even though it might feel that way sometimes."

"I know, Oma," I whispered, then closed my eyes and fell asleep.

ᘯᘯᘯᘯᘯᘯᘯᘯ

I SAT QUIETLY IN THE corner of the motel studio. Mama was looking through a stack of free newspapers. What was going to happen to us? I knew Mama had too much pride to take any job other than nursing. She would feel going back to Curaçao would be an embarrassment because we didn't have a home to go back to. We'd have to move in with my grandmother, something we had done a few times before, and something I would look forward to again. I knew Mama hated the feeling of being wrong—wrong about having a dream, wrong about taking a risk. I didn't like being wrong either, that's why I never said much and stayed out of the way.

Hendrika and I were watching television when Mama exclaimed, "Let's buy a car!"

"What?" Hendrika asked.

"Let's go buy a car!" she repeated. "We are driving to California!" Hendrika and I looked at each other and smiled.

Mama jumped up and said, "What are you waiting for? Let's go! We can't go to California in a taxi. Let's go buy a car."

"I know, Mama. Let's deal with Dan," I said, happy that I had useful information.

"Who's that?" Hendrika asked.

"The car dealer Serena and I saw on television," Mama explained. Minutes later we were in a taxi on our way to Dan's car lot.

A short, skinny man with a mustache met us at the entrance to Dan's Used Cars. He wore purple polyester pants held up by a white belt with a silver buckle. His tapered white polyester shirt made him look even skinnier.

"Welcome to Dan's Used Cars, home of the best deals in town. My name is Tony. How can I help you beautiful ladies?"

"We came to deal with Dan," Mama declared. "We want to buy a car."

"I'll be happy to help you," Tony said.

"But we only want to deal with Dan," Mama insisted. Tony walked to the office mumbling and came out a few minutes later accompanied by the man we had seen on television. Dan offered his hand to Mama.

"I hear you ladies would like to buy a car, and I'm here to make sure you get the best deal possible," Dan said, sounding like Gomer Pyle, another southern character from *The Andy Griffith Show* I had seen on Curaçao television. He was dressed in tight-fitting maroon-

and-beige plaid polyester pants and a beige tapered shirt. Where Tony's clothes emphasized his skinniness, Dan's clothes made his pudginess more obvious. A gold chain sparkled against his hairy chest, and his platform shoes made him two inches taller than he really was. With a big smile, Mama shook his hand vigorously.

"We're driving to California, and we need a good car," she said. "We saw you on television, and we came to deal with Dan."

"Well, ladies, you've come to the right place. I've got the perfect car for you. Follow me." Dan rhythmically slapped his palm against his thigh as he walked us down a line of cars to a bright-red 1971 Chevrolet Chevelle with a vinyl top. Mama's eyes opened wide. Dan opened the door and invited Mama to sit behind the wheel.

"I think this is the car for you. It's so fast that you will get to California before you know it. You'll save time, and, you know, time is money." Dan slapped his back pocket with his palm as he spoke. Then he walked to the other side of the car and opened the door for Hendrika and me, and we climbed in. "It has a radio and power windows, air-conditioning, and brand-new tires. It's only one year old. This is the best car on the lot." Hendrika snapped pictures of the car's radio and power window buttons.

Mama had her hands on the steering wheel as she looked at herself in the rearview mirror. Dan noticed and returned to Mama's side of the car, flipped down the sun visor, and pointed at the mirror built into it. Mama cocked her head to one side and winked at Dan with a half smile.

"Mama, let's buy this car. It's beautiful," I said, running my hand over the black-leather seats.

"Yes, Mama, this car is really *chulo*," Hendrika exclaimed. Mama sat up, took a deep breath, and turned to Dan.

"This car would be perfect," she told him.

"Excellent choice," Dan said. "I will even give you my personal ten-percent-off discount," he said happily.

"What's the price?" Mama asked.

"It's $2,220, and with my special discount of $222, it will cost you only $1,998."

"But we can't spend more than $500," Mama said, shocked.

"Just $500?" Dan said, slapping his hand on his pocket again. "Then this is not the right car for you. If you'll excuse me, I'll send Tony over to help you." Dan turned and walked away. Minutes later Tony reappeared with a bounce in his step.

"Please follow me, ladies," he called. We got out of the Chevelle and followed him to the other side of the lot. Hendrika pointed at a two-door red convertible with a black interior.

"How about that one?" she asked Tony as she snapped a photo of it.

"That's a 1965 F55 Oldsmobile. You seem to like the expensive ones," Tony replied. "That one is $999."

We walked past more cars. Finally, Tony stopped in front of an enormous blue car. "This is a 1963 Ford Galaxie. It has air-conditioning, power windows, and four new tires. It has a rear seat big enough to lie down on, and a huge trunk for your luggage. This is perfect for your drive to California, and it's only $600."

We stood there, examining the car.

"It's big inside," I said, trying to point out the good things about the car.

"It has a radio," Hendrika added, but she didn't take a picture.

"It's still too expensive," Mama reminded us.

Tony opened the door for Mama to get in. She sat down in the driver's seat. Then he walked around and opened the door to the passenger side. Hendrika got in and turned on the radio; Stevie Wonder was singing "Superstition." I got in the back. Tony was right—I could stretch out on the backseat and lie completely flat.

"It's nice, Mama. This is a nice car," I said.

"It's a big, safe car. You'll be glad you bought it," Tony reassured Mama.

"Sell it to us for $500," Mama said, putting her hand on his arm and smiling. "I have to drive these girls to California, and $500 is all I can spend on a car." Mama was almost begging. "I will light some candles for you. I will say a special prayer so that you will get more customers. It will be worth it to you. I have a special relationship with Saint Anthony, the saint you were named for. He helps me all the time—he could help you, too. The money you don't make with us you'll get back three times over in the next two weeks."

Tony stood in silence, his mouth slightly open.

"Let me talk to Dan," he said, and he walked back to the office. When he came back, he said that Dan would let us have the car for $525.

Mama shook her head and slowly climbed out of the car, her cheeks hanging, as they often did when she was disappointed.

"Saint Anthony, what am I going to do?" she said, almost crying, her hands raised in the air.

"I'll be right back," Tony said, turned, and hurried back to the office. He returned, smiling.

"You can have it for $500," he announced. Mama flung her arms around his neck and gave him a big hug. Tony looked startled. Hendrika and I cheered.

We drove back to the motel. Mama and Hendrika sat down to count the money we had left: $423 and some change would have to get us all the way to California. "We'll need to leave right away if our money is going to last," Mama declared. She said we had to leave by June 27th—only two days away.

We went back to the Publix supermarket, where Mama bought two cases of canned beans, four cases of canned corn, two cases of Coke, and four cartons of cigarettes. This would be our food for the next ten days. I liked sweet corn and loved Coke, but I hated canned beans. Hendrika and I tried to convince Mama to buy chips and cookies instead of the beans. She wouldn't hear of it, but I was happy when she let me buy a postcard of Miami Beach to send to Oma.

We felt independent with our own car stocked full of everything we needed. We bought a map of the US, and Hendrika and Mama plotted our route. It would take us seven to ten days, depending on how tired Hendrika got. Mama preferred not to drive; therefore we'd have to rely on Hendrika, who loved to drive. Driving was the only time she felt in control of her life. Mama, on the other hand, felt in control when she could give directions.

MAMA ARRANGED OUR POSSESSIONS IN the car with as much care as if we were moving into a new home. She took twigs of rosemary, dipped them in nutmeg and cloves, lit them, and used them as incense to bless the car. "Ah, I love the smell of these herbs, they remind me of my mother," Mama said. "She is so good with herbs. Let us hope they work as well for us as they do for her."

When she was done, I immediately stretched out on the enormous, soft backseat. The luxury of lying flat was delightful. From here I would be able to see everything when I sat up—it was the best seat in the car. I was excited about going to California, where my favorite television shows were made and where David Cassidy lived. I was a big fan of his and knew all the words to "I Think I Love You." However, I was sad that I would be even farther away from Oma, and I was also frightened that if we ran out of money there would be no way for us to get back to Curaçao. We would be stranded in a strange country.

Hendrika was singing "Anticipation" as she loaded her camera with film. She handed it to me and climbed in behind the wheel. We took the Florida Parkway. It was smooth and had a wide, grassy median that ran straight as an arrow, due north. This road was nothing like the country roads in Curaçao with their potholes and ruts; many of them were not paved at all.

Hendrika tuned the car's radio to the Spanish-language station that the Cuban taxi driver had played. Mama was enjoying the scenery. I read the large, green signs that announced the cities and towns. We passed miles of orange, lemon, and grapefruit groves. I liked the lush green landscape that was also very different from Curaçao. Occasionally I glimpsed a wild turkey, an alligator, and even an armadillo. I had never seen any of these animals before. We had driven three hours and we were only halfway across the state of Florida. It was beginning to dawn on me how big America was. You could drive from one end of Curaçao to the other on the paved main road in an hour and a half.

The Spanish station on the radio had faded. Hendrika fiddled with the radio dial trying to find some music we liked, but a loud hiss was all she found. Finally, she tuned in a station that was playing "She's a Lady" by Tom Jones. Another large, green sign indicated the turnoff for Merritt Island and the Kennedy Space Center. "Mama, look! Is that where they send off the spaceships?" I asked.

"I think so. That's where the rockets are launched. Remember three years ago when the astronauts walked on the moon?" Mama was stretching up in her seat, trying to see if she could get a glimpse of the rockets.

"*Eh-eh,*" I said in awe. I remembered the broadcast. Everyone stopped what they were doing in Curaçao and watched television. We were at Oma's, and the house was filled with neighbors, family, and friends. Toasts were made with Curaçao liqueur. Everyone wanted to see the astronauts land on the moon. "What did the astronaut say? 'One small step for man, a giant leap for mankind.'"

"Can we stop and take pictures?" Hendrika asked.

"*Ay nò*, we don't have time," Mama said. "This is not a vacation. We can't stop everywhere and take pictures. We'll come back some day." She wagged her finger as she always did when she needed to be assertive. I was disappointed; I would have loved to have told Oma we were in the very place where the rocket was launched. Just past Daytona Beach, we crossed over the Intracoastal Waterway to get to a gas station. Mama stayed in the car, talking to the attendant, while Hendrika and I walked to the bathroom.

"Did you see the signs for the wildlife refuge in Titusville and for the speedway? I wish we could have stopped. I wanted to take so many pictures." Hendrika had her camera hanging around her neck.

"Yes, I know. I wanted to stop and see the Space Center," I said, as we walked into the bathroom. "But Hendrika, what are you going to do with all the photos you take? Aren't you afraid you take too many?"

"I have to—to get that one perfect picture. The ones that don't turn out I throw away, but I always learn something from each picture I take. Things look so different when you see them in close-ups or from different angles."

"I love your pictures, especially the ones from Curaçao. I think some of them are good enough to go in a magazine."

"I hope so. I hope my pictures will be in a magazine one day."

We washed our hands and returned to the car. Saint Augustine and Jacksonville were the next towns we passed through. Mama hummed along with "Put Your Hand in the Hand," which was playing on the radio. We passed open meadows with cows and clusters of pine trees under which a shrub-like palm grew. Oak trees, hung with greenish-gray moss hairs, looked like they should be in the *Munsters* television show. I loved that everything was so green. We stopped just past Lake City and spent the night at a motel.

Early the next morning, we set out for Tallahassee. It was hot, even at eight o'clock in the morning. It was going to be a long day of reading billboards, listening to the radio, and looking at the scenery.

"Apalachicola Oysters, Next Exit. Take Highway 98 to St. George Island," a sign read. I was tempted to ask Mama to take a detour along the coast because I missed seeing the ocean already, and it was always cooler at the coast. But I knew she would say no.

There were other billboards advertising cars, hotels, and restaurants. One read "Tupelo Honey—Three Exits Ahead."

"Look, that's the second sign for Tupelo Honey we've passed," Hendrika said.

"What's Tupelo Honey?" I asked.

"I don't know, but there's a Van Morrison song about it."

"Really? Let's listen for it—maybe they'll play it on the radio."

We saw more Tupelo Honey signs along the road, but we didn't hear the song on the radio.

We continued west through Alabama and Mississippi. The landscape changed once again. Now there were rolling hills of emerald green, with groves of trees.

"Look! This is beautiful. This is what the south of Holland looks like," Mama told us. "They just don't have castles with moats here."

It was getting dark, and Hendrika was tired and needed to rest. Mama decided singing would help her stay awake until we found a place to stop for the night. The Dutch children's songs she had us sing made me homesick. I missed Johan's contagious laugh and the sound of his guitar, and I missed Willia's talks and advice, and the time we used to spend together while she brushed my hair and painted my toenails. They were eight and ten years older than I, and had stayed with Papa after the divorce. Willia had been like a mother to me when Mama was away delivering babies. I had felt so much safer when Willia was around. Willia and Mama didn't speak to each other anymore. She used to argue with Mama about everything.

Unlike Hendrika, Willia confronted Mama with every inconsistency, and Mama rejected her for it. Hendrika, on the other hand, never challenged Mama. It seemed as if Mama's mind had taken over Hendrika's body. I hated Willia for always fighting with Mama, and I hated Hendrika for never standing up to her. Yet I loved them both for doing what I didn't have to do. I could sit and watch and hide behind both of them.

A green sign announced that Smithfield, Louisiana, was two exits away. We left the interstate and drove slowly into town. Smithfield was illuminated by a few dim streetlights. At one gas station I saw a couple of black men leaning against the pump. We drove around searching for a motel. Some of the buildings had broken windows; others were completely abandoned, and in between them there were empty lots strewn with trash. I hadn't realized that places like this existed in America. The size of the stores reminded me of the little stores in Curaçao, only here the stores had neon signs advertising beer and cigarettes, and some of the lights didn't work. People stood on street corners smoking, drinking, and shooting dice. They stared at us as we drove by. My stomach churned; I didn't like this place. I could see Mama's worried face reflected in the passenger's side-view mirror as it was lit by the occasional streetlights.

"Let's go back to the gas station and ask for directions," Hendrika suggested. We traced our way back. She parked the car outside the office and got out; I followed her, hoping Mama would not call me back. I was scared, but I didn't want to miss anything. Hendrika walked with a sway, something she did when she was nervous but wanted to appear confident. Some of the tubes of the neon Coca-Cola sign in the window had burned out so that now it said "Co C la." A large, elderly black man sat behind a cracked Formica counter littered with empty cigarette packs.

"Good evening, mister, we're trying to find a motel," Hendrika said. "Can you help us?"

The man's eyebrows raised. "Down the road two blocks," he answered slowly in a deep voice. He seemed surprised to see us. "Turn left and go down till you can't go no more. I don't think it's no place for no white women, though." Hendrika thanked the man and we hurried back to the car.

As we got close to the motel, we could see the man at the gas station had been right. The building's paint was peeling and the doorjamb was askew, leaving the front door cracked open. A trashcan sat next to the door, garbage spilling out over its sides. A black woman with a large afro stood in a second-floor window. She wore a purple skirt that showed her thigh, and a blue top that looked more like a bra. She was talking and laughing with four black men who stood outside, watching our approach.

"*Ay nò*. This is nothing!" said Mama, throwing one hand up in the air. "We have to keep driving."

"Mama, my eyes are tired and burning—I don't know what's wrong. I can't see very well. Can you drive, please?" Hendrika asked from behind the wheel. My eyes were burning also; I thought it was from all the cigarette smoke while driving with the windows closed.

"Well, we cannot stay here. All right, I will drive." Hendrika stopped the car and switched seats with Mama. The men at the motel kept staring at us. I smiled at them, but they didn't smile back; their eyes narrowed and they seemed angry, as if we had done something awful to them. These people were different from the black people in Curaçao.

In Curaçao, people from Holland were the outsiders. Although Papa was from Holland, we were welcomed in the black community because of Oma. Her mother was Arawak Indian and her father was black. Oma was respected and loved in Curaçao's black community and so was her daughter's family, even though that wasn't a community Mama cared to be a part of. Mama said that black people were always serving white people. Even when a black person and a white person loved each other, like Oma and Opa, the black person ended up serving the white person. She said she had never seen it the other way around.

As we drove away, I glanced back and saw two of the men get into a car. I clutched the back of Mama's seat and turned my head. The men were following us. It was dark. There were only fields on both sides of the road. "Mama," I said, "the men from the motel are behind us." Hendrika looked back then stared straight ahead as she held on to the dashboard.

"*Ay Dios mío*," said Mama. "Saint Anthony, help us. We need to find the interstate."

The men drove up close behind us and honked their horn. Mama was shaking. "Oh, Saint Anthony, how can you let this happen to us? Are you asleep? Wake up and help us!" Our car swerved as Mama tried to get away. The men sped up and pulled alongside, laughing, screaming, waving their hands, and pointing at us. When we sped up, they sped up; when we slowed down, they slowed down. Mama didn't know what to do, but in situations like this she became more determined. She decided to outrun them.

"Now, Saint Anthony! Come and help. This is ridiculous. You can't leave us stranded after all I've spent on incense and candles for you. How can you do this to me? You should be ashamed of yourself—letting me down when I am counting on you!" Mama shouted as she gripped the steering wheel tightly with both hands. She leaned forward, her chin about three inches away from the wheel. We were flying, but the other car kept up with us. "Saint Anthony. I even named my son, Johan Anthony, after you!" Mama's fear had turned to rage. Hendrika slid down in her seat, her head barely above the dashboard.

Suddenly, we saw the sign for the interstate on-ramp. We had to slow down to make the turn. The men's car came up behind us and tapped our rear bumper. Oh God, I thought, they've caught us. I gulped, then looked ahead. We had reached the freeway. Mama floored the old Ford. Turning back over my shoulder, I saw the other car drop back. I felt like cheering, but instead I collapsed into the backseat. "Thank you, thank you, thank you, Saint Anthony," Mama screamed out in relief. "I knew I could depend on you." She took a deep breath and asked Hendrika for a cigarette.

My heart was racing. I had been holding onto the back of Mama's seat so tightly that when I let go, my hands tingled. I felt like crying, but I knew that was something that would upset Mama even more. I struggled to hold back my tears. Mama sat upright behind the wheel. Fear and determination had chased away her fatigue. Restless, I kept checking the rear window and was relieved to see darkness behind us and nothing but open road ahead.

ꙅꙴꙅꙴꙅꙴꙅꙴꙅꙴꙅꙴ

WHEN I OPENED MY EYES I could see the gray streaks of dawn across the sky through the rear window of the car. The heavy air of cigarette smoke made my throat itch. We had crossed another state line and we were now in Alpha, Texas. From the interstate, I could see this town had stoplights, a McDonald's, a Denny's, and even a Sears. I hoped Mama would allow us to rest here, and perhaps even have breakfast. I tried to think of a reason that would convince her.

"Should we stop for some coffee, Mama?" Hendrika asked.

"Yes, I think coffee is a good idea—but only coffee, we shouldn't have anything else. Let's find a cozy spot where we can have a delicious cup of coffee and a cigarette." Mama swung the Ford off I-10 and drove to Denny's. I knew breakfast would be cold canned beans and cigarettes in the car. I had found it difficult to look at the billboards on the highway. Every one seemed to be advertising food. The thought of more beans, corn, Coke, and cigarettes turned my stomach. I wanted a fried egg and toast. I wanted something hot to eat. At Denny's, we used the bathroom to brush our teeth and change our clothes.

As we sat down at a table for four, Hendrika grabbed the jelly packets from the table and stuffed them into the right pocket of her jacket. I envied the people in the restaurant with mounds of food on their plates; some didn't even finish what they had ordered. I stared longingly at the leftovers on the table next to us. "Look, Mama, can I take that plate? The man hardly touched his food."

"No, you cannot. You have no idea what diseases he might have. We're not in the war. And even then you should never take what is not yours," Mama answered firmly. Then her expression softened. "I know being in a new country can be difficult, but we must make the best of it. Anyway, you two have it easy." She took a sip of coffee and looked as if she had left us and gone back to a time we didn't know.

"When I was sent to Holland all by myself to study, I was scared. I was only seventeen." Her eyebrows rose and her head nodded with each word. "At first, I was treated as though I were an ignorant girl from the colonies. I could see there was a big difference between the way my new friends lived in Holland and my life in Curaçao. Everything there was bigger, better, and more beautiful. But I told them my father was a wealthy Jewish newspaper owner, and that if they came to Curaçao, they'd look just as ignorant as I looked to them—and they believed me! They came to regard me as a princess from a faraway island, and soon everyone wanted to be my friend." Mama smiled mischievously.

I thought about how we also were being treated as if we were ignorant. I wondered if we could change the way other people saw us, as Mama had in Holland.

Mama continued, "Then all the girls at the university wanted to help me. Once again, I was special. I was invited to vacation at my friends' houses. They were the high society of the Netherlands. Of course, I couldn't go back to Curaçao for Christmas or Easter—it was too far—so I would go to a girlfriend's house. Sometimes my friends argued about whose house I would visit. I had never been so happy in my life." Mama's eyes gleamed and she took another sip of her coffee.

"A few months after I started the nursing program at Voorburg, the war broke out. Overnight, the morgue filled to capacity. There were bodies lining the hallways. We all worked eighteen-hour shifts." I saw Mama's cheeks droop and the gleam in her eye disappear. "Astrid, my best friend, pulled me into an empty room that afternoon and warned me not to tell anyone again that my father was Jewish. Jews were being picked up and taken away—no one knew where." She winced. "The thing I was most proud of, I now had to hide."

"I saw how they treated the Jews. I saw how they were humiliated, ridiculed, and taken away. I kept my secret and my shame, and acted as if I were indeed a princess of the West Indies." Mama fell silent for a moment. I was spellbound. I looked across at Hendrika. She looked stunned.

My mother went on. "A lot of my friends who knew that my father was Jewish were afraid to talk to me anymore. But you see, when I left for Holland, Opa and Oma had given me a box full of jewelry. This was their way of ensuring that I would never be without. I hid the jewelry until near the end of the war, when no one had anything to eat. People were starving. Farmers were the only ones that had anything, and even they didn't have much because the Nazis took everything, everything. You should have seen how these girls who would not speak to me suddenly became my friends again when I had an egg, some milk, or a piece of cheese that I had exchanged for my jewelry. Sometimes I even had cigarettes." Mama smiled bitterly at the memory.

My heart went out to her. I admired Mama for her cleverness and courage. I couldn't even imagine how frightening it must have been to be Jewish in Europe during the Second World War. I wanted her to know how I felt, but the only words I came up with seemed inadequate. I didn't know how to tell her. She pulled a pack of cigarettes out of her purse and offered them to Hendrika and me. "During the war, watered-down coffee and a cigarette butt was a feast. We even have beans and corn in the car."

Hendrika's eyes met mine. I could see she was as shocked by this story as I was.

ع⋗عₔعₔₔعₔعₔₔ

WE CONTINUED OUR JOURNEY ACROSS America. Each day we drove until Hendrika became too tired to go on. Sometimes, Mama took over, but usually Hendrika found a rest stop where we could all sleep for a few hours. I spent a lot of time sleeping and often woke up with a sore throat and stinging eyes from the cigarette smoke that wafted back from the front seat. Each morning Mama changed clothes, fixed her hair, and put on lipstick as if she were going to work. We played a game of rating the rest-stop bathrooms. Some of them were nice, and in those we washed up and changed our clothes. Others were disgustingly dirty, with stopped-up toilets, missing toilet paper, writing on the walls, and used Kotex pads in the trashcan next to the toilet. In these we tried not to touch anything.

"Where are we?" I asked one morning, trying to orient myself.

"We crossed into New Mexico about a half hour ago," Hendrika answered. "See how far we have come!" She held up the map for me. I could see the line Mama had drawn from Miami to the Texas–New Mexico border. It was still a long way to California.

Hour after hour we drove west. The songs on the radio became monotonous. The landscape changed again, from rolling hills with trees to desert with gnarled shrubs and cacti. The excitement had worn off, and the distance between California and Florida was turning out to be much greater than I had ever expected. It felt as if we were never going to get there. At the next rest stop when Hendrika and I went in to use the bathroom, Mama decided to stay in the car to consult her crystal pendulum.

By the time we returned, Mama had decided that Hollywood, California, was going to be our new home. She had used the crystal to pick out the destination on the map. Hendrika and I clapped with excitement when we heard the news, although I suspected Mama had purposely guided the crystal. She often told us how she prayed for a child that would someday become a star, and she was continuously searching for some spark of extraordinary talent in one of us, but she was always disappointed, and never reluctant to tell us. Thank God my talents up to now had been more directed toward schoolwork. I secretly hoped she would focus on making Hendrika the star once we got to Hollywood.

The weather became hotter as we drove west. The landscape changed from a flat, gray desert to one of red dirt, large boulders, and cacti as tall as small trees. The air conditioner barely worked. There was nothing to read and nothing to do, other than memorize the songs on the radio. As we crossed the New Mexico desert, the song "A Horse with No Name" seemed depressingly appropriate. I stared out the car window and thought of Curaçao. The song reminded me of the riding club where I used to take lessons on my favorite horse, Tonka. I thought about my friends and wondered what they were doing. I missed them, but I kept telling myself I was special for being on this journey: only a few chosen people got to go to America, the Promised Land, and I was one of them.

Suddenly, the air conditioner quit altogether, and white smoke poured out of the vent.

"What is this?" Mama demanded. "Quick, pull over and turn the car off."

Hendrika turned off the air conditioner and took the next exit. As we pulled into a Flying A gas station, it hit me that gas stations across America had become our main source of information, safety, and hygiene—the places where all our most basic needs were met. The white building housed an office and a garage emblazoned with several signs with a large, winged capital *A*. Two red-and-turquoise pumps with circular metal tops stood on a raised island. We got out of the car. Inside the car it had been hot, but outside it was unbearable, as the sun's rays penetrated my skin. I couldn't believe it was actually hotter than Curaçao.

The gas station attendant, a wiry man in his thirties who reminded me of the American Indians I had seen in western movies, was standing by one of the pumps, turning the crank to reset the meter. These were the same kind of pumps we had in Curaçao. I loved watching the ball in the little round glass window as the fuel made it turn and the numbers changed below it.

"Hello, ladies," he said, as he strolled over to us. "Do you need gas?"

"No, but our air conditioner is broken. Could you fix it for us, please?" Mama asked. "Our air conditioner broke down here for a reason. It must be because you are such a kind and helpful person." The man smiled and stretched up a bit. Hendrika disappeared into the bathroom around the side of the station. I knew she was escaping because she heard Mama's tone. It made me uneasy, too, but I stayed. When Mama used this tone, she usually got her way. If she didn't, she'd be furious.

The attendant opened the hood and poked around the engine. He muttered, hummed, and talked to himself as he worked. Mama hovered right over him, as if she could give him special powers. He pulled on one thing, pushed on another, put water in a reservoir, then turned to Mama with a frown on his face.

"Ma'am, I fixed it for a while, but it's not going to be fixed for long. That air conditioner has to be replaced. It overheats the car's engine, so only use it when you really need it. You're going to have to get a new one real soon." He shook his head and shrugged his shoulders as he gave Mama the bad news. He closed the hood with a bang.

"*Ay nò.* That is not possible," Mama said, throwing her hands up in the air. "We can't drive in this heat without air conditioning. You have to do something. We have to get to California. Please check again. I know you can fix it."

"Nope, that's all I can do for you, ma'am," he said. "I'm sorry. That will be five dollars, please." He held out his hand with an apologetic smile.

"Five dollars!" Mama shouted indignantly. "Are you crazy? For water? Five dollars! That's outrageous. That is horrible. You are trying to take advantage of us. I was wrong about you. You are a cheat." Mama's face was red. "You know that if you do evil, evil things will come right back at you. That's right, they will."

Mama was in a frenzy, her hands waving madly as she tried to intimidate the man into not charging us. He seemed puzzled, as he thought about what Mama said. She saw him hesitate and immediately adopted her let-me-teach-you-a-better-way attitude.

"If you help us, God will pay you back ten times," she said. I could see her face relax. "He will smile on you. You know that a good deed never goes unnoticed in God's eyes." The man's expression softened. The promise that God would pay him ten times over was enough for him to let us be on our way. I let out a breath that I didn't know I had been holding. Hendrika came back from the bathroom. She raised her eyebrows inquiringly at me. I shrugged my shoulders, wanting to tell her that Mama had gotten her way again, but it would have to wait until the next rest stop.

We soon crossed into Arizona. Driving during the day became impossible because the engine kept overheating whenever we turned on the air conditioner. We decided to drive only at night. The desert stretches were long and dark, with very few gas stations along the way. Looking at the sky was comforting to me; the stars twinkled and gleamed just like they did in Curaçao.

Mama diverted herself by planning Hendrika's career. She could sing, even though she had an unmelodic speaking voice. She could play the guitar, and maybe even learn to act. "Perhaps she could be like Lucille Ball?" Mama fantasized aloud. I was curious how Mama planned to turn my melancholic sister into a comedian, but I certainly wasn't going to ask.

"We'll need an agent, Hendrika," Mama said. "And we'll need a portfolio of pictures. We can use your camera."

Hendrika frowned. "But I've used up all my film." She made this statement quietly—but not quietly enough.

"How could you use up all the film? On what? You take pictures of nonsense, and when we really need pictures we don't have film. I can't believe how irresponsible you are," Mama complained. I inched my way into the furthest corner of the seat. I felt bad for Hendrika. She didn't think her pictures were nonsense. She thought taking pictures was an art, and I thought some of them really were beautiful.

"Can't we buy more?" Hendrika asked.

"More, more, more. You always want more," Mama shouted. "You should be careful about how many pictures you take. You have a camera. That is more than most people have!" Her chin jutted out and her nose tilted up with pride.

Mama took personal offense at any mention of what we didn't have or couldn't do. She felt as if we were criticizing her, although we didn't mean it that way. We constantly had to be on our guard never to mention what we lacked, even if it was the most common thing, like a roll of film. Complaints about anything made her feel unsure of herself and might spin her down into a depression—a depression, inevitably, all three of us would share. The fear of being trapped in that dark hole was enough for me never even to think about what we didn't have.

There was silence for a couple of hours. I lay on the backseat staring at Mama as we drove. The moonlight shone on the left side of her face as she held her head in her hand, her elbow resting on the armrest. Her skin was khaki-brown in color. She would never expose her skin to the sun, always worried it would become darker. She had a scar on the left side of her forehead that she usually covered with her hair, but tonight it showed. It reminded me of the story Oma had told me about how Mama got the scar.

ᘔ♥ᘔ♥ᘔ♥ᘔ♥ᘔ♥ᘔ♥

MAMA'S SKIN COLOR CAME FROM her mother, who was half black and half Arawak Indian, but she preferred to acknowledge only her father's lineage. He was a Portuguese Jew. She was her father's favorite child because, of all his children, she looked the most like him. Of her nine brothers and sisters, she was the only one with his straight hair, which made her feel special. He had named her Gabriela.

When Mama was five years old, she climbed up onto a kitchen windowsill near the stove to watch a carnival parade. She fell from the sill and knocked a large pot of boiling water off the stove, spilling its contents over her. A third of her body was severely burned, and the doctors did not think she'd live, so Oma decided to take her home from the hospital. She treated her daughter's burns with egg white, glycerin, and arnica. She meticulously cleaned the sores and painted the mixture on with a feather, and brewed special teas made of lemongrass, oregano, and basil. She rubbed Mama's hair with *agua florida* and put cucumber slices on her body to cool her down. She sat by her bed and lit green candles made with plant oils. Then she smoked the room with frankincense and patchouli, and prayed.

Mama was ill for more than a year. Her liver and kidneys had been damaged, and because penicillin was not available yet, my grandmother's healing powers were critical. She stayed up with Mama at night, nursed her during the day, and loved her until she felt life coming back into her little daughter's body.

Opa peeked in on his daughter two or three times a day, and every evening at the dinner table he asked Oma, "How is my daughter? Do you think she will get better? Will the scars go away? Will her hair grow back?" Oma patiently reassured him, without making any promises. Opa was very demanding. Oma had to do everything for him. He insisted that she cook all his meals, serve his food, and sit with him while he ate. If he found a tiny bone in his fish, Opa would shout, "Are you trying to kill me, Elena?"

Because of Gabriela's illness, Oma became good friends with the six-foot-two, muscular black herbalist, Shon Mirto, who lived around the corner. Shon Mirto was a great admirer of Oma's. He knew she had special healing powers, and that she knew as much about herbs as he did. Opa was extremely jealous of Shon Mirto. Oma was a very beautiful woman, almost six feet tall. Her eyes were large, jet black, and glistened like sea glass in the midday sun. When she walked, her body swayed slowly and rhythmically, like the ebb and flow of the ocean. Her skin was the color of cinnamon. Her hands were always calm. There was a sense of aristocracy about her that was inborn, even if the dark color of her skin confined her to a lower class.

Oma was very fond of Shon Mirto. They discussed herbs and made decisions as to which ones were best for her daughter. Oma brought Shon Mirto *panlefi*, an egg cookie usually eaten at teatime with coffee. Occasionally, she brought him lunch, which was the big, hot meal of the day. Shon Mirto loved it because he didn't cook, and the cleaning lady who cooked for him was not as talented as Oma. Shon Mirto often said, "Oh, Elena, if only you were not committed, I would marry you right now!"

However, my grandmother was committed—although not married—to my grandfather. She had borne him nine children in the fifteen years they'd been together. They loved each other, but Oma also loved her independence.

I stretched out on the backseat and looked up at the night sky through the rear window. I wondered if Oma was looking at the same stars I was.

THE BRIGHT SUN, JUST RISING in the east, cast a golden glow in all directions over the rocky landscape of reddish dirt dotted with gray-green shrubs, towering, spiny cacti, and other plants that looked like giant aloe vera. Curaçao was dry and rocky, and although this Arizona desert with its red, yellow, and orange hues was very different, it felt strangely familiar to me.

I stared out the windows as the scenery whizzed by. The radio kept reminding us of the time every five minutes. In Curaçao my life had been full and it seemed as though time had an engine to speed itself up. Here it felt as if the engine had run out of fuel. We were stuck in a sea of time.

A road sign read:

Tombstone—Ghost Town
Exit 5 Miles Ahead

"Thank you, Saint Anthony," Mama said. She had her hands up in the air again, seeming to speak to the roof of the car. "Take that off-ramp, Hendrika. There is a message here for us. I can feel it." Mama leaned forward, looking for the off-ramp. When Mama had a feeling about something, there was no telling what would happen next. Hendrika took exit 303. Another sign declared:

Tombstone 24 Miles

"I'm telling you, Hendrika, Saint Anthony is looking out for us. I can feel it—our luck is changing. When we call the spirits at the ghost town they can help us with our future." Mama's face was cheerful. She often thought Saint Anthony put surprises in her path, just as *Sint Nikolaas* put presents in Dutch children's shoes. "Hendrika, what is that English word for calling spirits? Seems? Sans? Something with an *s*." Mama was making different *s*-sounds, hoping that the word she wanted would come to her. Hendrika nodded, but neither of them could come up with the word.

I didn't know what word they were looking for, but I knew Oma did not like the idea of calling spirits. They were supposed to visit on their own.

ᘚᘍᘚᘍᘚᘍᘚᘍᘚᘍᘚᘍ

OMA REFERRED TO SPIRITS AS *almas*, or souls. "*Almas* will find you if they have something to tell you," she used to say. "Otherwise let them rest, for their work in this world is done." Oma would never bother a soul, but Mama often would. Mama summoned them to ask about her future. When Mama called ghosts she frightened me, yet when the ghosts visited Oma, I was never afraid. At the House of Six Doors, *almas* often visited Oma. At the end of one summer I stayed behind with her after everyone else had left to go back to the city. I was helping Oma put things away and close up the house.

The House of Six Doors was a *landhuis*, or plantation house, that my grandfather owned. It was painted a brilliant cobalt blue, with white trim. They always spent the summer there. The house had been built in the early seventeen hundreds and its two-foot-thick walls kept the rooms cool even when the trade winds stopped. The entire house was encircled by a large veranda, where as many as twenty hammocks could be strung for extra guests to sleep after big parties. Many lives had started and ended at the House of Six Doors; the house was vibrant with souls. That summer day, as I was helping Oma put the hammocks away, a gust of wind came up, carrying with it the scent of the *kadushi* cactus flower.

"Where did that smell come from, Oma?" I asked. There were no *kadushi* cacti in bloom around the house, so it was impossible for their scent to be carried by the wind.

"I'm glad you can smell it, *dushi*. An *alma* is sharing its pleasures with us."

"How do you know that, Oma?" I asked.

"I can feel it," Oma answered as we stretched another hammock on the floor before folding it in half and rolling it up. "That soul loves to be here. She's letting us know that the pleasures we are feeling, she feels also."

"Does she live in this house with us, Oma?" I asked, not liking the idea that invisible beings were among us.

"It's not like that, *dushi*. When *almas* are free from their bodies, time is not as you and I know it now. All their lives are experienced at the same time." Oma smiled. My puzzled face amused her. I did not always understand Oma, but that never stopped her from trying to teach me. She continued to talk, hoping my ten-year-old mind could catch up. "Come, let's make ourselves some dinner and I'll tell you more about *almas*."

We passed through the large dining room into the kitchen. Oma took a plate of *funchi*, a kind of polenta, out of the refrigerator, sliced it, heated some butter, and fried it while I set the table.

"How can time be different, Oma?"

"Time was different before you were born and will be different again after you die. You just can't remember. Once you are born, you can only live one moment after another." Oma finished frying the *funchi*. She took one slice, covered it with Dutch cheese, and handed it to me. The cheese melted as I bit into the *funchi* with delight. She covered the rest of the *funchi* slices with cheese and placed them neatly on a plate. I took the plate from her, set it in the center of the massive kitchen table, and sat down, while she chopped cucumbers and tomatoes.

"But what good is it to have all these lives, Oma?"

"To learn empathy, understanding, and forgiveness, Serena. Souls remember all the lives they live. Souls are whole. Our minds remember only one life; that is only a very small piece of the whole. The mind is always wanting, yearning, needing. If you live from your soul, you will live peacefully, bringing joy and wisdom to those around you."

Oma sprinkled the cucumbers and tomatoes with vinegar and salt, and sat down next to me. "Souls are what we all truly are. You see, Serena, you have had many lives. You have been a king and a slave, you've been a warrior and a monk, you've been a thief and a judge, and much more. Do you remember all this?" Oma stared at me. I shrugged my shoulders, not wanting to disappoint her. She cocked her head and put her arm around me. "Do you remember me?"

"Yes, I do. I've known you forever." The words came out of my mouth before I realized it.

"That is it, Serena. That is the beginning of remembering that you have a soul, and that you know much more than you've learned in this lifetime."

"Can souls predict the future, Oma?"

"It is possible. Souls live in the past, the present, and the future all at once."

"Then Oma, when Mama calls the dead, who comes?"

"Often it is a soul that has lived a life guided entirely by the mind and finds it difficult to let go of that mind. An invitation from other minds is much too enticing to pass up." Oma stared through the kitchen window at the ocean as she ate. I knew she would never say anything bad about Mama, but I also knew she did not agree with everything Mama did. I knew Oma thought it was disrespectful to call the dead. She thought they should never be used. We finished our meal, and we went to bed.

Despite Oma's disapproval, Mama loved to call the dead. She'd invite two or three friends to spend the night at the House of Six Doors when no one else was there. They'd sit in the living room around the *mesita*, a petite, three-legged, round-topped table and spread their hands on the tabletop, touching thumb to thumb and pinky to pinky. Then, with eyes closed, Mama would invite a soul to come and visit. When the table moved, Mama would ask, "With whom do we have the pleasure of visiting?" The soul would spell out each letter of its name with a series of taps. Mama interpreted the number of taps with the sequentially corresponding letter of the alphabet. Once she knew who the ghost was, Mama would ask questions about the future.

I remembered the time Mama took me with her. She told me to go to sleep on the big couch in the living room. I lay down but I didn't fall asleep. I remember that night a soul told her she would spend New Year's Day in the hospital. It was three weeks before Christmas. Mama became furious at that soul and scolded him. "What do you think you are doing? You can't just show up and make bad predictions to scare us. That's not helpful. Go home!" Mama said a quick prayer to help the soul find peace.

That New Year's Eve, just before midnight, my brother Johan threw a homemade firecracker into the air to welcome the new year. When it didn't explode, he walked over to relight, it and as he bent over to pick it up, it exploded. His left leg was burned from his ankle to his knee. We spent New Year's Day at the hospital.

We were getting closer to Tombstone. I was not sure I wanted to visit a ghost town. I didn't want any bad predictions.

৵৵৵৵৵৵৵৵৵

"THERE IT IS. WE'RE ALMOST there," Mama said, her voice rising. The main road ran right through the town. With clapboard houses, wood-planked sidewalks, hitching posts, and water troughs, it looked just like *Bat Masterson* on television. A two-story, red-brick courthouse with a white cupola marked the center of town. People were dressed in turn-of-the-century outfits, and horse-drawn carriages were being driven up and down the road. Handsome cowboys with pistols in their holsters reminded me of *Bonanza*. I wondered if this was where they had filmed the series. I looked at every cowboy, hoping I'd see Little Joe.

We parked the car and walked up Main Street. Mama entered the Palace Saloon.

"Welcome to the Palace. That'll be one dollar each," a blue-eyed cowboy said at the entrance.

"Three dollars for what?" Mama asked.

"That's the fee to come in and see the saloon," the cowboy answered. He extended his hand and invited us in.

"I just want to know where we can call ghosts," Mama said.

The cowboy laughed. "Well, I guess you could go to the graves up on Boot Hill."

"No, that's not what I mean. Where do they call the ghosts?" Mama persisted.

"You mean like séances, Ouija boards, that kind of thing?"

"Yes, yes. That's it. Where do they do that?"

The cowboy slapped his thigh and burst out laughing. "They don't do that kind of thing here. Nobody calls them. Ghosts show up when they want to, mostly at night."

"No, no, no," Mama shouted. "I know they do that kind of thing here in America. Where can we do that?"

"Not here, ma'am. We just have good old fun here."

Mama looked disappointed. She pushed out her lower lip.

"Thank you, sir," she said as she walked out. "Why have a ghost town if they don't call ghosts here?" she muttered to herself as we walked past the shops. I looked in the windows at the many souvenirs; Mama looked around, her eyes searching. A poster in one store window read:

Shootout at the Livery Stable—Next Show: Ten O'clock.

"Let's go," Hendrika said, pointing at the poster.

"Yes, let's," I agreed. Mama's cheeks were sagging again, but she continued in the direction of the Livery Stable. At the entrance to the stable a sign said:

Adults: $1, Children Under 12: 50 cents.

Without saying a word, Mama turned around and started walking back to the car. Disappointed, Hendrika and I followed. "Should we buy some film here?" Hendrika asked.

"Why?" Mama snapped. "So you can take pictures of nothing?" I could see the hurt in Hendrika's face.

The sun was higher in the sky and it felt as if someone had turned on an oven. We piled into the car and headed back toward Interstate 10. Just outside Tombstone, Mama spotted a pink Victorian house with white gingerbread decoration. In the front yard there was a big sign in the shape of a tombstone with the inscription:

Haunted House
If you didn't see ghosts in Tombstone,
See them here.

"Let's stop here," Mama said. Hendrika pulled into the driveway. A woman with gray hair and pale skin opened the front door. She looked about seventy years old.

"Welcome. Come in. My name is Mrs. Wise," she said. The house was dark and smelled musty. It was difficult to see inside after having been out in the bright sunshine.

"Do you have ghost-calling meetings here?" Mama inquired.

"We don't have to do that. There are ghosts all around. They're right here as we speak."

Mama's eyes sparkled. "Do you communicate with them?" she asked.

"That will be one dollar per person. You can go on the self-guided tour, and you are bound to run into more than one." Without hesitation, Mama took out her wallet and gave the woman three dollars. Mrs. Wise put the bills into a metal box. Mama had great faith in her premonitions, and she would follow them even if they were only a remote possibility. "Please start at the door to your right and follow the signs."

We walked through the entrance and down a dark hallway. A door was opening and closing by itself. Further down the hall was a sitting room where the curtains were swaying even though the windows were closed. An arrow directed us up a flight of stairs, its treads creaked loudly. "There are no ghosts here. They are making fun of us," Mama said angrily. At the top of the stairs were three bedrooms. Mama peeked into the first one and as she did, a metal chamber pot fell over and a laughing voice came out of nowhere. Hendrika and I were startled. "This is ridiculous," Mama said. "They robbed us of three dollars." Mama walked into the next bedroom and we heard her scream. Hendrika and I hurried over to see what was wrong. A trap door had opened in the ceiling, and a mannequin with a rope around its neck had fallen out. It hung in front of her, its neck at an odd angle.

"I want my money back," Mama yelled as she stormed down the stairs. Hendrika gasped and covered her mouth with her hand to keep from laughing. I could not look at the mannequin. I ran down the stairs and out the front door. Mama was shouting at Mrs. Wise. Hendrika joined me outside.

"You're confusing haunted houses with guiding spirits, lady," we heard Mrs. Wise shout.

"What are they arguing about?" I asked Hendrika.

"Mama wants her money back, and Mrs. Wise won't give it back to her. She told Mama that we had gotten our money's worth. Haunted houses, she said, were supposed to be a good scare."

"I don't think that mannequin was funny," I said, annoyed. "Killing yourself is not a joke."

"Oh, Serena, you're right. I didn't even think of it that way." Hendrika stared at me for a moment, then put her arm around me. Mama turned away from Mrs. Wise, fuming, and marched us toward the car.

"I was wrong," she said dejectedly. "We cannot call spirits here." Mama looked exhausted. She had calmed down but her shoulders were slumped forward and her cheeks drooped again. When we reached Interstate 10 we headed west and searched for a rest stop.

It was dawn. The sign read, "Blythe, California."

"We're almost there!" Mama exclaimed, running her fingers through her hair. Then, twirling both index fingers as if she were leading an orchestra, she started singing, "California, here we come ..." I was glad her mood was up again. It was as if someone had opened the windows and let fresh air in. When Mama was down, it seemed as though I was suffocating. I sang along even though I really didn't want to.

"Let's keep driving," Mama said. "I want to see Hollywood. I'm so excited I couldn't sleep even if I drank a liter of basil and chamomile tea."

She shook a cigarette out of the pack. I scooted down and stretched out on the backseat of the car, buried my face into the seat back, and pulled my T-shirt over my nose to keep the smoke away. I was tired, and sleeping would make the time go by faster anyway.

"I wonder if we can find Lucille Ball's house? She must live somewhere in Hollywood. Maybe you can get a part in her show," I heard Mama say as I nodded off.

A ray of sunlight pulled me out of my nap. I sat up and asked where we were.

"We've passed Los Angeles; just a bit farther and we'll be in Hollywood," Mama answered, staring straight ahead, not wanting to miss anything. "If we see the Melrose exit, we have to get into the right lane because Hollywood Boulevard is only three exits farther," she said, quickly glancing down at the map and then up again at the street signs.

The way she said it made me feel that if we missed the exit, we would miss the best opportunity of our lives. We took the Hollywood Boulevard exit and stopped at the traffic light at the end of the off-ramp. We made a right turn onto Hollywood Boulevard. I was disappointed by what I saw. It was a wide street with two lanes in each direction, parking on both sides, and a lane in the middle just for turning left. Stunted, thin ficus trees with caged trunks and bushy tops grew out of the sidewalk. Square two-story buildings resembling giant, beige boxes lined the boulevard, with car dealerships in between. It didn't look as glamorous as I had expected. The car dealership reminded me of Dan, and I wondered if he had a car lot here, too.

A large marquee read: "World Theatre—*The Last Picture Show*." I asked Hendrika what the marquee said. Hendrika translated the title into Dutch and explained that the theater wasn't closing, but that it was the name of a new movie. On the next block there were more car dealerships and the Pix Theatre, which was showing *Dirty Harry*. The buildings became taller and fancier as we drove west. The banks were the most elaborate, with stucco decorations and marble façades.

As we crossed Argyle Avenue, we saw more pedestrians on the sidewalks. A large building displayed a colorful marquee. It proclaimed: "Pantages Theatre—*The Godfather*." King's Drugstore was across the street, and next to it was a store selling wigs. In front of that store a white man was disco dancing wearing an afro wig, a tie-dyed T-shirt, red pants, platform shoes, and sunglasses with large round lenses. A peace sign dangled from his neck as he waved at the cars driving by. Hendrika and I waved back. Hollywood was different from any place I'd ever been. I had never seen so many theaters on one street, and the people here were definitely out of the ordinary. Mama sat with one arm on the backrest, her other elbow resting on the door sill, enjoying the sights.

She spotted the World Import Bazaar. "Maybe they sell incense and oils there," she said. "We'll have to come back later." The Vine Theatre stood near the Bank of America, a shoe shop in between. We drove slowly, taking it all in.

The more we drove the more theaters we saw. There was the Fox Theatre and across the street The Pacific Theatre, and a block later Holly Cinema. Then we went past Vogue Records, Hollywood Books, and another wig store. Although the buildings were big and impressive, something essential was missing. It took a moment to realize that none of them had peaked roofs. It was as if someone had taken a giant saw and cut them all off, except for The House of Pies, which didn't have a real peaked roof either; just a triangle of painted wood stuck on the front. These buildings were going to take some getting used to. In Curaçao all of the buildings had peaked roofs of all different shapes and colors.

The New–View Theatre stood opposite the Vogue Theatre, with J. J. Newberry's on one side and Hollywood Toys on the other. Three people wearing ape costumes stood in front of Newberry's. Hendrika pulled over to the sidewalk and we all stared, but no one else seemed to pay any attention to them. Mama asked a passing pedestrian why they were dressed that way.

"This is Hollywood, lady. They're from the set of the movie *Battle for the Planet of the Apes*. They're probably on their lunch break," he said as he walked off. Hendrika and I clapped our hands in excitement. Now we were sure we were in Hollywood.

In front of the Swenson's Ice Cream Shop a man dressed in a silver suit juggled three balls while balancing a stick on his nose. Just driving down the street was entertaining. I didn't know whether to look at the buildings or the strange people. In front of the Egyptian Theatre stood four bald young men and a woman with long, matted hair, all dressed in orange robes. The woman shook a tambourine while they all chanted "Hare Hare, Hare Krishna, Krishna Krishna, Hare, Hare." I wondered what it meant. They all seemed so happy.

"What movie do you think they are in?" Mama asked.

There were more wig stores, shoe stores, drugstores, and banks. A large parking lot flanked Grauman's Chinese Theatre. Hendrika slowed down as we admired the tall, red-and-white, Oriental-style building. *Cabaret* was showing. The car behind us blew its horn. "Let's park and walk," Mama said, "There's too much to see from the car."

Hendrika made a left on Sycamore and another left on Hawthorne, and found a parking space on Highland. We put two dimes in the meter, which gave us two hours. Mama was smiling and her movements were determined and energetic. She could take on the world when she was like this. She seemed more comfortable here in California than she had been in Florida, even though she had never been in Hollywood. It must have been because she had worked for six months at a hospital about twenty miles east of Los Angeles. She hadn't seen much of California because she worked double shifts, couldn't afford a car, and shared an apartment with another nurse a few blocks from the hospital.

Maybe everything would turn out all right after all. There would be no more surprises. We were going to fit in and not be singled out as we had been by the customs officer, the motel owner, and the hospital receptionist; here, things were going to be different.

We walked three abreast, taking up almost the whole width of the sidewalk. Hendrika had her camera hung on her shoulder, hoping Mama would allow her to buy film. We gawked at the exotic lingerie in the window of Frederick's of Hollywood. I wondered how the pink push-up bra would look on me and saw Hendrika eyeing it also.

Mama suddenly disappeared up a set of stairs. Hendrika read the sign above the stairs to me: "H. M. Hollywood House of Magic." At the top of the narrow, dark stairway we saw Mama knocking on the door, but no one answered.

"*Ay nò*. There is nobody. We have to come back some other time," Mama said, waving one finger as she came back down the stairs.

"What are you looking for, Mama?" Hendrika asked.

"*Bruheria*. Maybe they sell what we need here for witchcraft. I could get the things I need to turn our luck around."

"It doesn't look like a *bruheria* store," Hendrika replied.

"I can see that, but they might have something inside. The way they were so strict about herbs at the airport, I would not be surprised if they kept *bruheria* things in the back where no one could see them."

As we walked on, a pair of checkered bell-bottom pants caught my attention at Lerner's; they had a matching beige halter top that would go well with my brown hair, and I imagined myself wearing the outfit. I was already five foot seven inches tall, and if I had platform shoes with the extra long pants, I surely would look tall and thin. In Curaçao, my oldest sister, Willia, was called "*guitara, guitara*;" that was the way girls were described who had big breasts, wide hips, and a narrow waist, which was the ideal body shape back home. My brother had said I would grow up to look like her, which I was happy about when we were in Curaçao, but I could see it was going to be different here.

Compared to the girls I had seen in American magazines and on television, I was chubby. I would have to lose weight to be like them. That way I would be able to fit in. The price tag on the outfit was $17.95; it would be a while before we could afford clothes like that. A few blocks farther on, Freeman's Shoes had the perfect platform shoes, which I pointed out to Hendrika.

"*Eh-eh*, neat! And look at the knee-high platform boots," she marveled.

"They have that wet look we saw in the magazine," I said. I was dying to talk to Hendrika about everything we saw, but somehow Mama tended to take over every conversation. I missed being alone with my sister. Mama constantly monitored and evaluated everything we said; she was fearful we might not agree with her point of view. She often questioned us and if she didn't like our answers, she tried to mold our opinion and she'd get mad if we didn't agree. It was just easier to talk to Hendrika when Mama wasn't around.

"Look! That store sells maps to the stars' homes. Let's get a map so we will know where to go," Mama said. We stopped at the shop. As Hendrika and I browsed through T-shirts with smiley faces, key rings with peace signs, and postcards of movie stars, Mama asked the sales clerk for a map. "Isn't it very clever the way they use the sidewalk as a cemetery?" Mama observed. "America is so practical."

"What are you talking about?" the sales clerk asked, staring at her in disbelief, raising only the right side of his upper lip as he spoke.

"The stars in the sidewalk," Mama said, pointing at one of them outside the store. "Aren't those for dead people?"

"No. Those are to honor actors and actresses. They don't have to be dead, and they certainly are not buried in the sidewalk," the clerk said, handing Mama the map and her change with a disdainful sniff.

As we left the store, I heard him comment to the next customer how dumb we were. It was a word I understood because in Dutch the word was almost the same. I was frustrated that even in a strange place like Hollywood we were different. I wondered where in America we were ever going to fit in.

We stood in front of the Capitol Records Tower and stared up, trying to decide if it really resembled a stack of records. Mama was getting tired and said it was time to find a motel. We went back to the car, and even though we had been gone much longer than two hours, we were lucky not to find a parking ticket on our windshield. Mama was determined to find a motel in the center of Hollywood, hoping we might meet an agent or movie star who could help us.

What we found was an L-shaped, dun-colored building with turquoise windows, called the Hollywood Star Motel. Mama loved the name, and although she was disappointed that the paint was peeling and the place seemed dirty, it didn't deter her.

"This is all we can afford," she lamented. The office was at one end of the L. The Mexican manager welcomed us and, in the same breath, warned us, "I don't want no trouble in my motel. No pimps, no drugs, okay?" I didn't know what a pimp was.

My mother stepped back. "What kind of place is this that you have to say that to your guests?" she asked.

"A very nice place. That why I make sure it stay nice!"

Our room was at the far end. Hendrika parked the car in front of the door, and we brought in our bags. In the room Mama sorted through our clothes to see what needed to be washed. Hendrika put the few cans of corn and beans that were left over from our trip on top of the chipped Formica table. I was craving a glass of cold Coke with ice but there were no Cokes left. I peered around the room. The worn bedspread was stained; its blue, yellow, and purple flowers had faded. The pale-yellow curtains were worn thin. The green carpeting had a gray cast to it, and the room smelled of a mixture of smoke, urine, and stale closet. I opened the windows and checked the bathroom to see if the toilet worked. I thought about the previous guests and was certain they were people Mama wouldn't want us to meet.

We heard a knock on our door and without opening it, Hendrika asked, "Who's there?"

"Elvira. I live next door," a voice with a Spanish accent said from the other side. Hendrika opened the door and in front of her stood a young Latino woman in her mid-twenties with ruby-red lips, false eyelashes, and blue eye shadow that clashed with her brown skin. Her hair was bleached bronze and her fingernails were long and painted a frosty red. She wore a wraparound skirt with a pink-and-red floral design, and a skin-tight T-shirt that made her plump arms bulge out.

"I hear you people are new in town, and I came to give you the *bienvenida*!" she greeted us, leaning against the doorpost. I was excited to see a friendly person that wanted to talk to us. It had been a long time since we had met anyone who wanted to socialize.

"Oh, thank you," Hendrika said, although she appeared baffled. I don't think she had expected welcoming neighbors.

"Well, aren't you going to invite me in? Where are you from?" she said all in one breath.

"*Pase.* Come in," Hendrika said in Spanish. "My name is Hendrika Brink. This is my younger sister, Serena Brink, and this is our mother, Señora Gabriela Ferreira-García," she said as she pointed to each one of us in turn.

"*¡Qué bueno que hablan español!*" Elvira said, smiling.

"How long have you been in Hollywood? What do you know about California?" Mama asked immediately.

"I have been here four years. I was an actress in El Salvador, and I want to be a star in Hollywood. I have already been in three movies as an extra, and I go to auditions almost every day. Soon I am going to be a star!" she said confidently.

"And how do you get these auditions and parts?" Mama asked.

"It's easy. You sign up with an agent. You pay them a little money, and they find you jobs." Hendrika was still standing, holding the door.

"How do you find your agent? How much does it cost?" Mama wanted to know.

"Fifty dollars. He will even make you a portfolio. I'll give you the name of my agent. He is really good."

"Ah! That would be *maravilloso*," Mama said. "Will you really do that for us? You are an angel. Thank you so much."

Elvira puffed her chest up with pride. She took a homemade business card out of her skirt pocket and handed it to Mama.

"Well, I'll let you unpack. I'm right next door if you need anything. *Chau, chau*," she said, as she walked back to her room.

"Oh, I think our luck is back," Mama said. "See how wonderfully things are working out. Now we know how to get the acting jobs. You two are lucky you are white; at least you have a chance of being recognized. Dark people like Elvira have a slim chance of being recognized even if they are exceptional. White people always have it much easier. Tomorrow we will use our map of the stars' homes, and we'll probably see them walking around and we will introduce ourselves to them. We'll also go to an agent to sign up. I'm sure by next week you'll both be in the movies. You are so beautiful and you are almost fluent in three languages. I think the agent will be begging us to sign up."

I never had any desire to act or to become a movie star, but if it was going to be this easy and it meant I could earn some money, and if it was going to make Mama happy, I was willing to try it. I imagined what it would be like if our faces were seen in the movie theater in Curaçao.

"We might not even have to pay. Let's see how much money we have. Here is thirty-five dollars," Mama mumbled, rummaging through her wallet. Her purse contained another one hundred dollars. It was clear that with only $135, we wouldn't be able to stay in the motel another night, especially if we had to pay agents' fees. So our '63 Ford would have to be home for a few more days. Later that evening, Mama got out of bed and counted her money again.

The next morning we put our things back in the car. We took showers before we left the motel, to be as pretty as possible for the days ahead. In our home-on-wheels, Mama lit a candle and sprinkled a few drops of a money-attracting infusion she had made in Miami. It contained cinnamon, cloves, and basil, but the patchouli was missing because she had not been able to find it yet.

She said a prayer: "Saint Anthony, please guide us and direct us to the homes of the stars. You have helped us before so many times, and we are grateful and counting on you, Saint Anthony." Mama's eyes were closed and her hands were folded in her lap. We sat in silence for a moment. I peeked at Hendrika, but she seemed to be praying also. "Let's go, we're ready now," Mama announced, sitting up and clapping her hands together.

Hendrika drove us down Sunset Boulevard to Beverly Hills. We admired the incredible mansions. "I Can See Clearly Now" was playing on the radio. Hendrika and I both hummed along, though we hadn't heard the song before. Mama was moving in time with the music and smiling. "This is it! This is what I want for you girls; someday we will live like this. This is why we came to America. Anything is possible here. And listen, this is the perfect song," Mama exclaimed. "From now on, it's going to be nothing but sunny days." When the song ended we listened carefully to hear who the singer was. The DJ announced that it was Johnny Nash from Jamaica. We let out a cheer. It was good to think that someone from the Caribbean was being played on the radio in Hollywood.

The houses in Beverly Hills were as big as public buildings. In Curaçao, schools and hospitals were that big, but these houses were even bigger than the houses on the American television shows. The houses were surrounded by wrought-iron fences with imposing gates that led up to enormous front doors. Some had large pillars and looked Greek, others resembled French chateaus, and still others looked like plantation houses. The lawns were mowed; the flowers were all in bloom; nothing was out of place, but all the doors and windows of the houses were shut.

All three of us wondered where the people were. Why were they not at home? In Curaçao, the doors and windows of a house stood open when people were home; even then everyone spent most of their free time outside on the front porch. Friends and acquaintances blew their horns and waved as they drove by, and in return you gave a loud "Hey, *kontá*" (How are you), to acknowledge the passerby. My mind searched for reasons why the houses were empty. Maybe everyone was on vacation. Maybe something happened and everyone had to leave.

"Something must be wrong with these houses—all locked up," Mama finally decided. "Why have big houses and beautiful lawns if you're not going to use them? This does not make sense," she said, looking out the window. Hendrika had driven us around for an hour, and we had seen only three people walking on the street. The sun started to go down and so did our gas gauge.

We went back to Hollywood and parked on Wilcox Avenue, a couple of blocks south of Sunset Boulevard, and started to set up the car for the evening. Hendrika took a couple of cans of beans out of the trunk; that was going to be our dinner. After we had eaten, Hendrika studied the classified ads in the newspaper she had bought.

"See here, Mama, you can earn twenty dollars a night for dancing. I'm not sure what go-go dancing is, but I could learn. I could do that to earn money."

"I thought we were going to earn money acting," I said, surprised.

Hendrika thought for a moment, and then said, "We might not get jobs right away. Remember, Elvira has only had three parts as an extra in four years." I thought it brave of Hendrika to offer to dance. She was the only one in our family that had not inherited the rhythm of the islands. I stared out the window at the parked cars. The street was deserted except for a police car passing by.

Mama took the paper from her and said, "Let me see—where is that? Here it is, the Pussycat Go-Go Club on Highland and Third. Let's keep that ad in case we need it." Hendrika folded up the newspaper and put it in the glove compartment.

Two hours later, as it was getting dark, a police car came by again, but this time it stopped and the policeman walked over to our car. "Are you waiting for someone? How long are you going to be here?" The officer was tall and thin, with blue eyes.

"We are spending the night here, Officer," Mama said innocently.

"Oh, no, you're not. It's against the law to sleep in a vehicle parked on a public street." He sounded as though he were quoting a rule book.

"Against the law? Why? I don't understand."

"If you want to spend the night in your car, you have to park on private property, at a campground, or at a designated sleeping area. You cannot park on the street and sleep in your car. I'll have to ask you to move on." Once again, Mama was exasperated by the laws of this country, which didn't allow her to live her life the way she wanted to. "If I drive by and you are still parked here, I will have to give you a ticket. Have a good evening." The officer turned around and got back in his patrol car.

"*Ay nò*, this cannot be. How is it possible you can't park on the street? Saint Anthony, what are you doing to me? Why are you punishing me like this? All I ask for is a little rest, and you send a policeman to chase me. Why me?" Mama fell silent for a moment. "That policeman must not like foreigners. Maybe he thinks we're lower class. That's why he treated us that way. Saint Anthony, where are you when I need you?" Her pleas filled the car and were quickly swallowed up by the night around us. Hendrika started the car and slowly drove off to nowhere.

༂ॐ༂ॐ༂ॐ༂ॐ༂ॐ༂ॐ

OUR GAS GAUGE WAS ON empty as we pulled up to a Mobil station on Highland and Sunset at two o'clock in the morning. A tall man, dark and slim with kind brown eyes and a narrow face came out to help us. "Hey, you ladies are out late tonight. What can I do for you?" he said with a heavy Spanish accent and a sweet smile.

"We need two dollars worth of gas, please," Hendrika answered. She eyed the man and asked him where he was from.

"Perú. What about you?"

"We're from Curaçao."

"My name is Ramón Rodríguez, *para servirles.*"

"I'm Hendrika, this is my mother Señora Gabriela Ferreira-García, and this is my sister, Serena."

Ramón offered his hand through the window and Hendrika shook it. Mama didn't waste a moment. Without any hesitation she asked if we could park our car at his gas station until morning. Ramón looked unsure, and then said with a slightly worried expression, "Oh, Señora, I don't know. If it were my place, I would say of course you could. But let me ask my boss. He's inside." It was nice that, for a change, someone was treating us with courtesy and respect. It felt as if we were being cloaked in a soft, warm blanket.

Ramón finished pumping the gas and went in to the office to talk to his boss. He came back with a smile on his face.

"You can park right there next to the bathroom, but you have to leave by six-thirty in the morning."

"Wonderful. Thank you. Saint Anthony will bless you. This is a good deed you are doing! You will see good things come to you. Thank you so very much! Thank you!" Mama said, leaning over Hendrika, trying to get closer to Ramón to ensure she got across her message of gratitude.

At six the next morning, Hendrika went to the office to get the key to the restroom. Inside, there was a mild smell of urine disguised by a strong scent of Lysol. I tried not to touch the sink as I brushed my teeth. I held my clothes under my arm as I changed my underwear and pants. I struggled, trying not to let them touch the floor. I could almost see the germs on the walls.

Ramón came out to say good-bye before he finished his shift. Mama quickly asked, "Do you think we could park here again tonight?"

"I don't know. Why don't you come around eleven tonight? I'll see if it is possible." He nodded his head and winked at Hendrika and me as a sign of encouragement.

Hollywood seemed deserted early in the morning. There were hardly any cars on the street. A gray haze covered the city, making the mountains that had been visible the previous day disappear. We parked in the big lot of the Ralphs supermarket, and Mama decided to wait there until it was time to go to the talent agency. I was both excited and nervous about going. Hendrika left the key turned in the ignition so we could listen to the radio. Cat Stevens was singing "Morning Has Broken."

Ours was the only car in the parking lot. I stared out of the window at the few people walking along the street. Our lives seemed so unpredictable. I hoped that once Mama got a job and had earned some money, our lives would go back to normal again. We were still a long way from a house with a lawn, but if acting was as easy as Elvira said, we could act until Mama renewed her license. In that case, it shouldn't take long before we were in our new home. I worried about how I would do in school. I hoped it wouldn't be too difficult to learn to read and write English.

Mama decided we should try Elvira's agent first. His office was on the other side of Hollywood, on Western Avenue near Clinton Street. We pulled up to the address. Mama stared wordlessly at the shabby building. The lobby had a stained linoleum floor and a 1920s cage-style elevator. We rode the elevator up to the third floor, where a wooden sign announced: "Suite 310: Daydream Talent Agency." Mama knocked on the door. We were welcomed by a short, gray-haired man with a pock-marked face. He was dressed in black.

"We're here to see the manager of the Daydream Talent Agency," Mama announced. Hendrika and I stood behind her.

"You have arrived at the right place. My name is Kent, and I can make you a star," he said with a big grin, sticking his hand out toward Mama.

"I want to find an agent for my two daughters." Mama turned around and showed us off as if we were the fresh catch of the day at Curaçao's fish market.

"That is what I do best. I wouldn't only be your agent; I give acting lessons, I set up your portfolio, and I send you to hundreds of interviews, all for one small fee of fifty dollars each. Please, come in," Kent said, holding the door open with one hand and waving us in with the other. Mama's face bore an expression of sheer delight, as if she had struck gold, but I wasn't so sure. We entered a room with a desk and walls covered with faded eight-by-ten photos of beautiful men and women. Kent sat down behind the metal desk. Mama sat opposite him and filled out the forms he handed her. Hendrika and I stood admiring the pictures.

"And you, Mrs. García, I see talent in you. I can think of three parts, right off the top of my head, which would fit you perfectly. Why don't you also sign up? It'll be worth it." Kent pushed another form toward Mama.

"No, I'm here for my daughters." Mama didn't want to spend another fifty dollars.

"I'll let you take acting lessons for free. I hate to see talent wasted," Kent moved around in his chair as he spoke, as if it had nails sticking up through the seat. Mama blinked her brown eyes, tilted her head from side to side and smiled, as if she were posing for a photographer. I was surprised to see she could be flattered by Kent.

"Do you think so?" Mama asked. "I never thought about ..." Mama did not finish the sentence. She was looking up, as if she were thinking about a career on the big screen.

Kent took Hendrika's and my pictures while Mama stood by, watching. He promised to arrange them in a portfolio and have them ready by the end of the week. "I could have taken our pictures and made a portfolio," Hendrika whispered to me. I whispered back that her photos would have been better but the real problem was that we didn't look anything like the beautiful people in the faded pictures that hung on Kent's wall. He told us to come back that evening to his acting class.

"I will have you auditioning by next week. You can be sure of that," Kent promised with a broad grin.

We freshened up in a JCPenney restroom before returning to the Daydream Talent Agency that evening. I was excited, and I thought Hendrika was, too—at least a bit. Perhaps we would learn to act and be in the movies, and one day Oma would see us at the movie theater in Curaçao. We arrived early for the acting class. In the room were two men, one in his thirties and another who was almost as old as Mama and had a beer belly, and three Hispanic women who were all short and fat.

The chairs were arranged in rows like a classroom, with Kent in front as our instructor and director. He handed out a couple of pages of dialogue. It was a romantic love scene in which two actors were to say a few lines and then kiss. Kent paired off the younger man, Jimmy, with one of the women, Laura. Hendrika and Mama paged through their scripts reading the lines to themselves. Mama leaned over to Hendrika and whispered, "We are much better looking than anybody here."

I tried to read the lines but I couldn't make out what they said. I listened to Jimmy and Laura.

"I want to spend the rest of my life with you. I love you," Jimmy read.

"I love you too and I want to be with you, but we have to be careful," Laura read. Jimmy put his arms around Laura and kissed her, but Kent immediately jumped up.

"No! No! No! Not like that. You need more passion. You need to think of someone you want to kiss, then close your eyes and let loose. Let me show you." Kent demonstrated how to do the scene, taking his time kissing Laura. Kent had an incredible ability to let loose. I wondered if he brushed his teeth between scenes.

Mama's turn came next and Kent paired her with the gray-haired, beer-bellied man, who introduced himself as Dick. Mama was in her fifties, and her body showed the wear and tear of having had four children. I cringed when it came time for Mama to kiss Dick. I felt humiliated seeing Mama kiss a man she didn't know. It was obvious Mama had no clue about acting.

"You're fine," Kent complimented her without much interest. "Just keep practicing."

I saw Mama's cheeks sag. "Practice what? Why start with kissing? I will practice but you must give me something to practice." Mama was now standing in front of Kent looking down at him. Kent ducked away and called Laura.

"Watch Laura and let her be your teacher. The best way to learn is by imitating," he said with a half smile. Mama returned to her seat.

The muscles in my neck and back were getting tired from sitting up straight. I was feeling light-headed from holding my breath each time a person was called to the front of the room because I was afraid I would be called before I could memorize the sounds of all the words. It was exhausting. Finally, Hendrika was paired with Jimmy. Jimmy shuffled his feet; they both seemed uncomfortable. Hendrika was blushing, and she played with the car keys in her pants pocket as she read the lines. Jimmy stood slumped with one arm hanging by his side while holding the script close to his face with the other hand. The script still in one hand, he put both arms around Hendrika to kiss her. Kent rushed toward them.

"Let me demonstrate."

Kent embraced Hendrika. Her body stiffened and she pulled her head back. I suspected that he was trying to put his tongue in Hendrika's mouth. She was probably counting the seconds until the scene was over. After the kiss, Kent rubbed Hendrika's shoulder and patted her hand in an attempt to relax her. But the more he touched her, the more rigid she became. Hendrika returned to her seat next to me, grabbed her camera from underneath her chair, and placed it on her lap. I tried to smile at her but she just stared at her feet.

Then it was my turn. My stomach simultaneously churned from hunger and twisted with fear, and my hands trembled slightly. I glanced at Mama as I walked up. She smiled and stretched up in her seat to encourage me. At the front of the room Kent handed me the same script.

"Okay. Serena and I are going to do the same scene. Serena, are you ready?" Kent came toward me and put his arm around me. "You'll do fine. Don't be nervous," Kent said as he pulled me closer.

I could feel the sweat from his armpit on my shoulder. I held my breath so I wouldn't have to smell him. My heart was pounding. Suddenly, Mama rose from her chair.

"Serena won't be doing that scene. She is too young!" Mama said, pointing her finger at Kent. There was silence while everyone stared at us.

"But why not? Teenagers are prime candidates for these kinds of parts. You will rob your daughter of her opportunity for stardom," Kent said. "There are lots of parts for teenagers out there. You should let Serena do this."

Mama hesitated for a moment. She put her hands on her hips. "I don't think so. Serena should get children's parts first, and then we can see about all of these love scenes. She is only thirteen years old." It was true, I was thirteen, but I looked much older. My body was developing rapidly. I now wore a 32B bra and had moved up to women's size six jeans.

"Fine. She will never get a child's part with that body. But don't listen to me," Kent muttered as he walked to the filing cabinet, pulled out a different script, and handed it to me. "Start reading the lines for Melissa," he grumbled.

I had memorized the lines of the kissing scene by listening to them, but now I had to read what was on the page in front of me. Terrified, I stared at the page. I read slowly, trying to sound out each word. The words made sounds that were unrecognizable to me.

"Ha-ve joo he-ard a-bot the bich hor-sa ra-sa?" is what came out.

"'Have you heard about the big horse race!'" Kent shouted at me. I felt like crying and I shrank with humiliation.

"This is ridiculous!" Kent exclaimed, storming toward me and grabbing the script out of my hand. "I can't do anything with you. You have the body of an adult, but you want a child's part. You want to learn to act, but you can't read the lines." He turned toward Mama. "I could cast her as an older teenager in romantic scenes in which she wouldn't have to say much. Otherwise, I can't use her in my agency!" Mama was speechless.

"That's it for today's session. I'll see everybody here tomorrow," Kent ordered, as he organized the scripts into a pile. Mama marched out the door; Hendrika and I followed without saying a word. We got into our car and drove toward Ramón's Mobil station hoping we would be able to park there again for the night.

"I could have done it, Mama," I said, from the backseat of the car.

"You could have done what?" she asked.

"I could have done the kissing scene. I just couldn't do it with Kent," I said, trying to bring some hope back into our car. The truth was that I had been relieved that Mama had prevented me from doing the scene, although I also desperately wanted to help change our situation. Mama took a slow drag on her cigarette, opening her mouth as she inhaled to let the smoke go deep into her lungs.

"Kent is the agent and he has to believe in you before he can represent you. I have a feeling if you cannot act with him, he will not represent you," she said.

I sat speechless. I knew it would have been impossible for me to act as if I were enjoying kissing Kent; anyone who could do that would have to be a great actress.

We drove to the Mobil station. The office had windows on three sides so the attendant inside could see the entire station. The front window had a crack that ran from the upper right corner to the lower left. Through the window, I could see a smiling Ramón waiting for us, as if he were an image in an old, cracked painting. He sat behind a battered, pressed-wood desk with four empty folding metal chairs surrounding him. When we entered the office, we could see why he was smiling. He had four Cokes and a large pizza with everything on it waiting for us.

"The boss went home early. Will you ladies join me for dinner?" he said as he stood, sweeping his right hand, palm up, across the display of food. He was so sweet, I wanted to run up to him and give him a big hug, but I was afraid Mama would find the gesture overly affectionate. I knew I could only show affection if she approved.

We hadn't had pizza in months. It was hot and the melted cheese dripped off the sides as we each took a slice and lost ourselves in the delight of food. Hendrika and I sat on either side of Ramón.

"So tell us, Ramón, where in Perú are you from?" Mama asked. She straightened herself in the metal chair, crossed her legs, and held a napkin under her chin with one hand and a slice of pizza in the other, trying to appear sophisticated.

"A beautiful pueblo in the Andes called Huancayo," Ramón answered, as he took another bite of his pizza. He paused for a second, as if he were remembering his boyhood home. His skin color and narrow eyes came from the Incas, but his face was long and thin, like the Spanish. I didn't think he was handsome, but I loved the way he had come to our rescue. I saw Hendrika stealing sideways glances at him, and I wondered what she thought of him.

"When I was sixteen, I was sent to live with my aunt and uncle in Lima. They said I was the smart one in the family, so Mama made a big sacrifice and sent me to the university." He cast his eyes down, as if he were humble about his intelligence. "I studied veterinary medicine there and learned about *los Estados Unidos* and its opportunities.

"Once I learned about California, I knew that's where I wanted to spend the rest of my life. I was told by my professors that my Peruvian diploma would not be recognized in the United States, so I decided it would be better for me to study in California." There was a sparkle in his eyes. He sat up in his chair and folded both hands behind his head. "Two years before I was to graduate, I bought a bus ticket to Mexico. I had to work in Tijuana for a while in order to earn enough money to hire a coyote to smuggle me across the border. I didn't know the coyote would be so expensive. I was lucky and got a job right away at a horse farm in San Diego." So Ramón knew about horses? He was even more wonderful than I had originally thought. I wanted to ask him about the horses, but I knew it would upset Mama if I interrupted.

"The people I worked for liked me," he went on. "After I had worked for them for three years, they sponsored me so I could get my green card." He smiled with only half his mouth, as if the experience had turned out to be less than he had hoped for. "After eight years of hard work at the same pay, I realized if I didn't go back to school I might as well have stayed in Perú. I heard about a two-year veterinary technician program at Pierce Community College in Los Angeles." Hendrika dropped her napkin. Ramón picked it up and handed it back to her, and continued talking. "So that's what I'm doing now and here I am, working nights to pay my way through school." Ramón raised his head and smiled.

"How long did it take to get your green card?" Mama asked.

"After I applied, about three and a half years—maybe a little more."

"That's a long time. How long will it be before you finish your studies?" She dabbed at her mouth with her napkin and shot Hendrika a dirty look for reaching for a fourth slice of pizza.

"I'm almost done with the program, but I want to transfer to UC Davis to get a BA, and then I'll apply to veterinary school after that. Here, they do not recognize my Peruvian education at all but that does not matter; learning things for the second time is easier, even if it is in a different language."

"Was it difficult to leave your parents?" Mama asked.

"Oh, yes. My father died when I was seven, and left my mother, my two sisters, and me behind." What a coincidence, I thought. We could be his new family here in California. "I was the man of the family and yes, it was very difficult for me to leave." We were all silent for a moment.

"Ramón, tell me, do you know where I can find a deck of tarot cards?" Mama asked suddenly.

Ramón raised his eyebrows in disbelief. "I have a deck in my car. It was my grandfather's. He gave them to me before he died." Ramón leaned forward as he spoke. "I've always carried them with me, but I don't know how to use them."

"Well, then, go get them. I'll read the cards for you and we can see what is in your future!"

Ramón pushed his chair back and stood up slowly, regarding Mama inquisitively. Then he slapped his right hand on the desk as if to reassure himself and said, "*¿Por qué no?*" as he walked off to his car. He returned with an old, faded deck of Spanish tarot cards.

"These cards have a lot of life in them," Mama said, as she studied the deck carefully and then handed it back to Ramón. "Here, shuffle them until you feel it's enough, then cut the deck in two, placing the bottom half on top. Then cut the deck into three piles: your health, your wealth, and your happiness." Ramón followed her instructions. Mama was good at reading tarot cards for other people, but when she read the cards for us she could only see what she wanted to see. I knew the general meanings of the cards. The Ace of Wands indicated a new project or career; the Five of Wands indicated trouble and strife; the Two of Cups meant the beginning of a new romance; the Nine of Cups meant contentment and well being; and the Ten of Swords predicted ruin, desolation, and deception. Mama had a talent for seeing much more than these general meanings. She could tell who was involved, and even predict the time of the events about to occur.

"Your health is good," she said as she turned the first pile over, "You're very strong and healthy." She turned the next pile over. "Your wealth is not so good." She took one card from the second pile to see what was underneath it. "Ah, still not so good." Ramón pulled back in his chair. Hendrika seemed uninterested. Then Mama pulled another card from the same pile. "It's going to take five years or more before you start making good money." Then she turned to the third pile. "Oh, look at this! You will have two marriages. The first one feels like a convenience. You will be happy for a while, and then I see trouble, anger, disagreements, disappointments, disillusion."

That's so sad, I thought. He was such a nice man. Some nasty woman was going to take advantage of him.

Mama shook her head and frowned. Then she rearranged several cards and continued. "But don't worry, in four or five years you will marry for love. This marriage will last. Oh, things will be very good then. I see a lot of happiness."

Oh good, I thought. He'll get rid of the nasty woman.

Mama smiled as she stacked up the three piles and put down the cards one at a time in the shape of a cross. "You'll be getting news from far away that a loved one is sick." She paused. "But it's not serious, although at first it will seem that way. You're going to have some arguments with your boss. Don't get too stubborn. Let him have his way. Someone is going to be asking you for money. And look, here is that love card again. You are going to be engaged very soon." Mama paused again, and then ran her finger over the cards one more time to see if she had missed anything. "That's it. Do you have any questions?"

"Yes. How do you do this?" Ramón asked, amazed. Then seeing the pride on Mama's face, he said quickly, "Wait, wait. I'm not saying I believe it." He pulled farther back into his chair. "I want to know how you make these predictions."

"*Ay* Ramón, let me tell you. I learned by watching my mother. She is an incredibly wise woman. She saved my life when I was five and she did not even have antibiotics." As Mama spoke a tender expression came over her face. "I would watch her every time she threw the cards. That is how I memorized their general meaning. Then I learned to listen to myself and I could hear what the cards had to say. My mother seldom had time to teach me these kinds of things. She had nine children, and even so my father wanted almost all of her attention. I wish she could have taught me more but the most time we spent together was when I was sick." Mama started shuffling the cards again. "Sometimes, I don't even know why I say things. Sometimes, words just come out. You should try it! Here, try it now. Not everybody can do it. Let's see if you have the gift," Mama insisted, pushing the cards toward him.

"No, no, no. Let's see if any of this comes true. Then, if you are right, I'll try to read the cards," Ramón laughed.

A car pulled into the gas station, and he jumped up to go to the pump.

"*Qué duerman bien,*" Ramón said, wishing us a good night's sleep as he went out to help the customer.

"We should get some sleep," Mama said, as she also got up. I didn't want to go yet. I wanted to ask Ramón about the horses.

"Can't we stay a little longer? Please, Mama?" I begged.

"No, it's late. Let's go to bed. Please throw these away," Mama said as she handed me the four empty Coke cans. She picked up the napkins and pizza box and threw them in the trash bin on our way to the car.

It was cold and I put on two extra layers of clothes. My throat was sore and my body ached from sleeping in the car at night and sitting in it most of the day. I curled up into a ball in the backseat and watched my breath as I exhaled. Hendrika and Mama were smoking cigarettes. Mama was looking up at the stars through the car window. I remembered the nights in Curaçao, when a cotton sheet was all I needed to cover me. I remembered the warm island breeze tickling my face and dancing in my hair. How I wished I could be there with Oma right now. She would have given me something for my aching body and my sore throat.

I closed my eyes. I could see her sitting in her rocking chair on the porch. She used to say, "Life is a paradox. Except for true love there is no good that doesn't have its bad, and no bad that doesn't have its good." I was beginning to understand what she meant. Here we were in America, a place Mama said was so good, yet things were going badly. I wanted to be with Oma. I'd rather be there, in a place Mama said was not so good, but where I didn't feel bad.

ᑐ᙭ᑐ᙭ᑐ᙭ᑐ᙭ᑐ᙭ᑐ᙭ᑐ᙭

I SAT WITH OMA ON the porch of her house at Penstraat 34. The ocean waves pounded hard on that side of the island, and I could taste the salt on my lips. Oma had lived in this house ever since my grandfather, Opa, bought it for her after the birth of their first child. I loved that house almost as much as I loved the House of Six Doors. Oma's house was a big, green, two-story building with three doors in the front, and a white stucco conch and feather decorating the peak of the roof. The back porch overlooked Curaçao's rugged, rocky southern shoreline. On cool evenings Oma made hot lemongrass tea and on hot evenings she made mint tea, which we drank sitting in our rocking chairs.

Twice a week, she walked from her house to the Kunuku Herb Gardens to buy fresh herbs, from which she made her teas and remedies. Sometimes I'd go with her. We always stopped at Shon Mirto's for salty licorice. While Oma and Shon Mirto talked, I sucked the pitch-black, strong-flavored candy until my teeth turned black. Then we walked through a small park with tall hedges of white, pink, and lavender oleander, which we called *franse bloem*. Oma had warned me the oleander was poisonous, but she had also taught me that if the leaves were boiled, the water could be used to treat skin rashes.

Although Oma was not Catholic, we always stopped to look through the office window of the bright orange-and-white church to see if Father Davelaar was at his desk. Oma did not believe in any specific religion; she was interested in all religions and eager to talk to those who practiced a particular faith. If Father Davelaar was there, he would wave us in for a cup of coffee. He was a six-foot-six, blond-haired, blue-eyed Dutchman who loved Curaçao. He even spoke Papiamentu. He always brought out his silver-colored cookie box to give us some of the Dutch cookies his family sent regularly from Holland. Oma and I both loved those cookies; they were so buttery they melted in your mouth. All of Oma's children had gone to Father Davelaar's parish school because it was the closest school to Oma's house.

After our visit with Father Davelaar, we climbed up the big hill called Berg Alterna. Colorful row houses stair-stepped up the hill, each house a half story higher than the next and each painted in its own vibrant color. It was hard to walk up that hill in the midday tropical sun. I did my best to keep up with Oma; somehow, the heat never seemed to affect her.

Once we got to the top of Berg Alterna, a cool breeze would greet us and we could see Punda and Otrabanda, the two sides of the harbor. They were linked by the Princess Emma Pontoon Bridge. An engine on the last pontoon allowed the entire bridge to swing out of the way whenever a ship went in or out of the harbor. From the top of Berg Alterna we could also see Scharloo, the fancy neighborhood where the wealthy Jewish merchants lived, and where my grandfather had bought his mother a house.

The house Opa had bought for Oma was in a different neighborhood. Oma was not accepted in the tight-knit Jewish community because of the dark color of her skin. But it didn't seem to bother her. She said, "It's not the appearance of the person that matters; it's the soul inside." Even though Oma had not been accepted in Scharloo, I loved the elegant houses. I looked forward to seeing them on our walks, until one day Oma told me the story about Mama and Opa's mother.

"When your mother was a bit younger than you are now, her father would take her to visit his mother and sisters at their house in Scharloo every Sunday morning. Your mother eagerly put on her special Sunday clothes, which she had laid out the night before. She combed her hair, braided it, and tied a large white bow at the end. Then she stood in front of my dresser and admired herself in the mirror. She wanted to be beautiful. She would ask me if she could borrow some of my cologne from Spain. I always told her she looked pretty as I spritzed her, happy to see how full of anticipation and joy she was. Then she would have breakfast with Opa in the dining room. She was proud Opa had chosen her, out of all his children, to visit his mother and his sisters.

"After breakfast, Opa would walk Gabriela to his mother's house. He always reminded her to be polite. He told her she was not to speak unless she was spoken to and she was not to take anything unless it was offered. If she were offered something to eat or drink, she had to finish it, even if she didn't like it. Trying to remember all of his instructions made your mother anxious.

"Every time they arrived at the front door, Opa's oldest sister came to greet them. He would tell your mother that he would be back soon, and to be a lady. Then he walked over to the press to work for a few hours. It took months before your mother told me what happened on those visits. She had never seen such a large and fancy house and described it to me many times in meticulous detail. The hall had a mahogany table with a marble top. White and pink vertically striped wallpaper covered the walls. The wide-plank wooden floors were polished to a high gloss, and two brass wall sconces hung on each side of the entrance to the salon.

"In the salon, your mother was always asked to take a seat on the couch, which was upholstered in gold brocade. The large room had high ceilings and was furnished with French antiques. A crystal bowl filled with bonbons sat on the table in front of the couch. Gabriela wanted to do everything right so that her grandmother would be pleased with her.

"She always sat perfectly straight on the couch, listening to every sound. Directly opposite the couch was the door to the rest of the house. She would stare at it with trepidation, wondering when her grandmother or one of her aunts would come in. She told me that her heart raced every time she heard footsteps or the creaking of the floors. Her back ached from sitting up straight for so long. After a while, the doorknob would turn and the heavy door would open slowly. A large silver tray with a porcelain teapot, one cup, and a silver tower laden with cookies, prune-filled pastries, macaroons, and fruit-shaped marzipan would be brought in by a heavyset black woman in a white cotton uniform. The woman would place the tray on the table in front of the couch, smile, and leave, closing the door behind her.

"For a long time your mother believed this meant her grandmother was about to come in. She would sit there, tantalized by the perfectly shaped marzipans on the tower, knowing she must not take anything unless it was offered to her, but her grandmother never came in. Finally, your mother told me, she would hear a knock on the front door. Then her oldest aunt would return to the salon and escort her back to the front door where Opa was waiting.

"On the walk home, he would ask about the visit. Opa thought she was developing a relationship with his family. Opa knew they did not approve of me and therefore would not associate with me, but he presumed kindness would be extended to his daughter. She was terrified he would be ashamed of her and didn't tell him how she would sit alone in the salon for hours, staring at the door.

"Your mother always hoped that one day her grandmother would spend time with her, but after many weeks she realized that although she was her father's favorite child, his mother and sisters would never want to talk to her, and it made no difference that she had done everything her father had told her to do."

That was when Oma turned to look at me and said slowly, "I wish I had protected her and not allowed her to go to that house. She was just a little girl, like you are now. I wish there had been more time to spend with her—time to let her know how much I loved her. I never had enough time to be the mother I wanted to be for my children." From then on the fancy Scharloo houses never looked beautiful to me again.

I missed Oma. She had a way of making sense of the world, and I needed her to make sense of what was happening to me now. Things in America might be better, but they were not the things I loved.

THE EARLY LIGHT OF DAWN woke me up. I was lying in the backseat of
the Ford while Hendrika sat with her eyes closed in the front. Mama
stood outside talking to Ramón.

"Ramón, I have a favor to ask," I heard Mama say, almost in
a whisper. "Could I use your address as the return address for my
nursing license? I need to renew it, but I don't have a permanent
address yet. Would you be so kind and let me do that?" Mama
cocked her head and put on a pained smile. Ramón looked down and
thought for a moment.

"*¿Por qué no?* I don't see why not, Señora. Let me write it down for
you," he said, and searched his pocket for a scrap of paper and a pen.
He wrote the address down, folded the paper, and handed it to Mama.

"*Muchísimas gracias*, Ramón. May Saint Anthony bless you and
keep you. Just wait, you will find happiness because you are so kind."
She put the paper in her purse. "You are like a son to me," Mama said
and hugged him. He returned her embrace and patted her on the back.

"Soon you will get your license, Señora, and everything will be
all right."

"*Si Dios quiere*, Ramón. God willing," Mama said, pointing
one hand to the sky. I closed my eyes as she got back into the car.
"Hendrika, Serena, it's time to go. Go use the bathroom." I pretended I
had been sound asleep. Hendrika and I took turns using the restroom,
and then it was time to find another place to park our car.

We drove back to the Ralphs supermarket parking lot. It seemed easier to return to a familiar spot than to find a new one. "Is it okay if I get a newspaper, Mama?" Hendrika asked.

"I think so," Mama answered, and opened her purse to find her wallet. She glanced up at Hendrika. "How much change do we have?" she asked. Hendrika scooped up the change out of the ashtray.

"We have $1.10 left in the ashtray."

"I only have $24.48 left in my purse. If we send in the renewal for my license, we'll be left with less than six dollars. We need to do something to make money," Mama said, almost to herself. She searched through her purse again, digging deep into every compartment. Finally she gave up. The empty purse rested on her lap.

Acting hadn't turned out to be as easy as we had thought, and it didn't look like we were going to get a part in a movie any time soon.

"I'll get the newspaper, Mama. We'll see what we can do for work." Hendrika returned with the *Los Angeles Times*. Once back in the car, she handed it to Mama, who kept the classified section and handed the comics to me.

"Here, read this. It will help your English," she ordered, as she opened the classifieds. I looked at the drawings. *Ziggy* only had one picture; most of the others had four. The *Doonesbury* characters seemed menacing. *Peanuts* was my favorite. I remembered seeing it on the cover of *Life* magazine years before at Oma's house. I tried to sound out the words, but I couldn't understand them and didn't have a dictionary.

Mama's eyes searched up and down the columns of ads. "Here is that dancing again," she said, tapping the ad with her index finger. "It says they pay twenty dollars a night. It seems that is the only way we can get cash right away. Usually you have to work two weeks before you get paid. I think we should go there this afternoon," she said confidently. Mama had a tendency to raise her voice to show certainty. I was not sure if she did that to discourage us from objecting or if she was merely trying to reassure herself. We had been poor before but we had never been this poor. After renewing her license we wouldn't even have enough money to call anyone. I wanted Mama to use the twenty-four dollars to call Oma; that was the only sane thing to do. It was time for us to go home, and Oma could send us the money to fly back to Curaçao, but suggesting that might enrage Mama and that would leave us worse off.

Through my half-opened car window I watched people walk in and out of Ralphs. Our radio was on all morning, and I listened to the lyrics of "Alone Again, Naturally." I memorized the sounds of the words, although I couldn't completely understand their meaning. We sat in the car until noon and then drove off to the address printed in the ad. Hendrika turned left onto Melrose and right on Western.

The fog and smog mixed, throwing a gloomy cast over the bleak surroundings. Square flat-roofed buildings lined the streets, and there were only a few pedestrians on the sidewalk. One man, dressed in rags, pushed a shopping cart filled with bottles. The address led us to a warehouse-like building. Next door was an empty lot surrounded by a tall chain-link fence, and across the street stood a Salvation Army thrift store. The side of the building facing the parking lot was painted black, and pink letters above a large pink metal door read "Pussycat Go-Go Club". Hendrika parked next to the door. Mama got out of the car and knocked, but there was no answer, so we sat in the car and waited.

"Why would they paint this black?" Mama said as she shook her head and pointed at the building. "This is so ugly. What kind of place is this? Someone needs to tell them black is in very bad taste. White and pink—that's what they should use. These people know nothing about color. They are not used to it," Mama said, shaking her head.

At three thirty in the afternoon a short, heavyset, dark-skinned bald man with a large nose opened the padlock on the front doors and went in. Mama took her lipstick out of her purse and painted her lips while examining her face in the mirror. She squeezed her lips together to let the lipstick spread evenly, and then handed it to Hendrika, who did the same thing. Mama fixed her hair in the mirror. "I'm ready, we can go in now," she said. Hendrika and I walked behind her like ducklings.

The pink front door of the club now stood open. I peered into the gloom. The walls, painted black, were covered with drawings of women with very large breasts, exaggerated lips, large buttocks, and practically no clothes. I jabbed Hendrika in the ribs to get her attention because I had discovered a painting of a completely naked woman in a corner. Hendrika glared at me and signaled me to stop bothering her. The place gave me the creeps, but I was curious about why there were women with barely any clothes painted on the walls.

"This art is terrible," Mama muttered as she looked around. "These people have terrible taste. Why don't they paint a Venus de Milo on the wall? There are so many famous paintings of naked women they could have copied. Why such bad taste?"

I saw a dark hallway leading into a large central room divided into three areas, each with its own bar. In the middle of each space stood a tall table with a pole in the center. I sniffed the air. It had a stale smell of alcohol mixed with cigarette smoke. The ceiling in the main room was about twenty feet high, and the upper half of the back wall was made of reflective glass. Behind the glass I could make out a desk, and the man who had opened the front door sat behind it. Mama waved her hand and shouted, "Hello! Hello!" The man waved back, stood up, and then disappeared. I could hear his footsteps coming down the stairs. Then he reappeared through a door behind the bar. Mama clutched her purse and announced, "Hi. We're here about the ad. Is this the right place?"

"The one for dancers?" he said in a Middle Eastern accent.

"Yes. Yes. That one."

"Which one of you is interested?" he said as his eyes fell on me. I took a step back to hide behind Hendrika.

Mama cleared her throat. "It's for me. I would like to dance," she said, moving a step forward toward him.

"Oh, no. You are too old—but you!" he said, pointing at Hendrika. "You would be good, and that one behind you, too. You two I can use." He stepped around Hendrika to inspect me.

"No, no," Mama said. "She is only thirteen. She is too young, but I am very good. What kind of dancers do you need? I can do cha cha cha, merengue, salsa, samba, you name it. I'm very good and I have a lot of experience." She stretched up to her full height and smiled.

"Honey, you don't understand. This is not ballroom dancing. This is go-go dancing."

"You mean striptease?" Mama's eyes opened wide. She stepped back, outraged. "We don't do that," she said, wagging her finger at the man.

"No, this not a strip club. I have two kinds of dancers. Some dance wearing a bikini and some dance topless. The topless dancers get twenty dollars a night and the others get ten."

"But you could have ballroom dancers here at your go-go bar. It would give your place some class. You would get higher paying customers—they would line up to dance with us. I could wear a low-cut dress, maybe even a little on the short side." Mama put her arms in dance position and moved her hips around.

"I told you, this is not ballroom dancing," the man repeated, clearly annoyed.

"Your place needs fixing up. The colors are terrible. The paintings are in bad taste. I could advise you." Mama stood erect and looked down at the man. She held her I'm-better-than-you posture, then cocked her head and smiled politely, but the man just shook his head and laughed. He was obviously not interested in what Mama had to offer. He looked at Hendrika.

"If she dances here she can wear a bikini or go topless, nothing else." His accent made the sounds of the vowels very sharp. "Look, if I have to explain it to you, you probably don't want the job. Let me show you out." The man put his hand on Mama's back and moved her toward the door. "The girls dance on the tables for twenty minutes at a time. They can accept tips. Dancers start at ten o'clock and finish at two o'clock in the morning. If she's interested, have her show up at nine o'clock." He continued talking until we got to the door.

Mama appeared frustrated. Hendrika turned to face her. "I can dance, Mama," she said.

"Thank you. Good-bye," the man said. He pushed Mama lightly with one hand and waved with the other.

Mama walked away, her posture erect. She didn't say a word. Disappointed, we returned to the car. We heard the big pink door slam behind us. "I will dance," Hendrika reassured Mama, but Mama did not answer. She stared straight ahead. I noticed her cheeks sag and I saw a tear run down her face. "It's all right, Mama," Hendrika said with strength in her voice. I felt Hendrika's urgency in the pit of my stomach. "I will pretend I'm on the beach in Curaçao. It will be good for my acting career." Hendrika had one hand on Mama's arm as she pleaded with her.

I knew she was not pleading to dance, and I knew she didn't want an acting career. Her pleading was for Mama not to despair, but Mama did not respond. Hendrika started the car and we drove back to Ralphs. The parking lot was full. I envied the people shopping for food inside.

My stomach was growling again. We were eating less often; we'd even run out of the cans of beans and corn. I felt like a caged animal in a run-down zoo. I remembered the Publix supermarket in Miami, where seeing the abundance of food had made me believe everyone in America was rich, but I was wrong and I had been wrong to believe the television shows: there were many poor people in America.

Mama and Hendrika were sharing a cigarette because Mama had rationed them to four a day for each of us. Mama was paging through the newspaper again. I felt helpless because there was nothing I could do to improve our situation. Outside our car, everyone seemed to have a purpose and a plan for their lives. I imagined them going to their cozy homes, being a father or a mother, cooking wonderful meals, reading together, talking to each other. Our lives had become so broken. I wanted to go back to Curaçao and see my friends, my grandmother, and my aunt. I wanted to see Johan and Willia; I missed my family. I didn't care about a nice house with a lawn anymore—I just wanted to go home.

My eyes fell on my small red-and-white purse on the floor of the car. I bent over, picked it up, and opened it. I pulled out a pink card, unfolded it, and ran my fingers over the logo of the Curaçao Riding Club. How lucky I had felt the day I had received it. Willia and I both loved horses. She was fourteen when Papa bought her riding lessons, and after each lesson she'd lead me around on the horse she'd finished riding. I loved the feeling of sitting on a horse; the rocking motion was soothing to me. A horse was large and powerful, yet so gentle. I loved the smell of horse sweat and leather and the feeling of running my hand across the strong muscles of its neck. Even at five years of age, I knew I loved horses and wanted to learn how to ride.

On the morning of my thirteenth birthday, I was sitting on my bed when Willia handed me an envelope. She was twenty-three then and had just gotten a job as a ticket agent for ALM, the Dutch Caribbean airline. "What is this, Willia, what is it?" I asked with anticipation. Willia smiled knowingly.

"Open it, Serena. It's for you."

I opened the envelope and pulled out a pink card with the Curaçao Riding Club logo and twelve printed squares on it. Each square was good for one riding lesson. My jaw dropped and I leapt up to hug her. "This is the best present I've ever gotten in my whole life," I said, jumping around and waving the card in the air. Willia beamed.

"I'm so glad I could do this for you," she said, holding her arms open for a hug. We held each other for a long time.

A tear ran down my face as I recalled the memory. I missed Willia and the horses. I yearned for that soothing, rocking feeling. Now the card was worn; the creases where it had been folded were wearing thin and the edges were tearing. Seven of the squares had been punched out; five were still waiting for me. Carefully, I refolded the card and put it back in my purse. Some day I would go back, to use up all the lessons and be with Willia and Oma again.

༯༄༯༄༯༄༯༄༯༄༯༄

WE SAT AND WAITED AS the sun went down ever so slowly in the sky. "Mama, dancing is the only way we're going to get money right away," Hendrika said. "And we need money now. Please let me dance tonight." Mama flinched, but she did not protest. Her eyes were glazed. I felt confused. If Oma had been here, she would have said, "*Kos ta tur bruá.*" Things are all mixed up. In Papiamentu the word for a mix-up and a witch are the same, meaning that when things are mixed up they are bewitched or bedeviled. Now I understood how people could be bewitched. Hendrika was begging Mama to let her dance, something she did not want to do. Mama did not want Hendrika to dance, but she wouldn't stop her. I still wanted to ask Mama to use our twenty-four dollars to call Oma for help but I was afraid to say anything. We were all bedeviled.

Hendrika started the car and she drove back toward the Pussycat Go-Go Club. The colorful lights flickering in the Hollywood Boulevard storefronts punctuated the darkness. I slouched in the backseat and peered out through the window. I wished we were driving somewhere else. Mama sat rigidly in her seat.

"It's going to be all right, Mama, don't worry," Hendrika reassured her, as she bit her lip and gripped the steering wheel tightly.

"What will happen to me?" I whispered.

"You're waiting for us in the car. You should go to sleep. We'll be back before you know it," Mama instructed.

"I can't go in with you? Can't I just wait inside, Mama, please?" I begged. "I don't want to stay in the car alone. What if someone sees me in the car all by myself and kidnaps me? Who will help me?"

"They don't allow anyone your age in. Please don't make things more difficult than they already are," she answered in a cold tone. "Just go to sleep, we will lock the car. You will be all right." But I was terrified.

As we drove south to Melrose Boulevard there were fewer and fewer streetlights, and when we turned onto Western Avenue there were no pedestrians on the sidewalk. All the shops had iron bars across their windows. The pink lights of the go-go club appeared, seeming to dance as they flashed on and off, beckoning us to come closer. The parking lot contained only two cars. We parked next to the big pink front door again. Hendrika smoked one cigarette after another. Mama sat listlessly and stared into space. Finally, Hendrika opened the car door. "I'm ready," she said, blowing out a big puff of smoke. She threw the cigarette on the ground and crushed it out with her shoe, cleared her throat, and walked to the door. Mama got out of the car slowly, smoothed her skirt and shirt with her hands, hung her purse on her arm, and followed Hendrika reluctantly toward the door.

"We'll be right in there, Serena," she said. "Lock the car and don't talk to anybody until we get back." I certainly wasn't about to speak to any strangers. I wanted to ask again if I could come in, but I knew better. I knew it was not a good time to be noticed. They wanted me to disappear, so I did.

ﮩ٠ﮩ٠ﮩ٠ﮩ٠ﮩ٠ﮩ٠

I DREAMT OPA STOOD IN front of me. "Let's go to the House of Six Doors!" he declared. The *landhuis* was a one-and-a-half-hour drive from town and down dusty dirt roads, and about half a mile from the ocean. Next to the house was a windmill to lift water from the well. There were no other buildings for miles around, just rolling hills and gray-green brush.

The house got its name because it had six doors, three on the ocean side and three on the bush side. The ocean-side doors opened directly on the center of the house. Here there was a large living room, a dining room, and a kitchen. The three bush-side doors opened onto a gallery that ran the entire length of the house. Oma had said all the plantation houses were built this way to let the trade winds flow through them. When I asked her why six doors and not four or eight, she told me each door had a purpose. The three ocean-side doors were to bring in gratitude, wisdom, and compassion, and the three bush-side doors were to let out greed, ignorance, and anger. I loved staying at the House of Six Doors.

I found myself sitting in the backseat of Opa's car, cradling on my lap the cake Oma had made six months before for his upcoming birthday. It was a *Bolo Pretu*, a black fruitcake soaked in rum, Curaçao liqueur, and Marsala wine, and decorated with snow-white icing and tiny silver balls of candy. *Bolo Pretu* was made only for very special occasions and tasted best six months to a year after it had been made. Opa's birthday must have been a significant one, although Oma didn't mention his age.

We traveled to the *landhuis* in my grandfather's car. Boxes were tied to the roof of the car with rope; the trunk was so stuffed that several boxes were hanging out halfway. On the way, we stopped three times. We stopped at Shon Pètchi's house, a modest mud house painted red with two green windows on either side of a green front door. The thatch on the roof was dry and sparse. Shon Pètchi came running when he saw our car arrive. He waved and smiled as if we were Santa Claus. Chickens and goats scattered in all directions.

Three dogs tied on long ropes under a tree barked furiously when Oma got out of the car and went to greet Shon Pètchi. She shook his hand and asked how he and his family had been since the last time she had seen him. His wife came out of the house with three of her children. Her oldest daughter stopped feeding the donkey and smiled at us. It was good to see familiar faces. "I'm glad everyone is well. Look how much the children have grown," Oma complimented him.

"Thank you, Shon Elena, thank you for your kind words. How long will you be staying at *Kas di Seis Porta*? Are you having any parties?"

"Oh yes, we'll be here for the summer, and this year Don Diego's birthday will be a big celebration." I listened from the car. I was bursting with impatience to see all of Oma and Opa's friends and my aunts, uncles, and cousins again.

"Would you like a goat for the party? I have some fat ones, really nice ones. They'll be ready two weeks from Saturday. That's the day, no?"

"Yes, that's the day, but I would like to cook iguana. This is a very important year." Shon Pètchi smiled and nodded; the whites of his eyes and his white teeth glittered in the sun against his black skin.

"Ah, Don Diego is having a special birthday? All right, I will find you the fattest, tastiest iguanas on the island." Iguanas once had been abundant on Curaçao but now they were difficult to find. "Don't worry, Shon Elena, I will catch them myself."

A mango dropped from the tree, just missing his shoulder. Everyone looked up. Hidden among the branches was a ten-year-old boy, one of Shon Pètchi's sons, trying to make himself invisible. I knew how much fun it was to climb a mango tree. Shon Pètchi frowned at his son and then turned back to my grandmother, apologizing and smiling.

We drove on down the dusty road lined with thorny, small-leaved shrubs. The occasional black-and-yellow *barika hel* flew from its hiding place, startled by the sound of the car. A turn off the main road led us to the beach and Shon Momo's house. His one-room house was painted light blue with dark blue doors and windows. The recently thatched roof was golden yellow. Shon Momo sat in his rocking chair under a big tamarind tree.

He was asleep as we drove up, but when Opa turned off the engine he opened his eyes and stared at us as if we were a mirage. His three short wooden boats lay in the yard, fishing nets scattered around them. Fishing lines were hanging in the trees and an old anchor leaned against the house. His dog, tied on a rope, barked and wagged his tail. Oma got out of the car and slowly approached Shon Momo, who recognized her as she got closer, and his face lit up. "Shon Elena, *kontá bai*?" How are you? Very kindly, he took my grandmother's hands in both of his and, nodding and smiling, he welcomed her and asked what he could catch for her.

His black skin looked like polished leather from being out on the ocean for so many years. He waved to my grandfather as he moved slowly and gently to Opa's car, as if he were a boat on a calm sea. He took my grandfather's hand in his, his big black hand covering Opa's slight white one, leaving only Opa's wrist showing. Shon Momo assured my grandfather he would bring him all the fish he could eat. With a smile and a wave, we were on our way again. Lizards scurried in panic as the car bumped along the dusty road.

Shon Tisha's tiny pink house had a corrugated roof and a car in the driveway. The antenna on the roof proudly announced she owned a television. A chicken-wire fence ran around her yard, confining her dogs, cats, chickens, and goats. Shon Tisha was a very large woman; her hips jutted out eight inches to either side. She could easily rest children or baskets on them. We picked up her daughter, Mirelva, who would clean and serve while we were at the *landhuis*. Mirelva and I had played together for longer than I could remember. She knew me so well we could communicate without saying a word.

"How long before we get to the House of Six Doors from here?" I asked Oma.

"Well, if we were traveling by horse and buggy, the way your grandfather and I used to go, it would be another hour, but since we are in a car, it will be only fifteen minutes more. Aren't you lucky?" Oma smiled. We turned onto another road. The House of Six Doors came into view as a speck at the top of the hill in the distance. A panoramic view of the landscape appeared as we ascended. Scrubby *divi-divi* trees, with their gnarly trunks and their branches all leaning in the same direction, were reminders that the trade winds always blew the same way.

Oma pointed out the window. "Serena, look at those trees. Curaçao doesn't get enough rain to grow big shade trees so it gets strong winds to shape the trees we have, into giving shade." It was true; a *divi-divi* tree had the perfect shape to lie under in the midday sun. As our car climbed to the top of the hill, a herd of wild goats scurried in front of us.

Opa blew the horn and waved his hands outside the window, trying to give the goats some direction, but they were confused and terrified as they dashed back and forth, bleating frantically. Opa stepped on the gas to scare the goats with the engine's noise, but the car surged forward, barely missing one of them. The cobalt-blue house patiently waited for us against a backdrop of green-blue ocean and light-blue sky.

As soon as we arrived, we opened all the doors and windows to clear out the musty smell of the closed house; it was immediately replaced with the smell of the ocean. I helped Oma take off the colorful sheets that covered the furniture. Mirelva was busy unloading and unpacking.

Opa went to the kitchen and came back with a large bottle of blue Curaçao liqueur and three tiny glasses. "*Ban dal un bríndis,* Elena," he said, calling for a toast as he poured. Opa always kept a large supply of Curaçao liqueur at the House of Six Doors. He put his arm around Oma and she raised her glass to meet his. "*Un bida largu bon bibá,*" he said. To a long life, well lived. Opa and Oma clinked their glasses, then each touched their glasses to mine, which contained only a tiny drop of Blue Curaçao. I pretended to drink: I didn't like the taste of the liqueur, but I loved the occasions on which it was served. Opa took Oma's glass from her and set it on the table. He hummed an old waltz as he took Oma in his arms, and they danced across the room. I sat watching them, giddy with joy.

I opened my eyes. The joy disintegrated. I was in the car, alone.

HENDRIKA DANCED FOR TWO WEEKS. The first week, we went to the go-go bar every other night, but the money wasn't enough so Hendrika had to start dancing every night. She was constantly smoking. Then the brakes on the Ford began to fail, and we didn't have enough money to repair the car. Kent had sent Hendrika on several auditions, and she got a part as a movie extra but it didn't pay anything.

After a week, Hendrika started smelling like alcohol when she returned to the car from dancing, and each day she seemed more distant. Mama napped more often, and from time to time I could hear her softly praying. I tried to cheer Hendrika up by finding her favorite songs on the radio or saving my roll of Life Savers for her when her roll was finished. I tried to tell her Dutch jokes, but she just brushed me off. "Not now, Serena, not now," she'd say. It had been weeks since I had seen her smile. She was not interested in eating and had lost weight. Mama had found a store with Indian incense cones to cleanse Hendrika, and Mama smoked her with it every night.

"That place is not good for you. All that needs to be cleaned out," Mama would say as the smoke swirled around Hendrika. She blamed Hendrika's depressed mood on *oyada*, evil eye. This happens, Mama said, when there is too much admiration that causes jealousy. In spite of Mama's incense, Hendrika's mood did not improve. I knew it wasn't admiration and jealousy that made Hendrika so troubled. I suspected Mama knew it also, but Mama needed to feel she was doing something about our bad situation, and so she did what she could.

One night, as we returned to the Mobil station Ramón ran up to our car with a big smile and a white envelope in his grease-stained hand. "*¡Mira, mira qué llegó!*" He waved the envelope and danced next to the car window.

"What is it, Ramón?" Mama asked.

"I think it's your license, Señora. It is from the California Board of Registered Nursing. Let's hope it is good news!" He handed Mama the envelope. She eagerly grabbed it and ripped it open.

"It is! It is! It is my nursing license! *¡Oh, Dios mío y todos los santos!* Thank you. Thank you." Mama was crying. Ramón bent over and hugged her; in this joyous moment she didn't even mind his grease-stained uniform.

"Everything will get better now. The worst is behind you," Ramón reassured Mama, patting her on the back.

Mama inspected the license carefully, and then she said, "Let's celebrate! Let's order pizza and have a little party!" Mama looked first at Hendrika and then at me with a big smile. The license washed away some of the bitterness she had been carrying. I could see the relief on Hendrika's face, and I felt as if the door to our cage had cracked open, and there was a possibility of our lives becoming normal again. Ramón ordered pizza and sodas, and we all sat in the gas station office enjoying our meal.

"I'll miss you once you have your own apartment and you don't need the gas station anymore," Ramón said quietly as he looked at each of us in turn. "But I'm happy for you and also relieved. I've been worried about you. Those go-go bars can be dangerous. I'm glad that is over." He nodded emphatically.

"You don't have to miss us, Ramón," Mama said. "You are our only friend here in Hollywood. Once we have an apartment you will come over every day, and we will cook for you. We'll make you our favorite dishes from Curaçao. We even know some Peruvian recipes: *Papas a la Huancaína*, *Ceviche*, and *Escabeche*. We'll cook them for you."

"Will you? Really? You know how to make that? *Papas a la Huancaína* are from my hometown. My mouth waters just thinking about them. Oh, we are going to have a good time," Ramón said as he rubbed his hands together in anticipation.

"Pull out your tarot deck, Ramón," Mama said. "I think it's time for another reading. I feel changes in the air."

"Oh, yes. That will be fun," Ramón said, getting up to go to his car. It was three o'clock in the morning, and I couldn't stay awake any longer. I gave Mama and Hendrika a kiss goodnight and walked out to the car. On the way, I passed Ramón and gave him a big hug.

"Thank you, Ramón," I said, almost crying. I held on to him as if I were holding on to dear life itself.

"It's going to be all right, *Chiquita*. The worst is behind you."

I wanted to believe him and hugged him as if I did.

ᘓᘓᘓᘓᘓᘓ

MAMA HAD FOUND A JOB as an OB nurse at Kaiser Hospital, and she had been working the night shift for about three weeks. Each day she became more confident, and like a bear coming out of hibernation, she slowly started planning our future again. Hendrika and I would pick her up in the morning, and we'd all go to Penny's on Sunset Boulevard because they offered all-you-can-drink coffee and a ninety-nine-cent breakfast. Our table would be covered with plates of hash browns, sunny-side-up eggs, and two baskets of hot buttered toast, with a double stack of jelly packs in the center. Mama and I enjoyed our meals but Hendrika hardly touched her food.

Hendrika had been searching the classified ads for apartments, and one morning she suggested, "Let's look at this one on Kingsley and De Longpre." We were still living in our car, with the occasional stay at a motel to wash our hair and get a good night's sleep. As soon as Mama had received her first paycheck, Hendrika stopped dancing at the go-go club. That's when Mama became impatient with Hendrika's mood and insisted she put the dancing behind her, but I could see it was hard for Hendrika. Mama was happy to be fully in charge again and told her to focus on her auditions. Although Mama looked tired from working all night and sleeping in the car during the day, she was smiling and joking, and even sang at times.

We had looked at many apartments, but the required security deposit plus first and last month's rent made it too expensive for us. We drove to the corner of De Longpre and Kingsley and parked in front of a beige stucco building that was completely square; it resembled a big, ugly cardboard box. It was nothing like the house I imagined we would live in. It made me realize how much I loved the colors and the intricate decorative trim of the buildings in Curaçao.

The entrance to this building was a square opening that led into a square courtyard with a square planter containing some sad-looking tropical plants. The building had three floors, with square balconies. Cement steps with hospital-green metal railings led up from the courtyard. The railing continued around each floor, becoming the balcony rails. Standing in the middle of the courtyard felt like being in a prison. A green door had a sign that read Manager and underneath another warned No Solicitors. Mama knocked and we waited until a stooped old lady opened the door. She was about four feet ten inches tall. "Hello. We are here for the apartment. Can we see it?" Mama asked.

The old lady put her hand up to signal us to wait, and said, "*Espera un momento*, one moment." Mama immediately switched to Spanish, and when she did the old lady smiled broadly and grabbed Mama's hand with both of hers, as if she were a long-lost friend. "Come in, come in," she said in Spanish and opened the door wider. "Let me get my son-in-law, Victor. He is the manager." I was grateful we spoke unaccented Spanish, which endeared us to most Spanish-speaking people even though we were not Latin. "Please come in and make yourselves at home. Here, sit down and let me get you something to drink." She called out for her son-in-law as she walked to the kitchen to get us three glasses of water.

Victor was a short man with black hair, dark eyes, and light skin. "*Mucho gusto, Señora, es un placer conocerla.* What a pleasure it is to meet you," Victor said, as he tilted his head, smiled, and shook Mama's hand. He and his family were from Bogotá, Colombia. He owned and managed the building, while his visibly pregnant wife, Isabel, worked as a secretary at an insurance agency, and *Abuelita*, his mother-in-law, took care of their apartment and their five-year-old daughter.

"We just arrived in Hollywood six weeks ago. I'm working as a registered nurse at Kaiser hospital. We have almost no cash because I had to wait for my license to be renewed, and you know how expensive it is to live in a motel. So between having to wait to get a job and living in a motel, we are having trouble coming up with the first, last, and deposit. Maybe if we could pay in installments? I don't know. We are really good tenants." Mama paused for a moment with both hands in her lap, leaning forward toward Victor with an earnest look. She was begging without words.

I glanced around the room and wondered if all managers' apartments were the same. The decor reminded me of the manager's apartment at the motel at Miami airport. Everything seemed to have been bought in matching shades of beige and brown. The only other color was the burgundy of the couch. There wasn't a trace of the family's Colombian heritage, and it was obvious they were proud that they could furnish their entire house from an American department store. Victor agreed we could pay the deposit and half of the last month's rent in installments. Then he invited us up to see the vacant apartment. It was a large one-bedroom, with everything painted off-white, and it seemed enormous in comparison to our car. Victor told us that once he'd checked with the hospital to verify Mama had a job, we could move in.

The last night we slept in the Ford felt longer than ever, and now that I knew it was coming to an end I finally allowed myself to admit how uncomfortable I had been, sleeping in the car these last two months. Mama was working the night shift, so Hendrika got to sprawl across the whole front seat. We lay lengthwise on our seats, facing in opposite directions, with pillows behind our heads. Hendrika had cracked open her window and was smoking a cigarette. I stared at her, wanting to start a conversation, but I couldn't think of anything to say—somehow we'd become strangers. We hardly spoke when Mama was around, and even when she was gone, we didn't communicate anymore. The go-go dancing had changed Hendrika. She had become distant. "How Can I Be Sure" was playing on the radio. "Do you like that song?" I asked.

"Kind of. It's okay, not my favorite." She shrugged her shoulders. I had the feeling she wanted me to shut up.

"You know which one is my favorite?"

"No."

"'Dancing in the Moonlight.' I love that song. Sometimes when Mama is upset, I try to imagine the three of us dancing our problems away." I sat up to see her reaction to what I had said.

"I like 'How Can You Mend A Broken Heart.' It's so sad, I feel like crying when I hear it," Hendrika offered. She took a last puff of her cigarette, turned away, and snuffed it out in the ashtray.

"Are you sad we left Curaçao?"

"Yes."

"Are you happy we're in Hollywood?" I asked.

"At first I was. I thought this was going to be a great place to learn about photographers like Richard Avedon or Annie Leibovitz. I expected there would be exhibitions and galleries to visit, and that it would be easy to find photography classes. But everything has been difficult here. Nothing is the way I thought it would be. It's all gone wrong. I never wanted to be an actress. I hate acting."

"Did you hate it when you were acting in that part you got as an extra in the movie, too?" I asked.

"Yes, I hate acting and I hated the dancing—it was awful. I want to be a photographer. Ugggh!" Hendrika said, from a place deep inside herself. "Ugh! Ugh! I feel so dirty." She wiped a tear from her cheek. I climbed over the backseat, scooted next to her, and put my arm around her.

"You're not dirty. You were the only one who could earn money, and without being asked, you did." She searched for another cigarette and lit it without looking at me. I remembered Mama telling her favorite story of Hendrika as a toddler. She told us that Hendrika was usually drawing or playing quietly in a corner, and she was never any trouble. She was so quiet that Mama had to call, "Hendrika, where are you?" to see if she was all right, and she would always respond, "Here you are, Mama." Mama loved that about Hendrika.

"If you could be anywhere, where would you be right now?" I asked.

"I would put film in my camera and go out and take pictures of all this." Hendrika took another drag from her cigarette.

"*Eh-eh*! That would be *chulo*. It's been a long time since you've taken pictures."

"I know. I would give up smoking to buy film, if Mama would let me. I was so upset that we didn't have money for film on our drive across America. There were so many pictures I wanted to take."

"Don't worry, you can still become a famous photographer," I encouraged her.

"I hope so. I would have to be really good to convince Mama to let me try, but I don't think that's what Mama wants me to be."

I wished I could help Hendrika to convince Mama, but there was nothing I could think of to say. She was right about Mama. We sat in silence for a while. "Do you think your records are okay?" I asked, to change the subject.

"I hope so. I can't wait to listen to them again. I miss them."

Her two boxes of records had traveled with us from Curaçao to Florida, and then to California, packed next to the cases of Coke, beans, and corn in the trunk. The boxes had not been opened since we left Curaçao, and we had no idea what had happened to them on our journey.

"I miss listening to them also," I said quietly. I loved having Hendrika's choice of music in the background of my life. I also missed being alone with her. When we were with Mama, Hendrika was agreeable no matter how outrageous Mama's ideas were. My sister gave up her desires and dreams to keep Mama happy. However, sometimes when we were alone, I could feel her sadness, something she'd learned to hide in Mama's presence. "Let's open the boxes and see what kind of shape the records are in," I said, sitting up.

"Okay. Let's." Hendrika got out of the car and walked around to open the trunk, I followed her. She cut the tape on the box with the car keys, then took a record, examined the cover, slid the record out, and checked both sides to see if it was warped or scratched. I saw how she handled it with care, as if it were an old friend. As she went through them one by one, I realized each record described something about her. When I listened carefully to the words of her favorite songs, I discovered that Hendrika had feelings that were only expressed in the music she loved. Most of the songs Hendrika liked were about lost loves and broken dreams. The ones she liked best were about love given but not acknowledged. Those records were more than her friends; those records were the way Hendrika held onto to that part of her self.

"Thank God Texas and Arizona didn't melt your records," I said, smiling, hoping she would cheer up.

"Or New Mexico or Barstow," she added. "We passed through some hot places, and believe me, I was worried about them. It made me sick to think my records were in the trunk, baking." She paused a moment. "I'm glad they're okay."

"Me, too," I said. "I can't wait to listen to them again." We got back into the car and stretched out. "Which one are you going to play first?"

"'La Bamba.'"

"I like that one, too. Can we play 'Oye Como Va' after that?"

"Yes, and Janis Joplin's 'Cry Baby.'" Hendrika bellowed out the title in the melody of the song. We were both anxious to move into our new apartment and play the old songs. She lit two cigarettes and handed one to me, then searched the radio dial and stopped at a station playing "Everybody Plays the Fool." We smoked our cigarettes and watched the sun come up.

That morning Mama looked angry when we picked her up at the hospital. Hendrika and I felt like disappearing as she flung open the door of the car, got in, put her purse on her lap, pulled her coat firmly under her legs, and closed the door. She opened her purse, took out a cigarette, and lit it. "Those doctors are butchers. There are no doctors here! All they want to do is drug, cut, and charge a lot of money. They have no respect for life. They only want to deliver babies when it's convenient for them. They induce and perform Caesarians for no reason. It's criminal what they're doing. They have no idea what harm they're causing, changing these infants' destinies by scheduling their births for their own convenience. And then, worse, they drug both mother and baby so neither one is aware of their first encounter.

"I've never seen anything so disrespectful. And these women all want the drugs. They don't know they're missing out on the most important part of life. They have a responsibility to be aware and to welcome these new beings into the world. When the umbilical cord is cut the woman has to be awake to look into her child's eyes and tell that little soul he is not alone; that she's there to take care of him. Here they take the babies away from their mothers, to clean them up right after a birth. They weigh them and do all these procedures to them as if they were dolls, never allowing them the time to connect with their mothers. It's unbelievable. I cannot imagine what these babies must go through. It must be a frightening experience to be born here in America."

Mama was in such a state I don't think she even noticed us. She looked straight ahead, puffing on her cigarette. I sat in the backseat, leaning up against the door. Hendrika had both hands on the bottom of the steering wheel, her head nodding in agreement. In Curaçao, Mama was a much-respected midwife and the first choice of expectant mothers. Mama's phone rang constantly, and as soon as a baby was on its way she'd leave the four of us with Papa, or sometimes alone, as she went off to welcome the new baby.

"And then that Dr. Waxen called me crazy. Can you imagine? He calls *me* crazy. I'm not the crazy one. He was the one delivering the baby, and just because he didn't want to come back later in the evening, he gave the mother Pitocin to speed things up. I cannot believe he did this. So I told him I would take care of the delivery, and he could go home and go to sleep. He said he couldn't do that. Then I told him he couldn't compromise a child's destiny because of a few hours of lost sleep. I told him he was in the wrong profession if he did that, and he got mad and started yelling at me and called me crazy. Meanwhile, the poor woman was in labor and needed us to help her, and this stupid doctor is yelling at me, keeping me from doing my job. If this is progress, I'm scared for the future."

She paused again. We were listening to her but were afraid to move. "Well, start the car. Let's go to Penny's. What are you waiting for?" She sounded irritated and impatient. Hendrika started the car immediately and drove off. I sat in the backseat and remembered the story my grandmother told me of Mama's birth. My grandmother had doubted if she'd done the right thing by delaying Mama's birth, while Mama had no doubt the delay had ruined her life.

꒰꒱꒰꒱꒰꒱꒰꒱꒰꒱

THE SUMMER OF MY EIGHTH birthday Mama told me she wanted me to stay with Oma at the House of Six Doors until school started again. She didn't want to worry about me every time she had to leave to attend a birth. I was delighted because I loved spending time at Oma's. Mama promised that she and my brother and sisters would visit often and that each Friday would be the day we would all have dinner together.

The first Friday Mama came over for dinner alone. My brother and sisters were out with their friends. Oma and I had cooked *Stobá di Kalbas*, squash soup, and baked a *Bolo di Kashupete*, cashew cake, Mama's favorite. I picked *cayena*, hibiscus flowers, from the yard and set them in a small vase on the table, along with candles from Oma's bedroom. I was excited to see Mama and I wanted everything to be perfect.

Mama arrived at six thirty. She looked exhausted, but she was pleased Oma and I had made such a fuss over the dinner for her. We sat down and started to eat when the phone rang—it was for Mama. One of her expectant mothers had started to go into labor. Suddenly, Mama didn't look tired anymore. With animated gestures, she reassured the mother that she would be there as soon as she could.

She hung up the phone, grabbed her purse from the chair, hurried over, kissed me on the forehead, and patted Oma on the shoulder. "I'm sorry," she said, "I've got to go. Shon Brandau has gone into labor." She ran out the door. It was as if a hurricane had just passed. The house was still.

Oma saw my disappointed face. "Serena, your mother loves you. It's not that you are not important to her. It's just that it's important to her to be available when babies are ready to be born. This time we'll have to make it our own party," Oma said, trying to cheer me up. But I was not hungry anymore. We blew out the candles, cleared the table, and put the cake away.

It was eight thirty, and Oma was helping me get ready for bed. I put on my nightgown and sat in the chair in front of Oma's mahogany dressing table. Oma always brushed my hair for fifteen minutes every night before I went to bed. I loved the feeling; it made me feel sleepy.

"Let me tell you the story of your mother's birth. I think it might help you understand why being on time as a midwife is so important to her. I was here at the House of Six Doors when I went into labor with my ninth child, your mother.

"It was Opa's birthday and the house was full of people celebrating. The maid was sent out to get Shon Clarita, the most experienced midwife. My best friend, Nadira, was with us. She kept Diego calm, made arrangements for the festivities, and took care of my other children. Diego was proud that this child was going to be born on his birthday. Nadira consulted her astrological books and found that date to be an auspicious day. Since this was my ninth birth, I expected my labor to be short. The maid came back with the bad news: Shon Clarita was on the other side of the island attending an emergency delivery.

"Nadira and I discussed the possibility of having the baby without Shon Clarita but when I told Diego about it, he panicked and begged me to take some herbs and wait for the midwife. He was terrified that something might go wrong and his panic frightened me. I asked Nadira to fill the tub with hot water for me to lie in.

Then I asked her to go downstairs to the kitchen and make a pot of chamomile tea with lots of honey and some valerian root. I went to my medicine cupboard and took out the bottles of skullcap tincture and hops tincture, put a couple of drops of each in a glass of water, and drank it. I asked Nadira to look after Diego and the children, and went to lie down in the tub so that the herbs could do their work.

"I hoped Clarita would be able to come soon. There were many people at the house that evening, but not one was a doctor or a midwife. Nadira made sure all the guests had plenty of food to eat and liquor to drink—after all, it was Opa's birthday. I spent a couple of hours lying in the tub before I moved to my bed. I lay in my room waiting for the midwife. Finally, at four thirty in the morning, most of the guests had gone to their rooms or fallen asleep in the hammocks. Nadira sat down in the chair next to my bed and asked me how my body was feeling. I told her that if I didn't move and kept taking the herbs, I could wait for Clarita. Nadira said she was sorry she could not do more.

"It was five fifteen that morning when Clarita finally arrived. She rushed through the door into my room, washed her hands, and checked the position of my baby. At 6:38 AM, as the sun rose in the Curaçao sky, little Gabriela Ferreira-García was born. She was blue and was not breathing. Clarita frantically worked on your mother to get her to breathe. We thought we were going to lose her, but slowly she took one breath and then another. After we were sure your mother was breathing, Nadira went downstairs to get Opa. Your mother was fragile, and it took over a day to get her on my breast.

"Opa was relieved that your mother and I were both fine, even though he was disappointed your mother did not share his birthday. When he first saw her, he was delighted at her light-colored skin color and fine hair. He hurried downstairs to announce the birth of his daughter to his guests. I could hear the cheering and toasting. There were so many toasts that six bottles of Blue Curaçao were consumed.

"Nadira retrieved her astrology book from her bag to look up Gabriela's new birth date and time. She sat in the chair next to me, studying. I asked her what position the stars were in when your mother was born. That's when she told me your mother had many contradictions in her chart and that she could easily become confused. Her chart had Aries ascendant and Mars ruling the first house, which meant she would be emotional, impulsive, and argumentative. I asked Nadira if it had been wise of me to wait for Shon Clarita. Nadira answered that when a soul returns to the world, it chooses the right moment to come in. If Gabriela had wanted to be born earlier, no herbs could have stopped her birth. I had done what I had needed to do, Nadira told me. I had felt frightened and isolated as I sat alone in that room upstairs waiting, and I always wondered if my waiting for Shon Clarita made your mother feel unwelcome and rejected. Babies can sense what their mothers are feeling. I've always wondered if it is a coincidence that overcoming rejection has been the main theme of your mother's life."

Oma paused as I lay down in the bed. "You see, Serena, stars shift in the sky, making every moment unique. They reflect the many energies and forces in the universe." Oma tucked the soft cotton sheet in around me. "Through our life we carry with us these energies and forces that were present at the time and place of our birth. The only way we can change these energies and forces is by going back to our essence and becoming aware of what forces and energies run our lives. Awareness allows us to choose the path of our life."

"You mean Mama thinks she should have been born at a different time?" I asked.

"Yes."

"Is that why Mama always leaves immediately—because a baby should be born when it wants to?"

"Yes, that's what Mama believes. But our time of birth does not determine whether we will perceive our essence. Each moment grants us a new opportunity to do that." Oma turned off the light and kissed me goodnight. I lay in bed wondering what Oma meant about essence, until I fell asleep.

Mama had finally calmed down by the time we pulled into Penny's parking lot, and we went in to have breakfast.

୨❥୨❥୨❥୨❥୨❥୨❥୨❥

WE MOVED INTO THE APARTMENT on Kingsley Avenue. Hendrika and I carried the boxes up from the car and placed them in the middle of the area that served as the living and dining room. *Abuelita* gave us a marmalade jar filled with daisies to welcome us, and I put it on top of a box.

Mama lit the ten incense cones she had bought at the Indian store on Vermont Avenue. In Curaçao, she used to make her own incense with coals, oils, powders, and herbs but here, the cones were all she could find. She walked around the apartment, carrying the smoking cones in the bottom of a coffee mug, pushing the mug deep into each corner of every room to chase away any bad luck that might have been left by the previous occupants. It was the nooks and crannies she paid most attention to; that's where she believed bad luck hid.

After the cones burned out, Mama spread her coat on the floor, sat on it, and rested her back against the wall, smoking a cigarette. She looked tired after having worked all night. I sat next to her. "I wonder what Oma would have done to clear this apartment. I wish she were closer at times like this," she said. "I cannot imagine Oma here in California or in Holland. I missed her so much when I was there."

"No, I can't imagine her here, either," I said, shaking my head.

"You know, when I came back from Holland I wanted to show Oma everything I had learned. I wanted her to know about the powerful and effective medicines they had in the Netherlands and how I had learned to use them. She always listened carefully but then always said, 'Healing power comes from the earth.' She would never try any of my suggestions. I wanted her to be proud of me but even after all that studying, it did not matter." Mama ground out her cigarette in the ashtray next to her on the floor.

"*Ay, Dios mío*, still so much to do. Now we have to get the electricity and phone connected. Next we'll buy groceries, kitchenware, linens, and towels." Mama looked around. "We have nothing and we need everything." She sighed. Our belongings amounted to the meager pile of boxes stacked in the center of the living room. This was going to be a completely new beginning for us, and it felt daunting.

There were quite a few things needed before apartment seven could become a comfortable home, but there was something magical about the almost empty room with only *Abuelita's* flowers, the candles, and the smell of incense. I felt hopeful. That evening, we ate by candlelight, and after dinner I took a bath since the water and gas were included in the rent.

Our bathroom was six feet by six with a sink, a toilet, and a short tub. One wall was covered floor to ceiling in mirrored squares. As I took my clothes off to take a bath by candlelight, I was surprised to catch my reflection. I hardly recognized myself.

The last time I had seen myself naked in a full-length mirror was at Oma's house on Penstraat. I had been a flat-chested little girl then. I swiveled around in front of the mirror and took a close look at the front, side, and rear views of myself. I couldn't believe my eyes. I knew I had been going through a lot of changes, but I hadn't expected to see large breasts with darkened circles around my nipples and a clump of black, curly hair between my legs.

I hadn't felt at ease with my body since I had my first period just before we left for America. I still felt embarrassed every time I had to wear a pad. I could not imagine ever getting used to it. It was uncomfortable, and I couldn't believe how grown-up women were so casual about it. I looked at myself again; it seemed as if I had turned from a child into an adult in less than a year. I sat on the toilet and stared at myself. For a moment I fantasized that if I went back to Oma's mirror, I would be a little girl again and everything would go back to the way it had been. The candlelight flickered, and the lights and shadows danced on my body and face.

Tears welled up in my eyes. Somewhere between Curaçao and here I had lost the little girl I had been. I never even got to say good-bye.

— Part II —

It was a cold, gray morning in January 1973. Hendrika and I were
waiting in the car, in the parking lot of Kaiser Hospital, for Mama's
night shift to end. She was usually finished by seven forty-five in the
morning, but it was eight thirty and she had still not arrived. We sat
in silence, worrying about what might have happened. Mama had
been complaining bitterly about how the obstetrics department was
run. We knew things couldn't last the way they were. Hendrika and
I were afraid she might come home from work one day, throw her
hands up in the air, and say, "That's it. I've had it. We are moving
to Texas to find an oil field. I will work as a nurse there until we can
buy our own oil well." I cringed at the thought of Mama dreaming
up a new way of finding her fortune.

The hospital's large glass entrance doors swung open and Mama
came marching out, her face contracted in frustration. She opened
the car door and dropped into the front seat.

"I have asked to be transferred to the nursery," she announced.
"I cannot keep working in obstetrics. It is degrading and making me
crazy. I am not doing it anymore. This is it. This madness needs to
stop!"

She spoke loudly and her hands were moving wildly, as if she
were pushing away all that had happened to her this past month. I
was glad the solution was only a transfer, and not Mama quitting her
job. I desperately hoped they treated babies in the nursery here in
California more like the way they did in Curaçao, so Mama would

feel comfortable doing her job. I had even asked Saint Anthony to help Mama because that was all I could think of to do. But from what I had seen visiting the hospital, there was little hope. All those babies lined up in plastic boxes behind glass windows, with no mother in sight, was something you saw only in an orphanage in Curaçao. I had visions of Mama waking up all the new mothers in the middle of the night to give them their babies, and then lecturing them that they had to keep their infants next to them.

"This baby wants you and you only!" I imagined her saying, as if she were a preacher. I wondered what the hospital would think of that, and how long her job in the nursery would last. Mama loved telling other mothers how to take care of their children, but she would not hear of anyone telling her that she should stay home and take care of us. She protected everyone else's children but never seemed to protect us.

We drove home to our apartment, with its vinyl couches and armchairs, glass coffee table, particleboard bookcases, and cheap posters on the walls—pristine rivers, wooded mountains, and golden sunsets over sand dunes by the sea—places most people dream of and few get to visit. There wasn't a picture, a blanket, or a trinket to remind us of Curaçao.

I had been sure that our family life in America was going to be as it was on television. Shows like *The Brady Bunch*, *The Waltons*, and *The Partridge Family* had me believing that any problem could be easily resolved and life was harmonious and happy. But that was not true. I had taken for granted the good things I had in Curaçao. Having Oma next door had brought me more comfort and joy than I had realized. The best part of our apartment now was Hendrika's record player. The music Hendrika played was the only memory we had of our old life.

Hendrika spent most of her days listening to music, smoking cigarettes, and sipping Coke. In the afternoons, she went to her acting class with Kent. After Mama got home from work all three of us watched the *Today Show* with Barbara Walters and Joe Garagiola. We drank tea and smoked cigarettes until Mama went to sleep.

After Mama was asleep, I helped Hendrika with the laundry and the cleaning, and we'd decide what to make for dinner. I tried to make Hendrika laugh as we did the chores, but she did not laugh at the things she used to find funny. In Curaçao, our imitations of Mama used to leave us rolling on the floor with laughter. Now, when I tried it, Hendrika would just shrug her shoulders and turn away. She had changed. She didn't do many of the things she used to do, like keeping lists of the top-40 hits, investigating the lives of famous photographers, and clipping pictures she admired out of magazines, and she no longer kept up with the latest photographic equipment.

I spent most of my time in front of the television. I got lost in each show's new episode and felt abandoned when they were over. After lunch, I couldn't wait to see what Erica Kane was going to do next on *All My Children*. When *Bonanza* was over I would close my eyes and pretend I was part of the Cartwright family, and I fantasized about marrying Little Joe. When I watched *Marcus Welby, M.D.*, I would get angry with Mama. If he had no trouble working in his hospital, why couldn't she work happily at Kaiser Hospital? I tried to encourage Mama to watch the show with me, hoping she would see how easy it was to work in an American hospital, but she was not interested.

I often imagined having a father like Marcus Welby—cool, confident, and kind. Mama's favorite television show was *Reverend Ike*. She insisted we all watch it together. She had received an envelope in the mail from the reverend, containing a letter. It promised if she returned the letter the very next day, along with a thirty-dollar donation, her good fortune was guaranteed, but failure to comply on time could bring doom. Mama sent in the thirty dollars and ever since then, Hendrika and I were required to watch Reverend Ike with her.

Reverend Ike was a tall, dark-skinned man with broad shoulders, who dressed in expensively tailored suits and wore a large gold ring on each hand. I wondered if Mama had a crush on him. She would never admit to having a crush on a black man, yet something about his elegance reminded me of Oma. He was a happy preacher, grateful for all the good things life had brought him. He claimed that if we adopted his way of thinking, good things would come to us. It seemed as if his entire studio audience had been touched by the same stroke of good fortune.

"Look at all these people being helped by Reverend Ike," Mama said as we sat in front of the television.

Reverend Ike explained, "The best thing you can do for the poor is not to be one of them. Forget about the pie in the sky; get yours here and now. If it's that difficult for a rich man to get into heaven, think how terrible it must be for a poor man to get in. He doesn't even have a bribe for the gatekeeper."

Mama encouraged us: "Let's all repeat after him," she said. "Come on, Hendrika, you need it the most. If a lower-class person like Reverend Ike can get rich, we should have no trouble at all." I liked Reverend Ike's sayings, but I wasn't sure how he was going to help us.

Reverend Ike shouted into his microphone: "The lack of money is the root of all evil! Thank you, Lord! Thank you, Lord!" He stood behind his lectern, both arms stretched out in front of him, his palms turned up.

"The lack of money is the root of all evil! Thank you, Lord. Thank you, Lord," Mama shouted enthusiastically, along with the Reverend. It was obvious she thought this was a brilliant statement. Hendrika and I sat with Mama and repeated his words whenever she told us to. I wished she would go back to her incense, herbs, and baths, and allow us to listen to Hendrika's music, but Mama was adamant, hoping Reverend Ike's positive thinking would raise our spirits and bring us the prosperity she was looking for.

I wrote letters to Oma and Willia, now that we could afford stamps, but when I sat down to write I couldn't bring myself to tell them everything. I was afraid Mama would be furious with me if I did.

⁊❧⁊❧⁊❧⁊❧⁊❧⁊❧

BY THE END OF JANUARY, Hendrika's and my tourist visas had expired. I felt uneasy, knowing that we were officially illegal aliens. I often found myself looking around, afraid someone would discover our status. It left me feeling excluded and unwanted. Even policemen, who were supposed to be there for our protection, were a possible threat.

Hendrika had looked for a job, but the only places willing to hire her were factories or restaurants that paid half the minimum wage and expected ten-hour workdays. Mama was outraged that Hendrika was considered just another uneducated, illegal laborer. In Mama's eyes, Hendrika was an educated European who had finished high school and was ready to start university.

Mama was trying to save enough money to pay for a private school for me. It was important to her that I go to a private girls' school so that I could socialize with the "upper class," as she put it. She had gone to the best private girls' school in Holland, and she wanted the best for me. But Hendrika had read that many movie stars sent their children to Hollywood High, so she convinced Mama to make an appointment to tour the school. Hendrika knew that no matter how much Mama saved, it would be crazy for her to send me to a private school.

Hendrika parked our car on Sunset Boulevard, and we walked up the concrete steps of the two-story, pinkish-beige building on Highland and Sunset. I was thrilled; it was the largest school I had ever seen and seemed to me more like a college than a high school. Going to this school would make me feel important. I wished my friends in Curaçao could see me now.

We opened the front door and turned left toward the office of Mr. Hugh Foley, the principal, who greeted us cheerfully. After telling us a bit about the school he escorted us upstairs to the math and science departments. There, off a wide hallway, opened classroom after classroom. I stood, amazed; this school was even bigger than it looked from the outside. Then the principal took us downstairs and outside, to a separate building that housed the library.

We entered through a lobby lined with photos of famous graduates. Mr. Foley proudly pointed out portraits of athletes, movie stars, singers, generals, and diplomats. I could not believe I would be going to the same school they had attended. But Mama was looking at the long-haired students in the hallways, dressed in tight, faded jeans and tight T-shirts. She did not seem impressed. Two large double doors opened into a high-ceilinged reading room; wrought-iron lamps hung on long chains from the ceiling. The walls were lined with books, and the room was full of chairs and tables, where students were reading.

We left the library and walked to the auditorium, which was professionally equipped and seated more than a thousand people. From the auditorium, Mr. Foley led us to the athletic fields, with bleachers twenty rows high. To me this school was as close to perfect as any school could be. Next to the fields stood the gymnasium complex, with separate locker rooms for girls and boys, joined in the middle by a large swimming pool. With this kind of facility anyone who wanted to could go to the Olympics. We returned to Principal Foley's office through the liberal arts building, and on our way he told us about the school's newspaper. I could not believe my ears. I had never heard of a school having a newspaper. If I went to school here, I could become a reporter after all.

"Mama, when can I start?" I asked excitedly, as we walked back to the car.

"That school is a breeding ground for drugs and badly behaved children," she declared. "Did you see how most of them were dressed? No movie star is going to send their children there." We got in the car and Mama turned around to look at me in the backseat. "You are not going to Hollywood High. I want the best for you," Mama declared, as Hendrika started the car.

"I'll study diligently. I promise, Mama. I won't socialize. I'll just study. Please, Mama."

"You are not going to that school. There are too many lower-class children there. You would have friends I would not want you to have," she said. We drove home in silence.

Mama marched up the stairs to our apartment, stabbed her key into the lock, and pushed the front door open. "That place is a playground for pregnant teenage girls. You are not going there."

She shut the door behind us, turned around, and looked right at me, wagging her finger. "I'm willing to sacrifice to send you to a private girls' school where you will get a first-class education and be protected!" Her breath smelled of cigarettes. I was furious. I felt my throat closing. I needed to get away from her.

"You're ruining my life, Mama," I shouted at her, and ran to the bedroom. I took out my backpack, stuffed in underwear, a bra, jeans, and a T-shirt, and my small red purse.

"What are you doing?" Mama said, following me into the bedroom.

"Nothing," I snapped and ran out of the apartment. I wanted to run away. But walking the streets of Hollywood frightened me— there were so many people I didn't know. In Curaçao, I knew all the people in my neighborhood. If I was ever in trouble, I could have knocked on any door and would have been helped. People in Curaçao smiled and took a moment to say *"Bon dia"* or *"Kontá bai."* Here everyone was in such a hurry, and they looked as if they had swallowed bitter medicine. For hours I walked the streets until it started to get dark. I stood on the corner and watched as people rushed by me.

I started walking again, although I had nowhere to go. I sensed someone following me. Out of the corner of my eye, I could see it was a black man dressed in a gray-checkered suit, a red shirt, and a black hat with a feather. He walked so close to me I could smell his cologne. Hendrika had pointed out these kinds of men to me and told me to watch out for them. She said they were called pimps. They tried to convince young girls they were beautiful and could be stars. But instead of making them stars, they forced them to become prostitutes. I was scared.

"Hey, baby, you are so beautiful," the man said. "You should be in the movies. I can make you a star. Let's work together, baby. We could make a lot of money, mama." He kept getting closer. "Hey, why aren't you looking at me when I'm talking to you?"

I didn't want to look at him. I wanted him to go away. I tried to walk faster, but he kept up with me. I was terrified. I walked into the

Vogue record store. He followed me in, keeping his distance while I pretended to search through the records. I sneaked out, but within minutes, he was walking next to me again. I went into a drugstore; he followed me. I hurried to the prescription counter and told the pharmacist a man was following me. The man saw me pointing at him, and when the pharmacist lifted the phone the man finally hurried away. I waited until I thought it was safe and walked out of the drugstore. I kept walking until I reached the corner of Hollywood and Western. On the corner I scanned the streets to make sure the man was really gone.

Defeated, I walked in the direction of our apartment. I didn't have a penny or a single friend to turn to, so no matter how much I wanted to get away from Mama, being with her felt safer than being alone.

₂❧₂❧₂❧₂❧₂❧₂❧₂❧

ANDREW McNAUGHTON SCHOOL FOR GIRLS was the place Mama chose for me. The private high school was housed in a green building on the corner of Franklin and Highland. It was so cramped that the front door led into the school office, and we had to go through the office to get to the rest of the school. Two wooden armchairs sat in front of the desk; a bank of file cabinets and a Sparkletts water cooler stood against the wall. A door behind the desk led to a shiny linoleum-floored hallway where a Coke machine stood next to a water fountain. Four doors off the hallway led to the school's three classrooms and the parking lot behind the building. The school's thirty-nine students were divided into three classes, each with two grade levels. The curriculum was mostly self-taught. There was no library, no theater, no laboratory, and no school newspaper.

I sat in the classroom at McNaughton School pretending I was reading, but in reality, I didn't understand much. I hadn't realized how helpful conventional teaching in Curaçao had been. Here, I was supposed to study on my own and ask questions if I didn't understand something, but with the lessons taught in English, I didn't even know what to ask. The fashionably dressed girls with their stylish hair and manicured hands treated me as if I were some kind of freak. No one would talk to me and everyone stared. I felt as if I were behind the glass walls of an aquarium, drowning.

One evening, when Mama had the night off and we were all watching *Happy Days*, the phone rang and Hendrika answered. "Mama," she shouted, "they need you downstairs—it's an emergency. Victor's wife, Isabel, is having her baby." Mama stood up and quickly walked out the door. "Hendrika," she said over her shoulder, "bring scissors, shoelaces, and the turkey baster. We will boil them downstairs. Serena, come with me and make sure they have clean sheets and towels, and a couple of baby blankets and a large bowl." When we got to their apartment, *Abuelita* let us in and led us to the bathroom where Isabel was sitting on the toilet screaming, gasping, and crying. Mama went in and washed her hands.

"The contractions are coming really fast. My water broke. I don't know what to do," Isabel gasped in Spanish.

"Do not worry," Mama said. "I am a midwife and have delivered many babies."

Abuelita stood by the bathroom door weeping. "Thank God you are here," she said. "Isabel has been having contractions all day. We just came back from the hospital where they checked her, but they sent us home because she wasn't dilated enough."

"Here, come with me," Mama said to Isabel as she helped her to the bathroom door. "Hold on to the knobs on either side of the door. You can support yourself as you squat down while you are having the contractions," Mama instructed her. I came over and put clean towels on the floor.

"Isabel, your body knows what to do. Your contractions are so intense because your baby is coming. If you need to scream do it in a low tone; that will mean you are breathing deeply." Mama looked at me and told me to get Victor. Victor came into the room, his face as white as the towels on the floor.

"Come, Victor, go behind your wife and support her," Mama ordered. Victor stood behind his wife apprehensively. He didn't look like he wanted to be there. Isabel was almost bent double from the pain of her contractions. "Victor kneel and slide your arms under Isabel's," Mama directed. She urged him to grasp Isabel firmly under her breasts. "I can feel your baby's head," Mama said. "Breathe, Isabel," Mama encouraged her. "Come little one, you are about to enter this world. We are here to help you and take care of you."

Victor's eyes were glued on Mama. Mama was calm and composed. We were all following Mama's instructions. "Another push, Isabel," Mama said, "and your baby will be here." Isabel grunted and the baby's head slid out, covered with mucus and blood. Isabel pushed again, and Mama gently guided the baby out and cradled it in her hands.

"Oh, Isabel, your baby is a big, healthy boy," Mama said, cleaning the baby's face gently. Isabel lowered herself to the floor with Victor's help. "And he is breathing well." His eyes were wide open, as if he were inspecting his new environment. Isabel looked down at her baby, crying and laughing with delight.

"Look, Victor, our son," she said. She touched his head, then ran her fingers over his tiny body. Mama placed the baby gently on Isabel's stomach. We all watched, spellbound. Mama put a receiving blanket over the baby and patted him dry, then covered him in another blanket. She put her hand under the baby's feet and supported him as his little legs pushed against her hand.

"It looks as if he is trying to crawl," Isabel whispered in amazement.

"He is," Mama said. "He is finding his way to your breast." The baby slowly scooted his way up, and as he reached her breast, his small head moved around until his mouth found her nipple and he latched on. Isabel had the sweetest smile on her face. Victor's mouth hung open in wonder.

Isabel had a few more contractions, and then her placenta came out. Mama tied the boiled shoestrings an inch apart across the umbilical cord. Then, handing Victor the scissors, she asked him to come around and cut the cord. Victor, his eyes moist, tentatively took the scissors and carefully cut the cord between the shoestrings.

Mama put the placenta in a bowl. I had made the bed and had it ready for Isabel, and Mama and Victor helped her into bed.

"*Gracias, Gabriela, un millón de gracias,*" Isabel said gratefully.

"Victor, would you call Isabel's obstetrician and tell him Isabel has had a healthy baby boy?" Mama said while cleaning up the room. She looked pleased; her face was glowing almost as much as Isabel's. It reminded me of the days in Curaçao when she came back from delivering a baby. I always knew Mama loved being a midwife, but I had never been with her when she delivered the babies. Now, for the first time, I was able to see how good she was at it.

IT WAS A MONTH BEFORE my teacher, Miss Lucy, realized that I had not completed any assignments. Alarmed, she tried to help. She decided to explain the first English assignment to me again. She sat down in the desk next to mine. "Write a letter introducing yourself," she said, mimicking the motion of writing a letter in my spiral notebook. "Tell me about yourself." She pointed at herself and then at me with her pen. "Tell me your hobbies, your interests, your likes and dislikes," she said, gesturing as she spoke, searching for a translation into a language I could understand. "It should be about two pages." She held up my notebook and pointed at two pages then returned it and stood up. I smiled and nodded, took out my pen, and started on the letter.

> *Deer Miss Lucy,*
>
> *My neem is Serena Brink. I just*
> *become fourteen yeers old.*

My pen felt heavier with each word I wrote. The burden of not knowing how to spell silenced me. What I wanted to say was impossible for me to write down. I took the dictionary from my backpack and looked up "yeers." I couldn't find it. Frustrated, I looked up "deer." I found it, but the word described an animal—it was not the "deer" I was looking for. Disillusioned, I sat looking at my work. I was ashamed to go back to the teacher for help. I didn't want her to realize how little I knew. Defeated and lonely, I sat in the classroom, looking around, wondering if anyone knew I didn't belong there. To look busy, I wrote letters in Dutch to Oma and Willia instead. At the end of the day, I packed up my books and headed home.

My daily route home started with a five-block walk along Highland Avenue to Sunset Boulevard, where I took the bus to Western Avenue. From there, I walked along Sunset to Kingsley Drive, and then down Kingsley two blocks to De Longpre to our apartment building.

After I had been followed by the pimp, I memorized every street and building so that I had an escape route worked out if I needed it. There was a strip mall on the corner of Sunset and Kingsley, with a dry cleaner, a liquor store, a loan office, and a Greek bar called the Gypsy Camp. Outside the bar, a sign announced "Greek Dancing Classes Tuesdays and Thursdays, 7:00 to 9:00 PM." Hendrika had explained what the sign meant. After that, every time I passed it I'd imagine how much fun it would be to learn Greek dancing.

Finally, I decided to ask Hendrika if she would go with me to watch the dancing class. I was bored sitting in the apartment listening to music and watching television, and I wanted to meet new people. To my surprise she agreed. We hadn't done anything together in a long time. Recently she had been irritable and almost angry, especially when she got home from Kent's acting classes.

Because Mama was working the three-to-eleven evening shift, we didn't have to ask for permission to go to the Gypsy Camp. We dressed in our best clothes. I wore my rust-and-beige granny gown, and Hendrika wore her blue painter's pants with a blue tank top and her thrift-store bomber jacket. I put on lipstick, blue eyeliner, and a lot of mascara.

"Do you think I look old enough to get into the bar?" I asked Hendrika.

"Yes, I think so. I can hardly recognize you," she said, and grinned.

I put on a couple of squirts from Hendrika's bottle of Jungle Gardenia perfume, and we were ready for the Gypsy Camp.

"What if they charge to get in?" I asked.

"I have some dollars. We'll see if that can get us in," she replied.

"Isn't that the money for your film?"

Hendrika shrugged her shoulders. "I have more."

We walked to the Gypsy Camp. There were a few people standing outside. More people were waiting inside for the class to start. The bar was to the left, and all the tables had been pushed up against the walls, which were painted a dirty red with fake beams, to make the room look rustic. The tablecloths were red, the chairs an assortment of styles from wood to metal, upholstered and un-upholstered. The bar was decorated with bright colors, to look like a Gypsy caravan. Posters of gypsies and horse-drawn wagons were scattered along the walls.

The Gypsy Camp had a festive feeling, as if we had walked into a neighborhood party. Everyone was smiling. A jolly, fat man with a black beard and a big smile stood in the middle of the room. "Come," he said with a heavy Greek accent. "Gather around, don't be shy." He beckoned us with his hands to move closer. He gestured to the man behind the bar, "Apollo, music, please." Everyone formed a circle around the man. "My name is Stefanos. Welcome," he said, with his arms stretched out to the side. He snapped his fingers as he danced around the inside of the circle. The music started.

Hendrika squeezed in between two men and started moving to the right with the circle. As I waited for a spot to open up, I tried to follow the dance steps from outside the circle, bending my knees, then moving two steps sideways and kicking with my left leg while twisting my shoulders from left to right, but I was always one step behind. A woman saw me struggling and broke the circle to allow me to join in. I put one arm around her shoulder and the other around the shoulder of the man on the other side of me. The music was loud and the people were even louder. I tried to listen to the different languages being spoken, but most were unrecognizable to me. After trying the same steps to three different songs, Stefanos announced a break. I was just starting to get the steps right and I was enjoying myself. The music stopped, the circle disbanded, and Hendrika and I walked to the bar.

"This is fun, isn't it?" I shouted to Hendrika.

"Yes. Not bad."

"Can you believe we are in America? There is not one American here," I said, leaning toward her ear as I spoke.

"It doesn't feel as if we're in America. It would remind me of Curaçao, if they didn't speak all these strange languages." Hendrika was actually smiling.

A man in his early twenties with black hair, dark eyes, and a black mustache approached us. "May I buy you girls a drink?" he asked. Hendrika looked at me and then turned to the man and said, "Sure. Why not?"

"Where are you from?" he asked.

"Curaçao."

"Wow! Where is that?"

"The Caribbean. Where are you from?"

"Romania. What would you like to drink?" He had one elbow on the bar as he spoke to Hendrika. I was excited for Hendrika, but I also felt as if I were in her way.

"A Coke, please. My sister will have a Coke, too," she said, nodding dismissively toward me.

"Let me introduce myself. My name is Radu. It's nice to meet you." Smiling, he offered his hand. It was as slender as a girl's, and on it were several silver rings.

"My name is Hendrika, and this is my sister, Serena."

We all shook hands. A tall, thin, blond man, also in his twenties, walked up to us and said something to Radu in what I guessed was Romanian. He looked at Hendrika, held out his hand, and said, "Hi. I'm Alexandru."

"This is my friend from Romania," Radu interjected.

Alexandru turned to me, holding out his hand. As we faced each other, his hazel eyes met mine and instantly drew me in. The noise in the room dropped away. I wanted to say something, but nothing came. I felt as if I were floating above myself in a quiet space. Alexandru didn't speak, either. As his hand touched mine, the noise in the room returned. I felt awkward about what had just happened and must have blushed.

"My name is Alexandru," he said, "but my friends call me Sandu."

"I'm Serena," I stammered, looking down. He had a big, strong hand with short, thick fingers, and a firm grip. I looked back up at him, and a tiny smile welcomed my gaze. I felt relieved. Maybe he liked me. I turned my head, hoping he wouldn't ask how old I was.

"Here is your Coke," I heard Hendrika say. Alexandru took the glass from her and handed it to me. He asked me where I was from and how long I had been in California. I answered, but we could hardly hear each other.

"Do you want to go outside?" he asked. "It's quieter."

"Is it okay, Hendrika?" I sounded more hopeful than I wanted, glancing at Hendrika to see if she had caught my eagerness. Hendrika agreed, saying she would come out in fifteen minutes. She wanted to talk to Radu and some other people she'd met. Alexandru and I walked outside and stood next to the Gypsy Camp's red imitation-leather-covered front door. For a few seconds neither of us spoke.

"Do you smoke?" I asked him, wanting a cigarette.

"No. That is not good for you," he grimaced. His accent was heavy.

"Why are you in California?" I asked.

"Doesn't everybody want to be in California?"

"I don't know. Maybe," I said, shrugging my shoulders.

"Why are you here?" he asked.

"My mother brought me here."

"Do you miss Curao?"

"It's Curaçao," I said with a smile and a nod. "Yes, I hope I can go back some day soon."

"I can't go back home. Ever." Alexandru looked down and kicked a cigarette butt.

"What do you mean?"

"Do you know anything about Romania?" He turned his face to me for a moment.

"No, not really. Isn't it near Italy?"

"No. It's east of Yugoslavia. It's a communist country, and you cannot do anything without the government's permission—nothing. Not travel, not own a business. We cannot even work harder to make more money if we want to. The government decides everything. There is no freedom." He paused. "That is a terrible thing." The corners of his lips turned down. "You are lucky you never had this experience." He pushed the cigarette butt with the side of his shoe, watching it while he talked. I had never lived under a communist government, but I understood what he said about oppression and not being able to do what you wanted to do. I understood his frustration about the lack of freedom. I felt that, living with Mama.

"How did you come here if you weren't allowed to travel?" I asked.

"I escaped." He paused, waiting for my reaction.

I saw that what he was telling me was painful for him. I wished I knew more about Romania and tried to remember my geography lessons, but the Eastern Bloc was something I had not studied in school.

"I escaped to France with Radu," he finally said.

"Was it far?"

"Yes. We trained for two years to be able to do it. First, we had to evade the border guards; then we had to cross Yugoslavia, and then from Yugoslavia to Italy. As soon as we got to Italy, we had to move on because Italy puts political refugees in camps. If you get stuck in a camp, it's difficult to leave."

Now I kicked at the cigarette butt on the ground. I wanted to ask more, but I didn't want to seem nosy. I felt him staring at me, and the urge to stare back was strong.

"It must take courage and faith to leave everything you know behind," I said, looking at him out of the corner of my eye.

"Or maybe desperation," he said, shrugging his shoulders.

"Hey, Serena. I think it's time to go home." I heard Hendrika's voice behind me. She came up to us, her eyebrows pulled together, frowning while studying our faces.

"Okay. Let's go," I said, afraid she would treat me like a child in front of Alexandru. I remembered how scared I had been when I first saw my changed body in the mirror of our apartment. Now I was happy I looked like a woman. I wanted to see Alexandru again. I felt noticed. This was new to me. No one had ever asked me questions about myself before. When I answered his questions I felt grown up.

"Come on," I said to Hendrika. "See you next time, Alexandru."

I waved good-bye to him and quickly left the Gypsy Camp with Hendrika following in my footsteps. I crossed Sunset and walked down Kingsley, past a run-down beige house with an old couch on the front porch. At the end of the block a brown dog barked as he ran up and down behind a chain-link fence.

"What's the hurry?" she said.

"I didn't want you to talk to him," I said, when we were half a block down the street.

"Why not? Is he strange or something?"

"No. I don't want him to know how old I am."

Scurrying quickly to stay ahead of her, I kept my head down and my arms crossed in front of me because I was cold. Sixty degrees was freezing to Hendrika and me—we were accustomed to balmy Caribbean evenings of eighty degrees. As we walked toward our apartment, I remembered the only other time I had ever gotten a feeling of floating, of time standing still, of complete silence.

૨ဝ૨ဝ૨ဝ૨ဝ૨ဝ૨ဝ

A MONTH BEFORE WE WERE to leave for America, Mama brought a *bruja*, or shaman, named Doña Dolores to our home. She was a short, fat lady of mixed race from the Dominican Republic. Mama had hired her to perform rituals and cleansings to ensure our success in America.

Doña Dolores arrived at our house early one morning with a large plastic handbag hanging from her shoulder; two giant suitcases, one in each hand; a cage containing a brown chicken; and two more cages with six pure-white doves in each. Her clothes were so tight it seemed their seams would rip if she made a sudden move. I could see the outline of her bra and the lines of her underwear through her red shirt and black-and-gold skirt. Long gold earrings dangled from her ears. A collection of gold, amber, blue larimar, and black and red coral encircled her neck. She smelled of cloves and cinnamon.

Mama and Hendrika helped her carry her suitcases into the living room. The cages were left by the front door. Doña Dolores walked around the entire room, stopping in each corner to fan herself with her hands, exhale loudly, and shake her fingers away from her as if shooing away evil things.

"Hay mucho que limpiar aquí," she said. There's a lot to be cleaned out here.

She walked over to her suitcases and opened them both. They were filled with bottles of colorful liquids, herbs, seeds, flowers, and bits of amber, larimar, amethyst, and sea salt. A burst of fragrance filled the room. She took a worn prayer rug out of her suitcase and placed it in the center of the room, and instructed Hendrika and me to move the furniture back against the walls. Then she arranged the stones, two incense holders, a tall candle and two shorter ones on the rug, and told Hendrika and me to bring two buckets each of cold and hot water into the room and place them on the corners of the rug. After we placed the buckets, she closed the curtains. In the darkened living room, she sat down on one side of the rug, and Mama seated herself opposite her. Hendrika and I remained standing against a wall, watching.

Doña Dolores lit the candles, then placed her incense mixture into the holders and lit them. She began to chant a prayer to Saint Jude, Saint Augustine, Saint Martin, and Saint Christopher. The room began to fill with smoke, and Hendrika and I finally slid down to sit on the floor, leaning against the wall. With Mama observing, Doña Dolores poured flowers, seeds, rocks, and the vials of colorful liquids into the four buckets of water.

Doña Dolores returned to the rug in the center of the living room and Mama followed her. They sat quietly with eyes closed for a moment. Then Doña Dolores stood up and walked to the front door to retrieve the brown chicken, now squawking in its cage. From one of her suitcases she extracted a burlap bag and placed it on the floor. She sprinkled it with a variety of leaves, salt, and some kind of green liquid. She opened the cage, reached in and grabbed the chicken by its neck, held it upside down, and tied its feet together. She let out an otherworldly screech and, with both hands, wrung the chicken's neck. The now silent chicken's body convulsed in Doña Dolores's hands. Hendrika ran out of the room.

I sat, horrified and perplexed, against the wall. I could not believe my eyes and burst into tears. Mama walked over to where I sat and put her hand on my shoulder. "It's just a chicken, Serena. We eat them all the time." She spoke rationally. I swore to myself I would never eat chicken again.

Doña Dolores gently wrapped the chicken's body in the burlap bag, tied it closed with a red ribbon, and placed it outside the front door. She informed Mama that Hendrika had to be there for the next ceremony. Mama left the room to find Hendrika. Now I was terrified to be alone with Doña Dolores. I tried to escape but just as I reached the door Mama came in and told Doña Dolores that Hendrika refused to come back. Doña Dolores told Mama that this was a particularly bad time to abandon the ceremonies. If Hendrika did not participate, she warned, she could set the universe against herself. Mama left to make another attempt to convince Hendrika to return, but Hendrika refused.

When Mama came back she ordered me to sit down against the wall again. She asked Doña Dolores to include Hendrika from a distance. Doña Dolores reluctantly agreed, but she warned Mama that she could not guarantee the effectiveness of her spells for Hendrika. Doña Dolores began to chant, and lit eleven more candles, sprinkled rose water, *agua florida*, and jasmine water around the living room. It smelled as if I were inside a bouquet of flowers. Doña Dolores's chanting changed into a softly musical murmur.

All of a sudden, the sound disappeared. I could see Mama, Doña Dolores, and myself sitting on the floor. I was floating, looking down on all of us. It was a feeling of being here, there, and nowhere all at the same time. I felt as if I didn't have a body, as if all that was left of me was my soul. I felt as if my soul were floating. The beautiful sound of Doña Dolores's chanting returned. She walked slowly over to me, with a smoking incense holder in one hand and a miniature crystal bottle of clear water in the other. She sprinkled me with the water and surrounded my body with smoke from the burning incense, while continuing to chant. Mama was looking over her shoulder at me. I loved the floating feeling, although there was a sense of being out of control that frightened me.

As she sang, Doña Dolores told Mama and me to follow her to the front door. There, she gave one of the cages of white doves to Mama and held on to the other cage. Together, they each opened the doors to the cages and lifted them above their heads. One by one the doves stepped out of their cages and flew a short distance away. Then slowly, each one took flight again and disappeared into the midday sun.

I was sad that Hendrika had missed the most beautiful part of the ritual, and afraid she had been left with only the trauma of the sacrificed chicken. I wished we could have shared the sensation of floating.

I turned my key in our apartment door. With Doña Dolores I had been leery about the feeling of floating, but with Alexandru it had been comforting.

꙲꙲꙲꙲꙲꙲꙲꙲꙲

"Please promise me you won't tell him how old I am," I begged, as we stood inside the apartment.

"Okay. I won't tell him, but you have to," Hendrika said.

"I will, but not now. I'll tell him later."

"You like him, don't you?" She put her hand on my shoulder and turned me toward her.

"We are going back to the Gypsy Camp again, aren't we?" I asked, suddenly worried.

"Sure. Why not? As long as we have the money, but only if you behave."

Hendrika scooped the car keys from the table and left to pick up Mama. I went into the bedroom and whispered "Alexandru" as I changed into my pajamas. What had he said his friends called him? "Sandu." I liked that better. It made me feel close to him, and I repeated it.

In the following days, I could barely sit still at school. I took out the classroom atlas and found the map of Romania. I worked up the courage to ask the teacher if she knew anything about the country, but Romania was a big blank to her as well.

I was excited when the day arrived for us to return to the Gypsy Camp. That evening, I took a long bath and spent an hour combing my hair in several different styles and trying on Mama's lipstick. I looked in the mirror and wondered how anyone could like me. I was nothing like the blond, tall, skinny models in the magazines. Frustrated, I tried on some of Hendrika's clothes, but they were all too tight and too long. Disappointed with my body, all the anticipation of the last couple of days turned into self-doubt. I hoped Sandu felt the same way about me as I did about him, but I didn't want him to discover that I was only fourteen. Suddenly, I was afraid to go to the Gypsy Camp.

"Are you ready?" Hendrika called.

"I'm coming. Just a second."

I put on a pair of flame-bleached jeans, a white tank top, and a dark-blue cotton poncho. I dripped some cold water on my face and pinched my cheeks to blush them up. Hendrika's bottle of Jungle Gardenia still sat on the bathroom shelf, and I smiled. That's it, I would use it again! I knew from Mama that gardenia petals were used in baths to attract love and establish romantic relationships. I sprayed it behind my ears, in the crook of my elbows, and all around my hair. I put on some eyeliner, and painted my lips sienna red.

"Serena, are you ready? Let's go!" Hendrika was waiting at the door.

"Okay, okay—I'm coming," I shouted, fluffing my hair with my fingers.

I could hear the haunting melody and slowly increasing rhythms of the Greek music as Hendrika and I stood across the street waiting for the Don't Walk sign to change. I felt my heart race as we approached.

"Here, stop. Does my breath smell okay?" I asked as I stood on my tiptoes, trying to put my mouth near Hendrika's nose.

"It's fine. Fine! What are you doing? You don't have to get this close." She waved her hand in front of her face. We made our way to the door, past people standing outside smoking cigarettes. The Gypsy Camp was crowded, and most of the people were standing along the perimeter of the dance floor. The dancing had just ended. My eyes scanned the room to see if I could find Sandu. I nudged Hendrika.

"Do you see him?" I asked.

"See who?" She frowned at me, as if I were annoying her.

"Do you see Sandu?" I said insistently.

"Oh, God! Don't be so desperate. I'm getting worried about you. Anyway, guys don't like girls who try too hard. Why am I even telling you this? You're only fourteen."

The music started again, and people lined up in the center of the room. Hendrika went to the dance floor and I followed her. I wondered if he had been here and already left. I walked across the floor, continuing to search every corner of the room. The dancing started, so it was difficult to cross the room again.

I sidestepped slowly around the edge of the dance floor in order to face the middle of the room. I spotted Sandu's blond hair and stopped for an instant. As I walked closer, I could see his broad shoulders tapering to his narrow waist, his pants and shirt tight, his back muscles visible through his thin cotton shirt. I stood behind him, not knowing what to do next. I waited and listened to him talk to his friend Radu in Romanian. I tried to decipher what they were saying, but I couldn't make sense out of it. They both sounded strong and confident. As I stood looking at Sandu, Radu saw me and waved. Sandu followed Radu's gaze until he saw me.

"Ah, Serena, I was afraid you wouldn't come tonight," Sandu said. His eyes sparkled.

"I was afraid you wouldn't be here, either," I said. He held one of my hands as he put his other arm around my shoulders and kissed first my left cheek, then my right cheek, and then my left cheek again.

"This is how we greet each other in Romania," he said, smiling.

"That's how they do it in Holland, too, but not in Curaçao."

"How do you greet in Curaçao?"

"We hug. We don't kiss. Just a big, strong hug."

Sandu nodded. "Do you want to dance right now?" he asked, but he sounded as if he was just being polite.

"Maybe later."

"Come, let's go outside." He grabbed my hand and started toward the door.

"No, wait. I've got to tell my sister," I said, letting go of his hand. He waited for me to return, and we walked out together. There was no one smoking outside.

"Oh, good. We're alone. That's nice." I pulled my poncho tighter around me.

"Are you cold?" He put his arm around my shoulder. "Here, I'll keep you warm." It was the safety that I had been yearning for. We stood quietly for a moment.

"Do you have family?" he murmured.

"Yes, I came to America with my mother and my sister, but I have one more sister and a brother back home in Curaçao." We were both staring straight ahead, letting our bodies sense each other.

"What about your father?" he asked.

"My parents are divorced, and Mama won't let me see my father." Not wanting to dwell on sad things, I changed the subject. "Tell me about Romania. I don't know anything about it."

"Well, I'm from a very old town called Sibiu, in the middle of Romania. It's about eight hundred years old—maybe even older. Sibiu is on a hill surrounded by thick forests and beautiful meadows." He frowned, then clicked his tongue and continued. "In the middle of town is a plaza. It's called Piata Mare … It's very beautiful to stand in the middle and look all around. It feels like you are at the heart of the earth." He paused for a moment. I saw sadness in his eyes.

"You miss it, *ja?*" I said.

He nodded, and we stood silently for a moment.

"Sibiu is like a fairy-tale city." His face tightened. "That dog

Ceauşescu has not yet destroyed it like he's destroyed everything else in Romania." There was anger in his voice that frightened me, and I pulled away slightly.

"Do you have any brothers or sisters?" I asked.

"Yes, I have a younger brother and an older sister. They still live in Romania."

"What about your parents? Are they divorced?"

He clicked his tongue against the roof of his mouth again. "No. They've been married for twenty-five years. My father works for the government as an engineer." He stopped. I felt his pain as though it were mine.

"Why are you sad?" I asked.

"Because of my escape, my parents' and my siblings' lives are difficult. My father has lost all of the privileges he worked for all these years. My family is blacklisted now because of me." His chin dropped and he spoke from the back of his throat, bitterness in his voice.

"Did you know this would happen before you left?" I asked, torn between asking too many questions and wanting to know more about him.

"No, of course not. I would never have done that to my family on purpose."

"I'm so sorry," was all I could say.

Silence settled between us, then he suddenly turned to me. "Dracula! Dracula—have you heard of Dracula?" His eyes lit up. "You know, the vampire?"

"No, what's that?" I was puzzled.

"Dracula is from Transylvania. Sibiu is in Transylvania. Transylvania is the county in Romania where Dracula's castle is."

"What is a Dracula?" I felt stupid having to ask.

"He's a vampire, but the story is based on Prince Vlad Tepes, whose father was Vlad Dracul. He named his son Dracula, son of Dracul. Dracula tortured people for fun, but he was not a vampire."

"What's a vampire?" I asked.

"A vampire is a creature that sucks blood from the necks of people."

"*Eh-eh*. That is strange," I said in disbelief. He saw that his story had made me uncomfortable. He smiled reassuringly.

"What about you?" he said, trying to change the subject. "Tell me about Curaçao." He spoke slowly and deliberately with careful pronunciation. I liked the way English sounded when he spoke it. For the first time, the language felt soothing to me.

"Curaçao is a small desert island." I shrugged my shoulders. His eyes fell on me. It felt good to have someone listen. Still, I was afraid to tell him the things I loved about Curaçao because they were so different from those he loved about Romania. I remembered reading in our Dutch school textbooks about emerald-green forests and meadows, sparkling snow, clear lakes, and delicious fruits and vegetables—things never seen or tasted in Curaçao. And I remembered wondering why things on our island were not important enough to talk about in our textbooks. Was it because Curaçao had nothing interesting to offer?

"Desert? Does that mean hot?" Sandu interrupted my thoughts.

"Yes, very hot," I answered. "We don't have weather forecasts. It's either clear, windy, and hot; or clear, very windy, and hot," I said, thinking back to the day when I had asked Mama what snow was like. She opened the freezer and scraped some ice off its walls and handed it to me. I watched the granules of ice melt in my hands. She told me snow was similar but lighter than freezer ice. "Know what you're getting out of the refrigerator before you open it, and then close the door immediately," she always said. Cold air was a precious commodity in Curaçao. I shivered.

"Are you okay?" Sandu asked.

"*Ja*, I'm just cold."

He took off his jacket and wrapped it around me. He tightened his arm around me, and I noticed how perfectly the contour of his body fit next to mine. I felt the muscles in his arms and on his chest. My soft body created a nest for him to fit into.

"Ah, that's why you're cold. You're not used to this weather," Sandu said, smiling as if he had made a great discovery. I smiled back.

"We have bright-colored houses in Curaçao," I continued my description of home. "It's not like this. The dull-colored houses in America make me sad. The houses in Curaçao are red, green, blue, yellow, pink, and orange ... like a big celebration. You look around and feel as if you're at a party. Not here. You can't even see the blue sky and the clouds because of that stuff called smog." I paused. "What colors are the houses in Sibiu?"

"I think more or less the same colors—but not orange." He raised his eyebrows and moved his head back, as if to say orange was a bit extravagant.

"*Ja*, we have orange, turquoise, and purple. The little one-room country houses have the most outrageous colors. The island almost looks like a Christmas tree. The view from the top of a hill is of grayish-green brush with brightly painted houses scattered here and there. They look like ornaments on a tree." I was pleased to see an amazed expression on his face.

"This is quite a place, this Curaçao." Sandu thought for a moment, as if he were trying to envision the island. "I think I will love it. I'd like to go some day. I want to see this Curaçao, and meet all your family."

I turned toward him. I was relieved my description had intrigued him.

"Is your father still there?" he asked.

"Yes," I answered.

"What is your father like?"

"He is a very quiet and kind man. When I was young he often traveled to the other islands for business. When he came back, I would run up to him and say 'Papa, Papa, did you remember me?' And he would always say 'A little something for my little girl.' He'd bring things, like soap from the hotel or candy from the airplane, in his pockets, and then let me search his jacket to see if I could find them."

I was surprised that that particular memory of my father had come up. I hadn't spoken about my father in many years. Mama hated him so desperately that it was easier not to mention him at all.

"Why did your parents divorce?"

I had to think for a moment. "My father wanted a simple life.

Mama wanted to live in luxury. Mama was constantly disappointed in him, and my father sometimes drank too much. I don't think he is a bad person like Mama says. He was never bad to me. I love him."

We turned toward each other, and I rested my head on his shoulder. We stood holding each other in silence. It was difficult to believe we were standing in front of the Gypsy Camp when in reality I had lost all sense of space and time.

"Serena, time to go!" Hendrika called. Her voice jolted me back into the present.

"I've got to go," I whispered sadly.

"Will you come back on Tuesday?" Sandu asked eagerly.

"Yes, I'll be here." I studied his face and tried to memorize all I could about his features, his breath, his gaze. I handed his coat back to him, and as we let go of each other, it was as if I was leaving part of myself behind. The cold air touched my body where he had been, and I felt myself stiffen. I crossed my arms in front of my chest. "Bye, I'll see you next week, okay?" I said, and started walking.

Hendrika and I crossed Sunset and walked down Kingsley, past the beige house with the couch on the porch. I thought about the conversation I just had with Sandu about my family. The last time we had all been together was eight years ago, right before Mama took us to Colombia.

ᴈᴗᴈᴗᴈᴗᴈᴗᴈᴗᴈᴗᴈᴗ

I WAS SIX YEARS OLD. We were not rich, but we had lived comfortably enough in Curaçao. Nevertheless, Mama was constantly looking for a better way of life. She had calculated that we would be twice as well off if we moved to Colombia and lived on the salary my father earned in Curaçao as the station chief for the Dutch national airline. Johan and Willia were not doing well in school. Mama decided the Dutch language was the root of all their problems, and if they switched to Spanish all their learning difficulties would disappear. My parents made preparations for Mama and the four of us to move to Bogotá, Colombia, and my father was to stay behind.

On the day we left, the Curaçao airport terminal was filled with our family and friends seeing us off. Oma took me aside and, in a whisper, told me to follow her upstairs onto the airport rooftop. There, benches were placed so that people could sit and watch the airplanes take off and land. No one else was on the roof as Oma and I sat down together. The Caribbean Sea glistened in the bright sunlight only a few yards beyond where the long concrete runway and the rocky shore ran parallel to each other.

"Serena, your mother is taking you away from Curaçao in search of happiness. She thinks happiness is found in prosperity somewhere out there, but happiness is found only here—in our hearts." She gently stroked the left side of her chest with her three middle fingers, as if she were reminding herself of where her own happiness lay.

I listened to Oma, and wondered why my mother thought happiness was something she had to search for. "You can travel the entire world, win the lottery three times over, and still never find happiness. Happiness is being true to yourself and recognizing those demons within that will drive you to look for happiness out there. I wish I had not forgotten this when I was raising my children, but I was so busy making sure Opa was happy, I forgot where happiness lay. We cannot give what we do not have, and we cannot teach what we do not remember. That is why I could not give this insight to your mother, but I can give it to you now. Happiness is in your heart and not somewhere out there. Remember this when you become confused. Your mother was very confused after the war, and she has not always been able to nourish her children with love and protection. When you are confused it is difficult to know how to nourish the light in your child."

The expression on her face was tender as she put her arms around me. She took something out of her purse. It was a small branch of black coral hanging from a golden safety pin. She pinned it to my collar. "This piece of black coral is lucky because I found it washed up on the beach. The lucky pieces of coral are the ones that are not taken out of the ocean but given by the ocean, and I give this one to you."

"Thank you, Oma," I said, rubbing the smooth, shiny branch of black coral. We sat gazing at the sea. I took in every ounce of protection and love Oma was offering. I was going to miss her terribly. "*Dushi*, if you miss me, just think of me. I'll know, and I will be with you," Oma said softly, her head resting on mine.

"You will come to Colombia, Oma?" I asked.

"No, *dushi*, I will be thinking of you and you will be thinking of me. That is almost as good as being together."

"Oh," I said, my heart sinking. I felt Oma was the only person who really understood me. We got up and slowly made our way back downstairs to the departure lounge where everyone was waiting.

The loudspeaker announced the boarding of our flight. As Oma and I walked back into the lounge, I saw my whole family standing in front of me: Mama and Papa, my eldest sister, Willia, my brother, Johan, my sister, Hendrika. The cage holding our parrot, Lorito, and Johan's guitar case and all our carry-on suitcases and boxes were piled around them. I left my grandmother's side and joined my family. A second announcement was made for our flight, and a confusion of hugs, kisses, and tears erupted. We proceeded to the gate with Mama leading the way.

On board the plane, Mama told me to sit down while she looked for a place to stow the luggage, the guitar, and the parrot. The stewardess seemed irritated by all of our possessions. I looked out the window and saw my grandmother and my father standing on the airport rooftop where only minutes before Oma and I had sat. I waved. Johan, who was sitting next to me, said, "Don't bother. They can't see you anymore." I lowered my hand to my lap, tears rising in my eyes. We buckled our seat belts and the plane taxied down the runway.

When the Fasten Seat Belt sign went off, my brother took out his guitar and quietly started strumming. The passenger behind him was an older Colombian lady. She asked if he knew the song "Guantanamera," and my brother played it for her. Then a man requested "La Bamba."

By now most of the passengers were clapping and singing along. Johan continued playing and even the stewardess, who had been so annoyed, was moving behind her service cart, dancing the cumbia to the rhythm of my brother's music. Johan let the parrot loose. Lorito hopped from seat to seat, squawking and occasionally letting out a few curse words. The pilot announced he was sorry he had to fly the plane and couldn't join the fun. Before we knew it, it was time to put away the guitar, put the parrot back in his cage, and fasten our seat belts again. The move to Colombia marked the beginning of the slow and painful dismemberment of our family.

Now only three of us were together here in America. I turned the key in the front door and walked into our stark apartment. It saddened me that not even the posters on the walls were of the island I knew and loved.

ּ₂♥₂♥₂♥₂♥₂♥₂♥₂♥₂♥

THE COLD AIR ON THE walk home from the Gypsy Camp had taken my sleepiness away. I took the notebook out of my backpack, sat down at the dining room table, and tried to work on an assignment for my English class. I wished English were easier. My difficulties with the language made me wonder if I would ever become a reporter. I had given up on living in a house with a lawn like *The Brady Bunch*, but I had Sandu as a friend now, and that made me feel less alone.

Still, I felt invisible, not being able to express myself in English. Frustrated, I let my pencil dash from one corner of the paper to the next, filling the page with dark pencil lines crisscrossing each other, leaving the page filled with shades of shiny gray shapes that revealed my confusion and anger. It wasn't the English assignment I was supposed to write, but it did express my feelings. I closed my notebook and went to bed.

Mama bought popcorn and sodas for each of us. She wanted to sit in the front row, to get a good view of Hendrika in her first movie. Mama had taken us shopping at Kmart for this occasion because she said we deserved new clothes—just like the movie stars at the Academy Awards. Mama stood out in the red dress she had bought, while Hendrika looked lovely in a white polyester suit. I couldn't wait to wear my new miniskirt and floral shirt to the Gypsy Camp.

Full of anticipation, we searched the screen for Hendrika. Finally, an hour into the movie, we glimpsed her back for a moment. Anxiously, we waited for her next appearance, but the movie ended. Mama sat in her seat with her mouth wide open. We left the theater, and no one said a word on our way home. Back in the apartment Mama sat down at the dining room table and lit a cigarette. She was as tense as a bull about to be released into the arena. As I walked to the bedroom Mama snapped at me, "Well, am I a painting or am I an insect on the floor? Am I not even worthy of a decent goodnight?"

"Goodnight, Mama. I was going to say goodnight. I didn't mean to be rude," I said, confused.

Mama turned to Hendrika. "I cannot believe this is all Kent found for you. And you went along with it. You need to stand up for yourself and be responsible." Mama slapped her hand down on the table. "I cannot do everything for you. How could you not know what kind of part this was? You must demand to be seen." Hendrika knew better than to try and explain to Mama that you don't get to demand parts in a movie. "You will never get anywhere like this. You are just like your father. He never stood up for himself either," Mama complained. I glanced at Hendrika who had gone into the kitchen. She was crying.

"What have I done to deserve this?" Mama lamented. "I do not understand. I do my best and look what I get in return."

Hendrika stormed out of the kitchen. "My God, Mama! What do you want from me? I've done everything you wanted me to do. I hate Kent. I hate acting. I'm doing all this for you. Everything I do is for you. Remember when the brakes failed and we didn't have enough money to fix them? The next day I told you I found some money behind the ashtray. Well, I didn't find any money behind the ashtray," Hendrika shouted as she walked toward Mama, the veins popping out in her neck. "I earned that money. I danced topless for it because you couldn't earn anything." Hendrika collapsed onto a dining room chair, sobbing. Mama sat in her chair, paralyzed, as if she had been struck by lightning.

"That is impossible. You are lying," Mama snarled in disbelief. "I was with you every night."

"No, Mama, you're wrong. That night before I 'found' the money, I went back for the second dance set alone—remember? You stayed in the car with Serena. That's when I went topless," Hendrika recalled bitterly. Mama sat motionless, except that her hand quivered as she brought her cigarette to her mouth. "That's how we got enough money to fix the car. That's how we could afford gas for the car, that's how we could buy groceries. I did help, Mama. More than you could with your useless incense. And I am responsible. You are the one who is irresponsible, taking us to a country you know nothing about," she shouted, and ran to the bathroom and slammed the door. Mama's face was red, the muscles of her jaw twitching as she stood still as a statue and stared out the window.

I watched silently from the bedroom door, horrified at what I had just heard. I saw the anguish in Hendrika's face and my heart ached for my sister. I felt sick. I wanted to run to the bathroom and hold Hendrika. But Mama frightened me; there was no telling what she might do next. I walked to my bed, curled up, and pulled the blanket over my head. I wanted to disappear.

ૐ૰ૐ૰ૐ૰ૐ૰ૐ૰ૐ૰ૐ

THE FOLLOWING SUNDAY, WE WENT to Ralphs and then to the cramped Cuban market at Vermont and First. We had grown accustomed to shopping in big supermarkets, where the amount and freshness of the foods always delighted me. At the Cuban market, like the markets in Curaçao, the tomatoes were often bruised and the bananas black. Ramón regularly stopped by the apartment for short visits, even though he was very busy with school and working nights at the gas station, but that night he was coming over for a special dinner, and we needed some things that Ralphs didn't have. We purchased all the ingredients for a big feast.

Mama had calmed down over the past few days. She was frying chicken for the *Escabeche* and cutting the onions, carrots, and celery that she would later add to the chicken while it was simmering in wine vinegar with mint, oregano, chilies, and garlic. Cooking often cheered her up. Hendrika was preparing *Papas a la Huancaína*. She made the sauce by adding chili, oil, and egg yolks to the feta cheese in the blender. The blender roared while she arranged lettuce under the boiled potatoes. She would add the sauce right before serving. These dishes were Peruvian and were two of Ramón's favorites.

I was making my own special dish. I sliced plantain bananas, fried them lightly, mashed them with garlic in a mortar, and then fried them again until they were crisp. For every three I made, I ate one. Hendrika and I were singing along to an Armando Manzanero record; the Peruvian singer-songwriter's music was famous throughout South America. The romantic ballads made me think of Sandu. The smells and sounds made me feel as if I were still in Curaçao, where we ate with friends from many South American countries. I closed my eyes. Our apartment finally smelled and sounded like home. Hendrika set the table. We all wanted to make the meal perfect for Ramón. We were very grateful that he had helped us when we first got to Los Angeles.

"I'm going to see if I can pick some flowers," I said, and walked out the door, a pair of scissors in hand. I returned with five yellow daisies. "It's difficult to find flowers around here. I finally found these daisies three blocks down the street," I said to Hendrika, pointing with the scissors. "When I started cutting the flowers, this old lady came out and yelled at me, telling me I was stealing her flowers. I was cutting from a bush of daisies that were hanging out over the sidewalk. I told her we were having a special dinner and wanted to decorate the table, but she didn't care."

"Yes. It's funny," Hendrika agreed. "People have so much here and yet they are so possessive, as if they don't have anything. The table looks pretty with the blue tablecloth and the yellow daisies. Some day we'll have enough money to replace these green-and-pink plates with Dutch Delft blue-and-white ones."

The doorbell rang and I ran to answer it. Ramón was dressed in his best clothes: a blue shirt with gray pants and black leather shoes. A light-gray wool sweater made him look elegant and tall.

"*Ramón, ¿qué tal?*" I exclaimed, throwing my arms around his neck and giving him a big hug.

"*Bien, bien. ¿Y tú, Chiquita?*" he said, hugging me back and lifting me slightly. "*Vengo con hambre.* I'm here with a big appetite!" He crossed the living room to the kitchen, sniffing with each step, as if his nose was telling him where to go. "It smells delicious. What are we having?" he asked in Spanish.

"*Escabeche, Papas a la Huancaína, y Plátanos Fritos,*" Mama said proudly, as she sliced cucumbers and tomatoes for the salad.

"*¡Qué delicia!* This is marvelous." Ramón put his hands together and lifted them up to his mouth in amazement. He looked truly grateful. I opened the bottle of Gallo wine and poured four glasses. Hendrika arranged the plantain slices on a plate and brought them into the living room. We all followed with our wine and sat down.

"So, how are things, Ramón? Any girlfriend yet?" Mama asked.

"*Ay,* Señora—I don't have time for a girlfriend. All I do is work and study. No girl is going to be interested in me while I'm this busy. Anyway, it would be too distracting to have a girlfriend right now." He smiled as he spoke, holding his glass in both hands, his elbows resting on his knees.

"You are such a sensible young man, Ramón," Mama observed.

"Thank you, Señora. How about you? How is work?"

"It is all right. It is work." Mama wrinkled her nose in dislike.

"You are not enjoying your job, Señora?" Ramón asked gravely.

"No, it's very different from what I am used to. I do not believe babies should be separated from their mothers or that all mothers need to give birth in hospitals. All of it seems wrong. The doctors are rude and in a hurry. The nurses take the babies to the nursery the minute they are born. *Ach,* Ramón, it is terrible. This is not what I am used to. I am a midwife and I know how to deliver babies. In Curaçao, the women in labor call me when they are ready to deliver. I deliver their babies at home, teach their families how to help the new mother, and explain to them what the mother and baby will need. I know the mothers because I have taken care of them before their babies are born, during the pregnancy, and after the baby has arrived. Here everybody is a stranger. Nobody knows each other. Such an intimate moment and only strangers around! *Ay nò,* this is not right. I do not enjoy my work." Mama shook her head while she was talking. We all sat quietly for a moment.

"I'll get dinner on the table," Hendrika said and went to the kitchen.

"I'll help," I said, and followed her. We were both worried that Mama would talk about nothing but her job, and we would have to listen to her complain all night. Mama and Ramón sipped their wine while Hendrika and I got dinner ready. Since only the counter separated the kitchen from the living and dining area, we could overhear their conversation.

"Ramón, we need your help," Mama said, putting her wine glass down. She folded her hands together on her lap and thought for a moment. Her expression was serious.

"Anything, Señora. You know if there is any way I can help, I'll be happy to do it. You are family to me," Ramón said.

"Well, Ramón, the situation is this. I have applied to the Immigration Service for green cards for Serena and Hendrika. With Serena, there is no problem because she is a child and I am her legal guardian. She will get her green card after a year or so. But Hendrika is too old for me to be her guardian, and her application will take five to eight years because she is considered an independent adult." Mama had a worried look on her face as she shook her head. "It is impossible for us to wait that long. If Immigration finds out that Hendrika is here without a green card they will deport her." She leaned forward as if she were going to tell Ramón a secret. "But if she marries an American citizen she also could have a green card in one year." Mama paused. Ramón nodded in agreement. Mama leaned forward. "Ramón, you are a citizen now. Will you marry Hendrika so she can get her green card?"

Ramón's eyes opened wide in surprise and he pulled back. He carefully put his glass down on the coffee table. "Señora, you have surprised me. I don't know. That is a very big question." He moved around in his chair and cleared his throat.

"No, no, Ramón. I do not mean it like that. I do not mean for you to be a husband and wife—just that you should marry on paper, so Hendrika can get her green card."

In the kitchen, Hendrika had stopped fixing dinner. Her mouth hung open; she was outraged. She almost dropped the plate with the beautifully arranged *Papas a la Huancaína* as she stormed into the living room. "Mama, what are you doing?" she hissed. "You can't just ask him to marry me."

Mama glared at Hendrika.

"Don't do this, Mama—it's not right."

"I am doing it for you, Hendrika." Mama stood up. She was fuming. "How else are we going to get your green card?"

Hendrika's body tensed in anger. I could see her teeth grinding together. Ramón stared, bewildered, at Mama and Hendrika. I wanted to do something to calm Hendrika and Mama down. "The food is ready, everyone," I said, bringing the dishes to the table and grabbing the bottle of wine to refill everyone's glass. Ramón didn't seem as excited about the meal as he had been when he first arrived.

"Come, Ramón, it is time to sit down and eat," I said. We took our places around the table without saying a word. The tension was palpable. I offered the platter of *Escabeche* to Ramón. Mama intermittently scowled at Hendrika. I could see Hendrika struggling under Mama's control. She looked as if she was about to explode. Ramón served himself and then I handed the platter to Mama; she put a tiny bit of food on her plate. I passed the platter to Hendrika, but she didn't take any food at all. I set the platter in the center of the table, served myself, and sat down. I was not really hungry anymore, either.

Ramón broke the silence. "I want to thank you for this beautiful meal, and I'd like to make a toast." He raised his glass so all our glasses could touch. "*Salud, amor, pesetas, y tiempo para gastarlos.*"

"Health, love, money, and time to enjoy them," I repeated in English, wondering if it would ever happen for us.

"Shall I put on some music?" I suggested, getting up and setting the needle back on Armando Manzanero. I hoped that the music would change the mood in the room but it didn't. After we finished eating, I took the dishes to the kitchen and brought coffee to the table. I couldn't wait for the meal to end. It felt uncomfortable and I felt terrible for Hendrika and Ramón.

"Señora, I have thought about it and you are family to me. It breaks my heart to think that you might be separated from each other. I will marry Hendrika if she wants to." Ramón paused. Mama's face changed instantly from a frown into a hopeful grin. Hendrika turned to Ramón, her face full of disbelief.

"I never expected to get married like this, but I know you depend on me. You need me and I will not let you down. I will help Hendrika get her papers," Ramón said. Hendrika leaned toward Ramón and touched his arm.

"Ramón, you don't have to do this. Mama is asking too much of you."

"It's all right, Hendrika. I will do it for you and your family. You will be able to get your papers," Ramón said in a sweet tone. I couldn't believe my ears. Ramón was truly an angel. I felt confused. I was happy Hendrika could get her papers, but I was angry with Mama for being so manipulative and disrespectful.

"Oh, Ramón, you are truly a saint!" Mama exclaimed. "Thank you, thank you. Oh, we are very lucky to have you as our friend. You are an angel sent from heaven." Mama got up, took Ramón's face in both her hands, and kissed him on the forehead. "Now you will be my son," she said. "Hendrika, you are getting married! We must make plans."

Hendrika glowered at Mama, speechless.

"What is the matter? Ramón is making a big sacrifice for you. Are you not grateful?"

Hendrika sat shaking her head. Mama's expression changed again. She turned to Hendrika with an erect, stiff posture to let her know she did not want any opposition.

"Ramón, do you think we could do it next weekend?" Mama persisted, turning back toward him. "We could drive to Las Vegas and you can get married there."

"I have to work, Señora," Ramón said. "I can't go to Las Vegas for the weekend."

"Mama, stop, please," Hendrika whispered. I wanted Mama to stop also.

"Could we not go just for one day? It would be much better if you two could get married as soon as possible." Mama wasn't going to give up easily. She wanted the wedding to happen soon, and she kept the pressure on.

"When do you have a day off, Ramón?"

"Sunday. I don't work next Sunday."

"Could we go then? Hendrika and I will do all the driving. You can sleep in the car. I will take care of everything. Please, Ramón?"

Ramón thought for a moment. "All right, Señora," he said reluctantly. He didn't seem excited about spending his day off driving to Las Vegas to get married.

"You don't have to do this, Ramón," Hendrika repeated. Exasperated, Mama flipped her head around to Hendrika, and her eyes looked as if they were on fire. When Mama was like this it meant she was about to blow up. I was torn: I wanted Hendrika to submit because there was no telling what would happen next if she didn't; yet I wanted her to stand up to Mama. Hendrika's shoulders slumped and she looked down.

Ramón turned to Hendrika and took her hand. "Pretty *Señorita*, will you be my wife on paper, so you can stay in this country without any troubles?" Hendrika smiled at him weakly.

"You are very sweet, Ramón. Thank you," she said softly, looking at her hands.

"Then, with that plan I will go home now. Thank you very much for this special meal." Ramón got up and kissed Mama first, then Hendrika, and me last. "*Compórtate Chiquita*, okay? Behave yourself," he said to me as he walked to the door.

I spent the next couple of days thinking about marriage and what it really meant.

ᘔᘔᘔᘔᘔᘔᘔᘔ

MY GRANDMOTHER DID NOT MARRY my grandfather for almost twenty years, although they thought of each other as husband and wife, even while living in their separate houses. At first, Opa did not want to marry Oma because of the dark color of her skin. Opa's mother and sisters wanted a say in who was going to be his wife. They were very possessive of their Diego, and found no woman good enough for him. He was the sole provider for his family and had been since he was twelve years old. He liked being the center of their lives and did not want to disappoint them. He loved my grandmother, and he felt torn between loyalty to his family and loyalty to his love.

At first, Oma was disappointed her love was not reciprocated in the conventional way. After the disappointment diminished, she decided their love was beyond convention and she would follow her destiny. "Love is something you feel deep inside your heart. Pieces of paper or ceremonies cannot change that. True love does not compare or calculate. It does not live by the rules of society. It is big and free, and when you fly on the wings of love you get a glimpse of heaven itself," Oma used to say.

Opa bought her the large house at Penstraat 34 when she had their first child. His life was divided between his mother's house and Oma's. Opa's mother and sisters referred to Oma as "that woman." It was very painful for him. He hated himself for not having the courage to show Oma the public respect she deserved. Tortured by doing the right thing for his family and wanting to follow his heart, he tried to live a dual life, until one day he could not stand it any longer and asked his Elena to marry him.

"Our lives are unfolding perfectly," Oma had told him. "I was hurt at first when you would not marry me. But I realize now that if we had married, I would have completely lost myself in being your wife. You have brought out the strength in me. Thank you for taking this journey with me. We do not need a piece of paper to prove you love me and I love you. The commitment we have is between us and no one else." For many years Diego kept asking Elena to marry him, but Elena's answer didn't change: "Thank you for asking, but I don't want to lose what we have."

It was on a Friday afternoon, seventeen years after their first child had been born, that Opa took her to Kranchi, the hall of vital records, to register as husband and wife. Oma told me that that afternoon the sun cast a magical glow over Kranchi, the bright-yellow *landhuis* with white trim that stood in a walled garden in town. Opa never walked Oma down the aisle; instead he walked her down the garden's path, over the threshold, and into the large, ornate entry hall of Kranshi. There, a massive, leather-bound register rested on an antique Dutch desk, waiting for them to sign. After they had both signed their names, thus recording their marriage, they drove out to the House of

Six Doors. They spent Friday night and Saturday alone together. On Sunday, Opa hosted a large party to toast his bride.

Opa and Oma knew each other well, before their marriage ceremony. It was different for Mama and Papa. They married in secret only four months after they had met. And seven months after their wedding they had been blessed with an eight-pound baby girl.

I wondered how Mama could end up hating Papa so bitterly when at one point she must have been passionately in love with him.

୬୬୬୬୬୬୬୬

I DIDN'T UNDERSTAND WHICH PART of marriage was the important part: the paper or the love. My parents' marriage had not lasted. As I thought back, I remembered Mama telling us once how Opa didn't approve of my parents' marriage. He was very angry with Mama for choosing a man who had been divorced. It was true that Papa had been married before, but he had only divorced his first wife after she was committed to an insane asylum.

"That is a man who cannot keep his promises. He will end up divorcing you, too, one day," Opa predicted. But he was wrong: Mama was the one who had asked for the divorce. I wondered if the divorce had been inevitable. When Mama told Oma she was marrying Papa, Oma wanted to have their charts read, but Nadira and Arjuna, the owners of the fabric shop where Oma used to work when she had first arrived in Curaçao, had returned to India. Oma didn't know anyone else who could do a marriage chart. I wondered if a chart could have predicted their divorce.

I thought about what life would be like if Sandu and I got married. I could leave Mama behind and start a whole new life. Maybe Sandu and I could live in a house with a lawn, and I could finally have a family. But Mama would never allow that. She might have, if Sandu had been rich and had a great education, some status that could set him apart from others and impress her—but he had none of these things. He just had my heart.

༄༅༄༅༄༅༄༅༄༅

ON TUESDAY, HENDRIKA AND I returned to the Gypsy Camp. It had been seven days since I had seen Sandu. He was waiting outside and his face lit up when he saw me across the street waiting for the Walk sign. He came toward me, we hugged, and our bodies melted into each other, like an exhalation after a long pause of holding one's breath. He put both arms around me and kissed my left cheek; when he went to kiss my right cheek, his lips brushed against mine.

"Mmm, your lips smell sweet," I said to him.

"Juicy Fruit for you," he said. He pulled out a pack of Juicy Fruit and offered me a piece. We stood holding each other, chewing our gum.

"How are you?"

"Okay," I said. "I missed you."

He pulled back and smiled at me. "I missed you, too," he replied.

I was curious to know more about him. I thought about what to ask. All I could think of was, "What do you love the most about Romania?"

"Well, let me think, there are so many things. I love the caves. There are many of them in Romania, thousands of them, scattered in the mountains. Some are huge and have ancient wall drawings; they say some were lived in forty thousand years ago. These caves are amazing!" His eyes shone as he spoke.

"Have you been to them?"

"I've been to some of them. They gave me a strange feeling. They have so much life, so much history. It's almost as if I could hear the stories while I was standing there. Some are so large that entire basilicas have been carved into them. I dreamed of getting married in one of those basilicas."

"Are you Catholic?" I asked.

"No—Greek Orthodox."

We were silent as I tried to imagine the caves.

"Well, we have caves in Curaçao also, but only one big one. It's called Grot van Hato. Hato is the name of the area and *grot* means *cave* in Dutch. It's long and dark, and they light it with lots of candles. You have to take a flashlight. There are tiny carved-stone dwarfs, about this big," I said, holding my index finger and my thumb about two inches apart. "They are lovely. It feels as if you are in a fairy tale ... that's the only big cave on the island."

"Caves with dwarfs, huh?" he said, nodding.

"We also have smaller caves on the north side of the island where the ocean hits the rocks. When it's low tide you can get into some of them, but it's very dangerous during high tide. There was one cave we used to go to a lot. It's round inside, with holes on the ocean side and an opening on top. We would climb down the opening into the cave, stand in the middle, and hold each other tight, to resist the force of the water that washed in through the holes. We would scream as the salt water rained down on us, as the waves broke over the top of the cave." Remembering made me smile.

Our faces touched, and then he gently kissed my cheek and forehead. I closed my eyes and imagined I was the sky with a thousand stars, each one being touched.

"I want to kiss every one of your freckles," he whispered.

"They're not freckles. They're angel kisses," I whispered back. He stopped and looked at me, puzzled.

"Which angel?"

"'Angel kisses' are what we call freckles in Curaçao. People with freckles are considered lucky."

"And beautiful," he added.

Flustered by his compliment, I changed the subject.

"Where do you live?" I asked. "I mean, here in LA?"

"Radu and I are sharing an apartment on Normandie and Sixth Street." He puckered his lips together and jutted his chin forward, indicating the direction. "I'll show you."

"Now?" I asked.

"No, now it's too late. Next time. First, I should meet your mother and tell her I want to go out with you. She should know. That way we can see each other during the day, and more often. When can we do this?"

"I don't know about Mama. We can try, but I'm not sure she'll be pleased. Maybe she won't let us see each other at all," I said, apprehensively. "Maybe it's better this way, that she doesn't know."

"Why? Why would she not like me?" Sandu asked, surprised.

"She's different. There's no telling how she will react. She's just ... different." I looked down, frustrated that Mama was the way she was.

"Don't be sad. She will like me," Sandu said confidently, and he kissed me again.

ᘒᘒᘒᘒᘒᘒᘒᘒ

ON SUNDAY, WE ALL PILED into the Ford at five thirty in the morning. I noticed that Hendrika did not take her camera, which she always brought on trips. We picked Ramón up at the Mobil station for our journey to Las Vegas and the wedding. I was excited about seeing Las Vegas, although I hated the reason we were going there. We brought clothes for the ceremony, coffee in a thermos, and bread and cheese in case we got hungry. Ramón was ready and waiting for us. He had a garment bag in his left hand, with his nice clothes, and a paper cup of coffee in his right hand.

"*Buenos días, Señora y Señoritas*," he greeted us with his usual smile.

"Oh, Ramón, you must be exhausted, working all night. Come sit in the car. You can rest while we drive," Mama said. Hendrika tuned the radio to a Spanish-language station as Ramón opened the back door of the car, but Mama opened her door and jumped out of the front seat.

"No, no, no—Ramón, you sit with your bride-to-be," she said. "I will sit in the back. You can rest." Mama got into the backseat next to me.

"Thank you, Señora. I am very tired."

We drove through Los Angeles and the San Gabriel Mountains. The landscape turned into a flat expanse of desert sand and sagebrush. I could hear Mama next to me, asking Saint Agnes to bless this marriage. I thought that was strange because Saint Agnes was the patron saint of sincerity in relationships. As far as I knew, this marriage was strictly for a green card. I wondered what Mama was hoping for. By midmorning it was hot, and the air conditioning wasn't working again, so I rolled down the window and tried to let the hot wind cool me down.

We stopped for gas at State Line, Nevada, on the border with California. I got out of the car to stretch my legs, and walked over to the edge of the pavement, where the desert sand began. I knelt down and lifted a handful of sand and let it trickle through my fingers. I remembered the time Opa had taken me to the synagogue in Curaçao.

❧❧❧❧❧❧❧

I WAS SIX YEARS OLD. It was one of the times Mama had left me at Oma's house. Opa invited me to take a walk into Punda, the main part of town, to see a big cruise ship come in and to buy some sweets. I was excited. Opa was a busy man and I didn't get to spend much time with him.

It took us about ten minutes to get to Punda. Opa stopped at a large, yellow wall surrounding a building with white trim, on the corner of Columbus Straat and Hanchi di Snoa. He looked at his watch, thought for a moment, and beckoned me to follow him through the arched wooden doors. They opened onto a walled courtyard that led us to another set of double doors that formed the entrance to the main building.

He told me this was the Mikvé Israel-Emanuel Synagogue, and that it was over three hundred years old, making it the oldest one in the western hemisphere. He told me Jews had been coming here to pray for all those years. Opa's words were fancy and I didn't quite understand them. He opened one of the doors and I followed him inside.

We stood at the end of a large, bright, white room with shiny mahogany benches lining each side. Above the benches were balconies with more benches. Four round, white plaster columns held up the roof, and four massive, three-tiered, polished-brass candelabra hung from the coved ceiling two stories above us. At the other end of the room stood an enormous, intricately carved mahogany cabinet.

The floor was covered with sand. Opa bent over and took a handful. He explained that the sand had come from the land of Israel and had been placed there to remind us of the forty years the Jewish people wandered in the desert after the Exodus from Egypt. The grains fell through his fingers. He stood up and pointed to the mahogany cabinet. Inside, he said, were the handwritten scrolls of the Torah. One of them had come from Spain and was six hundred and fifty years old. From the tone of his voice, I knew he was telling me things that were very important to him.

We stood admiring the beauty of the room. The sun's rays shone through more than forty narrow, arched windows, making the interior glitter as if we were standing in the center of a diamond in the midday sun. Opa told me he wished he could have married Oma in this synagogue. Confused, I asked him if he wasn't already married to Oma. He replied that they were married at the Kranshi city hall, but not in the synagogue. He walked over to one of the benches and sat down, and I sat next to him. I asked him why he had not married her here. He said Oma was not Jewish. I asked him if he came here often. He answered, "I used to, but I don't come much anymore."

He closed his eyes and I closed mine. We sat in silence. I felt light, like the instant on a swing when it reaches the highest point, just before it starts to swing back. I liked the feeling. Opa put his hand on my knee. I didn't want to leave, but he told me we would miss the arrival of the big cruise ship if we didn't go. The sand crunched under our shoes as we walked out.

The last grains of sand fell from my hand. I stood up and walked back to the car. The wind-blown sand on the pavement crackled under my feet.

WE REACHED JEAN, NEVADA.

"Let's stop at the casino and have breakfast," Mama announced.

"Are we there already?" Ramón asked in a drowsy voice.

"No, we're in Jean. It's another thirteen miles or so from here, I think," Hendrika answered.

"There, right there," Mama shouted, pointing at a billboard next to a motel. "All-day breakfast for fifty cents. Let's go there. Get off at the next exit, Hendrika," she ordered.

We pulled into what looked like a motel with a diner. The lobby walls were lined with slot machines, and they were jammed into every empty space in the diner. We walked in, and Mama told the waitress we were there for the fifty-cent breakfast.

"First you have to buy two dollars worth of tokens, then you will get the fifty-cent breakfast," she answered.

"But I don't want to play the slot machines. I play roulette, not slot machines. I just want the fifty-cent breakfast," Mama said indignantly.

"You should have read the sign more carefully. At the bottom of the billboard it says 'with purchase of two dollars worth of tokens.'" The lady sounded impatient, as if she had often run into this problem.

"I'll buy the tokens so we can try our luck and have breakfast," Ramón interjected, wanting to avoid conflict.

"Let's see if we're lucky," Mama agreed. Mama handed Hendrika a few tokens and offered Ramón some. "No, Señora, you are the lucky one. Please, you use them." Ramón closed Mama's hand and guided it back to her. I knew I was too young to play. I asked Hendrika to slip me a few tokens anyway but she said no. Mama walked over to the nearest slot machine and uttered a quiet prayer as she deposited the tokens. She pulled the handle firmly. The first reel stopped, revealing an orange, and then the second reel stopped, revealing another orange. "I won," Mama shouted and threw her hands in the air. The third reel came to a stop. It was a yellow lemon. She struck the slot machine with both palms.

"*Ay nò.* I almost had it but then I got a lemon."

A waitress wearing a black apron walked up to Mama.

"Please don't hit the machines," she said.

"But I got a lemon," Mama explained.

"Everybody gets lemons, honey," she said wearily. It took only a few minutes for all the tokens to be swallowed by the slot machines. Of course we had not been lucky. Mama resolved that when we got back to Hollywood, it would be time to look for some assistance from the world of the spirits.

"*Ay nò.* We're going to have to do something. Our luck is terrible. We have to find someone to help us," she said as the machine consumed her last token. "Where can we find a *bruja* here in America, Ramón?"

"I'm not sure, Señora. Maybe look under witches in the yellow pages? I don't know." Ramón shook his head as he spoke. I stifled a giggle. Was there a listing for witches in the phone book? We ate the fifty-cent breakfast without much enthusiasm and left.

After the last thirteen miles of desert, we could see a few tall buildings in the distance. As we got closer we could see large marquees and high-rise buildings sprouting out of the bare desert ground. The Tropicana Hotel and Dunes Hotel were on our left. Another hotel called the MGM was being built in the shape of a giant letter T. In between the high rises were one- and two-story motels with names like the Happi Inn, the Black Jack, and the Americana. The marquee of Caesars Palace hotel announced performances by Paul Anka and Joan Rivers. Across the street the Flamingo offered Leslie Uggams.

Hendrika drove slowly. We passed the Circus Circus Hotel and Casino. It was built in the shape of a circus tent. At the Lido casino we turned right onto Freemont Street. We were now in the heart of Las Vegas. The Freemont, the Mint, and the Las Vegas Club were to our left, and to our right were the Coin Castle, the Pioneer Club, with its forty-foot-tall cowboy covered in neon lights, and the Silverbird. Scrolling and flashing lights dazzled us. Many men wore suits and the women looked stylish in their summer dresses.

"Let's turn around and drive down this street again," Mama said. "We need to find a wedding chapel." Hendrika turned the car around in a large parking lot and we retraced our route, searching for a wedding chapel.

"Look over there," I said, "the Las Vegas Garden of Love Wedding Chapel." I pointed at a single-story white building decorated with red-plastic heart-shaped wreaths.

"Ah, good," Mama said. "Let's keep driving and see if there are any others." Then we saw the Little White Wedding Chapel. It was a collection of white buildings with a steeple on the roof of the entrance. A sprawling grass lawn and palm trees gave the chapel a lush look.

"That one must be too expensive," Mama commented as we drove by. We kept going. "That one, I like that one," Mama said. Cupid's Wedding Chapel was flat-roofed, with a steeple and a cross. Its sign was a giant red heart with an arrow through it. The air-conditioning unit poked through the roof next to the steeple, and bushes on either side of the front door were decorated with tiny white lights, barely visible in the bright afternoon sun. A sign at the entrance advertised a special price of $37.99. "Let's see if we can find something for less," Mama said. We kept driving.

The Chapel of Eternal Love was in a narrow white building without a lawn, trees, or a steeple. It was located next to the Desert Palm Motel. A flashing pink sign with two doves kissing hung next to the front door. Between the two doves the price of $29.99 was posted.

"We'll try that one," Mama said. Hendrika parked the car behind the building and we all went in.

We walked into the reception area. The man standing behind the desk wore a faded tuxedo, and he appeared as though he had worked all night. He hadn't shaved. Past the reception area was a cramped room with a table that doubled as the altar. It held no crucifix or saints, only some slightly faded plastic flowers on a plain white cloth. In front of the plain table were church benches of unfinished wood, on either side of a narrow center aisle. The chapel gave me the creeps. I was glad this was not my wedding, and I felt sorry for Hendrika.

"How much does it cost to get married?" Mama asked.

"It will cost you $29.99 without a blood test, and you're in luck, we can marry you at four o'clock today. That's only a half-hour from now."

"What do you think, Ramón?" Mama waited for Ramón to respond.

"Four o'clock is fine, Señora," Ramón answered.

Mama then turned to the man behind the desk and told him we would take the four o'clock wedding spot.

"You will need witnesses. That will cost an extra ten dollars, and if you want fresh flowers, a tuxedo, a wedding dress ..."

The man was running down his list of options when Ramón interrupted him.

"We'll just take the witnesses, please. Do you have a room where we can change?"

"Yes, over there." The man pointed briefly in the direction of the rooms, less interested in us now that he could see we weren't going to spend money on extras. We went back to the car to get our clothes and returned to change. Hendrika was quiet; she stared at her feet. I wondered if she was remembering someone else, maybe even someone she had hoped to marry. I felt sad for her. Mama was cheery as she accompanied Hendrika and me to the women's changing room.

"Here, let me look at you. Let me fix your hair. You've got to look pretty," Mama said as she moved around Hendrika eagerly. Hendrika was wearing her peach-colored wraparound dress. Mama was dressed in her white suit—the one she had made herself in Curaçao, for the trip to America. This suit came out on all special occasions. I wore a peasant skirt in red, blue, and yellow, and a yellow angel-sleeved shirt and platform shoes.

Mama returned to the office to meet Ramón and take care of any last-minute arrangements, while Hendrika and I went out for a cigarette. She leaned against the white stucco wall of the building. I stood next to her. She shook two cigarettes from a fresh pack and handed one to me. She struck a match, lit her cigarette, and handed me the still-burning match. We both stared straight ahead. Stretched out in front of us was a hot asphalt parking lot, and beyond it a lonely expanse of desert.

"This place is not what I had expected it would be," Hendrika said. A pitiful smile appeared on one side of her mouth and a drop of sweat ran down her brow. "Nothing here has been the way I expected it to be," she said. She took another drag from her cigarette and looked down at her shoes. It hurt me to see her so sad.

"You're doing this to get your green card," I said, trying to reassure her. "This isn't your real wedding." She didn't respond. "You're only doing this so we can all stay together in America," I said, putting my hand on her shoulder. She continued looking down.

"This is so humiliating," she sighed. A tear ran down her cheek. She looked away. She didn't want me to see that she was crying. I wanted to make her feel better, but I couldn't think how. She was right, it was humiliating, but I wanted her to do it so she could stay with us. She wiped her cheek with her hand.

"Things will get better. You'll see. This is our last bad day. From tomorrow on our lives are going to be perfect." I tried to sound cheerful.

Hendrika exhaled forcefully. "Our lives were supposed to have gotten better when we came to America. We've been waiting for months for life to get better, but it just doesn't." It was true—we were much further away from our dreams now than we had ever been in Curaçao. I was scared. Hendrika had let go of hope. I put my arm around her and pulled her close to me. Her body was limp. She took a last deep drag from her cigarette, dropped it on the pavement, and ground it out with her shoe. We slowly returned to the front door.

Ramón was waiting for us in his gray suit. "My three beautiful ladies," he said, holding out both hands. He turned to the man behind the desk and said, "I think we are ready." The man picked up the phone and called the witnesses.

"We'll start in ten minutes," he announced without looking up. Then he went into the other room to arrange the plastic flowers. The witnesses arrived, a man and a woman. They looked as though they might be related to him.

"Would you like the long ceremony or the short? It's the same price," the man asked.

"The short is fine," Ramón answered.

"Then let's start. You stand next to the altar," he instructed Ramón. "When the music starts, begin walking down the aisle," he told Hendrika. "The guests can take their seats on the benches." He looked at Mama and me. The female witness went to a boom box in the corner and started the music as Mama got seated. The man moved to the front of the altar. I stood next to Hendrika, waiting to see her walk down the aisle. She had aged. Her face had lost its radiance. The gleam in her eyes had disappeared. Her tall, skinny body hunched forward. She looked down at the floor. With each step she took down the aisle, more of the Hendrika I knew disappeared.

— Part III —

DAY AFTER DAY, THE SMOG-SHROUDED skies reflected the mood in our apartment. Hendrika was becoming more despondent. It had been more than six weeks since her wedding. Ramón's visits used to be a welcome relief from our dreary lives, but even those had become awkward. He now came less and less often, because every time he did, Mama insisted he talk to Hendrika. It was embarrassing; they had to tell each other everything. Nothing could be left unsaid, as if they were really a married couple. Ramón had to tell Hendrika how he slept, how he got dressed, where he kept his shaving cream and toothbrush, if he was neat with his clothes or messy, and Hendrika had to do the same thing. Mama wanted to make sure that on the day of their interview for Hendrika's green card they could pass for husband and wife.

Mama also gave Hendrika instructions about taking better care of herself because soon she would have a green card and she'd be able to get a good job, but Hendrika paid no attention. Hendrika and I hardly spoke. The only thing we did together was go to the Gypsy Camp, and even then we weren't really together because she had made friends with a different group of people. Her friends were two Turkish men and a woman from Panama. The men were large and domineering. They didn't say much and they never smiled. I couldn't understand why Hendrika liked them. They gave me an uneasy feeling. Sandu did not like them either. He mentioned this a number of times, but when I asked him why, he would just shrug his shoulders and shake his head, muttering she should not be with them. I told Hendrika what Sandu had said, but she dismissed his warnings. She was becoming absent-minded, forgetting to buy soap for the laundry, sugar for the coffee—even the coffee itself. Mama grew increasingly frustrated with her. Once she forgot to pick Mama up from the hospital at the end of her night shift. She arrived thirty minutes late and Mama was furious. In the evenings, Hendrika would leave the apartment by herself to buy a pack of cigarettes. She never let me go with her.

Television was my only escape. I still hadn't made any friends at school, although there was one girl who greeted me every day with a smile but that was as close as we got to conversation. I wanted to talk to her and sound American, but every time I tried I sounded stupid or my words would not come out right. She'd stare at me with a pitying expression on her face. The more I tried to be cool like the other girls in school, the more unlike them I felt.

ﭐﭐﭐﭐﭐﭐﭐﭐ

It was Thursday and I was flipping through a magazine, watching the clock's hands turn slowly. Hendrika sat on the floor staring at her record collection.

"Hendrika, I want to go with Sandu to his apartment tonight," I said.

"No way!" she said emphatically, shaking her head.

"Please, Hendrika. I promise nothing will happen. Sandu is a gentleman, and I know enough not to get in trouble."

"The answer is no. Seeing him at the Gypsy Camp is enough. Mama would kill me. No, she would kill herself and blame me for making her do it. Stop bothering me." Hendrika's voice was final. "Anyway, you're only fourteen. Why are you in such a hurry to go to his apartment? If he really likes you, he'll see you at the Gypsy Camp." She hunched over her records again.

"What are you doing? Why are you sorting the records?" I asked, wanting to change the subject.

"Because I feel like it, and I don't want you to touch them. Okay?" She glared at me as she spoke. Her bangs were too long and drooped over her eyes.

"Okay, I won't touch your records. Do you have any change? I want to go to the drugstore to buy some ex-lax."

"*Ja*, in my wallet, but why are you eating so much of that stuff? It's not candy." Hendrika pointed to her wallet on the dining room table.

"It's chocolate without calories because it goes right through you," I said, feeling clever. I wanted to be thin, and I thought the ex-lax would help. I ate a square of the laxative each day, sometimes two if I was feeling fat. It gave me terrible cramps and diarrhea, but also a flat stomach, and I wanted to look thin the next time I saw Sandu.

I took two dollars out of Hendrika's wallet and walked to the drugstore, a few blocks away. I wandered over to the cosmetics counter, ex-lax in hand, to browse through the lipsticks and eyeliners. I was always looking for things that might make me look older. Behind the counter was a tall, slender woman in her midtwenties, with chocolate-colored skin, a narrow nose, green eyes, and hair that had been straightened. She was elegant and her movements were graceful. She was arranging the display of sample cosmetics on the counter when she looked up and smiled at me.

"Is there anything I can help you with?" she asked. Her accent sounded vaguely Dutch to me. My eyes lit up.

"Where are you from?" I asked, hoping she might recognize my own accent. A smile formed on her face.

"I'm from Surinam. And you?" she asked. Surinam was another Dutch colony near Venezuela.

"I can't believe it. I'm from Curaçao! My name is Serena."

"*Ik heet Inez, en heb vijf jaar op Curaçao gewoont,*" she said in Dutch, telling me her name and that she had lived in Curaçao for five years.

"Do you speak Papiamentu?" I asked, referring to the language spoken in Curaçao.

"*Ja, kon por laga,*" she answered, and we switched languages again, this time to Papiamentu. Inez glanced over toward the manager who was looking at us suspiciously, so I gave her the ex-lax to ring up. She scribbled her phone number on the receipt, and I left. I was thrilled to meet someone who spoke Papiamentu. I had not had a girlfriend in almost a year, and even though she was older than me I imagined all the fun things we could do together. I hoped she liked the same things I did. I ran all the way home.

"Hendrika! Hendrika! I met someone from Surinam at the drugstore," I shouted as I ran into the apartment. My sister still had the box of records open on the floor. "Her name is Inez, and she lived in Curaçao for five years!"

"Oh," she said without much interest. "Small world." Hendrika stood up. I didn't understand why she didn't share my excitement. We commented all the time about how we never seemed to meet any Dutch people here in America.

"Would you like to meet her?" I asked.

"Sure," Hendrika said. "Maybe tomorrow." I sat down and told her what I knew about Inez while she continued sorting her records.

I waited until Hendrika left to pick up Mama from the hospital. Her secretive behavior had me curious. As soon as she had shut the door behind her, I walked over to her record box and searched through it. In the bottom of the box under the records was a cloth bag. I pulled it out and felt it; it was too light to be a wallet or coin purse. I opened the bag and saw sticks of incense and something that looked like tobacco. I had been smoking since I was twelve and knew that this was not tobacco. I sniffed it and rubbed it between my fingers; I suspected the only thing it could be was marijuana, although I had never seen it before. I couldn't believe my sister might be using drugs, but this could explain a lot of her distant behavior. I closed the bag, put it back in the box, and replaced the records exactly the way they'd been before. I went to bed worried about Hendrika.

The next morning, I told Mama all about Inez and she seemed eager to meet another Dutch person. Mama didn't have to work that day, so the three of us went over to see Inez after school. We walked into the store and I spotted her right away. She was wearing yellow, orange, and white–striped hip-hugger pants, a long-sleeved orange polyester knit shirt, a hip-length, sleeveless brown vest, and a chain belt. The way she combined the colors she wore reminded me of the way people dressed in Curaçao. She was helping a customer, so Hendrika and I pretended to shop for nail polish while Mama looked at face creams.

Mama called Hendrika over, waving a container at her. "This is criminal. They charge four dollars for face cream and nothing in it is natural. How is that possible? No wonder they have to come up with this hypoallergenic nonsense. This junk will make your skin dry up and fall off. I should start making my creams again. Maybe I could sell them here." Mama's eyes sparkled as she considered the possibility. She picked up jar after jar, reading the ingredients out loud. Her face had a severe expression as she studied the labels. Oh no, I thought. Please God, don't let her pursue another crazy idea. I could practically see our apartment stacked with cucumbers, coconut oil, oatmeal, and tea bags, with a sign on the door reading "Gabriela's Facials."

The year before we had left for Colombia, Mama had started making face creams from formulas Oma had used for years: oatmeal-and-egg-white masks to nourish the skin, tea bags to remove puffiness from around the eyes, cucumbers and witch hazel to close the pores and cool the skin. Mama had experimented with the creams on her friends and family. The word spread and soon Mama was booked with facial appointments in between delivering babies. Eventually, she had so many clients she converted Johan's room into a salon, which meant he had to sleep on the couch in the living room.

Mama was working very hard, holding down two jobs. But working hard wasn't her goal. Her real intention was to get rich by creating a best-selling cosmetics line based on Oma's formulas. The problem was that she couldn't figure out how to preserve her concoctions. Disappointed, she turned her clients away, letting them know she didn't have time to both deliver babies and give facials. The hundreds of jars with Mama's various attempts at preservation were thrown away. The house smelled like rotten eggs for weeks, but Johan finally got his room back and our life returned to normal.

Mama shook her head and made faces of disgust as she went through the shelves of cosmetics. I was relieved when I saw Inez finish with her customer. "She's ready!" I announced, pointing at Inez, who looked delighted to see us.

Inez raised both hands and said, "*Kontá, Kontá. Esta leuk nò,*" in Papiamentu, as she came toward us to give me a hug.

"This is my mother, Gabriela Ferreira-García, and my sister, Hendrika," I said in Papiamentu. Inez hugged Hendrika, but Mama held herself stiffly when Inez tried to hug her. That's when I realized I had not told Mama that Inez was not white.

"Let me show you some face lotion so it looks as if I'm working. My boss is not very friendly." Inez spoke hurriedly in Papiamentu. We walked over to the counter, where she showed us some cosmetics. She told us how she had met her boyfriend in Curaçao. He lived in Los Angeles, and she decided to move here for a year to see if the relationship would turn into marriage, although she claimed with a grin that she was not very domestic. I was excited to learn that her apartment was just a short distance from the drugstore, and only six blocks from our own.

Mama was less interested in where Inez lived than in her position at the drugstore, and immediately seized the chance to investigate the possibility of changing careers and starting a business making cosmetic creams. Inez was surprised at Mama's inquiries and seemed uncomfortable. Mama pressed Inez to ask her boss if he could put her in contact with some cosmetics companies. "I'm just a salesperson. I don't want to upset my manager. I don't want him to think I dislike what he sells in his store. I need this job," she said as she fidgeted with the items on the counter. "I've only been working here for a month, and I'm afraid to ask him. Please, I'll talk to him some other time." Her sentences came quickly. She was trying to get out of the situation, but she remained gracious.

"I'll make you some," Mama offered, nodding. "You're going to love them. Then you'll talk to your manager," Mama said.

"That would be fine." Inez smiled tentatively, and I saw her body relax.

"I think we'd better go before the manager realizes we're not buying anything," I warned. We said our good-byes and the three of us left and strolled toward our apartment.

"Let us take a walk up toward Hollywood Boulevard," Mama said, picking up her pace. She was energized and wanted to explore. We walked west on Sunset Boulevard, past the dry cleaners and the Copenhagen Adult Book and Film Store. We turned right on Hobart Avenue then on to Hollywood Boulevard.

The tall, skinny palm trees that lined the streets reminded me of helium balloons on long strings. Few people were on foot, and the sidewalks of Hollywood Boulevard weren't crowded. We were in the shabby section of the famous street, where there were no stars in the sidewalk. The smell of a Mongolian restaurant on the corner of Hollywood and Serrano made me hungry. A few blocks down, a Middle Eastern bakery had trays of baklava lined up in the window. Sam's Jewelry Store displayed cheap watches, whose dials were decorated with smiley faces and peace signs. At Grand Central Pants Station, faded blue jeans and T-shirts were strung up in the window on a clothesline, as if they were drying laundry.

We crossed Western Avenue and the smell of tortillas and refried beans assaulted us as we walked in front of El Taco. Across the street, between the Sunshine Thrift Shop and the Richard's Adult Theatre, I saw in a store window a statue of Ganesha, the Hindu elephant god, atop a table draped with a purple silk cloth embroidered with gold thread. In the corner of the window, black letters on a white board offered Vedic astrology and palm readings.

"Look Mama, an astrologer!" I said, pointing to the sign across the street. Mama had been looking for a fortune-teller ever since we'd returned from Las Vegas. She had consulted the yellow pages, inquired at the World Bazaar Store and at the Magic Store, but hadn't found anyone suitable. Mama always liked visiting astrologers, psychics, palm readers, and mediums. If an astrologer told her something good was about to happen, she would be happy for weeks.

"I cannot believe our luck," she replied. The door was closed, so we knocked. A heavy woman dressed in an orange-and-gold sari opened the door. She wore gold-hoop earrings, three gold necklaces, and about twenty bracelets on each arm. All her jewelry was crafted of intricately worked gold and the end of her sari was draped delicately around her head, concealing her hair.

"*Suswaagatam aayiye*," she said in Hindi. "Welcome. Come in, please." She held the door open. The singsong pattern of her speech made me feel at ease. She shuffled her feet as if it were difficult for her to move. We entered. "*Namaste*," she said putting her fingertips together in front of her chest and bowing her head to her hands with closed eyes. She pointed to the table. "Who is going first?" she asked, a faint smile on her lips.

"I would like a reading," Mama said, stepping forward. Hendrika seemed uninterested and stared out through the glass door at something on the other side of the street. Hendrika didn't like astrologers and fortune-tellers. I wasn't sure why, but I suspected there might be something she wanted to keep secret. I hoped Mama would let me have a reading also, because I wanted to know more about Sandu.

"Come," the astrologer said softly as she put her hands on the chair for Mama. She shuffled around the table to the opposite chair, exhaling as she sat down. "Please tell me, what is the time, the date, and the place of your birth?" the astrologer asked. Hendrika and I stood by the door, watching. We could barely hear her and I had to strain to hear my mother's whispered response. The astrologer opened a thick, old book that lay on the table and flipped through the pages.

"You have Aries ascendant and Mars rules your first house. You have a tendency to be blunt and overbearing. You're also very emotional, impulsive, and courageous." The woman paused as she turned to another page. "You tend to neglect relationships for work, and money is important to you." She closed the book, extended both of her hands, palms up, and asked Mama for hers. I was impressed by how accurate the astrologer was. Mama gave her hands reluctantly, her brows furrowed and her upper lip curled.

"One of your children ... will leave the country suddenly. There will be matters with the law." Mama's eyes narrowed. This was not what she wanted to hear. Perhaps our visit wasn't a good idea. That meant either Hendrika or I would leave. I thought about the possibilities.

"Your other child ... she will stay." As the astrologer spoke, she turned Mama's hands this way and that way. Her sentences flowed out in a musical and hypnotic voice. "You will work very hard, but prosperity will elude you. You have psychic abilities. You will find happiness if you use them to help others. Disappointment and disillusionment will come to you if you pursue worldly riches." Mama's eyes opened wide and her jaw dropped. "Try to understand your children. Try seeing things their way. Listen to what they have to tell you. If you don't, you will be left alone." Mama's body had stiffened, her mouth pulled down at the corners. She was leaning back, pressing into the back of her chair. She didn't like what the woman had to tell her. Finally, the astrologer looked up.

"Pay attention to what I have told you," she said, her head nodding as she spoke. "It is good advice." Mama wasn't interested in spiritual riches. She wanted worldly riches and was only interested in mysticism as a means to reach prosperity.

Mama pulled her hands away and opened her purse. "What do I owe you?" she asked, her lips tight with disgust.

"Any contribution is appreciated," the astrologer replied. "May I take a look at your daughters' hands?"

"I am not paying for it," Mama warned, placing two dollars on the table. I walked over and extended my hands to the astrologer. She studied my right hand carefully. "What is the date, the place, and the time of your birth?" she asked. I answered her questions. She picked up the thick book again and studied a couple of its pages.

"Come back another day when you have more time. I have some things to tell you." She bowed her head and closed her eyes for a second. Then she looked into my eyes and smiled. I smiled back, and looked to see if Hendrika was going to come over. She was leaning against the wall, both hands sandwiched safely between the wall and her rear end. No one was going to read her palms.

Mama stood by the door, her purse wedged in the crook of her arm. I turned to look at the astrologer, and watched her disappear through a door at the back of the store. I followed Mama out the front door. She marched down the street, shoulders back, head held high. "Overbearing! I'm the one that bears everything. I don't get along with my children! I give up everything for my children. I sacrifice and sacrifice. That woman is an imposter. She knows nothing about astrology. My mother knows more about astrology than she does. I know what an astrologer is. This woman is probably not even from India. What a waste of money."

Although we weren't really listening, we nodded and agreed as usual with everything Mama said. We trotted along on either side of her as we made our way back toward our apartment.

꙳꙳꙳꙳꙳꙳꙳

A DAY LATER, I SAT at my desk at school staring at the words in my English textbook, which still made almost no sense to me. The fact that my English was improving so slowly was disheartening. My mind started to wander to the Indian astrologer. I felt an urge to see her again. Something told me this woman had important information for me.

On the way home, I got off the bus early at Sunset and Hobart, and walked to Hollywood Boulevard. I saw her storefront across the street next to the thrift store, but it was dark. I crossed the street, wondering if she was there. I knocked on the door. A minute passed before I saw her shuffling from a back room. She opened the door but didn't immediately recognize me. Squinting, as if the bright sunlight streaming through the door were blinding her, she grasped my arm.

"Come in, please," she said, "I can't see in this light." As we walked away from the door she saw who I was and said, "*Namaste*. I'm so pleased that you came back!" She put her hands together in front of her chest and bowed her head to her fingers. She stood completely still. Then she gazed at me for a long time. "I have many things to tell you."

☙ *174* ☙

"But I don't have any money for a reading," I said anxiously.

"This is not about money," she said. "It is my pleasure to do this for you." She bowed her head again as she spoke.

"But I don't know you. I never even met you before yesterday," I protested.

"Oh, you know me well. You simply do not remember. I am not talking about this lifetime." She looked at me for a moment, and then, waving one hand, she said, "Other lifetimes. Other lifetimes. You will understand this many years from now. Please sit down."

She pointed to the chair by the table as she shuffled to the cabinet behind her. She took out a box of incense and placed several sticks around the room, lighting them along with two candles. I sat quietly, watching her as she moved slowly from stick to stick, striking a match for each one. Then she came to the table, pulled out the chair opposite mine, and sat down. She closed her eyes and put her hands in her lap, palms up. I could hear her breathing. I waited for a moment, and then I, too, closed my eyes. The scent of the incense reminded me of Oma. I felt very peaceful and let every muscle in my body relax.

A lightness came over me. I liked the feeling. I was swirling in a sea of colors: purple, yellow, green, blue, and gold. The ethereal sound of chanting surrounded me, and the scents of lavender, gardenias, and orange blossoms lingered in the air. It was complete bliss. I heard her shift in her chair, and I opened my eyes.

"Remind me of the date, the time, and the place of your birth," she said as she opened her book carefully. I told her. "Venus occupies the ascendant in Taurus, and endows you with kindness and patience, but you are also stubborn and persevering. You are a keen observer of people. You are also sensual. You are passionate, possessive, and jealous. You do not like to share. But be careful. There can be a tendency to overindulgence and laziness."

She paused as she studied her book. "The moon is in your Seventh House. You will marry someone who is very wealthy. He will also be passionate, and will enjoy having beauty around him. He will be ambitious and determined." She turned the page. "You will marry later in life. The man will be older." Sandu was older than I. So that meant he was going to become wealthy, and we weren't going to get married right away.

"He will love you, and you will love him." She told me, smiling. "He will teach you to live in this earthly world. He is good at it. You will teach him to fly in the other worlds. You will be good at that. He will be your partner, your friend, your lover, your mentor, your protector, your teacher, and all of this you will also be to him. His soul will grow because of you, and your soul will grow because of him." I knew she was talking about Sandu; he was all those things to me already. I was pleased that his soul would grow because of me. He loved me and I loved him. We would live happily ever after.

"There is a man in your life right now," she said slowly. I couldn't help smiling as I nodded, anxious to hear more. "You love each other very much. You have had many lifetimes together." I nodded again, agreeing with every word. The woman looked up something in her book. "When did you meet him?'

"Three and a half months ago," I answered.

"Saturn has been in transit in your Seventh House. This man will not be the man you marry. If you marry him it will not be good for either one of you."

I felt a huge lump lodge in my throat. With two sentences, she had ripped away the soft, warm blanket she had just put over me. I did not want anyone but Sandu. I did not care how rich he was—without Sandu my life was worthless. I felt like crying. I wanted to leave. I wanted to yell at her and tell her she was an ugly, old witch and that she knew absolutely nothing.

"I know this is not what you want to hear. I know you want to leave. But let me finish."

I was amazed as she repeated my thoughts. Then she asked for my hands. She looked at my palms.

"But what will happen to Sandu?" I said, almost crying.

"Is that his name?"

"Yes."

"His work is with other souls in this lifetime. But he will keep his promise to you."

She had seen Sandu's and my love for each other. She knew we had had many lifetimes together. Perhaps she was confused—she was old and getting very tired. The woman sat back in her chair, studying me, then she spoke again with a great intensity. "When we come into this world, most of us forget all of our past lives. We forget the promises we have made to each other. We forget our essence and the source from which we come. We disconnect. The more we forget, the farther we are from our inner light. The dimmer our light becomes, the darker we feel. Love is remembering. In each lifetime, there are people that help us remember and connect to our essence. They rekindle our inner light. Love comes in many forms: love for a child, love for a friend, and love for a father or a mother. Each one of these loves can illuminate us and make us feel whole again. Love reminds us of our true essence.

"You are much older than your years. You have a man in your life already. This man has promised to help you if your light dims. He went through many hardships to reach you. Be grateful for his love, but know that there are other relationships he has to attend to in this lifetime. The man you are with now is here to nourish your light."

I didn't understand what she was saying. It didn't make sense. I felt myself getting angry.

"Do not be angry," she said. "Someday you will understand what I have said, but only after many, many years. You will remember my words. Your life will be good. You will have help along the way. There is no need to feel sorry for yourself." She paused. Her breathing was labored. She was exhausted. As I looked at her, I doubted her words. If she was so enlightened she would not be laboring and exhausted; life would be easy for her. I didn't have to believe what she said. She was just an old, fat Indian woman.

"Do not look at my body. Try to see my light," she said softly, and closed her eyes again. I looked at her. For an instant, I could see a yellow glow surround her but when I blinked my eyes, it was gone. Had I been staring into the candles too long? I noticed it was dusk outside.

"I really have to go. My sister is probably worried." As I got up she put her hands together again and bowed her head. Then she looked up and smiled.

"One more thing," she said. "Someone you love will soon depart this world, but know that they will never leave you. *Namaste*. Remember the light within you."

I got up, grabbed my backpack, and walked out the door as fast as I could. I ran three blocks before I realized people were staring at me, wondering what was wrong. I slowed down to a fast walk. At our apartment building I ran up the stairs, pulled the keys out of my backpack, unlocked the door, stepped inside, and shut the door quickly, as if I could keep out what the astrologer had just told me. Hendrika sat on the couch, surrounded by three baskets of unfolded clothes. "Killing Me Softly" was playing on her record player. She must have spent the afternoon at the laundromat. "What happened to you?" she asked, but she said it as though she didn't really care.

"I went to visit that Indian astrologer again. She took a lot longer than I expected." Hendrika wasn't listening to me. She had closed her eyes and was singing along with Roberta Flack. I wondered whom she was thinking about as she sang. I didn't know any of the people she had been spending time with. Maybe she'd found a boyfriend. I was sad I didn't know who she was becoming. I carried my backpack to the bedroom and closed the door.

᷍᷍᷍᷍᷍᷍᷍᷍

MY FRIENDSHIP WITH INEZ WAS growing. I went to her apartment frequently, even though Mama didn't know it. Inez never did speak to her manager about Mama's cosmetic products. Mama was offended, and decided that Inez was not to be trusted and should be avoided. I thought that was unreasonable of Mama, and I wasn't going to let her prevent me from having a friend.

I liked Inez's apartment and I'd sneak over there as often as I could. It was a cheerful place with its avocado-green shag rug and its green, orange, and pink geometric-patterned curtains. Two yellow beanbag chairs and an oak Parsons table stood in the middle of the living room. In the bedroom an oak-framed waterbed was covered with a yellow, green, and orange afghan Inez had crocheted herself. Next to the waterbed, a red clock radio with flip numbers sat on her nightstand along with a paperback copy of *Jonathan Livingston Seagull*.

Inez had re-created the essence of a colorful Caribbean home, in Hollywood. Two plants hung from the ceiling in macramé hangers. Posters in metal frames of Diana Ross, Jimi Hendrix, David Bowie, and Cher hung on the walls. An oak bookshelf held two lava lamps and a moon lamp, an eight-track tape player with stacks of tapes next to them. A yellow-and-brown beaded curtain hung in the doorway to the kitchen.

Inez and I had fun together. We'd cook, give each other funny hairdos, and try different cosmetic samples. Sometimes she'd paint my toenails or fingernails. I never invited Hendrika along because Inez and my sister had almost nothing to say to each other, and Hendrika never felt like dressing up or looking pretty. On the other hand, Inez and I talked about everything. I told her about Sandu, Mama, and Oma. I even told her about the Indian astrologer.

One day, I complained to Inez that Hendrika wouldn't let me go to Sandu's apartment. "We always have to stay at the Gypsy Camp," I said, sitting on her waterbed as I removed the polish from my nails.

"Serena, you have to be careful. There is only one reason Sandu would want to take you to his apartment, and that's to have sex."

"It doesn't have to be the only reason," I protested.

"Don't be naïve—it is. Stay in public places." Inez came over and lay down next to me with her feet crossed and her toes pointed. She was suddenly very serious. "Do you know anything about sex? Has your mother talked to you about it?"

"No. But I know about it," I said, shrugging my shoulders.

"Have you ever had sex?"

"No! Well. Sort of."

"Okay, how far have you gone?" she said.

"Well, one night before we left Curaçao, we were with some

friends on the beach. Everyone was drinking beer. Anyway, there was this one guy who was kind of cute, and we started kissing. His hands were all over me. Then he put his hand in my underwear, and he stuck his finger inside me. He said he could feel I was still a virgin, and he asked if he could break my virginity with his finger. He had been moving his hand around in there, and it felt really good so I said yes. But when he broke my virginity, it didn't feel good. I got kind of mad, and I wanted to stop." I looked at Inez for her reaction.

"Is that it?" Inez asked.

"Yes," I said.

"Serena, sex is very serious. It should be a beautiful experience." She ran her hand through her hair. "Well, there are a few things you should know about it." She gently placed her hand on my lap. "Knowing how your body works is important."

"Tell me. I want to know," I persisted.

Inez thought for a moment. "Well, I'm going to tell you because there is nothing wrong with knowing, but you're much too young to do it. Have you ever seen a man's penis erect?"

"No, not yet, but Mama says it's the ugliest thing God created."

Inez burst out laughing. "Your mother would say something like that," she said, slapping her thigh. I had never thought of Mama as funny, but it felt good not to take her so seriously. "Let's not talk about her while we're having this conversation. In Curaçao people are a lot less open about sex than they are in Holland. Your mother would kill me if she knew I was telling you this stuff."

"No, she'd kill herself and let the whole world know you made her do it," I said, echoing Hendrika. We both giggled.

"Well, Serena, intercourse hurts the first time. Eventually, it becomes pleasurable to have a penis inside you. Some women can have an orgasm that way, but the clitoris is what creates the orgasm for most women."

"What's a clitoris?" I asked.

"There is a spot, it's kind of a bump between your legs. It's called the clitoris. One evening, when you can get privacy in the bathroom, bend over and look at yourself in the mirror. Get to know what it feels like when you touch it. Would it help if I got you a book?" she asked gently, tilting her head and studying my expression. I squirmed around and tried to look casual.

"No, I don't need a book. I know what you're talking about," I said. Inez's skeptical look made me think I might not know everything. "Well, maybe a book would be helpful," I said.

"So when you've found your clitoris—and you'll know when you've found it because it will feel good—get in the bathtub and turn on the water, as if you were going to fill the tub, but leave the drain open. Lie down in the tub, but all the way forward, so the stream of water hits you right on that spot. Stay under the stream until you feel an incredible explosion. That's called an orgasm." Inez smiled. I tried not to look embarrassed. "It might take a while. It'll feel even better if you touch your nipples at the same time. That is what sex should feel like."

She chuckled when she saw my puzzled look. "It is important to know there is a difference between just being sexually aroused and being in love. You see, it's complicated," she said, and stopped to think for a moment. "Being in love is overpowering, and it will arouse you sexually. But that's not enough. You must have a clear understanding of what you are agreeing to. If not, you can get hurt." Inez put her hand on my thigh. "That's why it's important to take precautions if you're not sure of your commitment. If you have sex you will become pregnant unless you are on birth control pills or your lover uses a condom."

"What is a condom?"

"It's a plastic glove that covers his penis."

"Weird." I squinted in disbelief. Inez raised her eyebrows.

"See, you're too young. You're not ready for all this."

"But I want to make love to Sandu. Can you get me some birth control pills from the drugstore?"

"Oh, Serena, you are much too young. You haven't known Sandu that long. Why don't you wait a couple of years? Talk to him about his plans for the future. You don't want to make love to him if he is not serious about your relationship."

"But he is serious. I know."

"If you have an irresistible urge to have sex, use the faucet—it's safer." Inez got up and walked to her bathroom. I heard her open the medicine cabinet, and she came back with a pink package that she handed to me.

"I feel very strongly that you should wait. But if you decide to have sex with Sandu you must start taking these pills before you do, and you have to be taking them for a month before they will work. I'm going to give you a pack of my own pills—I can get more. You take the pink ones when you have your period and the white ones when you don't. You have to take them every day or they won't work, and you'll get pregnant. You know what they say here in America—it's better to be safe than sorry. Please be careful and don't tell your mother where you got these. If you don't take sex seriously you could get hurt," she said. The sympathy in her voice took the edge off her words.

I stood up and gave her a hug. "Thanks, Inez. I'm really grateful. You are a true friend."

I walked home with my pack of pills, thinking over all that Inez had said. I wasn't sure I was going to take all her advice, but I appreciated the education. I seemed to learn more with Inez than I did at school. I put the pills in my backpack; that was a safe place where no one would look.

೭ೱೱೱೱೱೱೱ

HENDRIKA WAS COOKING WHEN I got home. The television was on and a child was singing about wanting to be a hot dog.

"Where have you been?" she mumbled. I could barely hear her.

"Inez's," I answered.

"Are we going to the Gypsy Camp tonight?"

"Of course. It's Tuesday isn't it?" I said, walking toward the bedroom to choose my clothes. I turned the water on for a bath, remembering what Inez had told me. I shook my head. After my bath, I put on my black bell-bottom pants and a white wraparound shirt. I walked over to Hendrika, who was waiting for me in the living room. "I'm going with Sandu to his apartment," I announced, and waited for her reaction.

"Are you crazy? Absolutely not! I've already told you I'll tell Mama."

"No, you won't. Because I'm going to keep your secret for you," I said.

"What do you mean? I don't have any secrets." She eyed me suspiciously.

"Oh yes, you do. What's the stuff in your record box?" I pointed to the box as I spoke.

"You rat! You sneaky little rat! You looked in the box when I told you not to."

"I did. So will you let me go with Sandu or do I tell Mama?"

My heart was pounding as I waited for her answer. I felt a loss, even as I heard the strength in my own voice. Something had changed forever between Hendrika and me. We were no longer two sisters trying to stay together while our mother dragged us from place to place. Now each of us was going in her own direction, and we were only held together by threats. She grabbed the keys from the table and stormed out the door without a word.

I panicked and started to doubt myself. I should have left things the way they were. I jumped up and ran after her. She had taken the car. I stood there crying and cursing myself for being so stupid. I looked at my watch. It was time to go to the Gypsy Camp. I ran upstairs, washed my face, and redid my makeup. Then I wrote Hendrika a note in Dutch:

> *Dear Hendrika,*
> *Please forgive me. I will keep your secret. It was*
> *wrong of me to look in your box when you had*
> *asked me not to. Let's forget this ever happened.*
> *Your sister, Serena.*
> *P.S. I'm at the Gypsy Camp. I'll be back at ten.*

I walked by myself to the Gypsy Camp and found Sandu standing outside, waiting for me. He walked toward me with open arms, and

I quickened my pace when I saw him. I threw my arms around his neck. He embraced me, lifting me off the ground.

"I've been waiting for you," he said as he looked at my face. "What's wrong? Have you been crying?"

"Can you tell?"

"Yes. I can see you've been crying. What's the matter, baby?" He held me tight and rocked me from side to side. Cradled in his arms, I once again felt safe. I told him what had happened with Hendrika, and that I probably couldn't go to his place anytime soon. I feared he wouldn't want to see me anymore if we met only at the Gypsy Camp. He kissed my cheek.

"It's all right, my love. I will go to meet your mother and then everything will be all right. I will ask her permission to see you. She will see I am a very nice guy." He grinned and kissed me, but this time he kissed lower on my cheek as he worked his way down to my mouth. His lips gently touched mine as our breaths merged into one.

"I knew you would be here!" Hendrika said in Dutch as she walked up behind Sandu. I pulled away. My heart was pounding. I had not expected to see her and I was afraid of what she might say. I took a step backward and looked at her. She didn't seem angry. Actually, she didn't look upset at all anymore.

"Did you get my note?" I asked.

"*Ja*, I found your note, and I have it here for you to throw away before Mama finds it," she said, handing it to me. I took it from her and raised my eyebrows. "Fine, go with him. I'll cover for you, but be back here by ten fifteen or we're both in trouble," she warned, pointing her finger. Her face was stern, her eyes narrowed. In contrast, I felt jubilant.

"I'll be back. I promise. Thanks, Hendrika." I gave her a hug, but she didn't hug me back. I shrugged and checked my watch. "We have two hours," I said to Sandu with a smile. He put his arm around me as we went inside to ask Radu for the keys to the car they shared. I was excited and frightened the same time.

Sandu drove down Normandie Avenue to Third Street. The buildings on his street looked nicer than the ones on Kingsley. His apartment was in a white building with a wrought-iron and glass entrance. He opened the door and I could see a well-kept patio with a fountain in front of us. Sandu held the door open for me with one hand and gestured me in with the other. We walked to the elevator, and he pushed the button for the third floor. He put his arms around me and kissed me on the forehead.

"Are you okay?" he asked.

I nodded my head yes. I couldn't help but think of what Mama would do if she found out about Hendrika's drugs and my being here with Sandu. The thought made me shiver.

The elevator stopped and the doors opened. The hallway was off-white with a carpeted floor. Pastel paintings hung on the walls. We walked to number 305, and Sandu opened the door to a big studio apartment. The living area was light and long, with a kitchen and dining area to the right. A sliding glass door opened onto a balcony surrounded by a wrought-iron railing. On the left was a bathroom, and at the end of the living area the wall jutted outward, making the room larger. The walls were freshly painted a bright white and the beige carpet was new. The wooden kitchen cabinets were painted white. A mattress and a table were tucked into the left-hand corner of the room, and in the right-hand corner of the living area lay another mattress. It was the nicest apartment I had seen in America. I liked the smell of the fresh paint and the absence of clutter.

"This is where I live," Sandu said with a smile.

"Nice," I said shyly.

"I'm sorry I don't have a proper bed or a bedroom to go to." He looked at me to see if I was upset. I was surprised by his assumption that we would make love. I wanted to make love to Sandu, but I wanted to be asked. I wanted both of us to acknowledge what we were doing.

"It doesn't matter," I said, shrugging my shoulders. Sandu walked over to the corner and flopped down on his mattress.

"Come," he said, patting it with both his hands. I hesitated, then lay down next to him and curled up in his arms. He held me tightly and kissed the top of my head again and again. It felt good to be held by him. Our bodies stretched out on the bed and slowly turned to each other. I lay quietly as Sandu gazed at me and touched my body with the fingers of his right hand, as if he were getting to know me all over again. "You're so beautiful," he whispered, and kissed my eyebrows. His hand moved slowly down my shoulder to my chest, and he untied my shirt. "You're so soft," he said, moving his hand down my stomach to my hips. His gaze never left mine. "I'm so glad we found each other," he said. Our eyes were conversing in a language in which there was no misunderstanding. "You are so sweet," he murmured. I felt myself opening to him completely. I wanted to give myself to him. He gazed at me with admiration, and I felt acknowledged. He seemed strong and understanding. I wanted every part of him that I was unable to find in myself.

He took my hand and ran it over his face, as if to invite me to get to know him. I moved my hand over his Adam's apple, down the indentation between his collarbones, and up over his shoulders. When I cupped my hand around his shoulder muscle, it left my fingers completely spread out. I felt shy, not knowing what to do. I ran my index finger down the crease between his triceps and biceps and marveled at how beautifully sculpted his body was. I played with the few blond hairs on his chest and traced the many little valleys between the muscles of his abdomen. I let my fingers trace from muscle to muscle, and he smiled. My hand stopped at the top of his pants, not sure what I was supposed to do next.

Sandu unzipped his pants and slid them off along with his underwear. I looked at his penis. He took my hand and placed it on it. I traced its outline with my fingers. He smiled. Slowly we discovered each other and ourselves. Sandu finished undressing me. Our eyes met and I was surprised to see the delight in his. "You are my delicate tulip, so graceful," he whispered. He was seeing things in me I had not yet seen in myself. I felt beautiful, sensual, desirable, irresistible—and loved.

I sensed we had done this before, in different bodies, in different times. As we mapped each other's bodies and tasted each other's mouths, our hearts held a steady beat. His eyes looked into mine. "I will go slow, we have time," he said as he covered my body with his. "Don't be afraid," he said, and I gasped as I felt his penis enter me. I was surprised how much it hurt. I tried to relax, hoping he wouldn't notice how uncomfortable I was. I smiled each time he looked at me. He didn't smile back. Slowly, the pain subsided as he kept moving. Suddenly, I could feel his penis pulsing inside of me. He kissed my lips, rolled off, and wrapped his right arm around my shoulders. "Come here, my baby," he said, pulling me close. Holding each other, we fell asleep.

ᶻ❤ᶻ❤ᶻ❤ᶻ❤ᶻ❤ᶻ❤

TENSION SEIZED MY STOMACH AND twisted it as I woke up. "What time is it?" I demanded.

"It's okay, my love. It's only nine forty-five," Sandu said, patting me.

"Oh my God, I was afraid we had overslept." I lay back down on the mattress, and he put his arms around me. I relaxed again and started to play with the hairs on his chest. Looking around the room, I imagined myself living in this apartment with Sandu. The thought made me happy. Then my eye fell on three framed pictures on the table next to the mattress. One was a portrait of a slender and beautiful girl with long, blond hair and green eyes.

"Who is that?" I asked curiously.

"Ah, that is Nadia. She was my girlfriend when I lived in Romania," he said. He took the picture and slid it into a drawer. A chill ran over me. The confidence I had felt only moments before disappeared.

"No, no. I want to see," I protested. He took it back out and handed it to me.

"She is lovely," I whispered.

"You think so?" Sandu said, sitting back, looking at me.

"Yes, she is. Why are you with me if you have a girlfriend in Romania?" I asked. I wasn't sure if I felt angry or if I was just confused.

"Nadia was my girlfriend in Romania. I will never see her again. Remember, I cannot go back, and she cannot get out. Her picture is here with the pictures of all the people I loved and left behind in Romania."

"Do you love her?" I asked, holding my breath.

"I loved her in the past. What do you want me to tell you? I loved her then, but it's over now." There was impatience in his voice, as if my jealousy was difficult for him. I wondered if I had made a terrible mistake. My eyes filled with tears. I tried not to show my insecurity.

"Serena, I have a new life here and I have you, and I am really happy. I did not know you existed when I loved Nadia. You cannot blame me for not loving you when I did not know you."

He looked at me as he tried to reason with me. He wiped a tear as it came down my cheek. He kissed my lips as he pushed me down on the mattress again and playfully wrapped his legs around me. "My new life," he whispered as he kissed me on the neck, on my hair, on my cheeks and my forehead, and then worked his way down the rest of my body. As we lay in bed, the other pictures on the table kept catching my eye. I pointed to one of a man with short brown hair, hazel eyes, and thin lips, and wearing a brown suit, and a woman with red hair pulled into a bun, close-set eyes, and a sweet smile. She was wearing a yellow dress with a lace collar. "Who are those people?" I asked. He picked up the picture and brought it closer.

"They are my parents. This is my mother. I really miss her. She took good care of us. She is an incredible cook."

"You have handsome parents," I said. "When was this picture taken?"

"I don't know exactly. Maybe ten or fifteen years ago. My mother was sixteen when she married my father, and he is five years older. They love each other very much."

"*Eh-eh*! Sixteen! That's young."

"That is not unusual in Romania."

I thought about this for a second. I was relieved that I might not be too young for him after all. "What does your father do?"

"Tata was a government engineer, remember? My parents lost everything because of my escape—all the privileges they had worked so hard for all those years. Now their apartment is bugged, and each month they are taken to the police station to be interrogated. Their friends are afraid to talk to them because they don't want to lose their own jobs. I've caused them a lot of pain." He was stroking the picture with his finger as he spoke, then he put it down and picked up another. Three children smiled out from the frame. "This is my older brother, Felix, that is me, and this is my younger sister, Reveka." Sandu pointed out each person. "They put my brother in jail for three months after I escaped."

"I am so sorry," I said, touching his hand. "Maybe one day they can all come here and everything you have gone through will have been worthwhile." I lay still, looking up at the ceiling. I could see Sandu was hurting and I wanted to comfort him, but I didn't know how.

"I'm going to work really hard. Maybe get a second job so I can go to design school. I'll become a famous designer. I have to do something big. I have to do my best because it cost my family so much for me to take this opportunity." Sandu was still looking at the pictures.

I understood what he was saying. Mama had given up a lot for us. She often told us how difficult it had been for her to raise us and that her life had changed forever once she had us. After we were born, she could no longer pursue her own dreams but had to pursue our welfare. Perhaps, if Mama had not had us, she could have been prosperous and happy. We both stared at the photographs.

"What time is it now?" I asked, worried again. Sandu looked at his watch.

"Ah, it's time to go," he said slowly. We got up quietly and put on our clothes.

"I wish I didn't have to go," I said.

"In my heart you are not going. You will be with me all the time."

I smiled at him wistfully. I felt a deep sense of loneliness at having to leave this oasis. I watched him retrieve the keys from the kitchen bar. His posture was erect and his demeanor self-assured. His thin, muscular body moved gracefully. Sandu put his arm around me as we walked to his car. As we drove back to the Gypsy Camp, I felt the joy draining out of me. The reality of who I was, and the fact that I still belonged to my mother, brought feelings of hopelessness.

"Are you all right?" Sandu asked.

"Yes," I whispered.

"No. Something is not right. Tell me, my beautiful. Tell me what's making you sad." He glanced from me to the road and back again as he spoke.

"I'm fine. Really, I'm okay. But I won't see you all week. I wish we could be together more. I feel empty when you're not with me." I looked at the road as I spoke. Sandu pulled into the parking lot of the Gypsy Camp and turned off the engine. He put both his arms around me. Our noses touched, then our lips.

"I will always be with you," he said again as he kissed me. I took in every bit of him I could, hoping it would somehow keep me full until the next time we met.

"I saw a fortune-teller last week," I said, looking at him sideways. "She said we wouldn't be together forever." Sandu grunted from the back of his throat.

"You went to see a Gypsy? You can't believe anything they say. They're only out to get your money. Romania is full of Gypsies." He turned to look at me. "They cheat, they steal, they tell you stories. They're bad people. I think you should stay away from them."

"But she didn't want any money."

"That's the trick. She'll probably ask for twice as much next time," he interrupted.

"She wasn't Romanian. She was Indian."

"That's exactly what I mean. Romanian Gypsies aren't really Romanians. They came from India. They're dark-skinned people, always moving around, cheating, stealing, and lying. They're vagabonds. They could be murderers or kidnappers. Stay away from them." Sandu spoke with contempt. "They are like the black and Mexican gangs here." I sat quietly, staring straight ahead, glad he didn't think the Indian fortune-teller was right, yet surprised and troubled by his angry words about Gypsies, blacks, and Mexicans. He rubbed my shoulder and pulled me closer to him.

Hendrika appeared at my window. "Where have you been? Do you know how late it is?" She was almost shouting as she directed me with her hands to get out of the car. Sandu looked at his watch and then at Hendrika.

"I'm so sorry. The time got away from us. I'm really sorry," he apologized. Hendrika wasn't listening. She jerked my door open, moving quickly and speaking in four different languages, something she and Mama often did when they were upset. She practically dragged me away from the car as I waved to Sandu. I wanted to say something to him but was too embarrassed by Hendrika's actions—I felt like a child being punished.

"I'm not doing this if you are going to be late all the time. This is going to get both of us in trouble. I knew it was a bad idea. I'm so stupid to think you're old enough to be responsible! You're much too young for this." Hendrika was switching from Dutch to Papiamentu to Spanish, with a few English words thrown in. Her words cut into me as we hurried back to our apartment on Kingsley.

"I am old enough," I protested. "It has nothing to do with my age, it was just an accident. I'm sorry, okay? It will never happen again, I promise."

"You need to do more than promise. You need to swear."

"Okay, I swear it will never happen again. Please forgive me. I swear, I swear I'll never be late again," I vowed. Hendrika didn't respond.

When we arrived at our carport, she got into the Ford and drove off to pick up Mama. I walked up the stairs to the apartment. I felt as if I were tied in knots. I wanted to be free of Mama and Hendrika. I wanted to follow my heart. I wanted to change my reality, but I was afraid; afraid that Mama couldn't survive without me. Hendrika and I were the last hope in her life. She reminded us almost daily of how she had sacrificed everything for us. Mama said she had given up the chance to realize her own dreams when she had her four children, and the two oldest had already failed to give her any sense of accomplishment as a mother. It was up to Hendrika and me to prevent her life from being a complete waste.

It just wasn't fair that Hendrika and I had to reassure her that her life was worth living.

When I took my clothes off, the scent of Sandu was all over them. I picked up my pants and shirt and crawled into bed. I clutched the clothes, holding them close to my nose, and imagined I was still in his arms. The sense of having known him before kept coming back to me, and my thoughts drifted to my grandmother.

ᘔᖯᘔᖯᘔᖯᘔᖯᘔᖯᘔᖯ

IT WAS A HOT SUNDAY evening at the House of Six Doors. The rest of the family had returned to town. Only Oma and I had stayed behind. We were in her bedroom. She sat in the rocking chair next to the window, meditating. I lay on her mahogany four-poster bed, running my fingers over the blue embroidery on the hem of the crisp white cotton sheets. I loved watching Oma meditate. She looked so serene, even the air around her seemed still. When she finished, she came to lie next to me. I asked Oma who had taught her to meditate. She put her arm around me and pulled me close.

"I learned to meditate when I first arrived in Curaçao. I found a job at La Moda Fabric Shop, which was owned by Arjuna and Nadira, a couple from India. Arjuna had come from India to work at the Shell Oil refinery. After his contract ended, he and Nadira opened the fabric shop. Nadira and I became close friends, as if we were sisters who had been separated at birth and only recently reunited. At first, my job was to sell fabric, but Nadira soon discovered I was a good seamstress. Nadira and Arjuna bought a sewing machine, and from then on La Moda was both a fabric and tailor shop.

"Nadira and I spent many hours working together, and during this time we told each other about our lives. I told Nadira about Arawak Indian traditions, and everything I knew about the African beliefs and practices brought to the islands by the slaves. Nadira told me about Hinduism, karma, astrology, and reincarnation. She taught me to meditate using a mantra, which is like praying. Emptying the mind allows one to discover one's purpose in life. Nadira believed that this earth is the only planet in the universe offering the ecstasies of love and the agonies of hate. Life constantly presents us with paths that require us to choose between love and hate. All the things she taught me seemed familiar, as if I had known them all along."

I asked Oma to tell me about reincarnation. A light breeze came through the window. Oma pulled the sheets over us and explained reincarnation means being born again in a different body. "It will become clear to you when you meet someone and immediately have a strong feeling of love or caring, or even anger or hate, without ever having met the person before. But you have met them before, in another lifetime. And those feelings were the last feelings you had for that person in a past lifetime. Each lifetime is an opportunity to create more love and less hate. Your mind does not remember but your soul does."

I asked Oma if this had ever happened to her. She smiled. "The very first person it happened with was Shon Mirto, the herbalist. I had no doubt I had known him before. Slowly, as we spent time together, we realized we had had many lifetimes together. The more I remembered, the clearer it became that in this lifetime we were destined to be friends." A full moon appeared in the window, casting a silvery light into the bedroom. Oma hummed an old Curaçao slave song. I tried to stay awake but was soon overcome by sleep.

Still clutching the clothes suffused with Sandu's scent, I sensed I had known him before.

MY SCHOOL ASSIGNMENT WAS TO read the newspaper for current affairs. For the first time since we moved to Hollywood, the *Los Angeles Times* piqued my interest. On the front of the sports section of June 10, 1973, a muscular horse stood in the winner's circle with a wreath of flowers around his thick neck, his jockey smiling. I read the article carefully, looking up every word I didn't understand in the dictionary. Secretariat had won the Belmont Stakes in record time. He had become the first Triple Crown winner since 1948. I had heard about the Triple Crown and the Kentucky Derby, and I was eager to learn more. Miss Lucy walked by my desk and saw me reading intently. She looked at the newspaper and smiled. "You like horses?" she asked..

"I love horses," I replied. This was one of the few times I was interested in what I was reading.

The other articles in the newspapers I had read were frustrating because I couldn't quite understand them. I felt tortured living in a world that made no sense. "Watergate" meant nothing to me. I recognized some of the more complicated words from Spanish. President Nixon had *conspirado* to stop an *investigación*. What did "Watergate tapes" mean? No matter how many words I looked up, all I understood was that the president had done something wrong and was being investigated. There were many front-page articles about the cease-fire in Vietnam and the return of the American prisoners of war, but I didn't know what they had been fighting for. There were other articles about the environment, smog in the Los Angeles basin, and preventing oil spills along the coast.

Curaçao had a large Shell Oil refinery, to which millions of gallons of crude oil were brought by tanker from Venezuela every day, but no one talked about the environment or oil spills there. Everyone knew to stay upwind of the refinery's smokestacks; downwind the air smelled bad and people often got sick.

I turned back to the picture of Secretariat and read the last line again. Secretariat was the most extraordinary horse of the twentieth century. I stared at the picture of this magnificent horse. I looked up at the clock; it was almost three. It was time to go home. After school, I decided to visit the astrologer again. I wanted to know more about the picture Sandu had of Nadia.

Crossing Hollywood Boulevard, I could see that her storefront was dark. I walked to the entrance and peered through the dusty window. The room was empty and the door was locked. Puzzled, I looked around, wondering if I was in the right place. But I was; this was where she had been. At the thrift store next door, I asked if they knew what had happened to her. No one did. How could she have disappeared? I made my way back to her storefront, cupped my hands around my face to see better into the dark room, and peered inside again. Disturbed, I stood in front of the now-empty storefront. No trace of her remained. Disappointed, I turned back and slowly started to walk home, wondering how she could have vanished.

ૐ૦ૐ૦ૐ૦ૐ૦ૐ૦ૐ૦

INEZ HAD GIVEN ME A key to her apartment, and I let myself in to wait for her. I turned on the lava and moon lamps and put a tape of Carole King into the eight-track, took a copy of *Ms.* from the stack of magazines on her bookcase, and sank into the waterbed. Shirley Chisholm was on the cover of the January issue. The article inside was about her attempted run for president of the United States. I liked paging through *Ms.* I wished I could understand more of the articles, but my reading was not yet good enough.

"Serena, *kontá*," Inez greeted me over the sounds of "It's Too Late" and placing her oversized purse on the floor next to the bed and settling into the yellow beanbag chair, legs crossed.

"I'll boil water for tea," I said as I jumped up and went to the kitchen. The beaded curtain clicked as I passed through. "Do you have any cookies? I couldn't find any," I called to her.

"No, I don't have any cookies," she called back. I took two Corelle mugs from the wooden mug tree, filled them with hot water and put a Celestial Seasonings herbal tea bag in each one, then walked back through the beaded curtain and set them on the Parsons table.

"How was work?" I asked.

"Good! I've been making a lot of sales. Customers seem to like the advice I give them and they keep coming back. My boss is happy with me." She took a sip of her tea.

"Do you think he will give you a raise?" I asked.

"He might. I could use it. I'm saving up so that I can afford to take night classes in fashion design." Her eyes sparkled. "How are you?" she asked, tilting her head slightly toward me and raising her eyebrows.

"Well, I'm happy and unhappy at the same time."

"Let me guess. You're unhappy because of your mother," she said, pointing her finger up in the air and raising her chin to the ceiling, as if she were getting this information from above.

"Yes," I answered in a tired voice.

"Okay, tell me what that woman has done now," Inez said, and rolled her eyes.

"She hasn't done anything. It's being her daughter. I hate being so tied down with rules that don't make sense. If they made sense, I could bear it, but nothing makes any sense," I said, relieved I had someone I could talk to. "I know I'm only fourteen, but I feel much older. I feel grown up."

"Okay," Inez said, changing the subject. She had heard all of this from me before. "Tell me why you are happy." I hesitated for a moment then I looked at her.

"Sandu loves me and I love him," I beamed.

Inez pursed her lips. "Did you make love?"

"Yes, we did."

"Are you taking the pills?"

"No, my period hasn't started yet," I said.

Her mouth dropped, she inhaled sharply, and put her hand over her heart. Then she stood up and walked quickly to the kitchen. She came back and sat down next to me holding a calendar with a "Love Is" cartoon on it. She looked distressed and started firing questions at me.

"When was your last period?" Inez tapped her fingers on the calendar. She wore a mood ring, and her long nails were painted burnt orange.

"Maybe two or three weeks ago. I don't remember."

"When is your next period due?"

"I don't know," I said, uncomfortable with Inez's panic. She was scaring me. "It's just been once. Nothing can happen in only one time," I said, reassuring myself.

"Just one time can get you pregnant. Serena, you are very fertile at your age. You have to be very careful. You've got to take the pills. You've got to!" Inez punctuated her words with emphatic nods.

"I'm sorry. I wanted to show Sandu that I loved him. I wanted to be with him more than anything in my entire life. When I'm with him my whole world changes. I'm happy. I love who I am. I feel beautiful. I can't keep my eyes off him. I get excited just thinking about him." Inez looked worried. "He loves me, Inez." I reassured her. She put her arms around me and spoke gently.

"Making love is a huge decision. You have to think about the consequences. I understand your eagerness. I was your age once, and I know. I'm trying to prevent a tragedy for you and for Sandu." Her eyes grew moist. "I don't want you to have to go through what I did." She said the words sorrowfully.

"What happened to you?" I asked.

"Many years ago I fell in love with a man. He was twenty-three and I was fourteen, just like you are now." She looked at me for a moment, then stared into space. "He was from a prominent family in Surinam, and my family was poor. So we saw each other secretly. After a year, we started to make love. I didn't know about birth control. I didn't know anything, and men really don't pay attention to these things. I got pregnant." She paused as if it were too painful to recall. "His family was very upset when they found out. They thought I had done it on purpose." The corners of her mouth pulled down. "They called me a *huru* and said they'd never allow him to marry me. They sent him to the Netherlands. They forced him to choose between me and his child, or his family and his inheritance. He chose his family." A tear ran down her face. "I was sent off to my aunt in Curaçao, where our baby was born and then adopted by a Venezuelan family. I've never felt so much pain and loneliness. I wanted to die."

She wiped the tears from her face with the back of her hand, sat up, and took a deep breath. Turning to me, she said, "I know being in love and being with the man you love is the most magical time in your life, but you must be safe about it. If you are not careful, it can turn into one of the most miserable times of your life.

"I was only supposed to stay in Curaçao until the baby was born, but I liked it there. I didn't want to go back to Surinam, with all that had happened. I think my parents were glad to be rid of me. I stayed with my aunt for five years."

"What was your boyfriend's name?"

"Sergio. Sergio Kooiman," Inez said, smiling at his memory. "When I was with Sergio, I wanted to be loved by him. I wanted his approval. My world was perfect when I was with him." Inez gazed down as she spoke, remembering those moments.

"Yes, yes. That's exactly how I feel," I interrupted. "I want to kiss and hold and touch Sandu, and stay in that feeling forever. I love being with him and being wanted by him. I never thought someone like Sandu would feel this way about me."

"I know how you feel, but that will change in time. At your age, acceptance is what you are looking for in love," Inez said. "Why don't we figure out when the first day of your last period was, and when the next one should start?" She looked at the calendar. "If you decide to make love to Sandu again before you start taking the pills, you must ask him to use a condom."

I knew I would feel awkward about asking him, and anyway, I didn't want any barriers between Sandu and me. I wanted to merge completely with him. I didn't want to consider the consequences, but Inez would not let me forget them.

"Serena, does Sandu know how old you are?"

I looked down. My age was a subject I didn't want to talk about. I considered my age an inconvenience and a misfortune. I felt imprisoned by my fourteen years.

"Do you realize Sandu could go to jail for making love to you?" The words came out of Inez's mouth carefully, as if saying them slowly would soften the blow.

"How could he go to jail for that? I want him to make love to me," I protested, feeling threatened.

"You are a minor. If you're under sixteen he isn't allowed to have sex with you."

I felt the walls of the room closing in. I had finally found someone who loved me, and it now was illegal.

"That's the law in this country. You are under your mother's guardianship, and knowing her, she wouldn't think twice about sending Sandu to jail. If you were in Curaçao, someone might be able to talk her out of it, but here you have nobody. She does not like me, and you know she wouldn't like him. She'd have him locked up faster than the Curaçao wind can blow your skirt up, and you'd have nothing to say about it. You need to tell him how old you are. He is taking risks he does not even know he is taking. It's not fair to him, Serena. He needs to know, and you need to protect yourself. If you love him as much as you say you do, you will use birth control, and you will tell him your age."

Inez's voice had an urgency I had not heard before. The thought of Mama finding out about Sandu and sending him to jail frightened me. I felt tightness around my heart, and the familiar tears welled up in my eyes once again. Inez put her arms around me.

"I understand. I understand what you are going through. I understand the ecstasy and the despair. That's why I'm telling you that you have to navigate your life very carefully, so no one gets hurt." Her hazel-green eyes stared right at me, and then she pulled me close. I was grateful to have her as a friend, but I felt overwhelmed by the burden she put on me. I didn't want to have restrictions or make decisions. I just wanted to be loved by Sandu.

ᔕᕗᔕᕗᔕᕗᔕᕗᔕᕗᔕᕗ

I THOUGHT ABOUT MY CONVERSATION with Inez over the next couple of days. She was lucky she had had someone in Curaçao to help her. Her story made me homesick for Curaçao and Oma. Even while watching television, my thoughts kept drifting back home, and Oma was constantly on my mind. Mama was still working the three-to-eleven shift. Usually I went to sleep only after she came home.

The phone rang one night, at four in the morning. Hendrika got up off the couch where she slept and picked it up. "Tante Dora ... Yes, it's Hendrika. How are you?" She was speaking in Papiamentu. Mama got out of bed, and I followed her to the living room. Our phone rarely rang; we still didn't know many people here, so its ring always brought all of us around, curious to hear who was calling. The fact that this call came so early in the morning made me worry. Hendrika's face went pale. She stood motionless, staring at us, holding the phone.

Mama grabbed it out of her hand and put it to her ear. "What is it? What's wrong?" Mama's body tensed. She looked at Hendrika with a furrowed brow while she listened. Hendrika looked down at the floor. "*Ay nò*. No." Mama gasped as if something had hit her right in the heart. Her eyes filled with tears. I felt my knees weaken and my stomach drop. I walked over to Mama, who had sunk onto the couch, weeping. I had seen Mama cry before but never like this. I took the phone from her hand. My aunt was on the line and I could hear her voice repeating "Hello, Hello."

"Tante Dora, it's Serena," I said. "What has happened?"

"Serena, I have bad news. Oma's body went to rest."

"Oma," I whispered. My chest tightened and I couldn't breathe; I gasped for air. Tears streamed down my face and I slumped onto the couch. I would never see Oma again. She was gone. I put my arms around Mama. Her body softened and she let me hold her. We sat sobbing. I stroked her hair and rocked her. Hendrika bought two glasses of water with drops of valerian root. I helped Mama drink from her glass.

"Come, Mama; let's go to the bedroom so you can lie down," I said. Hendrika helped me take Mama to her bed. She curled up like a baby. I sat next to her, stroking her hair until she fell asleep. I stared at her face while she slept.

I lay down in my own bed. I hoped Oma would come and visit me before she left this world completely, just as the spirits used to visit her. I wanted to tell her I loved her, and to know she had heard me. There were so many things I still wanted to talk to her about. My tears soaked the pillow until I fell asleep.

ﮞﮞﮞﮞﮞﮞﮞﮞﮞ

OMA LOOKED BEAUTIFUL, THE WAY she looked when I was five. She was smiling and radiant.

"I knew you would visit me," I said, exhilarated. She did not say anything but her eyes were full of love. I wanted to run up and hug her, but I chose to wait. "I love you, Oma. I'm so glad you came."

Her arms opened, inviting me to hug her. I did, and although I could see her outline as if she were in her body, when I touched her she felt airy, so I was very careful.

"Follow your heart, little one. Love is all there is in the end. Never turn love into anger or hate. All material things fade away and disappear. Love is powerful and transcends everything. If you keep love alive in your heart, you will never feel lost. Remember—life is like a game. If you leave this world with more love than you came in with, you win. If you leave with less, you lose." Her image was fading.

"No, Oma, don't go. Please, don't go yet," I begged.

"I'll always be near you, *dushi*. You won't always know it. Or maybe you will."

As she faded away I tried to run after her, but there was nowhere to go.

I woke up, and it took a few moments for me to realize I was in my bed next to Mama's bed. I was happy Oma had come to me, but heartbroken she was no longer in her body.

ᘏᕉᘏᕉᘏᕉᘏᕉᘏᕉᘏᕉ

MAMA WAS SITTING UP IN bed, smoking. She had lit three scented white candles and was staring at them intently. I wanted to tell her I had seen Oma, but I needed to go to the bathroom. As I sat on the toilet, I saw a big, purple bruise on my thigh. In Curaçao, they said that if a bruise appeared on your body but didn't hurt, someone you loved was about to die and was saying good-bye. I squeezed my lips together to hold back the knot in my throat as I realized Oma had pinched me good-bye.

I went back into the bedroom. Mama's hand moved from the bed to her mouth and back down to the bed again. I heard her sniffle, between the puffs of her cigarette. She looked listless. Her eyes were swollen and red from crying. Maybe if I told her what Oma had told me, it would help her. "Mama," I whispered.

"What?" Mama responded in a weary, uninterested voice.

"Oma was here. I saw her. She talked to me."

"Oh really! Oma was my mother. Don't you think that if she was going to appear to anyone, she would appear to me?" Mama glared at me and shook her head. Her response stunned me. I couldn't understand the sudden change from sadness to anger. I continued, hoping my words could console her.

"Oma told me life is a game, and you win the game by leaving this world with more love than you came in with."

"What nonsense are you talking about?" I saw her cheeks pull down in disgust. "Are you trying to hurt me? Is this some kind of joke? How can you be so cruel?" She took a puff, her mouth tense around her cigarette. "I don't even have enough money to buy a wreath for my own mother's grave. I will be the only one that will not be at her funeral.

ᖗ 202 ᖗ

People will think I did not love her." Mama's expression changed now, her face was gripped by tension. She was glaring at me. "Of course you would not understand. You do not know what it is like to love your mother." Her words devastated me. "I can't believe that not one of my children loves me. You have no idea what I'm going through. How could God have given me four such ungrateful children?" she cried out, her hands up in the air. She pulled her shoulders back. "I keep giving, giving, and giving until there is nothing left of me. How heartless, Serena. I seem to have lost the game already because I have given love my whole life and received nothing back. How cruel of you to say that to me." She looked away. I couldn't understand how my loving dream could be seen as hateful.

"Mama, I love you and I love Oma," I tried to explain again. "We're both going to miss her." I sat on Mama's bed and put my hand on her arm, trying to make her feel my love, but it seemed I just couldn't reach her at all. I pressed on and took her left hand, the one that didn't have the cigarette, and held it. I looked at her, but she wouldn't look at me.

"Mama, I love you. I love you so much. How can I show you that I love you?" I said, wanting desperately for her to recognize my love.

"What you said shows you have no understanding of what love is," Mama said. "You would never have said what you did if you loved me. And saying you love me does not make up for the cruel and hurtful things you do." Bewildered, I searched for a way to understand what she was trying to tell me.

Mama pulled her hand away, took another puff, and stared at the wall. I sat on her bed for a moment, devastated that my love was seen as cruel and hurtful. I walked back to my bed, crawled in, and pulled the covers over my head.

ༀༀༀༀༀༀༀༀༀ

I REMEMBERED MY GRANDMOTHER'S LIVING room at her house at Penstraat 34, with its red walls, rich mahogany bookcases, and elegant ebony furniture. When I entered the room, a large, gold-leaf-framed mirror greeted me, tilted slightly down, where it hung above a marble-topped table. That mirror, we were told, could reflect images of souls alive today as well as souls departed. To the right of the mirror a doorway led to the dining room. A glass-and-wood hutch guarded the fine china and crystal from sticky hands. It also protected the *Bolo Pretu* cake, liquor, and cookies from cockroaches and greedy fingers.

I had come to help Oma make *kala*, fried balls made of ground, peeled black-eyed peas and hot peppers, a great delicacy in Curaçao because of its labor-intensive preparation and its fiery taste. Oma stood at the patio table. This was where she did most of her preparations for special meals. The table was big enough to seat three or four helpers. We took turns taking handfuls of soaked black-eyed peas, carefully rubbing off the skins, and dropping the now perfectly blond peas, one by one, into a bowl next to the pot.

"People are like black-eyed peas," Oma said. "Under their skin they are all pure and unblemished."

I asked my grandmother why Shon Lulu, our housekeeper, was not helping us.

"*Shon Lulu su kurpa no ta bon,*" my grandmother answered in Papiamentu. Shon Lulu's body did not feel well. In Papiamentu, one refers to the body as a separate part of one's total being. I asked what was wrong with her body and Oma sighed.

"She went to *Tambú* again last night."

"Do you not like Tambú, Oma?" I had never quite understood the mystery behind Tambú.

"*Mi dushi*, it's not that I don't like it. It's a very old tradition. In the slave days, Tambú was used to call the rains and ask the spirits for a prosperous year. It was also a way for the slaves to protest their circumstances in a way the slave owners wouldn't understand. Nowadays, it is used to wash away the bad luck of the old year and assure good luck for the incoming one. That's why it's only done between October and February. The dancing, drumming, and chanting are very powerful."

She took another handful of peas from the bowl and continued. "Slave owners thought it was the behavior of savages, and it frightened them so they forbade it. Because of that, Tambú was held secretly. But curiosity brought people of all colors to Tambú." Oma stopped for a moment and looked at me. "Shon Lulu likes to attend Tambú, but when she goes she wants to have a good time, and she drinks too much rum. She thinks she's enjoying herself, but her soul tells her body this kind of entertainment is not good for her." Oma took another handful of peas.

"Have you ever been to Tambú, Oma?" I asked.

"Of course, *dushi*. It can be a wonderful release. A good Tambú can bring about all kinds of changes." She looked across the table, clearly wondering if anything she'd said made sense to me. I heard faraway church bells ring noon. After the bells stopped, the kitchen radio announced, "*A muri* Maurisio Claudio Jeserum, *mihó konosí komo* Shon Mau." At noon every day, a radio broadcast gave the names of those who had died on the island during the last twenty-four hours. The name, nickname, time of death, place of the funeral service, and, most importantly, the location of the wake was announced. No one we knew had died that day.

We finished peeling the last of the black-eyed peas, and I brought the bowl of peeled peas to the kitchen while Oma brought the pot containing all the skins. The kitchen was filled with the aromas of onions, tomatoes, and island spices. Shon Lulu had finally come to work. I put my bowl on the kitchen counter and stood on tiptoe to see what Shon Lulu was cooking. She was vigorously stirring *funchi*, a cornmeal mush, to keep it from sticking to the sides of the pot. *Kabritu Stobá*, goat-meat stew, was simmering on the back burner.

Oma took two glasses out of the cupboard and poured her specially brewed tea. "I think it's time for something cold," she said cheerfully. She took down the blue-and-white-painted tin box that was kept in the cupboard next to the window, took out some cookies, and arranged them on a plate. "Come, let's sit on the porch by the sea."

We retraced our way through the dining room into the living room. She paused in front of the mirror. A shiver ran down my spine; I was afraid she was seeing a ghost. She looked at me in the mirror. "Always remember to look back so that you know where you have been," she said. "Then look around you to see where you are. Only then decide where you want to go." She pointed at the mirror and continued. "There are plenty of souls to help you along the way." I looked in the mirror for souls, but I saw only my own reflection, and decided to trust Oma. The souls would come when they were needed.

I was sure Oma would be one of those souls for me. She would always be near me, especially when I needed her. I glanced over at Mama, curled up asleep on the bed next to me. Mama, still in this world, felt farther away from me than Oma ever would.

MAMA DIDN'T GO TO WORK after the news of Oma's death. After two days the hospital called, wanting to know where she was. Hendrika told them there had been a death in our family and Mama had become ill. Mama medicated herself with sleeping pills she bought at the drugstore, and spent the days either sleeping or smoking. I watched her carefully. Even Hendrika seemed concerned. Her staying home for five days meant we had to ration our food because even when she was working six days a week we could barely pay all our bills.

I lit candles for her and made her tea, but she showed no sign of getting over her grief. After a week of being at home, Mama ran out of sleeping pills. Hendrika had to tell her we had no money to buy more. We started giving Mama strong coffee, crackers, and soup. We needed her to get well enough to return to work. Slowly she began to eat, but it took a few more days before she was strong enough to return to the hospital.

A month after Tante Dora's call, it was still difficult for me to believe that Oma was no longer alive. My heart ached every time I thought of Curaçao without Oma. I couldn't believe Oma had died before I could return; I had thought Oma would never die.

Every day, Mama went to bed as soon as she got home and stayed there until it was time for her to go back to work. Hendrika also slept most of the time. The television had become the only cheerful voice in our house. I was glad I had Inez and Sandu, and escaped to Inez's apartment every chance I could. But I had to be careful and not go too often because that would arouse Mama's suspicion.

Tuesdays and Thursdays were the happiest because those were the days I met Sandu at the Gypsy Camp and we went to his apartment. Sometimes Hendrika and I would go on Fridays, if Mama was working the three-to-eleven evening shift that week. As soon as we arrived, Hendrika would go off with her friends from Algeria and Panama. We'd meet up again at ten fifteen, just in time to walk home together. Hendrika had become less depressed and her demeanor more easygoing; everything was "far out" or "groovy." If anyone asked her how she was doing, she'd say, "Excellent to the max," nodding her head and smiling with half a smile. Hendrika didn't seem to worry about Mama anymore.

One day when I got home from school, Hendrika was on the phone with Cayetano, a Bolivian friend we had met when he worked at the Texas Instruments factory in Curaçao. He had been promoted and now worked at the company's headquarters in Texas. We were surprised and delighted to hear from him again. He had got our number from Willia, and he was calling to tell us his mother and one of his sisters were coming to visit from Bolivia. They wanted to see the United States, but they didn't know how to drive.

Cayetano didn't have time to take them on a tour of the US and asked Hendrika if she would be interested in driving them around the country for three weeks in a car he would rent for them. Hendrika was excited. She was tired of her life of housekeeping. She immediately told him she would love to do it, and started telling him about all the places they could go. Then she realized she would have to ask Mama first, and told him she would call him back.

I crossed the room to the makeshift bookcase and turned the record player on. Carly Simon's "You're So Vain" began to play. I turned the volume up and sat down next to Hendrika. We sat staring at the ceiling, each of us in our own world while we listened to the same song.

That evening, Hendrika told Mama about Cayetano's call and asked what she thought of the idea. Mama was busy organizing the things on her night stand. "First of all, he should have talked to me. It was wrong of him to ask you. He should have asked me first. Second of all, I hope he is not expecting you to drive his family around for free. You have better things to do with your life." Mama's attitude was not promising. Hendrika and I were both surprised at her reaction.

"But Mama, I'd get a vacation for three weeks. I want to go. It isn't work for me," Hendrika pleaded.

"You don't know your own worth. You have obligations. If he is willing to pay for your time, you can go. I'll talk to him." Mama sounded definite. She pulled her bedcover down and folded it.

"But Mama, he's a friend. Please don't ask him for money. That is so embarrassing."

Hendrika spoke quietly. She didn't want to upset Mama any further. I was put off by Mama's opportunism, yet I could see her point: she was the only one working and we didn't have much money.

"You want to go on vacation for three weeks and have me pay for it. I cannot believe my ears. I work myself to death, then I come home and have to take care of you two, and you want to go on vacation! Don't you have any sense of responsibility? He should pay." Mama looked up at the ceiling, stretched both arms above her head, palms turned upward as she spoke. "God, what have I done to deserve this in my life? Am I the only one that has to kill herself working? Saint Anthony, please help me, God's not listening. Nobody thinks of me, they all think of themselves. I work—they play. God, please take me to you. I don't know how to raise grateful children."

Most of what she said was in Dutch, but she switched into Spanish to speak to God, and Papiamentu to speak to the saints. I had felt jealous of Hendrika, but now I was glad I had not been invited to go on the trip.

Mama took off her shoes, put them in the closet, and changed into her nightgown. She walked over to her bed and lay down. "Serena, get me a cup of tea!" she commanded, without even looking at me. I thought about how I was going to have to cope without Hendrika for three weeks. I had taken her for granted. She was the one who kept Mama steady and made our apartment a home.

The next morning, Mama called Cayetano and told him Hendrika could go if he would pay one hundred dollars a week, a total of $300 for the three weeks. Hendrika was profoundly embarrassed as Mama negotiated her vacation. Mama, on the other hand, thought she was giving Cayetano a bargain and should have charged twice that amount since Cayetano had money and we didn't. Cayetano didn't object and the dates were set. Hendrika would leave in two weeks for her adventure.

The evening before she left, I was awake when she returned after having dropped Mama off for the eleven-to-seven over-night shift. I was in the bedroom watching television. Hendrika lay down on Mama's bed. When Mama was working, Hendrika didn't have to sleep on the couch in the living room.

"Are you excited?" I asked.

"*Ja*. It will be cool. I can't wait to go."

It was funny hearing Hendrika use American expressions with a Dutch accent.

"Do you get to plan the trip?" I asked.

"*Ja*. I've mapped it out. I've already driven across America once."

"You're taking your camera, aren't you? This time you'll be able to take all the photographs you want."

"*Ja*. Maybe I will." She hadn't been taking pictures lately, but it still surprised me that she wasn't more excited about taking photographs on the trip.

"I'm going to miss you," I said.

"I'll miss you too." She closed her eyes as she took a puff from her cigarette. "You shouldn't walk to the Gypsy Camp alone. It's not safe." She turned her head slightly to look at me, waiting to see my reaction.

"I'll ask Sandu to come here while Mama is gone."

"Be careful with Victor, the manager. He might notice and tell Mama," she said. I didn't respond. She had a point—I hadn't thought of that. "Promise me you won't walk to the Gypsy Camp alone." She said and sat up.

"Okay, I promise. I'll ask him to come here. We'll watch out for Victor."

We stopped talking. The *Johnny Carson Show* was on, with Dan Rowan and Dick Martin as guests. At the commercial break I told her again that I was going to miss her. She didn't answer. I got up, took an Almond Joy bar from my backpack, and gave it to her. Hendrika smiled. It was her favorite candy.

"Thanks. Now let's watch." We watched Johnny Carson's next guest, Bob Newhart. I looked at her, wanting to say something to make the old Hendrika come back. I wanted to tell her to take her camera so she could finally photograph all the things she hadn't photographed on our trip across America. I looked at her as she lay on the bed; she had changed so much. Her tall, thin body and her freckles were the same, but her smile and her eyes had changed. Maybe this trip would do her good and she'd come back as her old self again, although I didn't want her to leave me. I promised myself I would spend more time with her when she returned.

Hendrika had fallen asleep. I put a blanket over her, turned off the television, and went to bed.

❧❧❧❧❧❧❧❧

AFTER HENDRIKA LEFT, SEEING SANDU became more difficult. He was attending Los Angeles Valley College and was working as a waiter at an Italian restaurant at night. Our meetings became irregular. Mama worked from eleven at night until seven in the morning, and her days off rotated. On the nights she worked, Sandu could come over. He would call me from the restaurant. If Mama was home, I would pick up the phone and say, "You have the wrong number," our code that I couldn't talk. If I was alone, I'd tell him to come over. We talked for hours. Sometimes he brought food from the restaurant, and we ate, listened to music, and made love. We told each other about our pasts, and planned our future together. Sandu often told me how innocent and sweet I was, and said he would always protect me and take care of me.

One night, he told me that, if we were in Romania, he would declare his love for me on the Liars' Bridge in Sibiu. He explained that Liars' Bridge was where lovers traditionally declared their love for each other, and if one of them were not fully committed, legend had it that the bridge would collapse. I told him I wouldn't be afraid to stand on the bridge and tell him I loved him too.

Knowing that he loved me gave me the courage to finally tell Sandu that I had just turned fifteen. He raised his eyebrows and looked surprised. Then I told him that it was a crime to make love to someone less than sixteen years of age, and if Mama found out, she could have him put in jail. He could not believe such a law existed in America, the land of the free. In Romania, girls got married when they were fourteen, and some girls had sex with their boyfriends even if they weren't married. He insisted that if he met Mama she'd see his good intentions, and everything would be all right.

"People fall in love at all ages. What is this that you can only start falling in love when you are sixteen? That's crazy!"

"No, you can fall in love any time but you can't have sex before you're sixteen," I corrected him, for once knowing something he didn't. I didn't have as much hope for his meeting Mama as he did.

"What if Mama doesn't like you?" I asked.

"Then we'll run away. I'm good at that. I have experience," he joked. "We'll get married and escape. I love you and nobody is going to come between us. We are together forever. You are the sweetness in my life." He held me close as he spoke.

I was amazed at how our apartment was transformed when Sandu was there. The gloominess disappeared. Everything looked the same but nothing felt the same.

After dinner, we'd crawl into bed and watch television. He'd put on some music and we'd make love and then fall asleep. I kept an alarm clock set for five thirty in the morning. When it rang we'd make love again.

The first, faint light of dawn was the signal that our time together was coming to an end. Sandu would gather his clothes and help me straighten up the apartment. We quietly turned back into the individuals we were without each other, and anxiously awaited the next time we could become one again.

ᴣᴖᴣᴖᴣᴖᴣᴖᴣᴖᴣᴖᴣᴖ

Life alone with Mama was monotonous. I was surprised how empty the apartment felt without Hendrika. I kept busy doing all the chores she had done: cooking, laundry, and cleaning. Now Mama had to do all the driving. Our special outing was the weekly trip to the supermarket. I knew what she liked and made sure we didn't forget any of her favorite things: a five-pound can of Spanish peanuts, waffle cookies, Lipton tea, and lemons.

Sometimes after school, if Mama gave me my allowance, I'd stop by the Indian imports store. For Mama, I bought purple candles scented with cinnamon for prosperity, and frankincense cones. For myself, I bought pink candles and sprinkled them with a bit of olive oil to ward off Mama's dark moods, blue candles, which I rubbed with rosemary to improve my schoolwork, and one white candle for Oma.

Mama worked six days a week, sometimes seven. If the hospital offered her overtime she always took it. She was determined to start saving some money. She was always tired and often fell asleep in front of the television. Since Oma's death, Mama had difficulty sleeping for more than a few hours at a time. She started taking sleeping pills. Having the pills around made me nervous, and I would count them when she wasn't there. Once a week, Mama would smoke the house with incense and light candles she had sprinkled with essential oils, but even that she did halfheartedly. I turned on *Reverend Ike* for her but she told me to change the channel.

Oma's death had left Mama resigned and withdrawn. I wondered if her resignation meant she was about to enter one of her dark moods. I almost preferred it when she was angry and ranting; at least that way, I knew she wasn't in danger. I kept a watchful eye on her. I tried to smile and look happy to cheer her up, even though my heart ached and all I wanted to do was grieve for Oma.

Two weeks into Hendrika's trip, the phone rang. It was Cayetano. He said he needed to speak with Mama and that it was urgent. She was asleep. I woke her and she picked up the phone groggily. "What? *Ay nò.* This is all your fault. You are going to have to set this straight. *Dios mío,* what are we going to do?" She was wide awake now and speaking in a loud voice. I was afraid to ask what had happened. I knew it was not good. She was crying and damning Cayetano in Spanish and Papiamentu. "Serena, get me a pen!" she shouted, wiping a tear from her face.

I ran to my backpack and got her a pen. Sniffling, she wrote down a phone number and hung up. I didn't dare to ask what was wrong. I knew I'd hear about it soon enough. I went to the kitchen to prepare a cup of tea for her, adding a few drops of calming valerian root, as my grandmother would have done. I set the cup on the table in front of Mama. She stared straight at the number on the paper. I didn't know if she was talking to herself, trying to understand what she had heard, or talking to me.

"Hendrika is in jail in Washington, DC. The police stopped her because she drove through a red light. They said they found marijuana in the car and they put them all in jail. Cayetano's mother and sister claim they know nothing about the marijuana. They are putting all the blame on Hendrika." Shaking her head she paused, her shoulders slumped. "Then the police found out Hendrika does not have a valid visa, and they are going to deport her."

Mama was tightly hanging on to the paper and firmly holding back tears. "I do not believe she was smoking marijuana. It must have been Cayetano's sister." She looked at me. "We have no idea who these people are. Now look at what trouble Hendrika is in." She wiped her tears. I reluctantly nodded in agreement, but I knew the marijuana could have been Hendrika's. "Cayetano is going to have to fix this. It is all his fault. He is going to have to pay."

Mama dialed the number of the police station Cayetano had given her. They wouldn't let her speak to Hendrika. My sister would have to call her. Mama fervently prayed to Saint Jude, the saint who helps people get out of jail. She repeated her usual litany about how amazed she was that God could do this to her. I prayed, too, hoping Hendrika would come back soon.

Early the next morning, Hendrika called. Mama stood as she spoke, a hand on her hip. At first, Mama was concerned for Hendrika's safety in jail. Then came the questions about the marijuana. "Tell me, Hendrika—you can tell me the truth. It was his sister, right? She had the drugs and now they are blaming you for it, are they not?"

I could not imagine Hendrika's response to Mama's question. I thought how difficult it would be to be truthful in her situation. I knew it was Hendrika's marijuana, and I doubted Cayetano's sister would have risked bringing marijuana from Bolivia into the US, even if she smoked it. Mama choked up, telling Hendrika she'd make Cayetano take care of everything. I wasn't sure how Cayetano could take care of Hendrika's visa problems. Mama panicked when Hendrika said she was sure she was going to be deported. "But they can't do that! You have to come back here. They can't send you back to Curaçao just like that. I'll call Cayetano and tell him to get you the best lawyer. I'll call him right now." When she dialed Cayetano's number, her right hand balled into a fist.

The thought that Hendrika might not return frightened me. It wasn't only that I would miss her; it also meant Mama's attention would be focused totally on me. I would have to agree with everything she said, have her meals ready for her, and make sure she had enough cigarettes. I was going to have to keep cleaning the apartment and doing the laundry. I would need to keep assuring her I was doing well in school and that I loved it. I was going to have to watch less television and look as if I was studying more. That would make her proud of me. She was going to need to be proud of me.

Now I would be her only hope, the only one that could make her feel like she was a good mother. I needed to be responsible, studious, achieving, organized, clean, polite, attractive, and ladylike. I wished I had helped Hendrika more and appreciated all she had gone through when she had been the focus of Mama's hopes. I went to the kitchen and prepared a cup of coffee, which I set on the table next to her.

"Cayetano, the least you owe us is to get my daughter the best lawyer possible. She needs one right now. She has to come back here and then we can fight the charges." Mama paused briefly to listen, then she said, "She is married to an American citizen. They cannot just deport her! She has a husband here who needs her!" There was silence again. "That marijuana was not hers. You tell your sister to speak the truth and leave my daughter out of her drug habit. I told her she should have never gone with your family!" Mama paced back and forth, her face flushed.

The intensity of the situation made me feel sick. I stepped out onto the balcony for a breath of air, and tried to think of how I could help Hendrika. I heard Mama phone Ramón. It had been weeks since we had last seen him. He had been coming around less and less frequently, and when he did come, his visits were uncomfortable.

"*Ay*, Ramón, something terrible has happened. We need your help. Oh, it is terrible. I do not know if I can even talk about it." Now, instead of raging, Mama was crying and sniffling. I could imagine the panic Ramón must be feeling on the other end of the line. "Ramón, no, everything is not all right. Can you come over? Hendrika is in jail in Washington, DC. I need to talk to you. Yes, tomorrow is fine. Thank you, Ramón, you are a blessing."

I went to the bathroom and sat on the toilet; it was the only place in the apartment I could be alone. I thought about all the different schemes Mama had tried, and how unlikely it was Hendrika would be coming back. I knew that if Mama could not bring Hendrika home, she might fall into one of her dark moods again. I knew what I had to do: I would watch everything she did; I would check all the pills in the house and count them; I would check to see if there was any rat poison in the house, and watch her very carefully around the knives. I felt my throat tighten. The double burden of being the only one who could make Mama's life worth living, and being vigilant enough to keep her from slipping into a dark mood was overwhelming. I longed for Oma, Willia, Hendrika, Johan, or even Ramón to help me, but I was alone.

When I came out of the bathroom, Mama announced that Ramón was coming over the next day to help figure out how to rescue

Hendrika. I pretended I was napping when Mama went to work. I didn't want to talk to her—I wanted to talk to Sandu. That night, he didn't call. Whenever I didn't hear from him, I felt unsure of myself. I knew he couldn't come over every night, but not knowing if he was going to call left me agonizing over whether he still loved me. It seemed as if everything in my life I really loved disappeared. I was afraid Sandu would soon disappear as well.

When Ramón arrived at two the next afternoon, Mama was still sleeping. "*Hola Chiquita*," he greeted me in a quiet voice, as if there had been a death in the family. We hugged, and I signaled him to step outside. We walked downstairs and stood in the courtyard next to the dying, untended tropical plants.

"Please tell me, Ramón. What is the problem? Why can't Hendrika come back here?" I leaned on his strong arm, cherishing his support. I needed someone to talk to.

"*Chiquita*, there are many problems. I have learned that Hendrika should have gone back to Curaçao immediately after our wedding. There she should have petitioned the American Consulate in Curaçao for a temporary visa to be with me, her husband, until her residency card could be granted. She didn't do that. Now there is this new problem of the drugs, and I can't help with that. I promised your mother I'd help Hendrika get her green card, but I don't know what I can do about this. And there is one more thing." He hesitated a moment, and looked down at me. "I have fallen in love. Her name is Maria. She is sweet and kind, and she is in love with me." A wistful smile lit his face as he spoke, the smile that only appears when one is truly in love.

"Why is that a problem? Doesn't she know you only married Hendrika so she could get her papers?"

"I have not told her anything yet. I don't know how to handle this."

"So Hendrika should have gone back to Curaçao?"

"Yes, you can't just stay here with an expired tourist visa. A green card usually takes two to three years. Sometimes they give it, sometimes not, depending on whether they think the marriage is real or fake. She never got that temporary visa because your mother didn't have the money for her to go back to Curaçao. Now the authorities in Washington, DC have discovered she has broken federal law by overstaying her original visa. This is not good." He shook his head. "She is in this country illegally. Then there are these drug charges. That is a disaster. When they review her case, they will look at all these issues, and probably say this lady is not respectful of our laws and refuse her green card application.

"*Chiquita*, I don't want to have to wait two or three years until Hendrika fails to get a green card in order to divorce her so I can marry Maria. I'd marry Maria tomorrow if only I could." A pained look crossed his face. Disappointing us was obviously difficult for him.

"Mama will feel betrayed and she will get very angry with you," I said, warning him his meeting with Mama was going to be extremely unpleasant.

"Will you forgive me, *Chiquita*?" he asked in a pleading tone, his head cocked to one side.

"There is nothing to forgive, Ramón. You are the best," I said and gave him the biggest hug I could muster. Then I pulled back and looked him straight in the eye. "I'm so glad you are in love. Isn't it wonderful? It makes all the pain in life go away, doesn't it?"

"Ah, *Chiquita*, you speak as if you also are in love."

"I am, I am, with the most wonderful man in the whole wide world." We were holding each other's hands as we spoke, as if we were children telling each other secrets.

"Does your mother know?" Ramón asked.

"No. Not yet," I answered in a sad voice.

"Then please don't tell me about it because I don't want to get in any more trouble. I'm very happy for you, but it's better if I do not know."

Again, I could sense he didn't want to disappoint me, but his need to disentangle himself from us diminished his ability to be my friend. "I understand, Ramón. Really, I understand," I said. We hugged again. I knew as soon as anyone refused to help Mama they would be banned from seeing the entire family. She had done that many times.

"*Pues ha llegado la hora*, the time has come." He stretched up to his full height as he pointed to our apartment door.

"*Suerte Ramón, mucha suerte y siempre estaré agradecida*," I said, wishing him luck and telling him I would always be grateful.

We climbed the stairs to our front door. He went in, but I stayed outside and watched through the closed kitchen window. Ramón and Mama sat down on the living room couch. Ramón's face was grave as he seemed to plead for her understanding. His hands moved and I guessed he was trying to explain his new situation to Mama. Slowly, the expression on her face tightened. She sat rigidly, her back no longer touching the sofa. Ramón leaned toward her and tried to place his hand on her shoulder. She stood up and looked down at him. He put one hand to his heart as he gestured with the other. He stood up. Mama wagged her index finger at him and then threw her hands up in the air. Ramón seemed to be shrinking. He took a step back. Mama moved forward. He took another step back and she moved forward again. Then he walked toward the front door and opened it. I heard Mama shout, "An Indian from the mountains of Perú should feel privileged to marry a European."

I wondered how we had suddenly become Europeans. Then I realized Mama was referring to our Dutch passports. Ramón didn't reply. He walked past me quickly and left.

I had watched as he appealed for her understanding about wanting to marry his newfound love. He needed to get out of the legal relationship with Hendrika, which, at this point, was hopeless as a means of getting her a green card, anyway. I got a chill—Mama had dismissed all the help Ramón had given us. She had even twisted the situation around to make it seem as if he was benefiting from the marriage because he was of a lower social class.

Ramón had looked devastated as he walked by me. My heart ached for him. Mama's words echoed in my ears, "An Indian from the mountains of Perú should feel privileged to marry a European." Mama had treated Ramón exactly the way Opa's family had treated her.

THE PHONE RANG. IT WAS the Netherlands Embassy in Washington, DC. I handed Mama the receiver. She sat with a straight back as she spoke her best Dutch without a trace of a Curaçao accent. In the pragmatic and unemotional manner of the Dutch, she explained to the embassy that Hendrika was married to an American citizen and should not be deported. She argued about the immigration rules and regulations, but the embassy must not have been interested because Mama fell silent; she stared off into the distance and I saw her cheeks sag. "But ... but ...," Mama tried to interrupt. Slowly her body slouched. "I understand," Mama mumbled. "I understand."

I got two glasses of water and dissolved ten drops of valerian root extract in each one. Mama was sitting on the couch. I handed her a glass. "Hendrika is going to be deported tomorrow," Mama said, her voice cracking as if the news was breaking her. I felt my heart in my throat but I held back my tears. I needed to be strong for Mama.

At seven o'clock in the morning, ten o'clock in Washington, DC, Mama called the jail. She demanded to speak to Hendrika but was told again she would have to wait for Hendrika to call her. I stayed home from school with Mama to wait for Hendrika's phone call. The television was on all day even though neither Mama nor I were watching. Mama was busy organizing bills, letters, and documents into neat stacks on the dining table. At three in the afternoon the phone rang. Mama picked it up on the first ring. "Oh, Hendrika, how are you?" Mama cried out. "I know. The embassy called me ... Call Tante Dora when you get to Curaçao. Maybe you will be able to stay with her ... Yes. And we will get you back here. God cannot do this to me. He will bring you back to me. Yes ... Okay. Here is Serena." Mama's words sounded reassuring, but she was crying. She handed me the phone but stood watching over me while I spoke.

"Hendrika, how are you?" I asked, my voice trembling.

"I'm okay, Serena. I'm sorry about all this. Look, you have to take care of Mama. Watch her moods and make sure she doesn't hurt herself. I'm sorry." Hendrika started to cry. "I'm so sorry," she repeated.

"But aren't you coming home first? Are they sending you directly back to Curaçao?" I was really afraid of being on my own with Mama.

"Yes. They're sending me back from here."

I squeezed my eyes closed, trying to push the tears away, and took a deep breath. "It's okay, don't worry. I can take care of everything here. You'll be back before you know it," I said. It was easier to deceive ourselves than to face the truth. "I love you," I whispered. She heard me.

"I love you too," she mumbled. I handed the phone back to Mama. She grabbed it eagerly out of my hand and was relieved that Hendrika was still on the line, even though there was nothing left to say but good-bye.

ᘓᕀᘓᕀᘓᕀᘓᕀᘓᕀᘓᕀᘓᕀ

I NEEDED TO STUDY IF I was going to do well in school, but it was difficult to concentrate even though it was very quiet in our apartment. Neither Mama nor I said much to each other. My mind would wander from Mama to Hendrika to Sandu. Suddenly, I'd get anxious about not having watched Mama carefully enough. When I was in school I wanted to call her, but I was afraid I might wake her up if she were sleeping. I kept thinking about Hendrika being deported and what she would do in Curaçao. I hoped that returning to Curaçao would be good for her and that Willia could help her. With everything that had been happening to us, I hadn't seen Sandu in two weeks. That worried me. The days crept by. I knew that if I were going to stay sane I would have to organize my life into compartments: my life with Mama, and my life with Sandu. I felt frustrated.

I knew Mama wanted me to get a good education, but no matter how hard I tried, I couldn't accomplish it. I felt guilty that she was wasting her hard-earned money. Mama had sacrificed a lot for me. Part of me wanted to succeed at school, but a bigger part of me wanted to run away and leave all this behind; I did both. With Sandu I was running away. When I was with him all my sorrows and anxiety were suspended and I was happy. When I was in school I tried my best to study, but it didn't make a difference. The school was terrible. It wasn't a school—it was a holding station. The teachers didn't teach, they just watched the students and answered questions. As soon as I got home I had to pay careful attention to Mama. I felt lucky to have Inez to help me navigate between my heaven and my hell.

A week after Hendrika's deportation, I told Inez the details of Ramón's last visit. She was not surprised at how Mama had treated him.

"Your mother probably considers me lower class too," she said mockingly.

I didn't tell her that Mama did indeed consider her lower class and not worthy of our association. I mentioned that Mama was still in a dark mood and that I was worried about her. Inez said that Hendrika's leaving was a huge loss for Mama, and that it was to be expected that she would be sad. She asked if Mama had any friends or if anyone came to visit. I told her Mama had no one. Inez thought for a moment. She suggested that it might be a good idea for Mama to meet Sandu. Mama might like him because of his blond hair and white features. She cautioned me not to introduce him as my boyfriend but just as a friend. If Mama liked him, it might cheer her up. Simply having a visitor might make her feel better. I was excited. Inez's suggestion brought the two most important people in my life together.

Mama was sleeping when I got home. Mr. McNaughton, the headmaster of Andrew McNaughton School, had given me a white envelope to take to her. I opened the kitchen drawer where she kept her unanswered mail. I noticed that there were several white envelopes lying under the stack of unanswered mail. They were the same as the one I held in my hand. Curious, I pulled a sheet of paper out of one. It was an overdue notice. Every month for the past six months the headmaster had given me an envelope, and here they all were, stashed away in this drawer.

I opened the one I had just received. There was more than three thousand dollars due. Mama had not paid my school tuition for eight months; she had been paying only the late charges. I couldn't see how she could possibly pay what she owed the school. I hadn't realized how difficult it was for Mama to pay my school bills, and I felt guilty that I wasn't learning anything. I stuffed the envelopes back in the drawer and started to make dinner. I didn't want to add to Mama's burdens, now that Hendrika was in trouble. I decided to cook something special for dinner—it was Mama's first night off in nine days.

Sandu was eager to meet Mama also because it had been so difficult for us to see each other behind her back. He was working hard and saving money. He wanted to move out of the shared apartment at Normandie and Third and into a place of his own in the San Fernando Valley. He had worked his way up as a waiter to serving at La Serre, the best French restaurant in Los Angeles. He'd tell me tales of serving movie stars and famous singers. He talked about transferring from Los Angeles City College to Valley College because it had a better arts program. Unlike my life, Sandu's life had gotten better. He was taking full advantage of the opportunities America had to offer him.

I pondered how to bring up the subject of meeting Sandu with Mama. Finally, I just told her that I wanted her to meet someone I knew. I explained that I had met him a while ago and he had become a friend.

"What kind of friend?" Mama asked.

"Someone I've been studying with. He helps me with my English."

"Hmm—a boy. Well, he can come over as long as you straighten up the apartment. I work all night. I do not have time to entertain your friends."

"That's fine, Mama. I'll take care of everything."

ᘔᗑᘔᗑᘔᗑᘔᗑᘔᗑᘔᗑ

SANDU WAS GOING TO COME over on Tuesday afternoon, Mama's day off. He arranged to work the closing shift that night at the restaurant, so there would be plenty of time for his visit. I was nervous but determined not to show it. I cleaned the apartment and baked Dutch cookies the way Mama had taught me. I took out teacups, saucers, sugar bowl, and teapot, and cleaned them. I opened a blue paper napkin and placed it on the serving tray to hide the scratches, then arranged the cups and saucers on it. I wanted everything to be perfect. Although I had done all I could to cheer Mama up, her unhappiness prevailed. I tried to tell her about Sandu's achievements, how he was working and going to school, how he was trying to qualify for a scholarship to the world-renowned Art Center School of Design. "Oh, an artist. How disappointing," was her only comment.

Sandu arrived with twelve white roses and a box of Swiss chocolates for Mama. I greeted him at the door with a casual hello. Mama was seated on the couch. As I introduced Sandu to her, she remained seated and stuck out her right hand for him to shake. After they shook hands he offered her the flowers and chocolates.

"Thank you," she said formally. "You may give them to Serena."

I immediately stepped in. "Here, let me put the flowers in a vase. They are gorgeous, Sandu. Thank you. They'll brighten up the apartment." I opened the chocolates and offered one to Mama. She refused. I felt she was trying to be superior. Disappointed, I offered Sandu one.

"Oh, thank you, no," he said. "I want you to enjoy them all."

"These are lovely," I said, taking one. "Thank you, Sandu." I hummed as I took a bite. Sandu appeared uncomfortable; it was obvious Mama was making no attempt to make him feel welcome.

"Nice painting," Sandu commented, pointing to the poster of sand dunes on our wall.

"I am not used to living like this," Mama answered, looking down her nose.

"I understand," Sandu said. "Serena has told me about the life you left behind."

I brought in the cookies and offered Mama one. She shook her head. I offered them to Sandu. He took one. I put them on the coffee table and sat down at the other end of the couch.

"Hmmm, these are wonderful. Did you make them?" Sandu asked me.

"Yes," I said proudly, looking at Mama. "It's my mother's recipe."

"These are very European. Your mother must be a great cook. You are learning from the best." Mama did not react to his compliment. She leaned forward and drew a cigarette from the pack on the table.

"Do you smoke?" she asked Sandu.

"No, thank you," Sandu said, but he jumped up to take a box of matches from the restaurant out of his pocket. "Please, allow me." He struck the match. Mama sat up straight with her legs crossed. She leaned forward. I could see a slight gleam in her eye. She liked Sandu's attentiveness. "Serena tells me you are a nurse. That is a noble profession," Sandu said as he sat back down.

"Actually, I'm a midwife, although at the moment I am working as a nurse. Nursing is not what it used to be. It used to be a privilege for a woman to be educated. Only upper-class women used to be nurses, but now anybody can become one. I have to work with Filipinos, Taiwanese, and Vietnamese." Mama looked haughty. I hadn't seen her adopt this attitude in a long time.

"I understand," Sandu said again. "My mother attended finishing school and then studied to become a school teacher, not because she was planning to work, but because it was important to have an education."

"Where are you from?" Mama asked, with mild interest.

"I am from Romania. Sibiu, Romania."

"Oh, Eastern Europe," Mama asked, raising one eyebrow. Her interest was waning.

"Yes. Romania is a beautiful country. I think you would like it."

"Hmmm," Mama grunted and looked away. There was silence. I poured the tea. Sandu was looking at me. We had discussed the best time for him to bring up the subject of going out with me. I nodded at him, encouraging him to ask the question. "Mrs. Ferreira-García, I would like to ask your permission to take your daughter out." He tried to sound honorable.

"Is that the purpose of this visit?"

Her stiff response was discouraging. I interrupted them. "No, no." I tried to backtrack. "When I met Sandu, I realized we had so much in common I thought you might enjoy meeting him."

"Sandu, tell me why you think I should let my fifteen-year-old daughter go out with you? How old are you?" Mama asked with authority.

"I am twenty-two." Sandu's face was serious.

"I do not think a twenty-two-year-old man has any reason to go out with a fifteen-year-old girl, other than bad reasons," Mama shot back, glaring at him. No one spoke. Sandu's face tightened. I could see Mama had offended him.

"I'll get some more tea," I said, rushing back to the kitchen. I brought out a fresh pot of tea, even though our cups were still full, and set it on the table. "It's nice and hot," I said, hoping to get the conversation going in a more amicable direction. "Would you like a cookie, Mama?"

Mama took a cookie but didn't say a word.

"Serena and I are good friends, Mrs. Ferreira-García. I really admire your daughter and only have the best of intentions," Sandu said earnestly.

"Best of intentions. Hah! What best of intentions? Don't be ridiculous! Don't you think I know what your intentions are? I was not born yesterday. If you think bringing me flowers and chocolates means I will allow you to go out with my daughter, you'd better take them with you and try another address." Mama stood, looking down at him contemptuously. "My daughter will not be going out with you."

Sandu immediately stood up. "But Mrs. Ferreira-García ..."

Mama crushed out her cigarette in the ashtray. "This conversation is over. Good-bye, Sandu." Sandu automatically offered his hand to her, but Mama had already turned around and was walking to the bedroom. I could see Sandu's jaw muscles clench and his lips tighten. The hand he had offered Mama was now balled into a fist.

"I'm sorry. That didn't go very well," I muttered, and tried to put my hand on his shoulder, but he walked to the door. "Wait, wait!" I called after him. He stopped halfway down the stairs. "So what does this mean?" I asked, looking down at him. He clicked his tongue and pushed his lower lip out.

"I came to do the right thing and all she did was act like an old Gypsy woman. She looks like one, too." He exhaled sharply in disgust. He was talking about Mama, but I felt as if he had just insulted me. He came back up the stairs, put his arm around me, and pulled me close. I resisted. His words hurt me.

"She will not keep us apart," he whispered. "Nobody can keep us apart." I felt reassured, although his anger made me uncomfortable. "I love you. I will take care of you and protect you. We'll see each other whenever we can." His body relaxed and he kissed me. Relieved that he still loved me, I kissed him back.

"Thank you for loving me," I said. I didn't feel worthy of his love and I was grateful for it. He kissed me on the cheek and left.

"I'll call you," he said over his shoulder.

I walked back into the apartment and picked up the teacups and cookies. I felt as if I were cleaning up a battlefield—all good intentions shattered, all hope demolished. I put a chocolate in my mouth and admired the ones left in the box. Each one was different, beautifully molded in a variety of intricate geometric shapes. The white roses were still in the kitchen. I put them into a tall glass vase, arranged them a bit, and carried them to the dining table. I sat down on the couch and stared out through the sliding glass doors.

I felt terribly lonely. Mama never seemed to be satisfied, and constantly sought something that remained always beyond her reach. I remembered the fiasco of the Colombian gold mine.

ɜɯɜɯɜɯɜɯɜɯɜɯ

AT FIRST WE WERE EXCITED, hopeful about our new life in Colombia. Mama rented a large house in the best part of Bogotá. She hired a housekeeper, a cook, a maid, and a chauffeur. The first months she spent decorating the house. Every day, she took us along on her shopping sprees. She was ecstatic. We visited the fanciest stores in Bogotá. The salesmen would offer her a glass of wine and bring us cookies and lemonade. Mama had great taste; she chose modern furniture, Colombian antiques, and indigenous Indian artifacts. The house was in a perpetual state of Christmas, with boxes arriving daily.

She taught the cook a few of her favorite European recipes. She trained the housekeeper in European etiquette: how to set the table, which glasses to use with which wines, what foods to serve on which plates, the difference between a fish knife and a dinner knife, and a salad fork and a dinner fork. Her staff adored her; they had never worked for anyone who had actually taught them anything. They usually learned in a haphazard manner from other housekeepers, and were yelled at if anything was wrong.

Everyone was impressed with Mama's taste and sense of style. She dressed impeccably and was happy when people admired her. She went to the hairdresser every week, and she had her nails painted red. She invited the neighbors over for tea and had weekly dinner parties, in her attempt to become part of the social circle.

At home we were treated like royalty. Our beds were made for us in the morning and turned down every night. A sweet snack and tea waited for us when we returned home from school. Even our underwear was ironed.

The money my father sent every month was not enough to cover Mama's extravagances. After about a year, the atmosphere in the house changed and life at home became very tense. Slowly, the dinner parties stopped and the meals were not as lavish as they had been. Mama let the housekeeper go. The woman cried and offered to work without pay until the situation got better, but Mama was adamant. Mama no longer went to the hairdresser every week and her nails were not painted. She seemed worried and irritable. Once again she searched for a way to get rich. Colombia was famous for its minerals, so she set out to buy a mine.

Now Mama dressed every morning in jeans and a T-shirt, and left with the chauffeur. They visited humble pueblos in the foothills of Bogotá, asking if anyone knew of mines in the area. She asked the villagers to spread the word to the Indians in the mountains that she was looking for a gold, silver, or precious-stone mine.

The mood in the house changed again. Two or three visitors showed up every day with information about mines. Mama was optimistic. She was sure one of these visitors would bring her the information that was going to make her rich. She had let the cook and the maid go. She was saving most of the money my father sent for our expenses each month to buy a mine. No one picked up after us anymore, and no snacks were waiting after school. We were cleaning the house ourselves and cooking our own meals. Our menu consisted of pasta with tomato sauce, beans and rice, and, once a week, chicken.

The chauffeur became Mama's right-hand man in the mine project, so he still had his job. Some of the furniture she had bought on monthly payments was taken back.

It was a Sunday morning. The seven forty-five church bells rang, warning there were fifteen minutes until Mass. There was a knock on our front door. My brother Johan went to see who it was. He let in a six-foot-tall Indian about forty years old, dressed in khaki pants and a green shirt. His hair was tied in a ponytail that hung down to his shoulders, and he wore a colorfully woven band around his head. The Indian explained that he owned a gold mine, but didn't have the money to develop it. He was willing to sell. He had brought pieces of gold from the shaft and photographs of many veins in the mine. Mama and the chauffeur were very excited. Maps were spread on the floor, showing the route to the mine. Two fistfuls of gold-bearing rocks lay on the coffee table next to scattered pictures of the mine and the deed testifying to the Indian's ownership.

Hendrika, Willia, Johan, and I peered from our bedrooms, listening to every word. Mama and the chauffeur excused themselves and went to the kitchen to discuss the offer. We couldn't hear what they were saying. They came back to the living room with determined strides and smiles on their faces. Mama told the Indian she'd buy the gold mine as soon as she could verify at the provincial courthouse that he really was the owner. The Indian was to return on Tuesday to transfer ownership and pick up the purchase money. The following Sunday, Mama and the chauffeur were to meet him at Pueblo San Joaquín, and from there the Indian would take them to the mine. He told them to wear comfortable clothes because part of the journey would be by donkey.

We all stood by the front door the next week, waving good-bye as Mama climbed into the car our chauffeur owned. She was dressed in blue jeans and a denim long-sleeved shirt, short boots, and a big hat. The chauffeur stuffed her large backpack into the trunk along with her thick, woolen poncho. "We are going to be rich," she said in Spanish as she waved back to the four of us. Although he was only fifteen, Johan was left in charge because he was a boy.

Two weeks went by slowly. We played games and invited friends to the house. We were afraid at night, so we befriended the watchman. All the rich neighborhoods of Bogotá had a watchman patrolling the streets from dusk till dawn. The house had become our playground and bore little resemblance to the orderly place Mama had left behind. There were clothes lying around, dishes left where we had eaten, books, records, and games scattered everywhere, and there was mud on the floor. After thirteen days, it was time to clean the house and put things back in order. Mama was due home any day. Sixteen days went by and Mama was still not back. On the seventeenth day, the chauffeur's car pulled up in front of our house. Mama and the chauffeur looked exhausted.

She got out of the car and asked, "Is everyone okay?"

"Yes, we're fine. Everyone is fine," my brother said. Without saying anything further, Mama walked through the house and into her bedroom and closed the door. The chauffeur sat down in the living room with all of us.

"The trip was a great disappointment," he said. "We drove to Pueblo San Joaquín. It took us two days to get there. At San Joaquín we met the Indian who guided us the rest of the way. We drove for another two days up into the mountains. The roads were bad. The last day there were only dirt roads. I was afraid my car was going to break down. Then we arrived at a village named Socorro. There we mounted donkeys to go the rest of the way. We rode all day, and in the evening we camped.

"Finally, at the end of the third day of riding, we came to the mouth of the mine. The entrance was located on the top of a four-hundred-foot cliff. A narrow ledge about a mile long led us to the opening. Your mother is an extremely brave woman. She never complained; she was never afraid; she was determined. When we got to the mine the gold was there, but getting it out was going to cost more than the mine was worth. She was devastated. We took what we could carry from the mine and strapped it on the donkeys. It was getting dark when we headed back down and the donkeys seemed restless. There was nowhere to camp for miles, so we had to continue in the dark on the narrow path, until it widened. By moonlight we picked a campsite. The next day we rode all day.

"That evening at about midnight, our campsite was raided. There were five men with pistols, and bandanas across their faces. Two of them stood pointing their guns at us as we lay on the ground, while the other three took everything. When they were finished, they shot their guns in the air and rode off. They obviously knew we had just come from the gold mine. We had to walk all the way back to Socorro. We were thirsty and hungry and had no water or food. Thank God my car was still parked where I had left it." The chauffeur pointed his finger up in the air. "You have to be clever in this world! I keep five hundred pesos under the seat of my car in a special compartment I made. When we got back we used that money to buy food and rent a room at the village pension. We barely had enough to get home."

The chauffeur stopped talking. We were huddled around him, listening as if he had been telling us a fairy tale. We couldn't believe this story was about our mother. "Now children, I must go home and see how my family is. Take good care of your mother."

With that, the chauffeur left. At about eight o'clock in the evening we still had not seen Mama. Willia decided to knock on her door, but there was no answer. She knocked again. She opened the door and found Mama sound asleep. Willia shook her to see if she was all right, but Mama didn't wake up. Next to her bed was an empty pill bottle. My brother called the doctor who came right away. When Mama opened her eyes, they were glazed and distant. She lay in bed, moaning repeatedly. *"Estamos arruinados,"* she said. We were ruined.

I looked at the white roses Sandu had brought. No matter how many times I told Mama that I loved her, she didn't believe me. Mama believed love was something that could not survive without money. Her willingness to distance herself from her family in order to chase prosperity around the world baffled me. She thought she could only be loved if she were rich.

ↄ♥ↄ♥ↄ♥ↄ♥ↄ♥ↄ♥ↄ♥

AFTER SANDU LEFT, I SAT in the living room, thinking how my brother and sisters had tried to earn Mama's love and approval. But each had finally left with injured souls and bleeding hearts, with no idea why they were not worthy of Mama's love.

Mama was busy in the kitchen, making herb tinctures. She hadn't found the same essential oils she had used in Curaçao, so she made her own tinctures with ethyl alcohol and ground herbs.

She was surrounded by cinnamon, cloves, and nutmeg; peppermint for wealth; lavender for chastity and tranquility; and star anise for psychic power. She ground each spice into a fine powder with a mortar and pestle. "Serena, what are you doing?" Mama called from the kitchen.

"Nothing, Mama. I was just resting," I said, startled.

Mama walked into the living room. "Resting from what? Why haven't you done the laundry? You haven't done anything today. Oh God, why me? What do you have against me?" Mama pleaded with God as she looked for her cigarettes.

I jumped up, went into the kitchen, and started washing the dishes. The kitchen sink was overflowing, herb bottles were scattered across the counter, and crushed herbs stained the grout between the counter tiles. Mama followed me back into the kitchen, a lit cigarette in her hand.

"Baking cookies for that man—that's all you've done today. Why aren't you studying? I'm paying thousands of dollars for your education. Serena, you are my only chance. Please try your best," she pleaded. "If you do not go to college my life will have been wasted. I will have sacrificed my entire life for nothing. Not one of my children has made anything of themselves," she said, her face only inches away from mine. "Serena, you can't let me down." She grasped my chin and turned my face toward hers. "You must do well, Serena. I am only living for you. I have nothing else left to live for."

The only way for me to show her that I loved her was to succeed in school, and I wasn't sure I could do that.

I LEANED ON A SHELF at the DMV, quietly checking off each answer on the multiple-choice driver's license test. I was fifteen and a half, and eager to get my learner's permit. I felt uncomfortable around government officials because I was afraid they might discover I was in the country illegally. Mama sat across the room, waiting for me to finish. By now I could read English slowly but writing was still difficult. I had to read each question two or three times and a few of them were tricky. For those I prayed to Saint Thomas, the patron saint of examinations, and Saint Louis, the patron saint of learning languages; then I guessed at the answer.

When I finished, I took my answer sheet to the test window to be graded, handing the sheet to the gray-haired man behind the counter and waiting as he checked it over. His pen circled an answer, then another, and then another. My heart raced. Finally, he looked up. "You've passed your written test. Please proceed outside to take the driving test." I felt like cheering when I also passed the driving test but I just said, "Thank you," with a timid smile. Mama let me drive home.

⁊ᴥ⁊ᴥ⁊ᴥ⁊ᴥ⁊ᴥ⁊ᴥ

I OFTEN STOPPED BY INEZ'S apartment on my way home from school. I would tell Mama I had been studying at the library, to cover my absences. Inez gave me tips on the latest fashions and asked me how things were going. There was amazingly little happening in my life, so I'd usually ask her to tell me about hers.

I lived vicariously through the stories Inez told me. I wanted to be old enough to live a life like hers. She and her boyfriend, Mark, had friends with whom they went out to dinner, to movies, discos, plays, and concerts. I used to close my eyes as Inez told me where she had gone, pretending I was there with her. Her life seemed luxurious to me. Mama didn't have money for such luxuries. Once every few months, Mama and I went to the movies. That was a very special treat.

Late one Tuesday afternoon, I was paging through one of Inez's magazines while she washed dishes. "Hey, Inez, does it matter if you're on the pink pills and you don't get your period?"

Inez stopped what she was doing and came to where I was sitting. "What? What did you say?"

"What happens if your period doesn't come while you're taking the pink pills?"

"Oh, Serena! It means you are probably pregnant! What happened?"

"I don't know."

"How long has it been since you started taking the pink pills?" Inez remained motionless as she spoke. She looked very serious.

"Well, I've started on the second set of pink pills and no period," I said quietly, not really wanting to say the words.

"Did you skip any days?"

"No. Well, maybe a day or two," I said. I had been hoping if I ignored the problem it would go away.

"Serena." Inez came to sit next to me. She put her arm around me. "We need to take you to a doctor, so we can find out for sure, and if you're pregnant, how far along."

"I don't know a doctor."

"I'll find you a doctor." We sat in silence. "How will Sandu feel about this?" she asked.

"I don't know," I replied miserably.

"What about your mother?"

"No. I'm not telling her." I shook my head. "If I'm pregnant I can't tell her." The possibility of Mama finding out that I might be pregnant sent shivers down my spine. She was working hard, and I knew that after Hendrika's deportation she would not be able to bear this. "How will you find a doctor?" I asked.

"Don't worry about that. I will make an appointment for you tomorrow with my doctor. We need to do this as soon as possible." Inez looked straight into my eyes. "Have you thought about what you are going to do if you are pregnant?"

"No. But I don't think I have many choices." Inez gave me a half smile and hugged me.

A week passed before I saw Sandu again. He still came over on his night off, but only when it didn't coincide with Mama's night off. As soon as he came into our apartment he noticed something was wrong.

"What's the matter, Serena? What's happened? Is it your mother again?"

"No, it's not Mama, Sandu. It's me. I'm pregnant."

The muscles in his jaw moved as he sat there, thinking. His silence worried me. I was afraid he was angry. "Did you not take your pills?"

"Yes, I did take the pills," I said. "I only missed two days. That shouldn't really matter, but it did. I went to the doctor on Monday. He said I was pregnant." I tried to hold back my tears.

Sandu took my hand. "Then it was meant to be. We will get married and have this baby that came to us."

My eyes opened wide in disbelief. I was speechless. I wanted to fall into his arms. Instead, I didn't move and all that came out of my mouth was, "What about Mama?"

Sandu didn't see the gravity of the situation right away. "I will ask your mother to allow me to marry you. She isn't going to want to leave you unmarried now that you're pregnant." He spoke with genuine affection.

I wished it could be as simple as he thought. "Sandu, if we tell Mama she will be very angry. She could even put you in jail." My voice was shaking. I felt weak.

"She wouldn't do that." He pulled back and he looked at me from under his eyebrows. "She wouldn't do that, would she?" he repeated.

"Yes. Yes, she would. She can be mean. She likes to feel powerful over others and this would be a perfect chance for her to show me, and you, who's boss." I was ashamed the person I was describing was my own mother. Sandu wiped away the tears that had welled up in the corners of my eyes and embraced me.

"Let's run away, Serena. Let's run far, far away. We'll find a church and get married. We'll go to San Francisco. I will get a job as a waiter, and I will work two jobs and we'll make it. You can keep going to school until the baby comes and, when you're ready and the baby is bigger, you can finish your school. We'll both work and I'll go to school and work."

Sandu spoke eagerly, as if the whole situation were ideal and all we had to do was make one decision: the decision to go. All I saw were the problems. I hadn't had any real schooling since I'd left Curaçao over two years ago. I didn't see myself graduating from anything, let alone getting a job. On top of that, I knew Mama needed someone to pin her hopes on or she would feel her life had no purpose. It frightened me to think that my running away could sink Mama into another dark mood. I didn't feel confident that Sandu would still love me if he knew all this. I loved who I was in his eyes, and I didn't want him to see the parts of myself that I hated. "I can't, Sandu. I just can't." The words fell like stones from my mouth.

He looked shattered. His eyes seemed to penetrate me. "Why not? What's the matter? I don't understand. Why won't you marry me? Tell me, Serena, why won't you marry me?" Suddenly insecure, he pulled away and looked at me sternly.

"There are so many other things that affect us. You don't understand," I pleaded.

"Then help me understand. What you're saying doesn't make any sense to me. If you loved me, you'd marry me and we'd have our baby." He looked puzzled. I cried. "Why are you crying? This should be a happy moment. What's the matter, Serena?" In between sobs and shudders I tried to explain to him about Mama. "I love you,

Sandu, more than I thought I could love anyone. I want to marry you and have this baby, but you don't understand." I paused. "Mama has made a lot of sacrifices for her children and she feels as if all her sacrifices have been in vain. Not one of us has turned out the way she wanted. I'm her last chance and if I disappoint her I don't know what she might do. My being pregnant would be too big a shock for her to bear." I wondered if he knew what I meant.

"Are you sure?" he asked.

"Yes, I'm sure," I whispered, wishing for a doubt. I needed Sandu to know that I loved him but that being my mother's daughter left me trapped.

He sat without speaking. Then he put his arms around me and held me close to him. He kissed my neck and my face and we both cried.

"I'll ask Inez to help me."

"Are you sure that's the only way?" he asked.

"It's the only way we will all be safe." I had to be strong even though I felt devastated.

❧❦❧❦❧❦❧❦❧❦

I WAITED FOR INEZ IN her apartment. I washed the dishes that were in the sink. In the bathroom, I organized her lipsticks, eye shadows, eyeliners, mascaras, and rouges, putting them in neat rows from light to dark shades. I put her curlers in the drawer and filled a basket with combs and brushes. I went to the kitchen to find a plastic container to hold her pins and bands. When I was done, Inez had still not come home. I glanced around to see what else needed organizing. There was a huge pile of magazines under the table. I took them all out and organized them by name and date, every now and then getting lost in the pictures of the elegant models wearing fabulous clothes.

I was startled when I heard the key turn in the front door lock. I had almost forgotten I was in Inez's apartment—and why I was there. Inez looked around, surprised and smiling.

"*Danki, dushi, bo ta lief,*" she said, thanking me and telling me how kind I was. She dropped her purse on the floor and put her arm around me as she led us to the bed in the corner of the room. "So tell me, what is the latest news?"

"Will you help me? I need an abortion," I blurted out.

"Oh, Serena! Of course I will help you, but tell me what has happened with Sandu?"

"At first, Sandu almost seemed happy I was pregnant, so we'd have an excuse to run away to San Francisco and get married. I told him I couldn't do that because of Mama. I think he understood that I was trying to keep him safe from my mother, and protect Mama from herself. When he realized an abortion was the only solution, he became very sad. He was really upset. Can you help me, Inez?" I pleaded.

"Yes, I will help you," Inez repeated. She hugged me and put her head on mine. It reminded me of how my grandmother used to hug me.

༄༅༄༅༄༅༄༅༄༅

EVERY DAY FOR THE NEXT few weeks I went over to Inez's apartment to see if she had found a place where I could get an abortion. I was discouraged because she couldn't find a clinic that would do it without the signature of a parent or guardian. I was having morning sickness and my breasts were tender. It was hard to ignore the fact I was pregnant, although I wanted to. I'd find myself daydreaming about having the baby and being Sandu's wife, and then I'd remember Mama.

Finally, Inez found a clinic in Santa Monica that didn't require parental consent. She told me she had gone to check it out and that it looked clean and well run. She had spoken to the doctor and asked him lots of questions to make sure I wouldn't be hurt during the operation, but she couldn't make the appointment. Sandu and I had to do that ourselves. I knew I should have been pleased that she had found a place but I was miserable, and when I told Sandu, I could see he was sad, too.

We both skipped school to make the appointment. He picked me up at the corner of Sunset and Western at nine in the morning. We didn't speak during the drive.

We walked into the clinic holding hands. I walked slightly behind him. A nurse sat at the reception desk. Sandu did most of the talking. Then the nurse handed me a form and asked us to have a seat. Sandu helped me fill out the form. I handed the completed form back to the nurse and we waited. Sandu looked nervous. I knew how he felt. I didn't want our love reduced to guilt. I wanted to think it was bigger and more powerful than Mama's control.

The nurse asked me a few more questions, and then told me to return in four days, with an empty stomach and someone to pick me up and stay with me after the procedure.

Sandu picked me up again at Sunset and Western at seven thirty in the morning on Friday, three months before my sixteenth birthday. "Are you sure you want to do this?" he asked as I got into the car.

I cried. I wanted to say no, I'm not sure, but I said nothing.

"We can go to my apartment, pick up a few things, and drive to San Francisco. We can still do that."

I tried to explain that there was nothing I wanted more than to drive away from my life and start over with him but that I couldn't. It was impossible to break the chains tying me to Mama. We drove in silence, both agonizing over what was about to happen.

Sandu parked near the clinic. We sat, neither of us saying a word, dreading what was coming. I had never seen him like this. He was somber and timid, not moving with his usual liveliness. He put a few coins in the meter, and we crossed the street.

I gave the nurse at the front desk my name. She told Sandu to have a seat and told me to follow her. I turned around and took one last look at Sandu. His eyes were glazed, but he lifted his fingers from his lap to wave me good-bye. I felt numb. My body was going through the motions but I felt as if my soul had abandoned me. The nurse gave me a gown and told me to change. Then she took me to a room with six beds and five women. I studied each one of the women. None of them was as young as I. The nurse brought a pill for me to take.

"This will make you relax and feel sleepy," she said kindly as she handed it to me. I took it and immediately felt drowsy, exactly as she had promised. I was scared. I asked the nurse if Sandu could be with me. She smiled and said, "No, that isn't possible." I was wheeled into the operating room, and the nurse put my feet in the cold metal stirrups. I whispered to myself, "Oma, help me. Am I doing the right thing?" Slowly everything went black.

I awoke, shivering uncontrollably. I looked around. I couldn't remember where I was. Then I heard the nurse's voice. "You're all done, Serena. Everything went well. Here are some more blankets. You're having a reaction to the anesthesia. It will go away after a while." She tucked another blanket around me. "Your boyfriend is waiting outside for you. You'll be able to go home soon." She went on to the next patient.

As I became more aware of where I was and what had happened, a terrible feeling of emptiness came over me. It was as if something or someone had left, disappeared, vanished without a good-bye, uncertain if we would ever meet again. While I had been pregnant, I wanted the fact of my pregnancy to disappear, but now I realized how full and accompanied I had felt. All of that was gone now and I was left empty. I wondered if I would have had the abortion had I not been afraid for Mama. Then I realized I was acting just like Mama—making choices with my head and not my heart. A huge wave of sadness welled up inside me and poured out as an uncontrollable stream of tears.

The nurse came back. "Dear, are you all right? Are you having any pain?"

I shook my head. The pain I felt was not a pain she could fix. I tried to compose myself. I tried to tell myself that what was done was done.

I asked the nurse what time it was, as I took some deep breaths to pull myself together. It was eleven thirty, leaving me six hours before I had to look normal for Mama. The shivers subsided, and I became more alert. It was time for me to leave the clinic. The nurse handed me my clothes, and I struggled into them. When I moved, I felt shooting cramps, painful reminders of what happened in my womb. The nurse brought a wheelchair and helped me from the bed to the chair, placing my purse in my lap. She rolled me back to the waiting room where Sandu sat, anxiously tapping his foot on the floor. He turned pale when he saw me and stood up quickly.

"Oh, my darling. What have they done to you?" I started crying again, hearing the fear in his voice. He knelt down and kissed my hand. His eyes glistened with the wetness of held-back tears.

"Do we still need to pay?" I asked, wanting to get out of there.

"Everything is taken care of. We'll go to Inez's so you can rest. I will take care of you, my baby. Come, I will look after you," Sandu said, just above a whisper, while he helped me out of the wheelchair and to the door. Those words, "my baby," wrenched my heart. I took a deep breath to send the tears back inside.

Sandu helped me up the stairs to Inez's apartment. She opened the door. I felt Sandu hesitate. Inez put her hand on his shoulder. "Nice to meet you, Sandu. Please come in. Let me help you." I realized Sandu had never met Inez, and his hesitation reminded me he was not fond of people with dark skin.

Inez had taken the day off and was waiting for me with warm tea and crackers. Her bed was made up, with the blankets neatly tucked in. Sandu and Inez helped me into it. I was tired from the ordeal and grateful for the tea. They spoke for a minute, then he crawled into the bed and held me while Inez went out to run some errands. He reassured me that, when the time was right, we would have many children, but his reassurance couldn't change how I felt.

"Do you believe in souls?" I asked, looking into Sandu's eyes. He nodded. "I feel so sad," I said.

"I'm sad too, but our love is big enough," he whispered in my ear. "This soul will come back to us. I promise you, this soul will be waiting for us." He sounded very sure of himself. I wished his words could override my feelings.

"Please keep talking," I asked. Listening to his words, I fell asleep.

ﻉﻭﻉﻭﻉﻭﻉﻭﻉﻭﻉﻭﻉﻭ

AT FIVE THIRTY THAT AFTERNOON Inez woke us up. "It's time to take you home, Serena," she said gently. "How do you feel?"

I tried getting up but the pain slowed me down. "I'm okay. It will just take me a second," I said, but Sandu had to help me. Inez brought me a Coke with ice to help me wake up, and a mirror and comb to fix my hair. They helped me to Sandu's car and the three of us drove to my apartment building. We pulled up, and they both accompanied me to the courtyard entrance.

From this point on, I was on my own. I had never felt so lonely. I shuffled through the courtyard and up the first set of stairs. I turned back and saw Sandu and Inez peering around the corner to be sure I got into the apartment safely. I smiled at them and gave them a thumbs-up as I tackled the rest of the stairs. I took a deep breath to prepare myself to face Mama, but I wasn't sure I had the strength. I wanted to tell her everything; I wanted all this sneaking around to be over.

I walked into the apartment and went into the bedroom. I saw Mama lying in bed, smoking a cigarette and watching television; she looked exhausted. "Hi, Mama. How are you?" I asked, trying to sound casual.

"Fine," she answered, without looking at me. I tried to move as normally as possible but stabbing jolts of pain made me hold my breath. I lay down on my bed and closed my eyes. "I must have eaten something that's making me sick." I paused. "I've been throwing up." Mama sat up and looked at me.

"You are not on drugs, are you?" she said as she examined me.

I stared back at her and pleaded, "No, Mama, I'm sick, and I really don't feel good." I was angry with her for scrutinizing me, yet I was glad she was concerned. She did care for me in her own way, but I wished her caring had more understanding and sympathy. I dozed off. When I woke up I found her standing over me, a cup of chamomile tea for me in her hand. She seemed worried as she stared at me. I wanted to be left alone.

"I'll be fine tomorrow," I reassured her. It was obvious she knew something was wrong, although she wasn't sure what it was. Mama opened the can of Spanish peanuts she kept on her nightstand. Eating one peanut at a time, she watched the television and intermittently glanced over at me.

I was too frightened she would find out what I had done, to feel sad. I imagined how she would have reacted if I had told her I was pregnant. I wondered if she would have advised me to have the abortion or to have the baby. I wondered if she would have offered to help me raise my baby. I almost started crying but stuffed my face into the pillow to hold back my tears.

I was anxious for her to leave for work; she was working the eleven-to-seven overnight shift. Mama stood by my bed before she left. I pretended I was asleep. I kept telling myself, she will leave soon, just keep pretending for a few more hours.

I lay in bed wondering what Oma would have done if she had been in my place. I wasn't sure I had done the right thing. I tossed from one side to the other, trying to find some comfort in my bed. I wanted to talk to Oma.

ᘒᗑᘒᗑᘒᗑᘒᗑᘒᗑᘒᗑᘒᗑ

OMA WAS DRESSED IN HER wedding gown, a simple, cream-colored dress with a lace collar. She walked up to my bed with a cup of her special tea in her left hand and a glass of valerian root dissolved in water in her right. She offered me the glass as she sat on the bed. I took it from her and drank it all, then she took the glass back and handed me the cup of tea. "I'm so glad you came, Oma. I miss you." She did not respond, but stroked my hair. "Oma, tell me, did I do the right thing? What should I have done?" I stared into Oma's eyes hoping to find answers.

She looked at me with compassion as she spoke. "We all do what we have to do, to learn what we need to learn. By the choices we make, we write the stories of our lives. You are writing the story of your life." Oma stroked my hair as she spoke. I felt comforted. She had not told me whether I had done right or wrong, yet I felt comforted.

"Oma, where did the soul of my child go?"

"That soul went to find another body. You see, *mi dushi*, a soul is really life force. We are all life force, that is what we all have in common. Be mindful, *mi dushi*, when looking into a stranger's eyes, because none of us are really strangers. Each one of us carries the same life force. We are all one."

"Did I choose to be Mama's child, Oma?"

"Circumstances were perfect for you to be your mother's child. You are learning what you need to learn so that you can become who you are meant to be."

"If I had known it was going to be this painful, I never would have chosen Mama."

"Someday you will look back and see this life is just one book in your library. You are the library. You are your relationships. Your relationships are much older than you remember. If you could remember, you would know why you chose your mother. Not remembering is what makes it painful." Oma held my gaze and slowly faded. I reached out to touch her but she was gone.

At midnight, the phone rang. "Hey, my love, how are you feeling? Can I come over?"

"Yes. I'd like that. I'll leave the door unlocked in case I'm asleep when you get here."

෨෪෨෪෨෪෨෪෨෪෨෪

I AWOKE WITH SANDU'S ARMS around me. I had no idea how long he had been there.

"Are you awake?" Sandu whispered in my ear.

"Yes."

"Are you hungry?"

"A little."

"I have something for you. Can you get up or do you want me to bring it to you?"

"I can get up. I have to go to the bathroom, anyway." As I turned

෨ 245 ෨

over, our lips met, and our bodies turned to each other while our arms and legs spun us into a single thread. "Is *that* what you have for me?" I asked jokingly.

"No, we're not supposed to do *that* for three weeks. How are we going to survive?" Sandu kissed me and jumped up. "Come here. I'll show you," he said. He took my hands and helped me to stand up.

"Wait, I have to go slow." Sandu waited for me outside the bathroom door and then escorted me to the living room. "Oh, Sandu! This is lovely!" I said, hardly able to speak. Sandu grinned, a bit of his old self returning.

"Come, sit down. We have to get you strong again."

The dining table had been transformed. A dark-blue cloth covered the wooden table Mama had bought at Sears. White candles surrounded a bowl of floating gardenias. Two place settings of white paper plates with blue trim were set opposite each other. Sandu led me to a chair and helped me sit down. "Where did you get all this?" I asked.

He poured Perrier into one of Mama's wine glasses. "I brought it from the restaurant. Tomorrow I'll return the tablecloth, the vase, the candles, and the platter." He smiled proudly. "Let me get the food." He went to the kitchen while I sipped my Perrier. A basket of bread and butter appeared on the table, and then a perfectly arranged serving plate filled with roasted chicken in tarragon and white-wine sauce, baby potatoes, and green beans. He served me first and then himself. "What are you thinking?" he asked.

"I'm thinking I love you."

We fell silent, comforted by each other's company, but aware of our sad hearts. It looked like a celebration, but it felt more like a wake.

I WAS DRIVING NORTH ON Highway 101 to the San Fernando Valley, listening to Elton John singing "Benny and the Jets." I had recently gotten my driver's license. Driving on the freeway with the radio on always reminded me of Hendrika—I wished she could see me drive. I thought of her in Curaçao and how strange it must be to be there without Oma. I still couldn't get used to the idea that I would never see Oma again. It seemed such a long time ago when I was the little girl who followed Oma around or played with Hendrika. I didn't know exactly when I had become a woman—was it the first time I saw myself in the mirror looking like a woman, or the first time I made love to Sandu, or the moment I got pregnant, or the moment I decided to have an abortion?

I looked over at Mama riding in the passenger seat next to me and realized how little I knew of the pain she had endured as a woman, just as she didn't know she was sitting next to a woman now.

We were on our way to visit San Fernando Valley College where Sandu studied. I wanted to convince her it was the best college for me. Two days earlier, we had visited Los Angeles City College. I had been successful in convincing her it was for low-achieving students and not at all the right place for me. Mama had taken one look at the students and immediately agreed, not because she knew their test scores, but because of their ethnicities.

I kept my fingers crossed, hoping the student population at San Fernando Valley College would be mostly white. I was sure race was the best way to convince Mama to allow me to enroll there. I parked the car and we walked to the administration office. To my relief, almost all the students and staff we saw were white. I went to the information desk and asked for a schedule of classes. The woman behind the counter was in her fifties, with dyed black hair and red lipstick.

"Are you planning to enroll here, dear?" She sounded friendly.

"Yes," I answered shyly.

"Would you like a student to show you around? I can make an appointment for you." The woman spoke in a high voice, as if I were a child needing some reassurance.

"No, thank you. We'll look around on our own."

"Are you sure?" the woman pressed, cocking her head.

"Yes, I'm sure. Thank you. Mama and I just want to walk around, if that's all right."

"All right then. But don't hesitate to ask if you have any questions," she offered.

I wanted to show my mother the school myself. I didn't want anyone to discover I was sixteen and had only graduated from high school in exchange for a year's back tuition. A month before graduation, I found out Mama had made a deal with Mr. McNaughton. He agreed that if she paid her outstanding bill he'd count some of the credits from my schooling in Curaçao so I'd have enough to graduate. Somehow, Mama came up with the money to pay for the tuition, the rental of the cap and gown, and the graduation pictures. I was relieved that my tedious hours in those awful classrooms were over.

I was hopeful about the possibility of going to the same school as Sandu, and I promised Saint Thomas I would do my very best in school. The previous evening I lit candles that I had sprinkled with rosemary and acacia leaves to strengthen my mind and improve my concentration. It felt like a new start. Mama was silent as we toured the library, the gym, the study center, and the various academic departments.

"I think we have seen the whole school," I said, checking the map on the back of the course catalog.

"If we have seen it, then let's go home," Mama said. I knew she was tired. She had worked all night and wanted to go home to get some rest before she had to go back to work again. I opened the car door for her first, and then I got in myself.

"Mama, I would like to go to this school."

Mama didn't respond right away. She sat for a moment, and then turned toward me.

"I hope you want to go to this school to get a good education." She paused. Pointing a finger at me, she said, "I hope it is not to see some boy or something like that. Look at me, Serena." I turned to her. "Look at me and promise me you want to go to this school for a good education." Mama clutched her purse on her lap. I hesitated, not wanting to lie. I felt guilty.

"I am not smart," she continued, "but I made something of myself. After I had gotten those burns, I was always sick and I missed a lot of school. Though I was terrible at school, the nuns loved me and they excused my mistakes." Her face was tense. I stared at the floor mat and listened. "They let me pass courses because they felt sorry for me. I knew I was not clever, but I asked my father to send me to the Netherlands to study nursing anyway. I was the first woman from the islands to attend a nursing program in Holland. Do you know what that is like?" Mama asked, her tone rising. She tilted her head and her eyes narrowed. I shook my head. "Imagine it! At seventeen, I went on a big ship to a place I knew nothing about, without anyone to help me. That took nerve. But I was not afraid, and I went." She said it proudly, her index finger now pointing at the horizon.

I wished I could be sent away to college. What a luxury it would be to have your parents give you your life and tell you to make the best of it. "Mama, I want to become a reporter and I think I can do it. No matter how hard it is, I want to try."

"I hope so, Serena. I really hope so," she said. I started the engine and put the car in reverse, then glanced at Mama as I looked over my shoulder to back out of the parking space. On the way home, I had a silent argument with myself. I tried to convince myself that I hadn't lied to my mother. I really did want to get an education, but I also wanted to go to San Fernando Valley College because Sandu went there. I felt guilty but, technically at least, I had not lied. She had never asked me explicitly if the reason I wanted to go to that school had anything to do with a boy—she had only expressed a vague hope that it did not. I had not lied to Mama, I decided.

"I am glad you care about academics. Learning is important. None of my other children cared about it. You are my last chance. I think you are making a good choice. I am proud of you. At least God gave me one child who cares about improving herself. You will show your brothers and sisters how you appreciate your mother and how your mother did everything she could for you."

Mama cracked the window open and lit a cigarette. Her high expectations made me nervous. I hoped I'd be able to keep up when I got to college.

ꜱꜱꜱꜱꜱꜱꜱ

THE SUMMER AFTER HIGH SCHOOL graduation, I took an eight-week nurse's aide course at Mama's insistence. It was offered at a hospital near Hollywood as part of the Adult Education Program. Sandu and I only saw each other six times that whole summer. We missed each other terribly, but he was very busy with school and I was busy with the nursing course. We talked on the phone and hoped the summer would go by quickly. I hardly saw Inez either.

The first two weeks were spent learning how to take and chart temperatures, blood pressures, pulses, and respiration rates. We learned to make beds with mannequins in them, and we practiced bathing them. I felt confident during those first weeks of the course because there had been almost no writing and not much reading. The next three weeks of the course were spent working in the hospital as an apprentice nurse's aide. The final weeks of the course would be spent working as an actual nurse's aide.

Peggy, the nurse to whom I was assigned, was about fifty years old and heavyset. She was motherly and had a loud laugh. "Follow me!" she commanded, as all the students scattered from the introductory meeting with our new teachers. "Let's get a cup of coffee and I'll fill you in on the day ahead." She took me to the nurses' lounge, stopping in front of the coffee pot to pour herself a strong cup of stale coffee. "Now darling, how old are you?"

"I'm sixteen years and two months old," I said.

"Mmm, that's what I thought. Why were you allowed to take this course?"

"I graduated from high school, and they said it was all right for me to take it."

"All right, then. I presume you have never bathed a patient before."

"No, but I've had lots of practice on the mannequins," I responded confidently.

"Well, I'll show you how to bathe a patient."

Peggy and I got along very well. We loved the candy machine, and she often brought special doughnuts, muffins, or cookies from home to cheer us up. The three weeks flew by and the time came for me to be assigned my own patients. I had four: a woman in room 413, two women in room 414, and a man in room 411. I was nervous as I introduced myself to each patient. Mrs. Cohen was eighty-four and alert; Mrs. Malley was ninety-four and slept most of the time; Mrs. Johnson was eighty-nine, skinny, and barely alive; and Mr. Newman was sixty-four and chatty.

"It must be my lucky day to have such a pretty nurse! And what is your name, angel?" asked Mr. Newman.

"Serena Brink," I answered, with what I hoped was a professional smile.

"And how old might you be?" he asked.

"I'm sixteen, Mr. Newman," I answered in a serious voice, trying to sound older. I decided not to mention the two months.

"Is that legal? Are you allowed to be nursing?" he asked, looking alarmed.

"Yes. I graduated from high school early, and this is my summer course."

"Well, you sure are pretty." Mr. Newman smiled again.

I went to the supply room to get all the things I needed in my cart. Then it was time to change beds and bathe my patients. I was exhausted by the time I got to Mr. Newman.

"Well, what do we have here?" asked Mr. Newman. "You don't think you are going to bathe me, do you?"

"Yes, Mr. Newman, I am here to bathe you," I said, closing the curtain around his bed.

"Oh no you're not! I'll do it myself! I couldn't stand having you bathe me. You're only a child! I'm quite well enough to bathe myself. Here, give me that pail and the sponge. Here, here, give all that to me and go to the other side of the curtain and wait!" Mr. Newman was grabbing things out of my hands and chasing me off. I was actually glad he had decided to bathe himself. I had almost thrown up while bathing Mrs. Johnson. The smell of her old body in a urine-filled adult diaper had nearly made me run out of the hospital.

I nodded shyly and thanked Mr. Newman as I closed the curtain and walked out of the room to wait until he had finished. By the time I returned the supplies from my cart to the shelves in the supply room, it was time to make my rounds again.

I went back to Mrs. Johnson's room. It was warm and a bit stuffy, so I pulled the curtains back and cracked the window open to let in some fresh air. As I opened the window, a puff of cold air blew around me from behind, and I thought there must be a draft. I walked over to Mrs. Johnson's bed, and gasped for air. My heart pounded and my body felt paralyzed. I wanted to run, but couldn't move. Mrs. Johnson was as white as the sheets on her bed. Her head hung loosely to the side of the pillow, her eyes were rolled back in her head, and her mouth wide open. Each hand gripped a side of the mattress, one arm extended down toward her feet, the other above her head. She looked as if she had been trying to hold on to her bed just before she died.

"Oh, Mrs. Johnson, you really didn't smell all that bad," I whispered. "I didn't mind bathing you—I swear." Now that she was dead, I was afraid she might have the power to read my mind, and she would know how I had felt about bathing her. I pulled myself together, took a deep breath and went to get help—Mrs. Johnson's chart said no resuscitation.

I dashed first into the nurses' lounge to look for Peggy, but she wasn't there. I ran down the hall and finally found her in Room 401. I slowed down as I walked in, took another breath, and went over to Peggy, who was taking a patient's temperature. Tugging at her arm, I signaled her to bring her ear down near my mouth. "I think Mrs. Johnson just died," I whispered. A wrinkle creased her forehead. She smiled reassuringly at her patient, and said she'd be right back. We rushed to Mrs. Johnson's room. I waited at the door. Peggy called the nurses' desk for help. She signaled to me with her hand. "Honey, go to the nurses' lounge and make yourself a cup of tea. I'll take care of Mrs. Johnson."

"Thank you, Peggy. Thank you." I felt my throat closing and tears welling up in my eyes. I was not proud of myself. I had bathed Mrs. Johnson for the last time, and instead of giving her comfort and sympathy, I had felt loathing. I begged Mrs. Johnson to forgive me, and promised myself that if I was going to work as a nurse, I would never forget that my patients were in need of care and love, no matter how repulsive their condition was.

꜀ꜟ꜀ꜟ꜀ꜟ꜀ꜟ꜀ꜟ꜀ꜟ

SMILING, I SLUNG MY BACKPACK over my shoulder and walked to the bedroom to say good-bye to Mama. I leaned over to kiss her. "It's my first day of college, Mama. I'll be back around four o'clock." She moved her head a couple of inches toward me so I could kiss her.

"Please do your best, Serena. That is all I ask. Do your best." I could detect a faint sense of pride.

"I will, Mama." I promised, and walked out of the room.

It was eight in the morning as I got on the freeway. That day I had three classes: English from nine to ten, Introduction to Journalism from ten to eleven, and American History from eleven to twelve. At eight fifteen I drove down the Coldwater Canyon exit ramp. For a moment, I debated whether to make a left turn at the end of the ramp—a turn that would take me to 4600 Coldwater Canyon Avenue, the address of Sandu's new apartment—or whether to go straight and get to school early. I felt torn between school and Sandu, and when I slowed the car as I tried to decide, the truck behind me blew its horn. Startled, I sped up and drove straight to school.

I listened to the lectures with interest, and I was eager to do the homework. In the library after class, I set my books down and looked over my English assignment. My reading was still slow, and having to write in English was frustrating. There was a lot I wanted to write about, but my thoughts got off track as I struggled to conjure up the spelling of the words.

⁊❧⁊❧⁊❧⁊❧⁊❧⁊❧

AT TWO O'CLOCK, I PACKED up my books and drove to Sandu's apartment, which was in a two-story rectangular building. The apartments on one side of the building faced the pool in the courtyard, and on the other side they looked over a creek. No one answered when I knocked on the door. My watch read two fifteen—Sandu was due home any minute. I checked under the mat and the potted plants for a key, but found nothing. The front gate slammed and I recognized the pattern of Sandu's footsteps, which I had memorized listening to him climb up the stairs up to Mama's apartment.

"Hey, baby girl. What a nice surprise. I've missed you." Sandu hugged me.

"I missed you too. That's why I came to see you."

Sandu opened the door and let me in first. "Come, I'll give you a key," he said. He walked through his narrow hallway to the kitchen, opened a drawer, and turned toward me, a key in the palm of his hand. "You can have this one."

"Really?" I said. "For me?"

"Yes, for you. Come, let me show you the apartment." Sandu covered my eyes with his hands as he guided me to the center of the room. "What do you think?" he asked, taking away his hands.

"Wow! Gorgeous! Oh my God. Where did you find that?" I gasped, staring at an antique queen-sized bed in the corner of the studio. Two large, carved angels gathering wooden fabric and scattering falling flowers crowned the imposing mahogany headboard.

"I found it in an antique furniture warehouse in Venice," Sandu said, putting his arms around me.

"It's beautiful. It reminds me of my grandmother's bed. It was big and heavy like this one, but it had four thick posts with a carved pineapple on each post. The wood was old—just like this." I stroked the bed with my fingers. I felt as if Oma were watching us.

"I'm glad you like it," Sandu said proudly. "I'm going to fill this place with special pieces of furniture—oh, and look over here." A hand on each of my shoulders, Sandu turned me to the right. In another corner sat a drafting table with a light and a chair. "That's my work corner. And here," he pointed to the middle of the room, "I want to put a couch and table. This will be our home, and over here we'll have lunch and dinner," he said, pointing to the patio outside a sliding glass door. "I'm going to get two large rattan chairs and a table, so we can share our meals al fresco." The patio was overgrown with honeysuckle and ivy. "If we leave the door open in the rainy season, we'll be able to hear the creek run," Sandu said. Then he kissed me. "I missed you so much, baby," he whispered. "I've missed your sweetness."

I wished his studio could be our home. He slipped his left arm under both of my legs and lifted me onto the bed. We tumbled in, kissing and holding each other, tossing and turning under blue and white sheets that were like clouds in a tropical sky.

HOLLYWOOD HAD BEEN TRANSFORMED IN anticipation of Christmas. Decorations hung from the streetlights. Salvation Army volunteers rang their bells, standing in front of their red kettles on street corners. Santa Clauses, reindeer, wreaths, snowmen, and Christmas trees were in every storefront window. Frederick's of Hollywood displayed its lingerie through snow-painted windows. At the Hollywood Toy Store, a man dressed as Santa Claus greeted customers with a "Ho-Ho-Ho" as they walked through the door. Christmas carols played on the radio from early morning until late into the night.

I remembered how much Hendrika and I had enjoyed listening to the carols during our first Christmas in America. With Hendrika's help, I had tried to memorize all the words. Christmas songs were all we had that first year, when there had been no money for a tree or presents. Hendrika and I wrapped our favorite flavors of Life Savers and placed them in each other's shoes. We couldn't celebrate Christmas the American way, and instead resorted to the Dutch custom of placing token gifts in shoes, the way we used to do in Curaçao when we celebrated Sint Nikolaas's birthday.

Hearing the carols made me miss Hendrika more deeply than usual. Ten days before Christmas, Mama instructed me to buy an inexpensive Christmas tree after school. With Hendrika gone, Mama was not in the mood for a big celebration, and since we had come to America, we had never had enough friends for a celebration anyway. She told me to get an artificial tree so we could use it again next year. When school was over I walked to Newberry's, where I found a large assortment of bread-dough ornaments: bells, snowmen, dogs, stars—everything imaginable made out of bread dough—but no Christmas trees.

I went on to Woolworth's and walked up and down the aisles. I found a selection of plastic trees with lights already attached, and chose one about three feet tall. On the shelves were a variety of dried flowers painted red. Some were sprinkled with glitter. Another shelf was devoted to wooden ornaments: cars, trucks, miniature houses, and animals. On the floor sat a bin full of Gingham bows, with tiny corn-husk dolls scattered among them. I wanted to buy some new ornaments, but there just wasn't enough money.

It was dark by the time I walked home. On the way, I admired the Christmas trees through the windows of the apartments. A few apartments were dark except for the lights on their trees. Those apartments looked magical to me, but maybe they were just trying to save electricity because of the energy crisis.

Mama was still at work when I arrived home. I set up the tree, found the box containing our old ornaments, and started decorating. I took out a tiny plastic record, an ornament Hendrika had bought, and hung it on the tree. I missed her, especially at times like this. She never wrote and it was too expensive to call. I wondered how she was doing. After I finished, I turned off the lights and sat on the couch with a cup of tea, staring at our meager tree, remembering what the holidays were like in Curaçao.

᠎᠎᠎᠎᠎᠎᠎᠎᠎

EVERY DECEMBER FIFTH, SINT NIKOLAAS sailed into the harbor on board a large ship, pretending he had come from Spain to celebrate his birthday with the children of Curaçao. He'd stand on the deck, dressed in his elegant bishop's robes and miter, his bishop's crook in one hand and waving to the crowd with the other. He was surrounded by his many black helpers, all dressed in sixteenth-century costumes, who were called *Zwarte Pieten*. His ship sailed carefully through the narrow harbor entrance, which was guarded on either side by massive stone forts. The entrance of the channel was lined with the brightly painted houses and shops that formed the center of Willemstad.

Sint Nikolaas was welcomed by the governor general of Curaçao, along with thousands of singing school children. It was a most impressive sight. The children sang Dutch Sint Nikolaas songs, which they had been practicing for weeks. Sint Nikolaas disembarked from his ship, accompanied by eight or ten Zwarte Pieten. He mounted a white horse, and as he rode through town the Pieten danced and jumped around him. With their wooden switches, the Pieten made threatening gestures at the children and then threw candies and marble-sized spice cookies from their burlap bags, as they encouraged the children to sing louder.

The Sint Nikolaas celebration was a kind of "day of reckoning" for children. If a child had behaved well throughout the previous year, there were gifts and treats. But if the child had not behaved well, Sint Nikolaas could command one of his helpers to put the child in his burlap bag, and take him back to Spain for a year of harsh discipline. I always wished for Sint Nikolaas to be kind-hearted and forgiving. The only presents I wanted from him were acceptance and understanding. The fear of being judged was overwhelming, and the promise of presents and the threat of punishment created a disturbing uncertainty that, for me, made the holiday a time of anxiety rather than joy.

Sint Nikolaas was a four-hundred-year-old Dutch tradition. In the Netherlands, Zwarte Pieten had to use large quantities of shoe polish to blacken their pale skin, something not necessary in Curaçao. I liked the Zwarte Pieten but I feared Sint Nikolaas. In spite of being disciplinarians, the Pieten were only following orders. To a Curaçao native, however, the image of a white man commanding his black servants to carry out his wishes was a familiar old story from the slave days.

Oma never celebrated Sint Nikolaas Day—she disliked it because she felt the celebration was hurtful for some and that a celebration should not be painful for anyone. Mama, on the other hand, loved everything Dutch. She celebrated Sint Nikolaas Day with great enthusiasm. I remembered the last Sint Nikolaas Day before we left for Colombia, when our whole family was still together. Because we were leaving soon, Mama wanted to make the day special. She invited fifteen families to join us on December fifth to celebrate Sint Nikolaas's birthday. She spent weeks in preparation. Mama and Papa's arguing increased during these weeks leading up to the party. Willia, Hendrika, and I could hear them from our bedroom every night, and it was always about money.

Mama didn't want to leave anyone out. For each child that was coming she wrapped a modest present: a car, a doll, or a game. She made centerpieces from grass, carrots, and sugar-cubes, the same things children put in their shoes to get the attention of Sint Nikolaas's horse and make him stop at their door. She created a throne for Sint Nikolaas out of a large armchair. She borrowed chairs and tables from friends, and made red tablecloths for each table. She had been baking in the kitchen for days, and there were cases of beer and spirits stacked outside the kitchen door. The day before the party, Mama prepared appetizers: meat croquettes, egg rolls, *empanadas* (meat wrapped in pastry dough), and cheese balls. We squeezed dozens of lemons to make lemonade. Mama rushed from here to there, giving directions and putting final touches on the dishes.

On December fifth we came home from school to a transformed house: our living room furniture had been moved into the garage, tables and chairs now filled the room and overflowed onto the porch, and a large throne on a raised platform occupied one corner of the room. The paper stars we had cut out and painted gold were now sprinkled all around the throne. The house was beautiful. Oma's housekeeper arrived with three of her oldest children to help serve and clean. Papa came home at three thirty and was shocked when he saw the house. He called Mama into the bedroom. We could hear them arguing again. Mama returned to the kitchen, her eyes red. We helped her cook and tried to cheer her up until it was time for the party to start. By the time the guests began to arrive at five thirty, Mama was smiling again. Beer, lemonade, and appetizers were served.

I waited with my friends at the front door, impatiently looking for Sint Nikolaas. We wanted to see him but we didn't want to be seen by him. Suddenly, candy and spiced *pepernoten* cookies came flying though the windows. Old and young were on their hands and knees, scooping candy and cookies from the floor. "He's not far away," someone shouted. Mama started singing the traditional Dutch welcoming song, "Listen who is coming children," and everyone joined in. More candy streamed through the window, thrown by the Zwarte Pieten outside.

The younger children stayed close to their mothers, frightened that the Zwarte Pieten might get confused and put them in their burlap bags. I tried to stay next to Mama but she was moving so quickly it was difficult to keep up with her. A car pulled into our driveway and everyone rushed to the front door. The singing grew louder. Eight Pieten helped Sint Nikolaas out of the car and into the house. A Piet led him to his throne, helped him to sit down, and then the Pieten lined up, four on either side of him. Burlap bags filled with gifts surrounded them. One of the Pieten handed Sint Nikolaas a large paper scroll. He signaled with his hand for the singing to stop. My heart was pounding as I hid behind Willia.

One by one, he called out each person's name, praising them for something they had done well during the year, and then commenting on something embarrassing about them. The adults always laughed at what Sint Nikolaas had to say, though I never understood why. Then he gave each guest a miniature piece of sculpted marzipan. For the children he did the same thing, but he also presented them with a gift from their wish list. Johan received a marzipan guitar and a book of sheet music, Hendrika a marzipan camera and a book on photography, and Willia was given a marzipan horse and a gift certificate for a riding lesson.

When Sint Nikolaas called my name I was afraid and didn't want to go up to his throne. Willia saw my reluctance. "He's not real," she whispered in my ear. "It's Mr. Brand, our neighbor. Go ahead, it's all pretend." Shocked, I turned to look at her. She winked as she pushed me toward Sint Nikolaas. Slowly, I walked up to him and sat on his lap. I examined his face and saw his beard was not real. Then I saw the large freckle I knew Mr. Brand had on the left side of his nose. I was relieved that Sint Nikolaas wasn't real. He handed me a marzipan doll as one of the Pieten extracted a pink bicycle from his burlap bag. It was exactly what I had hoped for. Papa walked up to the throne and helped me with the bicycle.

We took it outside to the driveway. We were alone. He held the handlebars while I climbed on. I sat up straight, trying to balance. He smiled down at me then walked alongside, holding the seat with one hand and the handlebars with the other. As I rode my brand-new bike, I felt safe with Papa holding me. We turned right, out of our driveway, onto the sidewalk, and down the street, leaving the commotion of the celebration behind. The night enveloped us with a blanket of stars.

That year, my fear of Sint Nikolaas vanished and I became fond of the holiday. Now, sitting in front of our tree in our apartment in Hollywood, I missed the people, the smells, and the sounds of Christmas in Curaçao.

ᘒᘒᘒᘒᘒᘒᘒᘒ

AFTER MY ENGLISH CLASS, I drove to Sandu's apartment, although it was early in the afternoon and he was still at school. On the counter sat the bag of lights, candles, ornaments, and the red satin sheets he had bought the previous day. I unpacked the bags as I listened to "Jingle Bells," "White Christmas," and "Rudolph the Red-Nosed Reindeer." I unwrapped the four Christmas candles, putting two on the bar, one on the coffee table, and one on the bookshelf. I cleaned the apartment and made up the bed with the red sheets. The studio was starting to look like Christmas. Sandu didn't have to work the lunch shift that day, so there would be enough time for us to buy a Christmas tree and go grocery shopping for a late lunch.

Sandu rushed into the apartment, his eyes glowing with happiness. "Let's go, baby. Let's get our own Christmas tree. And look, Chef Jean-Philippe gave me this great recipe for avocado and shrimp—I'm going to make for you." He kept his jacket on and was jingling his keys as he waited for me to get my coat.

"Do you just watch him cook, or does he actually teach you?" I asked.

"When the restaurant closes and it's our turn to eat, I ask him for recipes I might be able to make at home. He loves to talk about food, and now he saves all kinds of special recipes for me. He's a fantastic chef. Thanks to him, La Serre is the best restaurant in California." Sandu kissed his fingertips with a smack.

We drove west on Ventura Boulevard, looking for a Christmas tree lot, and found one near Topanga Canyon. Surrounded by the smell of pine trees, I imagined I was in a forest, but the sixty-degree weather reminded me we were still in dry and warm Southern California. It was not nearly as hot here as it was in Curaçao, where the Christmas trees arrived on the twenty-third of December and were dead before New Year's Day. We walked around the lot looking for the best tree. "That one," Sandu said pointing to a perfectly shaped fourteen-foot tree.

"That one is not going to fit in your apartment," I pointed out.

"Someday, baby, we will have a place big enough for that tree." He laughed and put his arm around me. "How about that one?" Sandu asked with raised eyebrows, indicating a tree that was twelve feet tall. I frowned at him.

"You've chosen the perfect tree," a salesman said approvingly. He was a big man with a beer belly, dressed in overalls and a Santa hat; one finger of his right hand was missing. He put his left hand on Sandu's shoulder and offered his right. "Hi, my name is Nick. Just imagine this tree all decorated in your home."

Sandu looked embarrassed.

"It won't fit in our apartment," I explained.

Sandu shifted from foot to foot, and then walked away, taking me with him.

"How about that one," I said, pointing at a six-foot tree.

Sandu stopped, then quietly walked around the tree, his left hand on his chin as he examined every branch. "Yes," he said. "Let's buy this one." I grinned, proud that I had found our first tree.

Nick was right behind us. "That size is my best seller," he said.

"How much is it?" Sandu asked.

"Eighteen dollars."

Minutes later we walked out with our tree, tied it to the roof of Sandu's car, and drove to his apartment to decorate it. Sandu placed the tree in the corner of the living room, next to the couch. I strung it with lights while he cooked. Every now and then, he'd walk over and help me straighten out a string of lights or shift an ornament to make the tree look better. I could see he loved to teach me, and I felt lucky he did. I thought everything he did was beautiful.

The lights on the tree were of many colors: blue, yellow, purple, and green, but all the ornaments were red. When we had finished decorating it, the tree looked great. The weather had warmed up, as it usually did by midday in the San Fernando Valley. Sandu set the patio table for lunch and carried his gourmet creation to it: avocado halves arranged on leaves of butter lettuce and scattered with cherry tomatoes, each avocado filled with bay shrimp and drizzled with a mustard-vinaigrette dressing. "*Eh-eh*, Sandu! That's so Christmassy! Look—red and green." He brought out a bottle of white wine.

"It's a special day today," he announced.

"Oh yes? Why is it special?" I asked. Sandu poured the wine and we toasted before we sat down to eat. I stared at him curiously, waiting to hear what we were celebrating.

"My best friend, Daniel, got out of Romania yesterday," he said with a gleam in his eyes and a big smile on his face. "We have known each other since we were three years old." He tapped his heart twice. "He is like a brother to me. He made it! He is in Italy, on his way to Germany." Sandu was smiling broadly.

"That's wonderful. When will he be here?" I asked.

"I don't know for sure. But it might be as soon as next month. It depends on how much money he needs to get here. Of course, I'll help him once he arrives in California."

We ate, drank wine, and admired our tree. After lunch, we slipped between the red sheets and Sandu serenaded me with a *Mos Gerila* song, which, he explained, was a Romanian Christmas song traditionally sung in honor of Father Frost, who brought presents on December twenty-fifth. "That was my mother's favorite Christmas song," he said as he finished. "She sang that song to us from the time we were born." His thoughts seemed far away. Then he started singing Romanian Sint Nikolaas songs. I knew some of the melodies because some of the Dutch songs were similar. We sang them together, each in our own language. We started tentatively, singing louder and louder until our singing dissolved into laughter. After a while, we fell silent. Sandu turned to me and leaned on his elbow. "I got a letter from my mother this week," he said. "Her letter was smuggled out of Romania and mailed to me by a friend in France."

"What did she say?"

"I had sent her a letter with your picture and told her all about you. I told her how innocent and kind you are, and how sweet and tender. I told her I fell in love with you the moment I saw you, how you came into my life when things were very hard and you were just what I needed. I also told her that you were the same age as she was when she met my father."

"How did you send the letter?"

"A few Romanians are able to travel. I found one who was willing to smuggle my letter in."

"And what did she think of me?" I asked.

"She said your picture was very beautiful and wrote that she liked your name because Serena comes from the Latin word *serenus*, which means calm or exalted. She said you looked very sweet and young, and she hoped I was happy with you." Sandu recited all the things she had said one by one, counting them off on his fingers, as if he didn't want to forget anything his mother had written.

"Does that mean she likes me?" I asked.

"Yes, she likes you and she is happy for me. She would love to meet you, and she is sad she can only meet you in pictures."

"Tell her I'd like to meet her, too."

We held each other, grateful to be together and sad to be apart from our families. I wished Mama were more like Sandu's mother. I imagined his mother was a loving, happy, kind woman dedicated to taking care of her family.

When I drove home after lunch the streets were crowded with people shopping. The shop windows overflowed with pretty things to buy: clothes, shoes, games, perfume, records, and jewelry. I didn't buy anything because we had no money for such things. Christmas in Curaçao was not about giving gifts, it was about singing, eating, and taking time to be together. In America, it seemed as if people thought it was more important to buy things than to spend time with each other.

๖ๅ๖ๅ๖ๅ๖ๅ๖ๅ๖ๅ

MY FIRST SEMESTER ENDED IN January. I had dropped two courses and earned an incomplete. I didn't show Mama my results. I told her I had passed all my courses and things were going well. I didn't want to lie to Mama but I couldn't tell her the truth, either. I had tried my best but I was not able to keep up with the classes. The lessons moved too fast. I was disappointed in myself, but thinking about it was too painful. I told myself a new semester was starting and I would do better.

For the spring semester I enrolled in four classes, scheduling them so I could spend more time with Sandu. We had established a routine of making love early in the morning before school started, and then, after school, going out for a late lunch. Sometimes we ate at fancy restaurants in the San Fernando Valley.

Sandu had friends who were waiters at almost every one of these restaurants. Fior d'Italia, where his friend Paolo was the headwaiter, was one of our favorites. He often brought us special dishes to test: butternut squash ravioli, shrimp scampi, and tiramisu. He'd tell us stories about Italy, and of course, there was usually at least twenty minutes of soccer talk. Most of the waiters at these restaurants were European, and the busboys Mexican. They all played in soccer leagues on the weekends and argued endlessly about their matches. I learned from them that Sandu was a very talented and passionate player. Sandu and Paolo boasted about plays each had made that weekend. I loved watching their intense conversations. Sometimes, it seemed as if they were angry with each other and were not going to part as friends, but their conversations always ended with a laugh and a hug.

"Let's go for a drive to the ocean, baby," Sandu suggested one cold day in January. "I'm in the mood for some salty air."

I was delighted. We often took this drive to cool off in the summer when it was over a hundred degrees in the Valley. We took Kanan Road to Highway 1, then made our way to Zuma Beach, where we parked the car and looked out over the ocean. We searched for pelicans. Sandu compared the California pelicans to the pelicans in Romania. He claimed the pelicans in Romania were larger, faster, and better at catching fish, but the biggest difference, he pointed out, was that the Romanian pelicans were snow white, while the Californian pelicans were a drab brown. After taking a short walk on the beach, we stopped at Moonshadows restaurant for coffee, and then drove back to the Valley.

On our drives to the ocean, Sandu always told me about Romania: the beautiful Danube Delta, with its hundreds of birds, and the many castles. He promised that one day, when Romania was a democratic country, he would buy me the biggest and most elaborate castle there. He'd drive me all over Romania until we found the perfect one. I'd be his princess, and we'd fill the castle with our twelve children. The sounds of laughter and joy would be heard for miles around. Sandu always made me feel good. It was as if, on those journeys across the mountains to the ocean, we'd take flight and visit faraway fantasy worlds where our love was safe and we could live our lives in peace—no boundaries, no obligations, no gravity to keep us down.

Sandu pulled up to his apartment. We sat for a moment, and then I stepped out of his car and into mine to drive home, where the sounds of laughter were seldom heard.

That day Mama was sitting on her bed with a big smile on her face, as I walked in the bedroom. "I have something for you, Serena. It's a surprise," Mama said mysteriously. She reached for the gift-wrapped box on her nightstand and handed it to me. At first I was confused. We had only had trivial gifts at Christmas this year because Mama said we needed to save money, but here she was, a few weeks later, handing me a surprise. I opened the box, trying not to rip the paper, and pulled out an envelope. Inside was a round-trip ticket to Curaçao with my name on it. I gasped and looked at Mama. "Go ahead, there is more inside." I took another envelope from the box. The return address said: "United States Immigration and Naturalization Service."

"What is this, Mama?"

"Open it, Serena. Go ahead, open it," she said, smiling broadly, her eyes sparkling.

I had not seen her this happy in years. I took the letter out of the envelope:

> *You are to appear on February 28, 1976, at*
> *1:30 PM, to receive your Resident Alien Card,*
> *Form I-551, at the American Consulate in*
> *Willemstad, Curaçao, Netherlands Antilles.*

"Happy New Year, Serena," Mama said. My jaw dropped. I stood speechless, delightfully surprised.

"Thank you, Mama, but how can we afford this?"

"Don't worry, Serena. I have my ways," Mama laughed as she stood up and hugged me. She had been so withdrawn since Hendrika's departure that I had forgotten how much I yearned for her affection. Surprised, I hugged her back.

"Let's celebrate, Serena. This is going to be the year our luck changes."

I EAGERLY WAITED FOR THE day of my departure for Curaçao. When I told Sandu about my trip he was excited for me and asked what else I was looking forward to doing there besides getting my green card. I told him that I wanted to see my sisters, my grandmother's house on Penstraat, and the House of Six Doors. He said he wished he could go with me. Part of me wanted him to come, but part of me knew he would not like most of the things I loved about Curaçao. Sandu loved castles, forests, and snow; Curaçao had *landhuizen*, shrubs, and heat. He loved opera, museums, and the symphony; Curaçao had Tambú, arts and crafts, and there were only two movie theaters on the whole island. Sandu liked white people; in Curaçao, most of the population was black.

Mama was happier than she had been in a long time. The week before I left, she took me to Lerner's to buy things I needed for the trip. We bought clothes, shoes, a carry-on suitcase, and even perfume as gifts for Hendrika and Willia. Money had been tight since before Christmas. I imagined she must still be paying off the loan for my high school tuition. I didn't understand how, all of a sudden, she could be so generous. I was both delighted and worried, and asked her several times if we could afford all this. Each time she answered, "Don't worry, Serena. I have my ways." We walked out of Lerner's, each carrying two bags. At home, Mama removed the tags from my new clothes while I packed everything into my new suitcase. All that week, I could hardly sleep; Eager to depart, I kept my packed bag on the chair beside my bed.

Mama drove me to Los Angeles International Airport. She walked with me all the way to the boarding gate and stood waving until I could no longer see her. I was nervous about changing planes in Miami and glad I didn't have to go through US Customs. At Miami International I walked along the concourses of the airport, looking down at my feet, hoping no one would notice me, terrified of anyone in a uniform. After all, I was still in this country illegally because I had overstayed my tourist visa long ago. My stomach still tightened at the memory of sitting in that stark room with Mama and Hendrika, not knowing what was going to happen to us. Just as I found the gate, I heard ALM announce the flight to Curaçao. I checked in, walked down the jetway, found my assigned seat, and took a deep breath, relieved that there hadn't been an immigration departure check.

The pilot's voice announced that our plane was starting its descent to Curaçao's airport, and that the local time was four forty five in the afternoon and the temperature was eighty-nine degrees with winds out of the northeast. I looked out of my window—there was nothing but ocean underneath us, but minutes later Curaçao came into view. The colorful houses dotted the landscape, and I could see a majestic yellow *landhuis* in the distance. The gray-green shrubs made the island look more desolate than I remembered. As we landed, goats scattered through the shrubs outside the airport fence, and I cheered silently, happy to be home again. At last, I would be in the place and with the people I loved and missed so much.

A strong, hot wind tried to push me back into the airplane as I stepped out onto the stairs leading to the tarmac. My skirt fluttered in all directions and I tried to hold it down with one hand as I held my carry-on bag with the other. Willia stood waving from the terminal roof, in almost the same spot where Oma had said good-bye to me so long ago. I waved back vigorously, holding back tears of joy.

A female immigration officer looked at my passport and then at me. "*Ta ruman di Willia bo ta?*" she asked.

"Yes," I smiled. "I am Willia's sister."

"*Bon biní,*" she said, welcoming me home. "Willia is waiting for you." She pointed across the arrivals area to where Willia was standing. Willia resembled Mama; she had khaki-colored skin and Mama's dark-brown eyes and hair. She was wearing red lipstick, which made her look striking. Willia worked at the airport as the sales manager for ALM.

I retrieved my bag from the carousel and made my way to the customs officer. "So you are Willia's sister who lives in California," he said. "Welcome. We have heard so much about you." The officer shook my hand vigorously and smiled.

"Thank you," I said as he waved me through. Willia stood in front of me with open arms. Both of us teary-eyed, we fell into each other's embrace. "I'm so happy to see you, Serena. I've missed you so much," Willia said between sobs. I had more than missed Willia. I felt as if I were regaining something I thought I had lost forever.

"I've missed you, too," I whispered huskily. The line grew behind us, until the customs officer helpfully redirected the passengers around us. Willia wiped away my tears, then picked up my suitcase. As we walked to her car, she put her arm around me. The sun was setting but the heat was still intense; only the steady, warm breeze made it bearable. It felt good to be in familiar surroundings, like sleeping in an old pair of pajamas.

"How are you, Serena?" Willia asked, looking me over as we walked along. "I want to know everything that has happened these past three and a half years." I wasn't sure I wanted to tell her everything. "Are you tired?" she asked once we were in her car. "Should we go to my place first?"

"I'm not tired at all, and I can't wait to see Oma's house again."

"Well, then, let's go," Willia agreed.

"Didn't Hendrika know I was coming today?" I asked.

"Yes, she did. But she is really struggling. You might see her at Oma's house. She lives in the cottage next door. She's been having a hard time keeping a job," Willia said, glancing at me out of the corner of her eye. "I hardly see her. I've tried to help her but it's been ... impossible." That was just what I didn't want to hear. I had hoped that returning to Curaçao would have been good for Hendrika.

We drove toward Willemstad. The road from the airport into town had been a rural two-lane road when I left. Now there were houses and small businesses on either side. I was surprised how crowded Curaçao had become in less than four years. There were stoplights where there had been none before, and some of the dirt roads that led to the beaches were now paved. As we got closer to town, I spotted my favorite snack bar. It was just a simple counter in front of a green garage, selling sodas, beer, popsicles, homemade local snacks, and ice cream. I asked Willia if they still sold coconut ice cream.

"Yes, and it is still homemade," she answered. It was good to find something that hadn't changed. Minutes later, we were standing at the counter, savoring our cones. Each bite of creamy, refreshing ice cream melted in my mouth and was a delightful relief from the evening heat. A slideshow of images of the many times my family had stopped at this snack bar flashed through my mind: the evenings when Mama drove us to the airport to pick Papa up from his business trips and we'd stop here on the way home; the Sunday afternoons when Papa took us for a drive and we'd convince him to buy us coconut ice cream.

"I'm happy you are back. It is so good to see you," Willia said again. We stood together, licking ice cream as we had countless times before. After we finished, we got back into the car and drove to town.

The narrow, winding streets were jammed with traffic, mostly compact cars and Japanese pickup trucks. We passed Scharloo, the old, fancy Jewish neighborhood where Opa's mother and sisters had lived so many years ago. The houses were as ornate as I remembered, but not as grand. Along the waterfront, just beyond Scharloo, was the floating market. I was surprised to see it consisted of only eight boats. When I was a child the market had seemed much bigger. Oma would sometimes take me here early in the morning before school started, to shop for fruits and vegetables. The floating market would be filled with the sounds of people bargaining for the best prices among the mounds of mangos, watermelons, cucumbers, and tomatoes that were displayed on the counters set up alongside the boats. But now the sailors had packed up for the day and were lying in hammocks onboard their boats, enjoying the evening.

On this side of the harbor channel, in Punda, the houses were still painted brilliant colors, although the paint was peeling on some of them. Willemstad seemed to have shrunk. Breedestraat, the main street of Punda, was only four short blocks. The pontoon bridge across the channel, which connected the Punda and Otrabanda sides of Willemstad, had been turned into a pedestrian bridge. A gigantic new bridge had been constructed farther down the channel, to carry cars and trucks; its arched steel structure was tall enough to allow the largest cruise ships to sail underneath. It majestically crowned the entrance to the inner harbor. Willia informed me it was the tallest bridge in the Caribbean. The governor general's yellow palace still had its detailed white-stucco molding. It had once seemed enormous to me, but it was no bigger than some of the houses in Beverly Hills. On the other side of the channel, in Otrabanda, I could see a few abandoned houses, their roofs gone and their walls crumbling. That side of the city had become a slum.

I was busy taking in every detail. Most of the stores had not changed. Penha, the perfume store, was still on Handelskade. The New Amsterdam Linen store, the La Ganga hardware store, and the Bata shoe store were still where they had always been. I asked Willia if the shops had the same owners. She explained that most of the shop owners' children had taken over the businesses. It was common for businesses to be handed down from father to son and owned by the same Curaçao families for generations.

Cinelandia, one of Curaçao's two movie theaters, was closed and a For Sale sign drooped from the marquee. The ticket window was boarded up and graffiti adorned the walls. When I was a child, it had been the only form of family entertainment other than gathering at friends' homes to talk, dance, or play games. I remembered dressing up in my best clothes to go to Cinelandia to see *The Sound of Music* and *The Jungle Book* with my family.

We drove along Penstraat, away from the center of town, toward Oma's house.

"How is Johan?" I asked.

"He's living in Amsterdam and doing well. He got married two years ago. Did you know that?" A shadow fell over Willia's face as she glanced at me. I pressed my lips together trying not to feel the sting of being excluded.

"No," I answered, surprised and upset that I hadn't known. "Why didn't anyone tell me?"

"Well, you know Johan has not spoken to Mama in years, and he knew that if he had told you about the wedding and not Mama, it would just cause more trouble between you. He felt it was better not to say anything at all."

"Is his wife nice?" I asked.

"Yes. I met her when they came here on their honeymoon. She's very nice." I was happy for Johan. He had found someone he loved.

Willia parked in front of Penstraat 34. I was shocked by what I saw. Some of the shutters were hanging askew from their hinges. A post was missing from the balcony railing. The green stucco of the walls was crumbling from the salt in the air. Now I could see why Oma had the walls lime-washed every year. "Doesn't Tante Dora live here?" I asked.

"Tante Dora had to move to a retirement home a year ago." Willia paused and glanced at the house. "She tried renting it out but maintaining it cost too much, so the house was left empty."

Of Oma's nine children, only Tante Dora still lived in Curaçao. They all had been educated in the Netherlands. The two oldest had died, five of them still lived in Europe, where the opportunities to work were better, and Mama lived in California.

I walked up to the front door and tried to open it. The wood was swollen and its white paint was peeling. The door was stuck. I kicked and pulled at it. Finally it opened. Inside, the house smelled musty. I walked into the living room where the mirror once hung, and stood facing a blank wall.

When I was growing up, this room had seemed large and elegant, but now it seemed cramped and devoid of the grandeur I remembered. There were rat droppings by the kitchen door. Flashes of memory came to me of the times I had spent in this house. I was standing in the very spot where all those wonderful memories had been created. I closed my eyes hoping to sense Oma, but I only felt emptiness. I walked to her bedroom and stood in the doorway, closed my eyes, and refurnished the room in my mind. I recalled her big bed and its crisp, white cotton sheets, the mahogany armoire whose door creaked as it opened, the ebony vanity, and the smell of her cologne from Spain. I opened my eyes.

The emptiness was overwhelming. Tears trickled down my cheeks. I realized that the only place I could still find Oma was in my heart.

I went to the back door and stepped out onto the porch. The ocean was the same sparkling cobalt blue it always had been, and the fluffy white clouds still danced in the baby-blue sky. The waves pounded the rocks, spraying white frothy water into the air. I had forgotten how loud the ocean could be. I licked my lips and tasted salt. The rickety boards on the porch floor creaked as I walked across them and sat down on the steps. Willia had walked around the outside of the house while I went through the house alone. We met on the porch steps. "This must be hard for you," she said, sitting down next to me. "It's the first time you have been here without Oma."

"*Ja*," I exhaled, as I looked down at my shoes. "What happened to all of Oma's things?"

"I have a few pieces, some things went to your aunts and uncles in Europe, and some were given to her friends."

"It's weird that I can't feel Oma here at all." I looked up at her. "Can we go see if Hendrika is home?" I asked.

"*Ja*. I left a note for her yesterday to ring me, but she hasn't." Willia stood up. We walked along the path to the cottage. The potted plants on either side were dead. Willia knocked on the door but there was no answer. She opened it a crack.

"Who is it?" I heard Hendrika's voice ask.

"It's me, Hendrika," Willia said as we walked in. "And look, I brought Serena."

The cottage was dark and dirty. Hendrika was sitting in a chair. She looked as if she had been sleeping. She seemed startled and disoriented for a moment, and then she jumped up, grabbed a cigarette out of a pack on the table and walked over to me. She wore a stained, gray tank top and denim cut-off shorts. She looked bony, thinner than I had ever seen her before. Her skin was so red and wrinkled that her freckles barely showed, her fingernails were long and dirty, her teeth were yellow, her hair looked dry and brittle, and she smelled of sweat. Nothing about her resembled the Hendrika who had come with Mama and me to America. Scattered everywhere were worn clothes, dirty dishes, records, empty Coke cans, magazines, and ashtrays full of cigarette butts. The air smelled stale. She hugged me, the unlit cigarette in her hand.

"It's so good to see you, Serena," she greeted me. As I hugged her I could feel her bony frame. I wanted to hold her tight but was afraid she would break.

"Hendrika, how are you?" I said.

"I'm fine. I'm fine, fine. How are you?" She shot the question right back at me. She seemed uncomfortable in her body. A stifling silence filled the room. She struck a match and held it to her cigarette. "Hey, we should go dancing," Hendrika said, patting me on the back. "I know this bar. It'll be just like the old times at the Gypsy Camp."

"That would be nice." I said, forcing a smile. I glanced at Willia. She raised her eyebrows, a troubled look on her face. I turned back to Hendrika. "How is the photography going?"

"Photography?" She hesitated. "Oh, I don't do that anymore. I'm on to bigger and better things. How are things back in California?" she asked. Without giving me a chance to answer, she continued. "I'll tell you, Serena, things are fine here. I didn't want to come back to Curaçao. But it's been great." She put out her cigarette and grabbed another from the pack. Her movements were jerky. "You don't have to worry about me. I'm fine." I could see that everything was not fine. I wanted to do something for her, but all I could do was talk to her.

"You must be tired, Serena," Willia said. "Let me take you to my house."

"Okay," I said, reluctant to leave Hendrika. I wanted to do something to change what I was seeing, but I didn't know what I could do. "I'll see you later, Hendrika. Okay?" I hugged her again.

"*Ja. Ja.* I'll see you later," Hendrika replied, letting me hug her. She stepped back, tapped the ash from the end of her cigarette with her index finger and waved good-bye with the other hand. I glanced over my shoulder at Hendrika as we walked to the car. She was puffing on her cigarette. It crushed me to see her so broken. "What's wrong with her?" I asked Willia once we were in the car.

"Cocaine," Willia said sadly. "She was using it in California, you know."

I gulped, fighting back tears. "No! I didn't know that. I knew she smoked marijuana."

"She was already addicted to cocaine when she came back to Curaçao."

"That explains her friends at the Gypsy Camp." I remembered Sandu warning me about Hendrika's friends.

I thought of all she had gone through to take care of Mama and me. She had tried so hard to make our dreams come true—all at the cost of her own. She was the one who had kept us from starving by go-go dancing when we needed money. She had never once complained about not being able to buy film for her camera. She had gone to those classes with Kent, she had driven us, cooked for us, and cleaned for us as if she had been a servant. Now I knew I needed to do something for her.

"I've tried to help her, Serena," Willia said, "but Hendrika doesn't want any help, and until she does, no one can help her." I realized Hendrika had good reason to be afraid of help, after all the help Mama had given her. I had only been home a few hours, yet I already felt as if I were picking up the pieces of a shattered treasure chest, some intact and shining, others disintegrated beyond repair.

We pulled up in front of Willia's house. It was painted yellow, with a large front porch and wooden shutters. It was built of concrete block and surrounded by a picket fence. She opened the door and ushered me in ahead of her. Her Airedale, Terrie, came up to greet us. The walls and the furniture were white. Colorful rugs were scattered on the floor, and bright, native Caribbean art contrasted sharply with the white of the walls. We sat and drank water with lemon. I told Willia I was in college. She shook the ice in her glass; she was surprised and very proud of me. I told her that I hadn't seen any movie stars and that I didn't play any sports, and I told her I had a boyfriend. She asked me a million questions about Sandu, and I answered almost all of them. Willia's eyebrows pulled together. "He sounds really nice, Serena. But he's much older than you are."

"It's okay. He'll wait for me until I'm old enough, and then we'll get married," I reassured her.

"As long as he's willing to wait, I guess it's okay." Willia sounded doubtful. I did not tell her we were lovers. I didn't want her to worry.

"How is Mama?" Willia asked at last.

"The same. I don't think she'll ever change."

"I'm sorry. It must be difficult to be alone with her." Willia scooted closer.

"Because I'm the youngest, I've been able to see that none of us have been able to please her. It's kind of a relief to realize it's impossible."

She took my hand. "I'm sorry, Serena. I know it must be hard."

"I miss Oma," I said.

"Mmmm. I miss Oma, too."

I pulled the pink card I had been guarding for the past three and a half years out of my carry-on bag and held it up for Willia to see. "Do you remember this?" I asked her.

"My God! You still have that?" Willia exclaimed in amazement.

"It's the best present anyone has ever given me." I flattened out the creases. "There are still five lessons left."

"I'm sorry you didn't get to use all of them," Willia said, pursing her lips.

"This pink card means much more than expired riding lessons to me," I said, holding the card up. "It's my reminder of the first time I dreamt of something I thought was impossible, and yet it came true."

"Don't ever be afraid to dream, Serena. Dreams can come true, no matter how impossible they might seem." Willia pulled me closer. I was happy she understood.

ﻉﻉﻉﻉﻉﻉﻉﻉ

THE NEXT DAY, WE ARRIVED at the American Consulate at twenty-five past one, exactly five minutes before my appointment. The consulate building was at the top of Berg Alterna, overlooking the harbor entrance and Punda, Otrabanda, and Scharloo. It stood out because it was a white building and had a slate roof. The lush grass and palm trees made the compound look as if it were in a tropical paradise, even though Curaçao was a desert island. Most houses in Curaçao had wood-shuttered windows to keep out the heat. The consulate had glass windows; the varnished shutters were only decorative because the building was completely air-conditioned. The Great Seal of the United States hung on the front of the building, next to the oversized teak entrance doors.

A blast of cool air greeted us as Willia opened the door. In the lobby a brass chandelier hung from the ceiling, reflecting the room below it. Mahogany armchairs upholstered in blue damask lined the white walls. Portraits of President Gerald Ford and Secretary of State Henry Kissinger hung on the wall in front of us. To our left, a wood-paneled counter topped by a glass partition separated the waiting area from where two consular officials sat behind ornate oak desks. I walked to the partition and gave one of them my name and the letter showing the date and time of my appointment. He handed me three forms to complete. I filled them in slowly while Willia watched, looking over my shoulder as I wrote. I felt self-conscious.

"Can I see that?" Willia asked.

"What?" I didn't want her to look at the forms.

"Those papers." She squinted slightly, trying to read them.

"Why?"

"Just let me see them," Willia insisted. She took the forms from me, frowning. "Serena, how can you be in college when you make these kinds of spelling mistakes? Here, let me help you fill these out." Willia corrected all my mistakes and handed the forms back to me. I was humiliated. The pride I thought Willia felt for me yesterday was now shadowed with doubt. Ashamed, I sat watching the minute hand of the clock on the wall jump every sixty seconds.

We waited for forty minutes before an official opened the door to the consul general's office and called my name. I was frightened he might see something in me that would make him deny my green-card application. I could hardly breathe as I stood up and walked toward him. When I reached the door and glanced back at Willia, she winked and smiled at me. I took a deep breath and followed the Consul General into his office. Twenty minutes later, I came out grinning. "He said I could expect my green card in a couple of days," I told Willia.

"Congratulations, Serena," Willia said with a smile as we walked out into the afternoon heat.

"So tell me, Serena, what's really going on with school?" Willia asked bluntly, staring at me once we were in her car. I swallowed to clear the lump in my throat, and told Willia about my graduation and my failed first semester of college. "It's not just you, Serena. Mama has done that to all of us. She has taken us from country to country, chasing improbable fortunes, never considering how difficult she was making it for us, changing languages and cultures all the time. And she expected her schemes to succeed, and expected great things from us." Willia's eyes narrowed as she remembered. "Then as soon as she was disappointed, she fell into one of her depressions." Willia was fuming. "You know, Mama is like one of those tropical strangler-fig trees in the rainforest. They wrap themselves around their host trees so tightly that they choke them to death. And without a host tree a strangler-fig cannot survive."

It was true; Mama could not survive without controlling her children. Willia's analogy sent chills up my spine. I stared out of the car window as she drove to her house.

Early the next morning, Willia dropped me off at the Curaçao Yacht Club, at Spaanse Water. I wanted to walk from the yacht club to the beach where Mama and Papa used to take us swimming when we were children. A boat with a blue-and-white sail was peacefully cruising the bay. The sun was rising fast and I could feel the temperature increasing steadily. As I got closer to the beach I could see the gnarled *divi-divi* trees standing in the sand, offering their shade, but it was a weekday, and no one took advantage of their offer. I thought about my conversation with Willia. Her story of the strangler-fig described exactly how I felt. It was such a relief to know that Willia felt the same way I did about living with Mama. I had missed Willia so much.

I found myself back at the yacht club at the spot where Willia had dropped me off. I waited for her to return, standing under a large *flamboyan* tree that was in full bloom, its bright-orange flowers scandalously flaunting themselves.

At five o'clock that evening, we arrived at the Avila Beach Hotel, where we were to meet Hendrika for an early dinner. The hotel was a converted pink *landhuis* on the beach. We made our way to the bar, which was made to look like a shipwrecked boat stranded on the beach. The bar overlooked a shallow bay, where the water lazily lapped at the white sand. Willia ordered a glass of wine and I ordered a virgin Piña Colada. Hendrika hadn't arrived yet.

"Mama isn't always wrong, you know," Willia said. "You're old enough to take care of yourself. You have to find help at your college. Help is always available, but you have to ask for it."

I felt as if I were listening to Oma, who had also reassured me that help would be available when I needed it. I appreciated Willia more than ever. She had always taken care of me, but I didn't remember hearing her speak like Oma before. I suddenly realized how big an influence Oma must have been on Willia. "You see, Serena, as crazy as Mama is, she does have good qualities," Willia said matter-of-factly, after she took a sip of her wine. She looked at me for a moment, as if she were weighing what she was about to say. "Mama sees no limits—that's the good part; but the bad part is that she acts on all her impulses without thinking them through. It is because of her you have your green card, and that's extraordinary." Willia leaned forward. "Living in America, you can become anything you want. Don't let the opportunity Mama has given you slip away." Willia's words pierced me. I was going to have to take responsibility for my own life. Feeling sorry for myself and running to Sandu for relief and comfort was not a solution.

Willia had made her own opportunities. She had worked her way up from ticket agent to head of sales at the airline, and she had done it through pure determination, working during the day and going to school at night. If Willia could succeed in spite of Mama, so could I. I decided to ask for help at school as soon as I got back to California.

The sun went down and we left the bar, to be seated for dinner. Worried, we sat waiting for Hendrika for more than an hour. Finally, we ordered conch fritters, fried plantains, and *Giambo ku Funchi*, a Curaçao version of gumbo and polenta. We were almost finished with our meal when Hendrika rushed in, a cigarette in her right hand. "I'm sorry, my ride didn't show up," she explained. She was wearing an old T-shirt with a yellow smiley face on the front, and shorts.

"We could have picked you up. Why didn't you call me?" Willia asked.

"*Ay*, it's okay. Don't worry. I'm here now." Hendrika pulled out a chair and slouched into it, puffing on her cigarette. The waiter came over and cleared the table. "A double vodka, please," she ordered.

"Aren't you going to eat?" Willia asked.

"I'm not hungry. I already ate," Hendrika replied, blowing smoke through the left side of her mouth. We sat in silence until the waiter brought dessert menus, along with Hendrika's vodka.

"How is Mama?" Hendrika asked.

"She's fine," I said. "She misses you. We both do."

Hendrika drank her vodka in one gulp and set the empty glass on the table. The three of us sat looking at each other. I picked at my cuticles, wishing Willia would say something. Hendrika stared straight ahead, a glazed look in her eyes. Suddenly she stood up. "I'm sorry, I've got to go," she said. "I have a meeting." She took a drag from her cigarette and ground it out in the ashtray as she blew the smoke, this time out of the right side of her mouth. Startled,

Willia and I stood up also. I hugged Hendrika good-bye and she hurried away, her frail body hunched over. Her elegant long legs, which once turned heads, looked like toothpicks. She stopped and turned back toward us and for a moment, our eyes met. Then with her eyes cast down, she walked away.

"How does she survive?" I asked Willia. "What does she do to earn a living?"

"She grooms dogs and gets other odd jobs."

"Does she take pictures anymore?"

"I don't think so."

"I wish I could help her."

"I try to help her, Serena, but she won't let me. I know it's hard to see her like this."

The next day I asked Willia if she would drive me out to the House of Six Doors. She told me it had been sold and was going to be knocked down, but that she would take me if I was sure I wanted to go. On the way, we drove by Shon Pètchi's house. He had passed away but the little red mud house with its green window frames was the same. It looked as though someone was still living there. As we passed Shon Pètchi's house I asked Willia if she could take me past Shon Momo's and Shon Tisha's houses.

We turned onto the road that led to Shon Momo's house. The light-blue house had been turned into a snack bar on the beach, and Shon Momo had moved to a retirement home. Shon Tisha had replaced her tiny pink home with a larger house constructed of concrete block. Four cars were parked in the driveway. I asked Willia about Mirelva, Shon Tisha's daughter, who used to help Oma and played with me. She told me that Mirelva had earned a scholarship to study in the Netherlands.

We turned onto the road leading to the House of Six Doors. Although the road had been paved, goats still ran free through the shrubs, sometimes dashing across the road. I was anxious to see the big blue *landhuis*. I hoped that somehow I would be able to feel Oma's presence there. Strangely, I felt further away from her here in Curaçao than I had ever felt in California. The gnarled *divi-divi* trees leaned over the grayish-green shrubs that covered the countryside. We crested the hill. I saw the cobalt-blue house imprisoned by a tall chain-link fence, its right side reduced to rubble and the roof gone. Only one of the six doors was still on its hinges. Debris surrounded the house. The trees and shrubs that had once adorned the grounds had withered. I couldn't believe my eyes. My heart plummeted. I was devastated to see the House of Six Doors in this condition and horrified to realize that soon it would no longer exist at all.

Willia stopped the car and I got out. A large sign posted on the fence declared "Coming Soon—the Country House Hotel." There was no one around. I walked around the entire fence, trying to find a way in. My fingers clenched the metal links of the fence as I looked to see if I could climb it, but barbed wire was strung along the top.

I stood there sobbing, mourning the loss of the house. As the trade winds caressed my face, the scent of *kadushi* cactus flowers enveloped me. I thanked Oma for sending it, and I thanked the house for the many happy memories it had given me. I bid the big blue house farewell and turned back toward the car. Willia was leaning against the car door waiting for me, tears running down her cheeks.

Four days later, Willia stood again on the airport rooftop waving good-bye. As I climbed up the stairs to the plane I waved back. I was sad to leave my sisters, but relieved that the Curaçao I loved was in my heart and could never be left behind. I was eager to return to California to pursue my rekindled dream of becoming a reporter. I took my seat and waved at Willia through the window, although I knew she couldn't see me anymore. I stuffed my carry-on under the seat in front of me and pulled out my wallet. Inside, I carried with me a few colors of the island: the folded pink card with its expired riding lessons, and next to it, my green card.

MAMA PICKED ME UP FROM the LA airport and greeted me as if I had been away for years. I held up my green card. She took it from my hand and read my name out loud, then examined it front and back, as if it were a precious artifact. "Congratulations, Serena. We've done it." She cheered. "We have to celebrate! Let's have dinner at Musso & Frank."

"Okay," I said, surprised. We had driven past the restaurant many times and read its olive green, neon sign: "Musso & Frank Grill, Oldest in Hollywood. Since 1919." At night, the letters on the sign looked as if they were floating in the air above the building. We had never eaten there because Mama had always said it was too expensive. A waiter dressed in a white shirt and black pants seated us in a booth against the wall. The large room looked elegant with its shiny wood paneling. The pristine white table cloths were a stark contrast to the paneling and the red-leather upholstery of the benches and chairs. At a table next to us sat a mother and father with their two teenage daughters. They were laughing and talking about all the things they had done on their vacation in Hollywood—the Universal Studios tour, shopping on Rodeo Drive, seeing a show at the Pantages—things I had heard about but which my family couldn't afford to see, even after four years in California.

After we ordered, I told Mama about Oma's house and about the House of Six Doors. She seemed to know that the House of Six Doors had been sold, but she was outraged to hear that it was being demolished and replaced by a hotel. "I would never have allowed that," she exclaimed. "Tante Dora should have put me in charge. Now see what has happened. *Ay nò.*" She slammed her hand on the table. "Tante Dora does not know anything. I would have told them they could not demolish it." Her face was tense with frustration, and she pulled out a cigarette and lit it.

Mama asked about Hendrika. I decided not to tell her that Hendrika was using cocaine. I just said she was fine.

"And Willia?" Mama asked, looking away. I told her how well Willia was doing. She stared at me, her upper lip tense and her eyebrows pulled together, her face full of disbelief. "She is doing well only because of all the languages she learned while she was with me." Mama examined the check the waiter put on the table between us. "And Johan?" she asked, without looking up. I told her he lived in Amsterdam and was married. Her eyebrows went up and the corners of her lips pulled down. I could see she was hurt, but she didn't say anything. I watched Mama pay the bill and wondered if our improved financial situation was because of the sale of the House of Six Doors.

We arrived home and I went straight to bed, exhausted. I had missed the third week of my second semester and was anxious to return to school. I wanted to make an appointment with a counselor as soon as possible.

On the day of my appointment I went to the administration building and knocked on Mrs. Huffman's door. "Come in," Mrs. Huffman said. She was standing behind her desk when I pushed the door open. She was a short, slightly overweight woman with a big smile and glasses, her gray hair pulled back in a bun. I introduced myself and handed her my transcript. She invited me to sit down. I was nervous.

"I detect an accent. Where are you from?" she asked, glancing from me to the transcript and back again over her glasses.

"Curaçao." I waited for a response, playing with my fingernails.

"I've never heard of that country. Where is it?"

"Near Venezuela. It's a Dutch island," I said.

"That sounds exotic. How can I help you?" I told her about all the difficulties I was having with school. She listened attentively. "Your spoken English is quite good. We have students here from all over the world. Some of them don't speak English nearly as well as you do. I will arrange for you to take placement tests to see what classes you should be in, and I'll set up an assessment test that will tell us if you have any learning disabilities that might make writing hard for you."

Mrs. Huffman took me over to the student center and scheduled tutoring sessions. She explained that the school offered special classes for students who spoke English as a second language. Willia had been right. I had no idea so much help was available.

A week later, I met with Mrs. Huffman again. My test results had come back and she advised me to drop my English and math classes, and transfer into Advanced Remedial English and Algebra 1.

Sandu had always presumed my studies were going as well as his. He was excelling in all the classes he took, his English was steadily getting better, and he loved his job. His apartment was the only place where I felt I belonged. I spent a lot of time there while he drew, painted, and worked on his art projects. I loved watching him and he loved showing me his work. He always looked very proud when I praised him. Now I was going to be able to do my school work while he did his. I was looking forward to doing better in school so I could show him my work and he could praise me.

One Friday afternoon, I was at his apartment, sitting in the bathroom watching him get ready for work at La Serre. I sat on the counter while he was shaving. We glanced back and forth at each other in a silent conversation. His eyes were searching for mine, but I was busy making mental notes of every bit of his body. "What are you looking at?" he asked.

"You. Every inch of you. And I'm committing it to memory. I want to remember all of you," I said with a smile.

"Why do you need to remember me?" Sandu asked, furrowing his brow. "We are together. You see me almost every day. Why do you need to remember?"

"I don't know," I said. "I just feel the need to look so I can remember you." I shook my head as I spoke as if I were awakening myself from a daze. "I want to remember you the way you are now.

We won't always be the same people." Sandu shrugged his shoulders, puzzled. "I don't know why I feel this way, but I do," I said.

He turned on the shower, stepped under the stream and reached out his hand invitingly. I unbuttoned the shirt I was wearing and joined him. We stood holding each other as the water hit our bodies and streamed off. Sandu rocked me back and forth, and slowly we found ourselves dancing to the rhythm of the drops tapping against our skin.

ᘓᘍᘓᘍᘓᘍᘓᘍᘓᘍᘓᘍ

IT WAS THE BEGINNING OF summer and the end of my second semester when I opened the envelope that contained my grades. I had earned Cs in Remedial English and Algebra 1, and Ds in American History and Introduction to Psychology. I was proud of myself for having completed all my courses. I wanted to show Mama, but I knew she would not be proud of Cs and Ds. I wanted to tell Sandu, but I was afraid he would also be ashamed of my results. My confidence wavered because I could not share my progress with the people I loved most, but I needed to talk to someone. I knew Inez would be encouraging, so I decided to call her. We had not spent much time together because my school work had kept me busy, and she was spending more time at her boyfriend's apartment. Now that she and Mark were engaged and making wedding plans, she was seldom home at the times I could visit her.

Inez invited me to stop by for dinner. We started talking while we made spaghetti and meatballs. She already knew how Mama had paid the headmaster for my high school diploma, and how difficult college was for me. She shared my delight in my academic progress, as I thought she would. I was touched when she praised me, grateful that she saw how hard I had tried.

ᘓᘍᘓᘍᘓᘍᘓᘍᘓᘍᘓᘍ

THE SUMMER HAD BEEN HOT and I was looking forward to the cooler weather of fall. I had taken two summer courses: Spanish Literature and English 100, and was studying for finals. The day of my Spanish Literature exam, I arrived at Sandu's apartment early in the morning. The studio, normally so neat, had a large suitcase open on the couch, a coat I didn't recognize hanging on the back of a chair, and unfamiliar shoes on the floor. A mattress lay in the corner where our Christmas tree had been. Sandu was still in bed. "Who is here?" I asked, surprised.

"My friend, Daniel. He arrived yesterday," Sandu said, half asleep. It had been almost a year since we'd celebrated Daniel's escape, and I had forgotten about it. Sandu was lying on his stomach, and he turned his face to me as he spoke. His left arm crawled out from under the sheets and signaled me to come closer.

"Where is he now?" I asked, since there was no one on the mattress.

"He's in the bathroom."

I slid under the covers with Sandu, upset I hadn't been told about Daniel's arrival. Sandu fell asleep again, not noticing my reaction. Daniel came out of the bathroom in his underwear. He didn't see me and casually walked back to his mattress. I peeked out from under the covers.

Daniel had dark hair and was much shorter than Sandu, but he had the same athletically sculpted body. Sandu had told me Daniel had been a gymnast in Romania and that he loved to play the guitar. I watched him getting back under the blankets on the mattress. I felt left out—Sandu had not told me Daniel was going to be staying with him. I closed my eyes and tried to sleep, but my mind raced until Sandu woke up an hour later. "What exams do you have today?" he asked as he rolled over me and put his arms around my body.

"I've got a final at eleven," I answered.

Sandu sat up. "I want to introduce you to my best friend. Hey, Daniel! I want you to meet Serena." Daniel got up from the mattress, wrapping the sheet around him.

"Serena, please excuse!" he said, his hand holding his sheet. "Nice to meet you. You are very beautiful young woman. Sandu is lucky man," he said with such a thick accent I could barely understand him.

"Very nice to meet you, too, Daniel," I responded. "What did he say?" I whispered to Sandu.

"Just that you're pretty and I'm lucky." Sandu kissed me.

"Please excuse," Daniel said again, bowing his head slightly. He picked up some clothes and went into the bathroom.

"Why didn't you tell me he was coming?" I asked Sandu.

"I didn't know. He called me the day before yesterday and told me he was here. When would I have told you? I haven't seen you since finals started. Why are you being so difficult?"

It felt awkward with the three of us in the tiny apartment, but Sandu wasn't going to ask Daniel to leave. I was angry our world had been invaded, and sad we had lost our privacy.

ᘔᑫᘔᑫᘔᑫᘔᑫᘔᑫᘔ

I EARNED AN A IN Spanish Literature and a C in English 100 that summer. Because English was difficult for me, I was as proud of the C as I was of my first A. For the first time I had taken responsibility for my future, and it felt good. That fall I enrolled in English 101, Intermediate Algebra, and History of Western Civilization. I now felt I belonged at San Fernando Valley College. I was asking questions and finding answers, and I spent most of my days in class, at the library, or at the student center.

Two months had passed since Daniel's arrival and he was still living in Sandu's apartment. There was no sign of his moving out. Sandu kept reassuring me that soon things would go back to the way they had been, but I was frustrated—I wanted to be alone with him. I couldn't grasp why Sandu allowed Daniel to share his apartment for so long. I felt displaced and abandoned.

Now when I wasn't at the library or the study center, I went home. Mama noticed I was home more often. Just as I was doing better in school, she began to worry about my studies. She asked about my classes and my grades. I assured her I was doing well and that I was home because I had taken easier classes this semester. The more I was home, the more Mama tried to direct my life. She suggested I learn to play the guitar, take singing lessons, and resume my interest in modeling and acting. Mama was annoyed that I didn't act on any of her suggestions and offended that I didn't take her advice. When I told her I was not interested in modeling or acting and that I wanted to become a reporter, she was disappointed.

I wasn't going to pretend to be someone I wasn't—Hendrika had done that and it had destroyed her. I was determined not to end up like Hendrika. Mama warned me that I was throwing away once-in-a-lifetime opportunities if I didn't listen to her, but her words did not affect me the way they used to. I knew she wanted me to be successful because, in her eyes, anyone successful was loved. But I was slowly learning that my only chance of success lay in following my own dreams.

ᘉᕽᘉᕽᘉᕽᘉᕽᘉᕽᘉᕽᘉ

IT WAS SIX MONTHS BEFORE Daniel finally moved out of Sandu's apartment. I cheered silently as I helped him pack his things. Every time the two friends spoke Romanian I had felt left out. In the beginning, they'd talk and watch sports on television as if I weren't there, but after a few months even Sandu started to show signs of frustration that his space had been invaded. Helping Daniel get started in America had proven to be more difficult and expensive than he had expected.

Sandu graduated from San Fernando Valley College, and was one of the few students admitted in the fall of 1976 to the prestigious Art Center School of Design. Because he had to save every penny for tuition and supplies, he could no longer afford to take me to fancy restaurants. Now our outings consisted of going to the grocery store and returning home to cook. He spent hours and hours on his art projects, meticulously addressing every detail. I still sat next to him, but instead of just watching him, I was studying.

It was February 1977, exactly one year since my trip to Curaçao. Willia had been right, once I decided to look for help I had found it. I had earned Bs in English 101, Intermediate Algebra, and History of Western Civilization. I was proud of my college-level English grade. Although this was going to be my fourth semester at San Fernando Valley College, I was just barely starting my college education.

I was grateful to Mrs. Huffman for all the help she had given me and often dropped by her office when I needed to talk to someone. I told her I wanted to become a reporter and she assured me I would be good at it. One afternoon she informed me that the school paper had a section for articles and poems written by foreign students about the experience of being an immigrant in the US. She suggested I submit something. "This could be the start of your writing career," she said with a big smile. I was surprised by her confidence in me and didn't want to disappoint her.

I thought about everything that had happened to us since we had come to America five years before. I remembered how everything was so different than it had been in Curaçao, how we had been treated as if we were stupid because we did things differently, how disorienting it had been suddenly not to know how much things cost, or how Mama could get a job, or what the laws were. It had taken courage and perseverance to make a new life.

Two weeks later, I handed Mrs. Huffman my poem.

My mother led me to America
With the promise of a better life.
I didn't know what she wanted.
I just wanted what I had left behind.
I felt lonely and insecure,
Distant and misunderstood.
All I wanted was a place to hide.
My fear was overwhelming—
It left me immobilized.

One day someone told me:
"Be brave. Let go of what you've left behind.
Dare to take the opportunity.
You'll be surprised at what you'll find."

The words were tempting, but I was afraid—
Afraid to let go of what I had left behind.

I took a breath of courage and closed my eyes.
I waited for fear to pass me by.
I waited, but the fear did not subside.
I had to leap and let faith be my guide.
I made the leap.
When I opened my eyes, I was surprised.
I still carried in my heart
Everything I thought I'd left behind.

After she read it Mrs. Huffman looked up at me. "This is beautiful, Serena. I'm very impressed." I smiled, relieved that she had liked it. It had been difficult for me to write, not only because it was in English, but also because it was painful to remember how scared and lost Mama, Hendrika, and I had felt when we arrived. My poem appeared in the school paper a week later. When I showed Mama the newspaper, she seemed happy for me that my poem had been published but she was puzzled.

"Serena, what did you leave behind that was so good?" I shrugged my shoulders. She didn't understand, and I didn't know how to explain it. When I showed Sandu my poem in the newspaper he looked proud, but after he read it he said, "It's beautiful, Serena, but isn't our being together here better than what you left behind?" I could see that he didn't understand, either. I wondered why everyone focused on the same line in the poem. I picked up five copies of the newspaper, sent one to Willia, and saved the rest.

I still found it difficult to live with Mama, even though she was no longer depressed. Every now and then she'd call Curaçao to talk to Hendrika but she seldom reached her, and the few times she did, the calls ended with Mama upset because Hendrika had no interest in trying to return to the United States. Mama couldn't understand why, and she'd be upset for days, until something new would divert her attention. Usually they were money-making schemes advertised on television or in magazines, ones that started out "Get Rich in Ten Days," "Work from Home," or "Start Your Own Business." I'd listen to her explanations of the investment each of the schemes required. I'd ask her as many questions as I could, trying to point out the risks, but she'd grow frustrated with me and send off her check anyway.

One afternoon when I came home from school, Mama handed me an envelope. It was from San Fernando Valley College, and it was addressed to me. I speculated about what could be inside. It was the end of March—too early for grades. I opened the envelope and inside was a check for five dollars and a letter announcing that my poem had been awarded the school newspaper's annual prize for foreign students who had taken English as a second language. "I can't believe it. I can't believe it," I cried, jumping around the living room and waving the check in the air. "Look Mama, I won a prize." She took the letter and the check from me.

"Oh Serena, that is excellent. What is the check for?" she asked.

"That's the prize for my poem. It was published in the school newspaper, Mama, remember?"

"Oh, really? That's wonderful." Mama sounded surprised. "I think that deserves a celebration."

"I've got to go back to school and show Mrs. Huffman," I said eagerly.

"Who is Mrs. Huffman?" Mama asked. I retrieved the letter and the check from Mama.

"She's my counselor at school. I have to show her," I said as I gathered my backpack, keys, and sweater. "I'll be back soon."

"Can't you just call her on the phone?" Mama asked, disappointed. I could see she felt excluded.

"No. I want to see her face when I tell her," I said, running out the door.

Once I got to school, I peeked into Mrs. Huffman's office. She was sitting at her desk. "Serena! Come in. What can I do for you?"

"Mrs. Huffman, look," I exclaimed, holding out the letter and the check. She rose from her chair with her arms open.

"I'm so glad you won," she said smiling. "You deserve it. You worked hard."

"But Mrs. Huffman, I don't understand how I won this prize. I didn't enter any contests. How could I have won?"

"Serena, I really liked your poem, something about it spoke to me. I entered it for you," Mrs. Huffman said as she hugged me. "Do you know that the newspaper will want to run a profile of you?" she asked.

"No," I answered. "What kind of profile?"

"They'll want to know about where you came from and how long you've been here—so you'd better start thinking about it." I felt my heart thumping with excitement. I was a long way from my goal of becoming a reporter, but now at least the prospect felt within reach.

I drove to Sandu's apartment to show him my prize. It was four o'clock in the afternoon. I swung open the door to his apartment and rushed in waving my letter and the check in the air.

"Sandu, look! Look what I won!" I shouted. What I saw stopped me in the doorway. Sandu was sitting on the couch, a blond woman next to him. I stood frozen. She seemed somehow familiar to me but I could not figure out why. My mind raced as I tried to place her. My eyes darted across the room and fell on the picture of Sandu in Romania with his family. I remembered the other picture he had on the table next to his mattress years ago. That's why she was familiar: it was Nadia. Sandu rose from the couch and walked over to me.

"Serena, this is Nadia, a friend from Romania. Nadia, this is Serena, my girlfriend." Sandu put his arm around me. I stood limp, my prize dangling from my hand. Nadia stood up, her tall, thin body elegant. Her posture was that of a ballerina, her gray-green eyes had a translucent quality, and her shiny blond hair hung down her back in a thick braid. I stepped back and gazed at Sandu with questioning eyes.

"Come, I'll explain everything," he said. I followed him outside and we walked to my car. I opened the door and placed my letter and the check on the dashboard. He hadn't asked what it was. I closed the door and leaned against it. "Nadia was my girlfriend in Romania,"

Sandu said as he stood next to me, also leaning against the car, looking down.

"I know. I remember her from the picture."

"Well, I had told her before I left that she had to forget me. The Romanian authorities picked her up and questioned her after I escaped. They questioned everybody who knew me. They suspected Nadia knew about my plans to escape because she had been my girlfriend. But she didn't know anything." His eyes met mine. "My plan to escape was a secret between me and my friend Radu, who escaped with me. When I got that letter from my mother, she told me that Nadia was still waiting for me." He raised an eyebrow and shook his head in amazement. "She spent many years trying to escape and follow me to California. She thought if we were together again everything would go back to the way it had been."

My heart ached as I wondered if perhaps she was right.

"Finally, Nadia met an older American man from Florida, who traveled to the Black Sea on business. She seduced him. He thought he had found the love of his life. He married her and brought her to Florida. Two days ago I got a phone call from her. She was crying and begging me to send her money so she could get away from him. She told me he was fat and ugly and he wanted to have sex all the time. She told me she hated him." Sandu paused, watching my face closely. "Nadia had nowhere to go. I felt sorry for her and I wired her money so she could come here." He paused.

I took in everything he said. "Is she going to be staying with you?" I asked without looking at him.

"I'll take her to Daniel's," Sandu answered. "Don't worry, you're still my baby." Then why am I standing outside? I asked myself. He pulled me close. A line from my poem came to me: "I still carried in my heart everything I thought I had left behind." I wanted to believe that there was nothing to worry about, but somehow I couldn't.

NADIA MOVED INTO DANIEL'S APARTMENT, but a couple of days later there she was again, in Sandu's apartment, sitting on his couch. She smiled at me triumphantly, as she flicked the ash from her cigarette into the ashtray. A wave of anger washed over me. I glared at her. "Where's Sandu?" I asked. Before she could answer, Sandu came in from the bathroom.

"Aren't you going to say hello to Nadia?" he said as he kissed me.

Irked, I asked, "What is she doing here?"

"I'm taking her to fill out job applications. You can come with us if you want to." He walked over to the drawing table and sorted through some papers.

"Hello, Nadia," I said, looking past her. She looked stunning with her blond hair and a forest-green dress that clung to her body and revealed every curve. The green of her dress matched her green eyes. She looked at me with contempt, then turned to gaze out the glass doors leading to the patio.

"Hello, Serena," she replied flatly. She spoke English well and had a lovely accent.

Sandu retrieved his keys and wallet from the drawing table and put them in his pants pockets. "Okay, let's go," he ordered. I felt as if I should go to school or go home, but I didn't want to leave them alone together. Besides, I wanted to know what was going on. Nadia ran her fingers through her hair, pulled a lipstick out of her purse, and applied it to her lips. Sandu walked to the door and held it open for both of us. Nadia said something in Romanian to him and he responded in Romanian. I felt excluded. There was a comfort in the way they communicated, an unconscious familiarity Sandu and I had never reached. But our relationship had something different: it had magic.

"Why can't she speak English when I'm here?" I asked.

"It's just a habit," Sandu responded. "I'm sorry. We'll speak English."

As the three of us walked to the car, Nadia walked right next to him and I found myself lagging behind. Sandu stopped to wait for me. Nadia stopped next to him. Sandu began to walk again, ignoring both of us. He seemed frustrated, and he opened all four doors of his car.

I sat in the backseat, watching the magic of our relationship evaporate. Nadia was redefining everything. I wanted to slap her and scream "Go away!" I realized Sandu was struggling with both Nadia and me; he did not want to reject Nadia after all she'd been through to be with him, and he didn't want to abandon me. He was like a frustrated child, awkwardly and clumsily trying to juggle two balls. He was doing the best he could to make both of us feel at ease, but I could see that it was going to be more difficult than he had anticipated.

We stopped at Bullocks. While Nadia went in to fill out a job application, Sandu and I sat in the car and waited. I opened my door and slid into the front seat next to him. "How did Nadia meet her American?" I asked.

"Six months after I left, things quieted down. The authorities had given up on trying to get information out of her." Sandu spoke with his head down and his hands clasped in his lap. "Nadia used her ability to speak English to apply for a job at the Black Sea hotels. She waited years to get one. Finally, she got a job as a waitress at the Lido Hotel, and that's where she met the American.

"The hotels on the Black Sea are the only places in Romania where foreign tourists are allowed; they fly into Bucharest and then are bused to the hotels. It's a way for the government to earn hard currency. It's ironic, isn't it? The tourists want to see Romania, but the government wants to keep them away from the Romanian people. But of course, that is impossible." Sandu looked across at me to see if I understood, but I was not in the mood to understand.

When Nadia returned, I didn't move from the front seat. She threw me an angry look as she opened the back door and got in. We drove to Robinson's department store so Nadia could fill out an application there, and then we drove back to Sandu's apartment. I walked into the kitchen and started washing the dishes that had been left in the sink. Sandu followed me in and put his arm around my shoulder.

"It's going to be all right," he reassured me. We walked back into the living room, where Nadia was playing a record she'd brought from Romania. I wondered if it was a record they had listened to when they were in love in Romania; maybe they used to dance to it. The phone rang and Sandu picked it up.

"Hi, Lucas, how are you?" he asked, looking at me as he spoke. Lucas was the manager at La Serre, the restaurant where Sandu worked. "Oh, that's wonderful. Thanks. I'll get her. No, no, it's okay. She's right here. Thanks again." Sandu held out the phone for Nadia. "It's Lucas from La Serre, for you," he said.

"What's going on?" I asked, angry they were sharing information I knew nothing about.

"Yesterday Nadia asked me if she could apply for the hostess job at La Serre. Lucas called to tell her she got the job."

I stared at Sandu, frightened that I was losing him. I felt a wave of rage come over me.

"How could you do that?" I asked, shaking my head. I couldn't believe his naiveté.

"Baby, I'm just trying to get her a job as fast as possible so she can make her own life."

"You two will be working together all night long. You'll be spending more time with her than you do with me." I tried to make him understand that Nadia's working at La Serre felt threatening to me.

"I don't know what you want from me. How can working at La Serre matter? We're so busy at the restaurant I probably won't even see her. You don't understand—we are running from the moment we get there to the moment the restaurant closes. Sometimes there isn't even enough time to go to the bathroom." His body was tight. "I don't understand what you want." He stood up, went to his drafting table, and started working.

"I've got to go." I said, crying. "I'll see you later." I was angry. We were starting to see things differently. He ran after me.

"Let me walk you to your car." Outside, he put his hand on my shoulder and gently turned me toward him. "I love you. We have to work this out. You just have to believe in me." Sandu said. I nodded. When we reached my car he put his arms around me, and as he held me I could feel our bodies relax.

"Sandu, Sandu. Where are you?" I heard Nadia calling. I pulled away. Sandu's jaw muscles clenched. I let go of him and got into my car. He prevented me from closing the door. Nadia walked up behind us. He shouted something at her in Romanian. She stopped, then turned around and walked back to the apartment. I looked at him through my tears.

"Daniel is picking her up in a couple of minutes to take her back to his apartment," he reassured me. "Come on, let's go for a drive." He got in on the passenger's side. I was glad he would not be in the apartment with Nadia waiting for Daniel.

༄༅༄༅༄༅༄༅༄༅

ON THE DAY OF MY eighteenth birthday, in the spring of 1977, I arrived at Sandu's apartment early. It was a cold and rainy day. He was still sleeping. I took my clothes off and slid into bed with him. My hair was wet from the rain. He snuggled around me to warm me up.

"Happy birthday, baby," he murmured in my ear. "You're all grown up now." He unwrapped his right arm from around me and reached behind his back to recover a gardenia he had hidden. "For you, my love," he said.

ॐ *299* ॐ

"Oh, I love gardenias. Thank you." I breathed in the divine scent.

"Because you love them so much, here is one more." He brought out another gardenia he had hidden under the sheets. I smiled and thanked him again. "And here is another one for your hair and one for the other side." He put a flower behind each of my ears, and then he kissed me. The fragrance of the gardenias lulled us to a heavenly place. He brought out three more and placed them on my breasts and my navel. I felt shy. His hand tenderly stroked my body as he gently placed eleven more flowers all around me. Slowly, he kissed my feet, my legs, my knees, my stomach, my breasts, my neck. He worked his way to my mouth. Eighteen white gardenias surrounded me on the white satin sheets. Sandu kissed me and caressed me as if I were a goddess. With him I felt beautiful and loved.

We spent the morning in bed. Sandu finally got up around noon. "I'm cooking for you," he shouted from the kitchen. "My special salmon dish!" I put on his white waiter's shirt and went to the kitchen to help.

"Is it one of Jean-Philippe's recipes?" I asked. He took out a bowl and put the gardenias in one by one, floating them in the water.

"Of course; I cook nothing but the best for you," he joked. He kissed me and then turned to prepare the salmon. "I'm sorry I can't afford to take you out, my love," Sandu said in a sad voice.

"I know. I don't care if we go out or stay in, as long as I'm with you. I almost like staying home better." I took the lettuce from the fridge and started washing it. The kitchen was narrow and, as we worked, we'd bump into each other, which was a good excuse to stop and kiss again.

"Now that you're eighteen, we can get married," Sandu announced. I didn't reply. He put the salmon in the oven and rinsed his hands. As he dried them he moved in front of me, blocking me from the sink. I felt both hopeful and trapped: happy he still wanted to marry me, but not ready to say yes. I was becoming independent of Mama at last, and I didn't want to become dependent on someone else; I longed to be my own person and make my own choices. I wanted to believe that Sandu loved me but the way he behaved around Nadia made me wonder. I was unsure about everything.

"Will you marry me?" he insisted. "Let's run away. I know this church. It's small and white, and not too far from here. It's a beautiful church." His eyes sparkled. "We'll get married and then we'll tell your mother. What can she do? She can't put me in jail anymore—you're eighteen!" He had both his arms around me and was holding me close.

"What if we get married and my mother goes into one of her dark moods?" I asked. "What then?"

"She won't do that. She's just using those moods to control you." Obviously annoyed, he turned his back to me and started cleaning the vegetables. His sudden irritation alarmed me.

"I will need to break this to her little by little," I explained. "First, I'll tell her I'm seeing you, and then after a while, I'll tell her we're getting married. It will take time."

He turned to me, pointing a stalk of Brussels sprouts. "Okay, we'll do it your way." My body relaxed in relief. He put the sprouts on a baking sheet, sprinkled them with olive oil and garlic salt, and set them on the stove, waiting for the oven to get hot. "Let's go sit on the bed and you can tell me how you are going to convince your mother." He opened a bottle of white wine and poured two glasses.

As we sat on the bed, we sipped the wine and listened to the raindrops beat against the glass door. It was raining hard outside.

ᘔᗷᘔᗷᘔᗷᘔᗷᘔᗷᘔᗷᘔᗷ

FOR DAYS I THOUGHT OF ways I could tell Mama about Sandu. I mentally rehearsed telling her, and imagined every response she could possibly offer. I would need to wait for the right moment because once I told her, there would be no going back. I realized I used to think I couldn't survive without her, but that was not the case anymore. Now my anxiety came from being unsure whether she could survive without me. It was time for each of us to learn to live without the other.

After winning the prize for my poem, I had started spending time at the school newspaper office in the basement of the Humanities building. There I had made two new friends, Claudia and Jessica. Claudia was a German girl from Berlin who was twenty, almost six feet tall, blond, and muscular. She was an English major and her English was impeccable. It had been her idea to run a column featuring the stories of immigrant students, and she asked me to write something about myself that she'd be able to run in the column to accompany the announcement of my prize. Jessica was the editor of the paper. She was short and stout but full of energy. She also had a full-time job at the weekly *Valley Sun* newspaper, working nights in the classified advertising department.

I was impressed with how many students went to school while working full time. I thought about the jobs I might be eligible to apply for. How free it would feel to have my own money.

ح٭ح٭ح٭ح٭ح٭ح٭ح٭

EXACTLY ONE WEEK AFTER MY eighteenth birthday, at seven twenty on a Thursday morning, I unlocked the door and walked into Sandu's apartment. Nadia jumped out of our bed. She covered herself with the sheet. Sandu leaped up as soon as he saw me.

"Why didn't you knock?" he said sharply.

I stood paralyzed. "I never knock," I said. My heart pounded as my chest tightened. I wanted to escape but I was trapped, watching what I didn't want to see.

"Wait. It's not what you think. Please, let me explain," Sandu said, distressed. Nadia said something to him in Romanian, her words coming quickly. He snapped back at her. She took a shirt of Sandu's that was hanging on his drafting chair and put it on, then took a cigarette out of her bag, lit it, and walked out onto the patio.

"It's not what you think," he repeated. He came to stand next to me. "A couple of friends came over after work last night." He put his hand on my back. I shrugged it off. "Nadia wanted to stay and

❦ *302* ❦

talk after everyone left. We talked, we remembered, we cried, and I didn't mean for this to happen. But it did. I'm sorry." He gently turned my face towards his with his hand. I turned away. "You are the one I love. I want you. She means nothing to me anymore. It was a mistake." Sandu's eyes begged me to understand.

"Did you make love to her?" I asked.

"It just happened. We had a bottle of wine," he said, as though this explained everything.

"I can understand everything else but I can't understand why you had to make love to her," I said coldly.

"It was a mistake, but it's done and there is nothing I can do about it now." He was becoming impatient. "She escaped for me. She did all this for me. I can't tell her that I don't care anymore and that I won't help her. I can't just tell her to just go away."

"No. You have to help her. But you didn't have to make love to her." Suddenly he didn't seem so confident. Nadia was still on the patio. I could see her watching us through the glass doors.

"She's been through a lot," Sandu said and paused. "You don't understand. You don't understand what it is like to take risks—big risks—to get to freedom." He looked down. He was asking me to understand her, but what I understood was that he was still imprisoned by his past.

"Nadia didn't escape to get to freedom. She escaped to get to you," I said.

"No, she's just scared. She needed a place to escape to. It's very frightening to leave everything behind and go to a place you know nothing about. It's easier if you have a beacon. I was her beacon." Sandu came closer. "She knows you are my baby and that I love you. I'll tell her she can't see me anymore, even casually. I'll tell her to stay away from me." Sandu half-smiled as he tried to wipe the tears from my face. I pulled back. "Once she has a boyfriend everything will be all right."

"I'm going to be late for school," I said. It wasn't true. I had almost two hours before class, but I couldn't bear to be there any longer. I stood up and walked out the door.

"Wait, wait," Sandu called, but I didn't stop. I decided not to go to class. I drove home.

ઝ૰ૐ૰ૐ૰ૐ૰ૐ૰ૐ૰ૐ૰

THE PHONE WAS RINGING AS I walked into the apartment. It was Sandu. "We need to talk, baby. Please, can I come over? I need to see you." Mama had already left to work the day shift at the hospital.

"I don't know if that's a good idea," I said. "I need to be alone and think."

"Please, let me come over," he begged.

"All right," I said, not wanting to argue.

Forty-five minutes later, Sandu arrived. It had been a long time since I had heard the sound of his footsteps on the stairs to our apartment. He knocked, and I opened the door. He held a bouquet of red roses. He tried to kiss me. It was difficult to resist kissing him back. He handed me the flowers. "Thank you," I said and I took them to the kitchen. I remembered my mother's words: "If you think bringing me flowers and chocolates means I will allow you to go out with my daughter, you'd better take them with you and try another address."

I placed the flowers in a vase and set them on the coffee table in the living room. We sat down on the couch; he put his hand on my knee. I turned and looked at him. We spoke with our eyes but our eyes weren't speaking the same language they used to. "I'm sorry for what happened, Serena. You are the one I love," Sandu said.

"I know," I responded.

"Then you forgive me?"

"There is nothing to forgive."

Sandu's eyebrows pulled together. "What do you mean?"

"You told me what happened and I understand. And it still hurts. You have been so definite and sure about everything in your life, and I know you are sure about your love for me. But you have not been definite and sure about our commitment. Ever since Nadia arrived, you've been unsure of yourself."

Sandu hesitated. He didn't seem to know what to say. "Things have been happening very fast. You don't understand how difficult this is for me. I want to help Nadia, but that doesn't mean I am in love with her."

"Let's be honest with each other, Sandu. You never expected her to come and find you. You thought you had lost her. It's obvious to me you never stopped loving her. And here you are, loving both of us." The words flowed out of my mouth as if someone else was speaking, and I realized how true they were. Sandu did not dispute it.

"I think it is only fair that you know everything about me before you tell me again that you love me. My grandmother was half black and half Caribbean Indian."

Sandu's face betrayed his surprise. "But you're Dutch," he protested.

"I am Dutch. And so was she."

He nodded. "So that's why your mother reminds me of a gypsy."

"I've never told you about my family. My grandmother was a very wise and spiritual woman and she used to say life is like a game. She said that to win the game you have to leave this world with more love than you came in with. She said never turn love into hate." I paused. "Things changed between us the moment Nadia arrived. Our love is quickly turning into frustration, anger, and pain. It seems to me that what we used to have has vanished. I don't want to turn our love into hate. I think we are all confused, and time and distance might give us some perspective."

We sat in silence for a moment.

"But if I love you and you love me, we should fight for our love." His choice of words seemed awkward. He didn't understand that love is not something you fight for. I took a deep breath.

"Sandu, I love you but I don't think we should see each other anymore," I said bluntly.

"It's over with Nadia," he argued.

"No, it's not only because of Nadia," I said. "There are a lot of things that have happened these last few months. I've done a great deal of thinking. You've changed, and mostly I've changed."

Sandu frowned and pursed his lips. "That should not matter," he said. "We should be able to work this out."

Suddenly nothing I said made sense to him, and nothing he said made sense to me. "I'm going to miss being with you," I said.

"Are you telling me this is it?" he asked. My heart was in my throat. I swallowed twice trying to dislodge it.

"Yes, I am."

"I think you're making a mistake."

"The time we had together was perfect," I said softly. "I wish it could have lasted forever." I stood up from the couch. "I don't know what I would have done without you."

His jaw clenched. His eyes narrowed. They pierced my heart and shattered it into a million pieces. I watched Sandu walk out the door. As it clicked shut behind him, I collapsed onto the couch, sobbing.

I COULD STILL HEAR THE sound of the door clicking shut behind Sandu, signaling the end of our four years together. Although it had been a long time since he had come to the apartment regularly, I vividly remembered each one of his visits. They were the happiest memories I had of this apartment: the dinners he brought from the restaurant that we ate in the middle of the night at Mama's dining table; holding each other on the couch; talking and dreaming of our future together; and making love in the early-morning hours. We had been different people then. We were both lonely and grateful to have found each other. But now our lives were taking different directions: I was finding more of myself and he was finding what he thought he had lost.

The fragrance of the twelve red roses Sandu had brought me as a symbol of his love filled the room, and it was beautiful. Sandu had the talent to recognize beauty and surround himself with it. He had taught me how to use my senses and to enjoy smells, tastes, sounds, and what pleases the eye. That was something I wanted to keep in my life forever.

I turned on the radio, hoping the sound of music would replace the emptiness. Jim Croce was singing "If I Could Save Time in a Bottle." My head was throbbing. I needed aspirin, a sleeping pill, something—anything—to make me feel better. Mama was not home yet. I looked in the lower cabinet of her nightstand. There was incense, a couple of herb-tincture bottles, erasers, glasses, paper clips, pencils, pens, candles, and matches. When I opened the top drawer, bunched-up papers sprang up. I pulled them out and piled them on the bed, still looking for the pills I knew my mother usually kept near her. The handwriting on a light-blue airmail envelope caught my eye. It looked like Oma's writing. The letter was addressed to me from Elena Ferreira-García.

Oma had sent me a letter! I touched the stamps on the right-hand corner of the envelope. The portrait on the stamp, of Queen Juliana, was smiling. I imagined Oma licking the stamp and placing it in the corner of the envelope. I looked at the date. The letter had been mailed more than two years ago. I turned the envelope over. It had been opened. I held my breath as I delicately extracted the two translucent blue sheets from the envelope. Eagerly, I began to read:

Dear Serena,

I miss you and I realize we will not see each other again in this lifetime. There are so many things I still want to tell you, but the time to release my body is drawing closer. I will not be here for your eighteenth birthday so this letter will have to speak for me.

When it is your time to become independent, remember your mother loves you and that everything she did was done out of love. She never got over the pain of the rejection of Opa's family and the rejections she suffered in the war. She has spent her whole life battling to be accepted.

Rejection has imprisoned her life. Her control of and expectations for her children have been her way of protecting all of you from that rejection. But by trying to save you from that pain, she has inflicted a greater pain: the pain of her not accepting you the way you are. She does not understand that by trying to spare you, she has hurt you.

*Nothing that I am telling you will ease the
pain, but I hope it will bring understanding.
You will have many feelings, but blaming your
mother for the pain will only perpetuate the
darkness. Rejection has been passed on for many
generations. It was your mother that helped me
realize that I carried that rejection in me.*

*My mother left her body as soon as I came into this
world and my father died when I was two years
old. My sweet grandmother did everything she
could to shield me from the pain of that rejection
and instill independence and self-reliance in me.*

*Celebrate your time together. Being with each other
in acceptance and understanding is what brings
about happy hearts—we are all interconnected.*

*Let your feelings flow freely, and accept each one
of them; know that they are your feelings and no
one is to blame for them. Live from your essence
and watch your feelings flow; only when you accept
them can you understand the story of your life.
Happy birthday,* mi dushi.

*With all my love,
Oma.*

*P.S. I am including a gift, as my grandmother
did for me. Enclosed is a check for fifteen
thousand guilders for your eighteenth
birthday. Put it in a savings account so
that you have it when you need it.*

Tears filled my eyes. I wished I could have been with Oma before she died. I looked in the envelope for the check, but there was nothing. I leaned back on my mother's pillow, the tears spilling down my face. Oma had been the only person who had accepted me totally. I could talk to her about anything. I could hardly remember what that felt like, it had been so long since anyone had understood me completely. Even with Sandu I had always hidden part of myself.

I walked to the dining table, took my pen and a notebook out of my backpack, and started writing. I wrote to Mama telling her how angry I was that she had not told me about Oma's letter. I wrote that I hated being accused of not loving her, of being ungrateful and uncaring. I told her that I was grateful and that I did love her and cared deeply—but I was frustrated because she could not see it. Tears streamed down my cheeks as I wrote furiously. I told her I knew she loved me but the way she showed her love hurt me. I told her I wished I could talk to her and tell her how I felt. I asked her if Hendrika, Willia, Johan, or I had done anything right—anything that had not hurt her. Had we done anything to make her proud?

My pen finally slowed down. Out of breath and drained, I stopped and read through the letter. To my surprise, I found that I had said things I would not have said to Mama in Dutch. I realized that when I spoke Dutch to Mama I was still a child, but in English I could express myself as an adult. My English was finally good enough—I had learned the words I needed to describe my feelings. It was in English that I could understand and explain my life. There were many things that I had learned in Dutch, Spanish, and Papiamentu, yet it seemed that English was the language in which all the things I had learned became clear. From now on, I'd speak to Mama in English.

I read the letter again and realized that each statement I had made, Mama could have made about me. I debated whether to give Mama the letter. I decided not to. Just writing it had been a revelation. I thought about how my whole life revolved around Mama and the apprehension I felt while living with her. I didn't really know who I was without her.

I felt suffocated and wanted some fresh air. I put on my jacket, grabbed my backpack, and went for a walk. As I came down the steps, I could smell the coffee that *Abuelita*, the apartment manager's mother-in-law, always brewed after dinner. I walked along Kingsley Avenue. It reminded me of the many times Hendrika and I had gone this way. I stopped at the corner of Sunset and Kingsley. The Gypsy Camp was across the street. It had been years since I had been there. Wanting to see if it had changed, I crossed the street. The red front door was now beige. It was open. Inside, the room no longer resembled the Gypsy Camp. Two pool tables stood on the old dance floor. I walked on and stopped at the drugstore where I had first met Inez. She had married Mark and moved to San Diego. I bought a pack of gum at the counter and continued down Sunset.

As I passed Hobart Avenue, I remembered my visit to the Indian astrologer. I struggled to recall our last meeting. At the time, I hadn't wanted to hear what she had to say, but now it seemed important. She had been right: Sandu and I were not going to live happily ever after. I remembered her saying he had promised to help me when my light grew dim, and that he had gone through many hardships to reach me, but there were other relationships he had to attend to in this lifetime. Now I understood what she had meant. And she had said more, so much more.

I walked faster, as if the effort would help me remember. The astrologer had spoken about how we forget our past lives and the promises we have made to each other as souls. Oma also had told me about reincarnation and about how she could remember her past lives. And Oma had said that our souls are pure life force. That's why the astrologer's words had sounded so familiar to me. She had said the more we forget, the further we are from our inner light, and the dimmer our light, the darker we feel. And Oma had said the darker we feel the more we blame others for our pain.

Now I understood what the astrologer and Oma meant. They meant that love is the ever-present light of the life force within us, and anger and hate is the darkness that conceals that love. I realized that it is in our relationships that we can see the love and hate that is within us reflected back to us. That's why Oma always said to be grateful for love and never turn love into hate. And that is why the astrologer had said remembering is love. I was feeling how difficult it was not to turn love into hate. It was painful to let go of Sandu. Letting go of him would be so much easier if I blamed him, but blaming him would lead me to hate him.

I returned to the apartment and started cleaning the kitchen. The apartment had become a place in which I no longer belonged. Nothing here reflected me. I wanted to start a new life, a life with less of Mama and more of Oma, a life of my own. I heard Mama's key turn in the lock. She greeted me as she closed the door behind her.

"I'm tired," she said, walking past me and into the bedroom. "The nursery was full of babies tonight. Three of them were in incubators." Seconds later, she returned from the bedroom. "What have you done?" she demanded. "Why have you been looking through my things?"

She was frightened. Her face was tense, her eyebrows pulled down.

"It's all right, Mama. I found Oma's letter, and I'm not mad at you." I held the letter up. She reached over and ripped it from my hand. I wanted to pull it back, but I was afraid it might tear.

"Why did you go through my things?" Mama went into the bedroom. I followed her. She collapsed on her bed and I sat down next to her. It was time for me to tell her the truth.

"Mama, I need to talk to you. Can you listen, please?"

Something had shifted inside me; I wasn't afraid anymore. I was going to tell her everything. I wanted her to see me as I was. She lit a cigarette. "Remember the Romanian friend I brought over that day?" Mama didn't answer. "He has been my friend and my lover for the last four years."

My mother's head snapped toward me and she looked at me, shocked. "What did you say?"

"He has been my friend, my lover, and my savior all these years."

"*Ay Dios mío. Ay Dios mío*," my mother moaned. Then she slumped back on the bed as if she were too weak to hear more.

"Mama, I found the letter while I was looking for a bottle of aspirin. I wasn't going through your things to spy on you." Mama looked at me disbelievingly. "I broke up with Sandu tonight. That's why I was looking for the aspirin. I was upset and had a headache. That's how I found the letter."

"I told you that man was no good," she hissed. "I wanted to protect you from him." She pointed her index finger in the air.

"I know, Mama. I know and I understand," I said. "But I did what I needed to do," I added in a soft voice.

"You needed to act like a prostitute? All that man wanted was your body. I know his kind."

Her words stung like needles and I felt the pain, but there was no use in arguing. "There is more," I said.

"*Ay Dios mío. Ay Dios mío*," she kept repeating.

"Do you remember my high school graduation?" My mother didn't answer. "I hardly knew how to read or write in English at the time. When I got to college, I couldn't do the work. It was Willia who encouraged me to get help, which I did when I got back from Curaçao."

"Saint Anthony, help me. All I have done to give my children an education, and nothing. *Ay nò*, I failed! Did you hear that, Saint Anthony? She didn't even bother to learn to read in high school. Nobody cares what I have sacrificed. My life is worthless!"

"Your life is not worthless. I'm grateful for everything you've done for me, and I'm sorry if I have hurt you." I was overcome by pity, as I tried to convince her that her life had not been wasted.

"You're not sorry! You wouldn't have done all these things if you loved me, or at least respected me. I'm not worth your respect or your love—sleeping with that man while I paid the bills."

"I'm sorry, Mama," I said again, seeing her point of view for the first time.

"Nonsense," she shot back.

"No, it's not nonsense. I'm sorry for everything that's gone wrong and the part I had in it. I was wrong in doing what I did because it hurt you. But it was what I needed to do. You don't have to protect me anymore. I know you want me to be successful so I will be loved and you're trying to protect me from getting hurt. I'm talking about what Oma wrote in her letter." Mama turned toward me, squinting. "Mama, I'm grown up now," I said.

She looked at me as though she understood, and more importantly, as though she accepted that I was now an adult. And perhaps for the first time, I felt that I really understood her. Oma had been right. In her own way, Mama did love me.

She stood up and walked over to the television. Under it was a box. She pulled it out, opened it, and took out an envelope. She handed it to me, turned on the television, and sat down on her bed again. I looked in the envelope: it contained ten one-hundred-dollar bills.

"And the rest of the money?" I risked asking, knowing it might infuriate her. To my surprise, it didn't.

"Some of it I used for your trip to Curaçao, and some of it paid your tuition. Now you have what's left," she said, never taking her eyes off the television.

"Thank you," I said, and I meant it. She had spent all the money on me. I wanted to talk more, but I sensed it was too much for Mama right then. I decided to go to bed.

The next morning, I bought a copy of the *Los Angeles Times* on my way to school. It felt odd to know that Sandu's apartment was no longer my haven, and it was painful that Sandu was no longer part of my life. I wondered if Nadia had already moved in. At the school's cafeteria, I took out the classified ads and circled all the jobs I was possibly qualified for. I was surprised at how many there were. I circled jobs for nurses' aides, housekeepers, retail sales clerks, fast-food workers, and waitresses. Then I looked up studio apartments for rent and circled the cheapest ones near San Fernando Valley College.

After I finished, I went to the office of the school newspaper, which was now the place where I spent most of my time. Claudia was working on her column. She said I looked tired and asked if anything was wrong. I told her I had broken up with Sandu. She asked if I wanted to talk, and I was glad she wanted to listen. It was hot in the office, and we climbed up the stairs out of the basement and sat down on a bench outside the Humanities building. I told her all that had happened since Nadia's arrival, and that I was looking for an apartment. Claudia offered to ask her roommates if I could move in with them. I couldn't believe my luck.

That afternoon, I filled out a number of job applications after class. I returned home late. I liked being busy; it made me feel productive. In the evening, Claudia called to tell me her roommates wanted to meet me, so the next day we got together on campus at lunchtime. The other two girls, one from Encino and one from Tarzana, were friendly, and we got along well. At the end of lunch, they agreed I could move in. Now all I had to do was tell Mama.

Mama was home when I returned in the late afternoon. It had been her day off. She was watching *All in the Family*. We greeted each other without much enthusiasm. I sat on the bed next to her. I took a deep breath trying to gather strength, and asked silently for Oma's help. "Mama, can we talk?" I asked. "I'm going to be moving out next week."

Her eyes grew wide. "Where are you going?"

"I'm going to live with three other college girls."

"Why?"

"I want to be independent."

"I won't allow you to go," she declared, sitting straight up in bed. I could sense her fear.

"Mama, I'm leaving next week." I paused. Every muscle in Mama's face was tense. She sat, rigid. "I'll visit you often. You can call me anytime. I'll come and help if you need me for anything." I tried to reassure her, knowing that she must feel I was rejecting her.

"Will you be safe?" She stared at me.

"Mama, I have to go out on my own, but I am not abandoning you," I said in a soft voice.

"But what will you do? How will you pay your bills? You don't know how to take care of yourself." She shook her head as she spoke. I could feel her insecurity.

"I've filled out some job applications, and I'm sure I'll find something."

"What sort of jobs? Why a job? I'm working so you can go to school."

"I've applied for a job as a nurse's aide and a nanny. I've filled out applications for a job as a waitress and as a sales clerk. I'll clean houses if I have to. I don't know yet."

"*Ay nò* ... a maid. You could be so much more if I help you. Don't throw away your life," Mama pleaded. I put my arm around her. I could see Mama's sense of worthlessness.

"I will be more some day, Mama," I reassured her. "This is just a start." I felt my strength growing. The limbs of the strangler-fig were peeling off me one by one. I wondered if she could survive without me. "Thank you for everything, Mama. I love you," I said, rubbing her arm.

To my surprise, her face softened a little. She looked up at me with tears in her eyes.

"Please, let me help you," she begged.

"No. I need to do this on my own, Mama, all on my own. You have done everything you needed to do, and I'm grateful for all of it." I kissed her as she stared down at the bedspread.

The following week, I moved in with Claudia and her roommates. They had a two-bedroom apartment on the second floor of an L-shaped building. I shared a bedroom with Claudia. I had bought a bed, white sheets, a cobalt-blue bedspread, and a wooden chest of drawers. That shade of blue was my favorite color because it reminded me of Oma, the House of Six Doors, and the color of the ocean. The bedspread stood out nicely against the white walls and the cream carpet of the bedroom. On the wall above my bed, I hung a collage I had made of all the old family pictures Willia had given me, along with photographs I had taken the last time I was in Curaçao, and my pink riding card. I surrounded them with a wooden frame that I had painted cobalt blue. On the chest next to my bed I placed a branch of white coral I had picked up from the white-sand beach at Spaanse Water.

I sat quietly on the bed. I realized everything I had chosen reminded me of Oma. I closed my eyes and found myself in that timeless space. It was evening when I opened my eyes again. Full of joy, I put my hand on my heart, and thanked Oma.

I took out my notebook, and started writing:

> *Mama's hands fluttered like flags in the island's*
> *trade winds, as they always did when she was*
> *nervous. She smiled at the Miami International*
> *Airport customs officer, who asked her again*
> *whether she had anything to declare.*

ACKNOWLEDGMENTS

LIFE GAVE ME ONE STORY. Being an author gives me the privilege of creating many stories. I want to thank the many people who have touched my life and who inspire endless characters who live in my world of stories.

I will be forever grateful to Janet Lucy and the women in her writing group, without whom this book would never have been written. They held the space in which my stories were born, and their encouragement and enthusiasm filled me with creativity.

My deepest gratitude for Dan Smetanka, who skillfully guided me through the editing process. As soon as I started working with him, I knew I was working with a master of his craft. I'm lucky to have a beloved friend and marvelous editor, Maeve Cooney, whose commitment and support have been invaluable.

Special thanks go to Justine Cook, for her insights and encouragement. Thanks to Ray Castellino and Mary Jackson for keeping me grounded throughout this whole process. My deepest appreciation to Cecile Barendsma for being there just at the right time, to keep me believing in this project; and to Gretchen Miller, for painstakingly typing up hundreds of pages of scribbles.

My appreciation goes to Kate Saltzman-Li for steering me in the right direction after reading the first rough draft. Many thanks to Erika Römer for her research, commitment, and dedication. Thanks to Elizabeth Lyon and Ariele Huff for seeing potential in the story. Thanks to Jessica Incline for her suggestions, and to Michael

Hague for bringing to my attention the art of emotional rhythm in storytelling. Special thanks to Jack Wise and Eric Rosoff for their insights on Florida.

My heart is overflowing with gratitude for Nancy Black and Isaac Hernández. A million thanks to Nancy, for her contagious enthusiasm, and for finding all the right people to help bring *The House of Six Doors* to light. Special thanks go to Isaac, for so beautifully interpreting the story, not only by painting the cover illustration, but also for the beautiful cover and interior book design, the book trailers, and the photographs of Curaçao.

Thanks to my friends, Nancy Koppelman, Zev Nathan, Joshua and Cindy Odell, Julie Bergman, Peggy and Don Bollinger, Paul Clay, and Deborah Hutchison, who read early drafts and gave me encouragement and advice.

Thanks to the incredible team who put the marketing package together: web guru Alicia St. Rose and publicist Jeanna Zelin.

Lastly, thanks to booksellers everywhere, for making this story available to the world … and to all who have spread the word around, including the Curaçao Tourism Board.

Finally, I want to express my loving gratitude to my husband, Jim, and my two sons, Stefan and Spencer, for their love, support, and patience during the many years I've devoted to this project. You are my inspiration.